Nury Vittachi is Hong Kong's most popular contemporary writer in English – hailed by CNN as 'the beat reporter of the offbeat' and described by the BBC as 'Hong Kong's funniest commentator'.

Born in Sri Lanka, Vittachi escaped the civil war and emigrated to Britain. He later returned to Asia and began his career with the *South China Morning Post* in the late 1980s. Well known for not pulling any punches in his journalism his gossip column was deemed too dangerous to publish in the 1990s after Hong Kong was handed over to China.

Vittachi now lives with his English wife and three adopted Chinese children in Hong Kong. His whole life has been dedicated to breaking down cultural barriers and promoting freedom of expression, and he has written many fiction and non-fiction books for adults and children.

He did not win the Vogel for his first novel, was not shortlisted for the Man Booker Prize with his subsequent books, and has never been nominated for a Nobel Prize for Literature. 'I hope to make it a clean sweep by not winning the Pulitzer next year,' the Hong Kong-based novelist says.

NURY VITTACHI

THE
SHANGHAI UNION
OF INDUSTRIAL
MYSTICS

Polygon

First published in 2006 by Allen & Unwin, Australia

This edition published in Great Britain in 2007 by Polygon,
an imprint of Birlinn Ltd

West Newington House
10 Newington Road
Edinburgh
EH9 1QS
www.birlinn.co.uk

9 8 7 6 5 4 3 2 1

ISBN 10: 1 84697 023 7
ISBN 13: 978 1 84697 023 8

British Library Cataloguing-in-Publication Data
A catalogue record for this book is available
on request from the British Library.

Typeset by Hewer Text UK Ltd, Edinburgh
Printed and bound by Clays Ltd, Bungay, Suffolk

1

In ancient China in the first century, a criminal was caught robbing the emperor's palace. He was sentenced to twenty days in jail. But the jail turned out to be no jail. There were only white squares painted on the bare ground.

The robber was put into the centre of a painted square. The only other person there was an old man with a long beard in the next square.

The robber said: 'What sort of jail is this?'

The old man said: 'The worst in the world. If any convict steps outside his lines, all the demons of hell come and eat him up.'

The robber was terrified. He stayed inside the painted lines for the full twenty days. At the end of that time, the bearded man stepped out of his square.

The robber said: 'Why are you not being eaten by all the demons in hell?'

The old man said: 'I am not a convict. I am the jailer.'

Blade of Grass, people think they react to what is around them. But the truth is that they react to how other people react to what is around them. The worst demons live inside a ma —

Crash! There was an ear-splitting roar of destruction and the world ended. Well, that's what it sounded like. What actually happened was that the building shook so hard that CF Wong's pen jumped in his hand, prematurely closing his elegant final line with an out-of-place dash. He jerked upright, suddenly alert. *Mut yeh si?* What's happening? End of the world? Office falling down? Someone drop an anvil upstairs? He noticed that the tremor had pushed his cup of *gok fa* right to the edge of the table and he reached out to pull it back.

'*Cheese*,' said his assistant Joyce McQuinnie as her headphones rolled off the desk and bounced on the floor. 'What was that? Like, an earthquake?' She started chewing a fingernail.

'*Aiyeeaa!*' screamed his secretary Winnie Lim, emerging from a deep vegetative state and jumping out of her seat. 'Each person save herself first.' She scrambled around her desk and tottered out of the office. 'If I killed I sue you,' she warned her employer from the corridor. She click-clacked down the stairs in her high heels. Then the sound of her footsteps stopped: she was evidently having second thoughts. The brittle noise restarted as she clattered back up again. Bursting back through the office door like a small aftershock, she started rooting around in her drawer for something important she wanted to save: a frosted silver-pink lipstick that was not available in this country.

At that moment, a second huge thump sent even greater shock waves into the building, running through everything sentient and non-sentient in the room. It tipped Wong's teacup right off the desk, and he watched it smash with a musical tinkle on the floor. The clear tea produced a stain on the threadbare carpet which was blackish, like blood. Why do liquids which are not black so often produce black stains? Wong stored the question away for a later session of pondering. Joyce's iPod joined her headphones on the floor. She now had four fingers in her mouth.

Winnie squealed and click-clacked out again without her cosmetic treasure. 'You owe me one lipstick compensation,' she screeched.

'I die first before I pay you,' Wong shouted back.

'Yes, I hope,' Winnie said, cantering unsteadily down the stairs. 'Today.'

Joyce, frozen in a state of indecision, stopped biting her fingers, took them out of her mouth and started nibbling her lower lip instead. Following Winnie's lead, she began looking for prized possessions. She groped under the magazines on her desk to find her most treasured item: her mobile phone, or, more accurately, the digital address book inside it. Joyce was a slow-motion panicker. The more urgent things became, the more slowly she reacted. This did not seem to be a wise habit, nor was it a good argument for the survivalist theory of evolution, but that was just how she was made. She had no idea how to react in this situation. 'We better, like, split the scene?'

Joyce was scared, but she was also just plain annoyed. She didn't know whether to scream in fear or out of frustration. An earthquake! Would you credit it? It didn't say anything about earthquakes in *Lonely Planet*. She had been feeling unnerved all week, finding Shanghai hard to adjust to after slick, English-speaking Singapore. Here, few people spoke English, most of the signage, shop names, menus and everything else was in Chinese only, and so much of life in the city seemed unreal. The buildings were straight out of *Thunderbirds* – or perhaps *Batman Begins*: ancient and futuristic squeezed together side by side. One iconic Shanghai skyscraper looked like a giant pair of steel tweezers holding a ball. Several were globe shaped, and one was a globe halfway up a stick: a weird, giant Cantonese skewered fishball, with people scurrying around inside. The Park Hotel looked as if someone had built a replica Empire State Building and then stamped on it, collapsing all the floors together. Almost next to it was the Radisson, a tall white tower on which a huge UFO from a 1950s sci-fi flick had apparently landed. A pair of thin ropes hung from rods on the roof, as if the aliens were fishing.

And the culture seemed as weird as the architecture. Every day she encountered something new and strange and totally unbelievable. Was the world ready for the Hezhenin Heilong-jiang salmon fish-skin suit? Or for taxis which had little English signs in them saying 'No drunkards or psychos without guardians'? Should shops really be allowed to display dried pig faces – surely no one wanted to see those, let alone eat them? When she told her Shanghainese associates that she'd stopped eating meat, they replied suspiciously that vegetarianism was a cult traditionally associated with violence, gangsterism and the underworld. China was such a totally different planet to, well, *Earth*, that she felt dangerously adrift. The more she failed to make sense of her new home, the more she felt that fissures were spreading under her feet. And now Shanghai was becoming *literally* unstable. The bowels of the city were rocking and the same thing was happening to hers: she discovered she desperately wanted to go to the toilet.

Across the room, Wong did not reply, as he didn't know what Joyce meant when she said they should 'split the scene'. If this was an earthquake, the scene appeared to be splitting by itself.

He was shaken, but only physically. He was not panicking: he was pondering. He had lived through earthquakes before. The sensation was not easily forgotten. It is impossible to convey the horror of an earthquake to someone who has never experienced one. It's beyond frightening. The one thing you have always always *always* trusted turns into a lethal enemy. The ground, the firmament, the rocks and trees and mountains, the world, the steady foundation of everything you have ever known starts playing the fool, shimmying and tangoing around for minutes on end. It's the physical equivalent of your mother telling you that she is not your real mother because you are actually the offspring of the Kanasi Lake Monster in Xinjiang province. Earthquakes touched the deepest, darkest part of one's soul. And this was not doing that.

'I think not an earthquake,' Wong commented, mostly to himself, tugging at the straggly hairs on his chin. 'I think demolition ball.'

He moved to the old sash window and pulled it open, not without a struggle. The chill air of a Shanghai April rushed into the room, as did the signature tune of the city: whining soprano drill-pieces harmonising atonally over the staccato rhythm of massed baritone jackhammers. And, oddly, a New York-style police siren was wailing a fugal tenor counter-melody in the distance.

In the muddy wasteland in front of their small block, just off Henan Zhong Lu in an unfashionable bit of Huangpu district, stood several unfamiliar pieces of heavy machinery. He immediately spotted the culprit: a rusty green crane was idly swinging a wreckers' ball into the rooms next to them on the fourth floor. It was instantly familiar yet unfamiliar. On any given day there are twenty-one thousand construction sites in Shanghai, and their office block had just become the twenty-one thousand and first. To be demolished by heavy equipment along with one's premises was definitely not good feng shui – especially not today, the official opening day of CF Wong and Associates (Shanghai), a feng shui consultancy retained by a major international property development company, East Trade Industries Company Limited.

'*Wei*,' Wong called out to a pot-bellied man with a dirty yellow hardhat and a clipboard who appeared to be directing the operation from ground level. 'You cannot demolish this building now. People are inside. People are here.' He spoke in southern-accented Mandarin.

The foreman languidly lifted his megaphone and directed it at their window. 'Get the people out quick-quick,' he replied in the same language, pointing to his mud-spattered watch. 'Have deadline.'

Joyce, joining her boss at the window, shook her head in disbelief, pleased to have finally summoned up enough courage to move a few metres. 'This is so, like, totally not done,' she said.

'You have to tell us in advance,' the feng shui master shouted down in Chinese to the uncaring men 12 metres below. 'You must give us warning. You can't just knock down the building.'

To their left, the man operating the crane swung the iron ball away from the building but remained waiting at the controls, while his senior colleague gave the condemned building's occupants the full extent of the bad news: 'Building is coming down. Today. Better you go.'

Seeing the two shocked faces remaining defiantly at the window, he continued: 'We sent you a letter telling you that we would knock the building down on this date. But it got lost in the post.' A nasty half-smile appeared on his face.

'Oh.' Wong thought about this for a moment. He translated for Joyce: 'He says they sent us a letter. But it got lost in the post.'

The feng shui master's eyes crinkled as he weighed his options. Hmm. So. Now he knew what was happening. This was a round of one of the most popular games in mainland China. It was called Bureaucracy, and you could find yourself in the middle of a life-and-death round at any time of the day or night, without warning: this was what made life in China so, well, interesting. Performing well in the game required great skill which could only be acquired through active play, as there were no books or teachers who could give you lessons. Fortunately, Wong had played it before, although not for a long time.

Joyce blinked. 'Hang on a tick. He may have sent us a letter, but how does he know it got lost in the post?'

It was a logical point, but probably too predictable to be of any help. Wong decided to pursue it anyway, in the absence of other inspiration. 'How do you know it got lost in the post?' he shouted out of the window.

'That sort of letter *usually* gets lost in the post,' the demolition man replied, his unpleasant smile becoming a notch more evil as he delivered what he thought was a knockout punch.

Wong nodded. It was an excellent answer, and one that was hard to gainsay. But he had to try. If the man below could use fine points of uniquely mainland logic against them, he needed to follow suit. 'Actually, it *didn't* get lost in the post. We received it,' he said, raising his chin and lowering his brow to show that he was not going to be a soft target.

It was the turn of the foreman's brow to crinkle. This was not an answer he expected. It was not a move which had been attempted before by victims of Bureaucracy. He was not prepared for it. He lowered his megaphone to consult with the man next to him, a thin individual holding sheaves of paper plans. How should we reply?

Wong, seeing the growing discomfort on the men's faces, realised he had snatched the initiative and had to hold on to it with all his knobbly fingers. 'Yes, we *did* receive it. Also we replied to it, asking for extension of time. Also we received a reply *granting* us extension of time.'

The foreman lost it. He snarled in fury: 'Ach! No, no, *no*. It *did* get lost in the post.'

'It did not.'

'It did. It *must* have done. Because we never—' He stopped dead. He knew that he had nearly given the game away, and he knew that his opponent knew it, and knew that he knew he knew. The man's expression altered as he changed tack, becoming calmly belligerent. 'Letter doesn't matter,' he shouted. 'Whether lost or not. You get out. We have *permit* to do this.'

Permit. A trump card in China. But Wong had lived in Singapore. He knew all about permits. 'You must show me three signed permits from the three relevant ministries,' he replied calmly.

'Ah. We have exemptions,' the foreman said. Now it was clear that both sides were achieving a sort of equilibrium in the game. Thrust. Parry. Thrust.

'Then you must show me the permit that exempts you from having the three signed permits.'

'We are exempted from that one, too.'

Wong gritted his teeth. His enemy was highly skilled in the

fighting techniques used in Advanced Hand-to-Hand Bureau-cracy, Black Belt, fourth dan. What line to take now? Of course: chops, seals, stamps: nothing happened in China without pieces of paper bearing official splodges of pressed red ink. 'But you can only be exempted from that with chopped paper. Show me your chops.'

The foreman lowered his megaphone to think. After a few seconds, he raised it and declared, less confidently: 'I have chopped papers. They are back in the office.'

'You go get them.'

'Cannot. Too busy. No time.'

'Then I will call my friend Mr Zhong who is head of security for the Secretary-General of the Communist Party of China and his men will come and explain to you why you need the right chops. I call him right now, okay?'

A sneer in reply: 'If you are best friends with the immortals in the Politburo, why are you in this poky office in the cheapest street in town?'

'I am humble feng shui master,' said Wong, displaying his *lo pan* in the window. 'But these days everyone needs feng shui – even the President.' With his other hand he reached into his pocket and pulled out what looked like a business card, which he also held to the glass, although he knew it would be impossible to read at that distance. 'One month ago I had a meeting with the most powerful people in this country.' The card was actually a piece of junk mail urging him to get his plumbing from Wu The Number One Wonder Water Work-er, but Wong spoke with conviction – because he had indeed advised the premier's head of security on feng shui matters on a preparatory visit the previous month.

'I don't believe one word of this,' said the foreman in a nervous voice that revealed that he did in fact believe some of it. He stared at the oriental compass and the card Wong was displaying and the cockiness in his face started to evaporate.

'I call him now,' said the feng shui master, putting down the *lo pan*, picking up a phone handset and starting to press the buttons.

There was a tense moment of frozen inactivity – one second that was somehow ten seconds long. 'Stop,' the foreman said, apparently speaking to both Wong and his colleague in the crane. 'You got one hour to clear out. Then we pulverise this building to dust, and anyone inside with it. This project is for the Central Military Affairs Commission. You can't stop it. You got one hour.' The emphasis he gave to the title of the organisation he was name-dropping was clear evidence of the power he believed it carried.

The feng shui master quickly jerked his upper body back through the window like a turtle whose head had been struck. 'Victory, but very minor,' he said to his assistant. 'Just got time to grab our stuff and go. One hour.'

Joyce was already dialling a number on the phone. 'If we gotta go, we gotta et cetera. I'll call Marker PDQ.'

'Peedy-queue?'

'Colloquial English term. Means pretty damn quick. He can help us move our stuff again.'

'Yes,' said Wong, sitting down and lowering his chin into his hands. 'Call Marker, peedy-queue.'

It was a shame to have to leave. This office was quite good. His life was an endless search for spots where energy flowed in precisely the right ways that would make his life work. People these days often designed their offices with large windows and open-plan layouts which made ch'i energy move quickly in straight, fast streams: and then they were surprised when they felt tired and burnt out all the time. In contrast, older offices were often maze-like rabbit warrens of filing cabinets and old papers, where ch'i stagnated – and people were surprised that their businesses failed to thrive. What he looked for were environments which allowed the ch'i to flow and pool and meander, like a stream dipping in and out of small lagoons. And of course cheap rent. This office had both. But evidently luck was not with him this time. He must check his pillars of destiny to find out what had gone wrong.

Today had been a time of great *yin* – calm, cool, smooth, watery energy flowing around him, enabling him to do some useful work on his literary masterpiece: a book of educational, inspirational, ancient Chinese anecdotes called 'Some Gleanings of Oriental Wisdom'. Yin was intellectual, yin was creative, yin focused the brain marvellously. And yet the yin day had been interrupted by a demolition ball – probably the single most *yang* object imaginable, other than a ballistic missile. Yang energy was forceful, hot, unyielding, heavy, and had hit his yin space with the force of a meteorite. How could such extreme contrasts exist? Then he recalled the ancient text which said that extreme yin was but one step from being yang, and extreme yang was but one degree from being yin. He quickly flicked through his book of notes and found the passage he wanted. It came from the writings of Chou Tun-yi in the eleventh century: 'The Ultimate Power generates yang energy through movement. But what happens when movement reaches its extreme limit? It becomes tranquillity. Tranquillity increases. But what happens when tranquillity reaches its extreme limit? It becomes activity. Thus yang becomes yin and yin becomes yang. Each is the root of the other.'

But dreadful though it might be to say it, this was no time for mulling over classic Chinese philosophy. They had to move. Their brief time in this office was over. He saw that he may have won a small skirmish, but there was no way he would win the whole battle – not against the Central Military Affairs Commission. What a start to the week. There are few things more depressing for a feng shui master than to painstakingly arrange a set of premises to maximise good fortune only to find, on the day of completion, that it is about to be demolished – unless, of course, the client has paid for the examination in advance and will have to pay again, which didn't apply in this case as he was his own client. His only hope would be to pass the additional costs upwards to the company paying his retainer.

Something else occurred to him: there had been a strange omen that morning that he had been struggling to understand. The local newspaper had carried a picture of a white elephant on the front page – no doubt imported into the city for some circus or other. The image had stuck in his mind: when one made a big change in one's life, such as setting up a new business in a new country, one naturally took care to see what sort of omens presented themselves. And white elephants carried a host of different but important implications in various branches of Asian esoteric thought: Chinese, Thai, Indian, Vietnamese. They were connected to royalty, to longevity, to magic, to heaven, to all manner of things. But what did this mean to him, at this time, in this place?

He had even asked Joyce what a white elephant signified to a European (to Wong, like to most Chinese, all Westerners, whether from Australia or Canada or Argentina, were 'Europeans'). 'In Western culture a white elephant is a thing which is totally useless,' she had replied. 'It means, like, a silly mistake.' So much for Western culture.

Setting the omen to one side, he had decided to write an ancient Chinese anecdote for his book, which would be his first work published in English. And it had been that classic tale which had been so rudely interrupted by a thunderous metal ball of yang.

☯

Fifty minutes later, a removal team led by Marker Cai, a small but stocky young man who had moved them into that very office eight days earlier, was moving the same boxes out again, to put into storage until they could find another office. It was an easy job. Neither of Wong's two staff members were efficient or fast workers: many of the boxes had not even been opened, let alone unpacked.

The young man's real name in Chinese was Cai Ma Ke, but he'd changed the word order for Westerners to Marker Cai. He was attractive: Joyce thought of him as Mister *Sigh*. She fantasised about one day getting to know him so well that she could persuade him to change his name from the absurd Marker to the more acceptable Mark or even the sexy Marc or Marco. And there was a chance they would stay in touch. For Mr Cai was not just a removal man. He was a weigher of bones: a practitioner of one of the most ancient Chinese arts of divination, and thus a professional contact of CF Wong's. But an ambitious young man cannot make enough money as a bone-weigher in modern Shanghai, so he shifted crates during the day.

Joyce McQuinnie was packing the few things on her desk into a cardboard box. It was the last one. She had more or less finished and was working as slowly as she could, given the urgency of the situation. Marker Cai was moving each box downstairs as they finished packing it. He was twenty-five years old. She was five and a half years younger. They were both taking surreptitious glances at each other. At that moment, they were both supremely beautiful in each other's eyes, which would mean nothing at all to anyone else. Each was hoping that the other would not notice his/her furtive but powerful interest in her/him, while at the same time half praying for the opposite. It didn't make sense, but what was there in the business of love that did?

Marker was also in a thoughtful mood, and he too knew the removal operation had nearly finished. His darting eyes revealed that he wanted an excuse to interact further with the young *lao wai*, but he couldn't think of what to say. He knew that she spoke little Chinese, so realised that their conversation would have to be in English, which was not his best language. His upper arms were clamped to his sides when he was in the room with her. He was hot and sweaty and was worried that he would smell odd to her, in the same way that Western people often smell unattractive to Chinese. He took the second-last box downstairs.

Joyce had a feminist ideological aversion to wearing much make-up but was wishing she had worn a bit more of it today. There was a physical pain in her chest but she wasn't sure why. It was something to do with Marker's beauty, and the fact that it/he made her heart beat so fast it felt like it would burst, and it/he would shortly vanish again. She wanted to make sure that she had another reason to meet him as soon as possible. This was the second time they had met, and the second time his presence had triggered an attack of breathlessness. But it was not like they could move office every week. Or perhaps they could? They'd have to move the stuff out of storage and into a new office again eventually. But that might take a week or two. Or three. Too long.

It appeared possible that Wong would invite Marker to join his union of mystics, but that wasn't due to meet until Thursday – two days' time. The way Joyce felt now, even waiting one day would be too long. She felt she should say something, take the initiative, ask him out even. Chinese guys were supposed to be too shy to start anything. But what should she say? She couldn't think of a thing. She picked up a gold-leaf longevity vase, wrapped it in newspaper, and placed it in the box. How long did they have now? Only another minute or two. She looked for something else to pack, but the desks were all clear. She slowly taped up the final box.

The young man re-entered the room. 'Nearly finish,' said Marker, picking up the box. Joyce looked up. For seven-tenths of a second they held each other's eyes.

At that moment, there was intense activity in Joyce's head and heart (which in her case was only a single location, two sides joined with an always-on organic broadband cable). She felt the weight of her youth upon her, and the real heaviness was, perhaps surprisingly, the weight of mathematics, or more particularly, of statistics. For Joyce had five different choices she could make at that moment (it would have been seven had she not had three glasses of Tsing Tao at O'Malley's the previous night). She could hold the young man's gaze and touch his soul with enlarged, puppy-dog eyes, sending him an unmistakable message that something important *relationship-wise* was happening between them; she could continue the movement of her hand towards the tape that she no longer needed; she could cough (there was a tickle in her throat which had sent a memo to her brain: please cough immediately); she could let her eyes go out of focus as she continued a thought running through the back of her mind which contained, among other things, a memory of a forgotten song she'd heard on the radio; or she could do none of these things: she could do nothing at all, emptying herself, not even thinking.

Or could she? A couple of years ago she would have said no. Since all moments contain a portion of time, it should not be possible to do nothing – a portion of conscious time, however small, can't be empty, and the brain never really shuts down. But time spent in Asia with Buddhists and other meditators would these days inspire her to say yes: we can empty ourselves completely of thought and movement, and can actually stop time working for that particular moment. But it wasn't easy. Once a moment has come into existence, it is already fading to make space for its offspring – another moment, similar to the first, but not the same. Each newborn moment offers us yet another raft of possibilities to study, choices to make.

But youth: now that's when this whole issue of time becomes a serious challenge. You see, Joyce was nineteen years, four months, thirteen days, eleven hours, nine minutes, two seconds and one and a half moments old. She had (demographic experts tell us) another sixty-one years, two days, six hours and two minutes of life ahead of her. With an open-ended number of possibilities in each moment, and sixty-one years of moments ahead of her, her spread of choices was almost incalculable – certainly, it ran into googles. Compare CF Wong, who (the same demographic experts tell us) had only fifteen years, seventy-five days, four hours and nine minutes of life left. For him, the number of permutations was far less, and was falling fast. This basic mathematical principle has a powerful effect on the lives of people who are close to the beginning or end of their lives. Yes, it's true that most individuals are incapable of adding up a $2.90 coffee and a $3.00 sandwich without computers. But the answer is that we can calculate it and we do it all the time.

All human brains constantly do advanced maths, whether they know it or not. On a subconscious level, we know exactly how fast time passes, and how quickly our choices are disappearing. It is the subconscious realisation of this which brings about the pressure that makes a teenager's life such agony. Those are the years when we become dimly aware of the fact that every choice made every moment has consequences that could, nay, *will* crucially shape the rest of our lives.

Joyce subconsciously knew that if she caught Marker Cai's eye and held it for another seven-tenths of a second, she would be sending him a clear message that there could be a potential overlap between several trillion (at least) of the possible permutations of his life and a similar number of hers. This overlap could last a minute, an hour, a day, a month, a year, or, should they get married, the rest of their lives. So it was no wonder that Joyce was having a hard time deciding what to do.

Across the other side of the room, Joyce's boss was sitting, smiling to himself. CF Wong was fifty-seven. The main part of his life was over. The number of permutations possible for him had fallen, from googles to quintillions and then to mere trillions, billions and millions. The pressure of having to pick from an almost infinite number of choices had faded. It had been replaced by something equally affecting: a growing subconscious desperation born of the knowledge that since there were relatively few choices left, all of them deserved extra care and attention. But by then, one was *so tired.* And the kettle's on the boil. And what's for dinner, anyway? By the age of fifty-seven, we are tempted to choose the safest option for each moment, the do-nothing option, the perfectly blank do-not-move, do-not-think action, the choice that empties the time from each moment. (That's one of the reasons why television is such a helpful device: it blanks out thought and action, quietly eating our lives while we pretend nothing is happening.)

Wong was rescued from the worst of the pressure of the passage of time by being unusually focused: he had a fervent desperation to accumulate money, despite the fact that much of his writing dealt with the superiority of spiritual and natural wealth over material riches. This need in him was so deep that there was no room in his life for unnecessary trivia (like hobbies, television, relationships and so on). He hadn't the patience to do anything that didn't earn him countable, collectible, strokeable, fondleable cash. He had been poor most of his life, and the thing that drove him was a determination to earn enough not to be poor, for a little while, before he died.

Poverty grants many benefits which the wealthy miss. For a start, it toughens the soul marvellously against adversity, and sharpens the part of the spirit that bounces back in a crisis. He may be being knocked out of his office by a wrecker's ball, but Wong had already fully recovered. He was focusing on the positive: it had occurred to him that it might not be a bad thing to move office again. In truth, he was rather embarrassed about having accepted an office on the fourth floor of a building, so perhaps he should not be too upset about having a chance to change that. In low-brow Chinese superstition, four is a negative number, but in classical feng shui it is positive. Yet he has more simple, superstitious customers than intelligent, well-read ones, so he might be wise to cater for their ignorance.

And, inconvenient as it may be, another move could turn out to be good news – the property company who was sponsoring his stay would be forced to finance replacement accommodation for them. He knew the accounts department would be irritated at having to go through the operation again, so he would once more offer to take the money and arrange it himself, and they'd probably agree this time. Lack of change was eventual stagnation, whereas change always brought with it the opportunity for personal enrichment. He would argue for a large premium over the standard accommodation budget, explaining that he urgently needed somewhere nice to recover from the inconvenience of having to move in and out so quickly, and he'd say that places with good feng shui always cost more. Then he'd find a cheap hovel with a reasonable flow of ch'i and pocket the difference.

He was a natural salesman, and squeezing money out of people was something Wong was good at. His consultancy was small, but survived. Whenever he met someone who needed a feng shui reading, he rapidly tried to read them before feeding them the most suitable line. He had learned that a come-on phrase which was perfect for one customer instantly turned off his neighbour. Fortunately, feng shui was an amorphous, shape-shifting concept that lent itself to multiple interpretations. There were basically four types of customer.

1 The Superstitious. Their basic driving force is fear of the future, and their weapons against it are magic totems. They are mildly agoraphobic, a term which to him was interchangeable with the word 'American'. These people are worried about 'Bad Guys' and like being told that they need statues of the Four Kings of Mount Sumeru by their doors to guard against poor luck entering. They want a Curved Knife in their office desks to fight the invisible demons of the world (which these days include the taxation department and computer viruses). For them, life is a battle against a massive horde of invisible evil forces, and they need spiritual weapons of mass destruction for self defence. Fundamentalists of all religions can generally be included in this category.

17

2 Then you have your Futuristic Primitives. (For some reason, there are many IT and computer people in this category, plus many Europeans, plus young Indian people who were educated in California.) They are deeply religious but do not realise it. They passionately express their contempt for organised religion while devoting considerable amounts of time and money to filling their homes with items which are ostensibly non-religious. They like to have transcendental experiences. They need to feel correctly allied with the forces of Destiny. They enjoy having a place in their home which is shrine-like without being a shrine. They need regular rituals which are not recognisable as religious rituals. They scoff at people who carry rosary beads, but are happy to be sold Mystic Chinese Knots to rub before going out to greet the world.

3 Then we have the Shoppers, one of Wong's favourite categories. Twelve or fifteen years ago, this category was filled with the idle rich. But these days, many of the middle class have picked up the Shopper mentality, particularly in Australia, Hong Kong and Singapore. These people are only averagely superstitious and have little interest in hanging plastic tokens around their homes. But they already own all the basic necessities of life (an apartment, nice furniture, a car, a gym membership) and yet are so addicted to shopping that they desperately hunt for more things to buy. They are particularly partial to spending money on items which have no practical use. They are driven by the thought 'Some people are buying this, therefore I could, too.' On these people, Wong would unload large amounts of the high-end stuff: elegant, overpriced statuettes made of white jade, *objets d'art* in hammered metals, figurines in silver, gold, copper or bronze, symbolic items inlaid with 'good luck' gemstones. He had learned, over the years, not to sell too many items to Shoppers at once, tempting though it may be, for they have no interest in what they purchase, but enjoy shopping for its

own sake; so the right thing to do is to sell them stuff at regular intervals, enabling them to maintain a steady flow of hits for their spending habit. A periodic phone call is all that is needed to bring the money in: 'Era Eight has started. People are buying gold-leafed wealth vases and booking cleansings to welcome in the energy from the southwest. When can I arrange yours?' No Shopper can resist such a line.

4 The next group is what Wong called the Scientific Eclectics. These he found frustrating at first, but they had become good contributors to recurrent income once he had learned how to deal with them. They are highly intelligent and analytical and are violently opposed to superstition of any kind. They find it hard to suppress a giggle if you suggest hiding eight gold coins under their beds. But if you tell them that a 'ley line' of energy runs through their study, they are fascinated and want to hear more. They feel they know most things about modern physics, and have moved on from the study of the material world to the study of non-material things. They put feng shui in the same category as quantum physics, dark matter, reiki, extra sensory perception, chaos theory and so on: these are all things that you can't actually see, but there is enough evidence to suggest that it makes sense to be aware of them, and to pay them some credence. Scientific Eclectics cannot be sold solid items of any sort, but will pay large fees for services. They take a strictly psychological view of feng shui. If they can pay a fee for an expert to make their premises into happier, more creative places in which to live or work, then why not do it? They place feng shui masters on their service-providers list along with ergonomics experts, somewhere after architects and plumbing engineers, but before interior designers and art suppliers.

Wong had also discovered that even people who were entirely sceptical about feng shui could also be a source of income, as they would pay for feng shui readings to satisfy their staff or spouses. This is Asia, so we suppose we have to shell out for this, even though it's probably a load of mumbojumbo. We guess it's a small enough price to keep her/him/ them happy. *Geez, is that what it costs? Hell's bells.* Wong found non-believers a good category on which to exercise his negotiating skills. They usually have no idea how important or not feng shui is to their staff. Any situation in which the purchasing party has no idea of the value of what they are buying gives a huge advantage to the selling party; one which Wong would play to maximum benefit. 'I think better you order gold plus package, sir. Or else staff will maybe definitely walk out, possibly, for sure, no doubt about it. All will walk out, probably definitely.' They usually pay by gold or platinum corporate credit card.

Wong felt that he and the fellow members of his union tended to fall into the Scientific Eclectics category: very discriminating about what they hung in their offices or homes, yet always studying the esoteric arts to discover what their different areas of expertise had in common. Actually, it was the thought of Wong's professional association which was the biggest contributor to the smile on his face at that moment. The nearest thing he had to an actual gang of buddies was the small cluster of individuals who made up the Union of Industrial Mystics, an association which started in Singapore but which was spreading to other countries and city-states in Asia. Wong had moved to Shanghai a week earlier partly in order to set up a fully operational chapter of the union here – after his initial raft of high-paying assignments were complete, of course.

Other than Wong himself, the most active members of the union were Dilip Kenneth Sinha, an Indian astrologer and *vaastu* expert who was due to arrive in Shanghai from Singapore that night or the following morning, and Madame Xu Chong-Li, a Singaporean-Chinese fortune teller who was also due to arrive some time in the next thirty-six hours. They were due to meet Shang Dan, a Shanghainese *ming shu* expert whom they hoped would become the main contact in this city in which a new branch would be formed. Then there was Marker Cai, bone-weigher and removal man. (Bone-weighing, despite its gruesome-sounding name, did not involve the handling of corpses, and was largely a numerology-based technique.)

A group of the mystics planned to meet for dinner somewhere nice on Thursday – perhaps Emperor Xiangfeng's Kitchen in Yunnan Lu. Wong wanted to introduce his Singaporean friends to the delights of *xianji* (cold salty chicken) and *hupi jianjiao* (tiger skin chillies). Then of course there was the squirrel fish – Sinha would enjoy that. Most of them were at the age when food was the main carnal interest they had. It would surely be a wonderful reunion and an excellent meal. For although he would hotly deny it, Wong was not an entirely one-dimensional character. On the rare occasions he was not obsessing about money, he was thinking about his stomach.

Gastronomic interests were going very well for him at the moment. In addition to the dinner meeting of the union planned for later in the week, he also had an invitation for a meal that night at a new ultra-high-class dining club called This Is Living, based at a fancy new restaurant in a Shanghai skyscraper. He had done the feng shui for the new eatery over a series of flying visits, and was delighted when the manager invited him to be a guest at the founding meal of a club of gourmets which would 'sample the most exciting menu in China'. Further, Wong had presented him with a truly outrageous bill and the manager had promised to pay him in cash at the meal that night.

Life was good, and it was wonderful to be here in Shanghai at this time. Wong loved Shanghai architecture, which looked from a distance like a jumbled mess but was often built with well-hidden feng shui traits. The heart of town was an open area called the People's Square and the People's Park, but if you took a helicopter and rose above it, you would see that the road surrounding the square formed a neat half-circle. Neighbouring Zhejiang Lu and Nanjing Dong Lu formed the other half of the circle. And running from north to south exactly in between the two semi-circles was Xizang Lu. The whole construction thus formed a squareish circle with a line running through it: yes, the character *zhong*, meaning 'centre' or 'heart', and the first character in the word China: *Zhong Guo*. This was usually translated into English as Middle Kingdom, but that missed the point entirely. The true meaning of *Zhong Guo* was Land at the Centre of the World.

The main buildings in the People's Square were the Shanghai Grand Theatre, the Shanghai Museum and the Shanghai Government Building, and all three had south-facing doors, following the best feng shui tradition. The Grand Theatre looked like a bowl held up to heaven, and the Museum like a *ding*: a ceremonial bronze container with three legs. In a different part of town, the Shanghai Centre was clearly built in the shape of the character *shan*, meaning 'mountain'.

Yes, the feng shui master's schedule was packed with good things at the moment: two good, long, stretched-out dinners in three nights. A reunion with his friends. And the official founding of the Shanghai Union of Industrial Mystics. So that was why Wong was sitting in his about-to-be-demolished office and smiling broadly.

Another deafening crash reverberated through the building. The bare light bulb started to swing. The sound of shattering glass followed as window frames fell out of neighbouring walls. The demolition men were back at work. The Central Military Affairs Commission could not be kept waiting.

Marker Cai picked up the last box and handed it to a colleague, a fat, sweaty youth, to take downstairs.

'Finished,' Cai said.

'Ah – thanks, well done,' Joyce stammered. 'That's great. Er.'

'Okay.'

'Great. Thanks. You've done a great job. Can I ask. Er. D'you want to . . .'

'Yes?'

'Um. I just thought. You know, maybe . . .'

'Ah.'

'Wanna go for a coffee or something, sometime, or something?'

'Okay. Go for a coffee or something sometime or something.'

'Er. I'll call you. Or you could call me.'

'Yes.'

Joyce started feeling around in her pockets for something to write with. 'Er. Let me get a pen or something and I'll give you my mobile.'

But all the pens had been packed. 'I don't have a . . . do you have a . . .'

Marker tapped his pockets and found nothing. Then he discovered half a pencil behind his left ear. He gave a short embarrassed snort of laughter when they both notice that there was a ring of teeth marks around the top.

Another crash shook the building, but the two young people didn't notice. There were far larger explosions – we're talking 100-megaton nukes – happening in their glands.

'Now let me find a piece of paper,' said Joyce. Problem: all the pieces of paper had been packed.

Marker handed her a bent, slightly damp business card from his pocket. 'You call me. I write my mobile phone number on the back of my card. We go for coffee. Or something. Sometime.'

'Yeah. Great. Ha ha,' she said. 'Cool. Okay. Well, bye. See you on, on, er, sometime.'

As he backed away, she held his gaze for one point nine seconds longer than was absolutely necessary and her heart did a set of triple backflips as a trillion new delightful possibilities added themselves to the google which were already there. Life was rich. Then he was gone.

Seconds later, she and Wong were running down the stairs as the building crumbled around them.

2

Heading into work when everyone else is heading home should be depressing, but sometimes it isn't. At certain times in our lives, we discover that there's something oddly energising about swimming against the current.

These days, Lu Linyao felt like that all the time, which was a bit worrying. She felt she was literally charging against the flow of a major river as a Yangtze of people poured out of an office block on the built-up side of Zhongshan Dong Yi Lu, the road that skirted The Bund, and she had to shoulder her way through the bodies like a fifty-eight-kilo salmon powering upstream. Being the sort of person she was, Linyao only half stepped out of the way, leaving the person coming towards her to contribute the other half of the manoeuvre.

A number of men – through carelessness, sleep deprivation, world weariness or for other reasons – preferred to brush heavily against her instead. This was bad news for them, as she was deliberately carrying a hardcover book under her right arm, its sharpest pair of edges scratching painful tramlines on anyone who made the mistake of encountering her right breast. When she saw a trio or longer string of people heading directly for her, she lowered her head, bullet-like, and careered through them, forcing them to break formation and regather behind her, their heads turning. *What's the matter with her?* As the pavement obstacle course grew more dense (for that's how she saw most people: as obstacles), she did not slow down, but marched faster, punishing people for being in her path.

Yet once she was through the crush of people on the main road and had turned into a quieter side street, she found her footsteps slowing down. Was she going the right way? Was she doing the right thing? *Perhaps I should just leave it to the others.* After all, they were young people with time on their hands; she was a thirty-one-year-old woman with a professional job, a mortgage and a child. These were big responsibilities, adult ones that had to be taken seriously.

Her steps slowed even more. Should she be doing this sort of thing at all? She never had enough time for herself and her offspring. Yet here she was, heading for her second job, the voluntary running of the Shanghai Vegetarian Café Society. The group she chaired ran a small canteen and catering operation on Hankou Lu, a road just off one of the main arteries that carries traffic towards The Bund.

Lu Linyao was divorced and had an eight-year-old daughter whom she adored, and who hated her, or acted as if she did. This was no surprise to people who knew them. The girl had been excessively needy from birth (most of her friends, being childless, did not realise that all children were excessively needy from birth), and Linyao was not cut out to be a mother, as she and her friends knew long before she had a child of her own. She had never developed the ability to build a rapport with small children that other females seemed to acquire in their teens or twenties.

As a result, Linyao's daughter Jia Lin (Julie to her mother's ex-husband and English-speaking friends) was always angry with her mother for one reason or another – the biggest sin, of course, being to have got herself divorced. Surrounded by rich friends in an English–Mandarin private school in the north of Shanghai, it was only natural that Jia Lin wouldn't be able to understand why she had to do without a father or a high income, while most of her friends had both and seemed to live charmed lives filled with extra ballet classes, chauffeurs, electronic toys and age-inappropriate videos.

Linyao's velocity decreased, her lower limbs seemed to go into slow motion, and then she came to a complete halt, like a steam train reaching a station. Should she skip this assignment?

Should she turn back? Here was an opportunity to win some much-needed brownie points with her sullen and angry daughter. She had managed to leave her job as a government veterinarian early, and yet was going to spend some rare free time doing a task that was strictly voluntary. Although she was chair of the Café Society, she could easily leave it to her deputies, Joyce and Philip. All she would have to do is give them a quick call on her mobile.

Yes. She'd turn around. They could do the assignment tonight. Be good for them to have the extra responsibility. Instead, she could go to Jia Lin's school – actually, her after-school tutorial club – and meet her at the gates. On rare occasions when she had done so in the past, Jia Lin had never said anything, but Linyao knew the girl found the extra attention significant.

She was almost ready to spin on her heels when another thought struck her. The catering job tonight – to make a sumptuous vegan dinner for an important group of eleven visitors staying temporarily in Shanghai – was no ordinary booking. The visitors were a much talked-about group of international animal rights activists called the Children of Vega. The visit of this group was the most discussed event in recent memory, as far as vegetarian circles in this city were concerned. The charismatic boss of the group was said to be extremely sensitive about his food. Woe betide anyone who served him an ill-conceived meal, or one with anti-ideological ingredients. This thought made her feel uncomfortable. Perhaps it was too risky to leave it to the youngsters.

To ponder over intractable dilemmas is like doing the cha-cha-cha. Two steps north, one step south. Pause. Turn around. Two steps south, one step north. Pause. Turn around. Linyao was performing this complex manoeuvre in her head, and her feet were starting to do the same thing as she twisted her body one way and then the other. Then she made up her mind.

She started walking forward again. No; she couldn't skip it.

On this occasion, she had better oversee the catering job herself, and leave the job of collecting her daughter to her domestic helper, who did it automatically unless informed otherwise. Can't risk the Children of Vega being upset. A link with Vega could put their café on the map as far as vegetarianism in China went – perhaps even internationally. She'd pick Jia Lin up from school tomorrow, or another day.

And so, with a few seconds' thought, we make quick decisions we are to bitterly regret over long hours ahead. For perhaps this is the biggest dilemma of creatures who live temporal lives. Trapped in mono-directional time, we have no ability to step outside and see our lives from more useful angles. Linyao is an over-busy woman eleven and a quarter years older than Joyce, and her problem is not her awareness of the number of possibilities ahead of her, but her lack of awareness of them. Her life has become a high-speed sequence of decisions, huge numbers of them a day, almost all of which are made with little or no thought. Life is not a box of chocolates, but a lucky dip containing an infinite number of tightly wrapped packages, some of which hold diamond rings while others harbour miniature nuclear bombs. You just keep absently picking out the packages, every minute, every day, your whole life long. Lu Linyao, on this occasion, picked a ticking package out of the lucky dip of life and slipped it in her bag to explode later.

☯

First came the sauce inspection. Linyao had always been a meticulous person, but today she was excelling herself. She stood on the staff deck of the small, closed restaurant and prepared for battle. The nine years she had spent in Canada (during which time she acquired a Canadian passport, a child, a Filipina domestic helper and – temporarily – a husband) had given her an easy fluency in English.

'Ingredients check,' she barked. She started grabbing the

28

bottles and jars from the condiments tray and tossing them to the two young people standing in the centre of the room.

'I'll do them. Let me do them,' Joyce McQuinnie said guiltily, snatching bottles from the air. The British-Australian teenager had replenished most of the items on the condiments rack, feeling that important guests needed fresh, clean jars and bottles, not grubby, half-empty ones. As a child, she had always been told off by her older sister for her constant desire for *brand new* things. Her sister had sneered that *brand new* meant the same as *new*, but she still felt the two words together conjured up a delight lacking in the word *new* on its own. It wasn't until years later that it became obvious to her that firstborn children place less value on the virginity of mundane items, while younger children, inevitably dressed in hand-me-downs with 'not too many stains', considered it an issue of great importance.

One of the things Joyce most liked about staying in hotels was the way staff sneaked into your room and tried to make everything new, doing absurd things such as folding the end of your toilet roll into a triangle. It was a delicate little attempt to make a singularly unattractive object – a half-used toilet roll – look brand new again. She had thought of adopting the technique for home use, but decided her guests, most of whom were rather slovenly young people, would laugh at her. And besides, she was not a details person, nor was she a person of consistent habits. She knew she would have done it for three days and then dropped it.

Joyce's failure to pay attention to detail often jumped up and bit her on the bottom – and it looked as if it might do so again on this occasion. In the past week she had already been caught out once by the presence of an illegal ingredient in the small print on the label of an item she had bought for the vegetarian café. And she had a sinking feeling that she might be disgraced again. The worry drove thoughts of Marker Cai out of their pole position at the centre of her thoughts. Had she carefully checked the label as she bought each item? Probably not. But it was too late for her to take over the job of checking the ingredients lists herself. Linyao had already tossed several items to Philip 'Flip' Chen, given a third of them to Joyce, and retained the rest to examine herself.

The young woman looked at the collection of condiment containers in front of her: ketchup, dark soy sauce, Japanese chilli powder, sesame seed powder, and some sort of bottled satay sauce. At first glance, it all looked veggie enough. But Linyao had drummed it into her troops: the utmost vigilance in label-reading was the only way to maintain physiological and ideological purity.

Joyce had been in way too much of a hurry to do the shopping properly. After they had abandoned their crumbling office block on Henan Zhong Lu, Wong had said that he was going to the opening of some sort of new dining club tonight – it had a stupid name, 'This Is the Good Life' or 'Really Living' or something like that. So she had taken the opportunity to stop work early too. How could she work without a desk or an office? She had raced to a food store, grabbed some fresh condiments, and then walked briskly to the café.

'Remember this is a Code 3 meal,' the chair of the society said, pursing her lips and staring coldly at each label.

Joyce nodded. Code 1 meals were strict vegetarian. Code 2 meals were strict vegan. And Code 3 meals were restricted vegan meals, conforming to the vegan code with extra conditions attached by the client who had ordered the food. In this instance, the client had given Linyao strict lists of possible ingredients, and she had thus classified the meal as Code 3.5, also known as hyper-vegan. Joyce bit her lip as she read the ingredients list on a product without taking in a single word. When she became stressed her brain seemed to wipe itself clean, a process she could never repeat when she tried meditation or yoga. She shook her head to get her brain working and started reading again.

On the other side of the room, Phil Chen nodded his head to a heavily syncopated rhythm audible only to him as he read the back of a jar of Dijon mustard: water, mustard seed, vinegar, salt, citric acid and potassium metabisulphite.

'I tink you be lucky today, sista,' he said in a broad Jamaican accent. 'Dis stuff be mostly ohkay.' He put it down and picked up a jar of Lee Kum Kee Chilli Bean Sauce and traced his finger down the ingredients list: chilli, water, fermented soy bean paste, fermented broad bean paste, sugar, garlic, spice, modified corn starch, soybean oil, food acid, disodium 5 inosinate. 'And dis one too.'

As usual, Phil's accent put a broad smile on Joyce's face.

Although one hundred per cent Chinese by blood, Phil Chen had learned English while spending most of the past year as an exchange student in New York. He had lived with the family of Royston Marley Lewis, seventeen, in an apartment off 125th Street, and found the environment of Harlem so fascinating that he had spent more time studying Royston's happy and creative family (five adults, only two of whom were related to each other, and four children, most of whom had different fathers) than focusing on what he was there to do: business studies at the City University of New York.

Raised in a small town north of Beijing, Phil (his name was an Anglicisation of his Chinese name Fei) spoke no English at all when he arrived in the United States, although he could read and write it quite well: such is the situation of people who learn languages largely from books. So he naturally assumed that the pronunciation of Royston's family was the best way to speak the words he knew so well from his English textbooks. None of the Lewis family had much time for him (nor did the teachers at CUNY) so he spent long hours with Salvation Preciousblood Constance Lewis, Royston's eighty-three-year-old grandmother, who had moved to New York from Jamaica only three years earlier. It was a joy to finally find out how people in the United States pronounced the words he had written in hundreds of exam answers over the past six years.

I ask, he asks, they asked = I arks, he arks, dey arks.

First, second, third = fussed, secun, turd.

A, B, C, one, two, three = air, bee, see, one, two, tree.

Baby, you and me = Mama, I an' I.

As he became more relaxed about speaking in English and mixed with more people at the university, he was pleased to discover that his value judgement was correct. The Lewises' English *was* the best English. The young men (of any colour) who spoke like Royston's family members were the popular ones, the ones who were looked up to, the ones who set the style for others to follow. While most of the teachers spoke in the softer, more sophisticated, affricative accents he heard used by Westerners in movies and on the BBC World Service, the coolest of the boys and hottest of the girls spoke like the Lewises. So he did too.

Now he had been back in China for seven weeks, and was delighted to show off his fluency in English. But although most English speakers understood what he said, they always looked faintly surprised at his *Yo, homey* greetings and Jamaican accent. This rather upset him. He had never understood why his speech patterns were considered odd until Joyce commented a few days earlier that it was funny to hear *that* sort of accent coming out of a Chinese face.

'Wot chew mean?'

'You know, like a, a, a, a, whatdoyoucallit, a West Indian accent sortofthing,' she had stammered awkwardly.

'Indian? I not speakin' *Indian*, gul.'

'No, I mean like *black* people and all that,' she said, her shoulders creeping upwards with the embarrassment of having said something that was probably un-PC. 'You know. Africa. Jamaica. Around there.'

'I lairned me to speak English in Noo York.'

'New York, yeah. That's where I meant.'

But his family and friends were getting used to his accent, and since he had also picked up New York teenage fashion sense, copying his garments precisely, label by label, from Royston's younger half-brothers Washington and Stevie, he dressed the part too, in baggy trousers and shapeless XXL T-shirts. He had shocked his Chinese friends by declaring that blue denim jeans were out of fashion. 'Nobody wear dem. Only de moms. De hip people, dey doen wear dem. Dey wear udder casual clodes. Usually yellow or brown colour like dis. Dem call car-keys.' He yanked the spare folds of cloth on his voluminous low-crotched khaki Chinos and left his Shanghai contemporaries gaping. Phil, everyone decided, had become totally cool. He was never without a backpack containing two items – his skateboard, and a megaphone used for declaiming rap poetry on the streets. The boy who had been born Fei, and who had then become Philip, now asked people to call him Flip, but most were too taken aback at the transformation to call him anything at all.

Linyao gave out a yelp, followed by a sharp intake of breath. Joyce and Flip froze and turned to stare at her. For a few seconds, nobody breathed. Linyao was holding a thin, dark brown bottle with a black and orange label. 'Who bought this?' she asked, her voice dangerously low and calm sounding.

Joyce recognised the product. It was a bottle of Lea & Perrins sauce, a brown, dark-tasting liquid which her father used to pour onto sausages and steaks. Her shoulders flopped. 'Er. It may have been me,' she said in the shrivelled voice of a child admitting to an illicit visit to the cookie jar. She'd assumed it was made out of vinegar and cornflour – that's what it tasted like.

Linyao stretched out the unpleasantness by reading out the ingredients list extremely slowly: 'Vinegar. Molasses. Sugar. Salt.' She paused. 'And *anchovies*,' she added in a whisper.

There was silence for a full two seconds.

'Oops. Oh dear,' Joyce said nervously. 'Ha ha.'

'Anchovy am wot?' Flip asked.

Linyao turned her head to him while somehow managing to keep her hurt, accusatory eyes fixed firmly on Joyce. 'Murdered fish,' she said. 'Fish who were caught, skinned, decapitated, murdered and put into tins, all while they were still alive, in all probability.'

Joyce shook her head in wonder. 'Ha ha. Anchovies. How on earth did those get in there?'

Flip stared. 'Lemme see de bottle.'

Linyao held it up. Now it was Flip's turn to give a squeal. '*Aiee!* I put some of dat stuff on my snack yesterday – ach, mardered fish.' He began spitting theatrically into a sheet of kitchen paper, and then scraping his tongue with his fingernails. 'Ew, ew, ew,' he whined. 'I can't believe I eating poor little live fishes.'

'They're not alive,' Joyce said, wondering whether it would make the situation better if she admitted that many times she, too, had consumed Lea & Perrins sauce, not realising that it was not strictly vegetarian.

'They were once,' Linyao said, icily, 'before they were murdered to be put into this sauce.'

'I better go tro up,' Flip said. 'I *hate* dis.'

As he left, Joyce considered running after him to explain that it was too late to scrape his tongue or throw up. If he had eaten the sauce the previous day, the material would surely no longer be in his stomach, but would have moved on to his intestines, or been purged. But she decided to keep quiet. She had sinned. She was in disgrace.

'I guess I didn't——' Joyce began.

'Read the label,' Linyao barked. 'That's obvious enough.'

'Sorry. It's really low on the ingredients list, which probably means there are only a few, like, *molecules* of anchovy in it. Not even adding up to one whole fish per bottle, probably.'

Linyao said nothing. Joyce bowed her head and tried to look contrite. 'Sorry.'

'I will not have a bottle of meat in this restaurant,' Linyao shrieked. In direct contradiction to her words, she threw the bottle across the room, where it hit the wall with a crash, leaving ugly splodges of brown all over the restaurant's east wall. 'Now clean it up.'

'Okay.'

Linyao turned to go back to the pantry, but then faced Joyce again. 'And when you've cleaned the walls, throw away the cloth or sponge you used. Throw it away *outside* the building.'

'Okay.'

Tears pricking behind her eyes, the young woman dropped to her knees and started picking up pieces of broken glass, while reflecting, not for the first time, that the reputation vegetarians and vegans had for being gentle animal-lovers had some spectacular exceptions – Linyao being an obvious one. Yet she felt that the chairperson of the Shanghai Vegetarian Café Society was even more tense today than she had been the past few days. Was there something in particular irritating her? Or was it the already-known fact that she was a grouch, having messed up her life fairly comprehensively by the age of thirty-one? Fortunately, Linyao's outbursts of temper usually disappeared as quickly as they began. Joyce had barely finished picking up the pieces of glass when Linyao joined her, scrubbing the wall with a dishcloth, even though it meant that the 'meat sauce' was likely to touch her skin.

'Sorry I'm so uptight,' Linyao said. 'It's just that Vega is—' She paused to try to find the right words. 'Vega is – very particular. He's very careful. And he has a foul temper. I mean, I've never actually met him. But I've heard he's got this hot temper.'

Joyce asked herself: *Worse than yours?* Then she blushed, wondering if she had uttered the phrase out loud. But the older woman did not immediately react, so apparently she had not.

'Worse than mine,' Linyao volunteered. 'Much, much worse.'

That's hard to believe, Joyce thought.

'You probably find that hard to believe,' the other woman continued, 'but—' She stopped, as if she realised that it would be bad manners to speak ill of an honoured guest who was soon to grace their restaurant. 'If he had found an anchovy in his sauce – but never mind. He'll be here soon enough. We'll all meet him.' The tone in her voice was unmistakable: a one hundred per cent solution of pure, undiluted awe.

The two continued to clean up. Flip returned to the scene, announcing that he had changed his mind about throwing up and would just try to struggle through. 'I tink I will have nightmares about de ghosts of anchovies 'aunting me and saying, "Why you eat me? I doen do nutting to you". I feel like a cannibal.'

Joyce was going to say that he could only consider himself a cannibal if he, too, were a fish. But looking at his pasty face, blubbery skin and shiny hair, she felt that the comment would have been a little too accurate. And besides, Linyao's vegetarian ideology stressed the basic unity of all sentient beings.

The three of them worked fast, knowing that there was not much time before Vega and his team of animal liberation activists were due to arrive.

But the brown stain was not coming off the wall.

'Dis meat sauce, it stick,' Flip said.

'It's *not* meat sauce. It's got one molecule of—'

'I teasing you, sista.'

'Go and get some stain remover,' Linyao said. 'Something really strong. There's a hardware store on Sichuan Nan Lu which will probably have something.'

'Will do.' Joyce picked up her bag and headed to the door.

'And read the ingredients,' Linyao barked.

Flip sniggered. 'Yeah, careful. A lot of cleanin' fluid ackshally made of stek, you know.'

'Har-har-har,' Joyce said. 'I'll search high and low to find one which is entirely meat-free.'

As she put on her coat, Linyao's mobile phone trilled – the ring-tone was a Cantopop tune. She burrowed around in her handbag to find it and quickly stabbed the answer button. Lines appeared between her eyebrows as she listened to the caller. 'Not home yet? Probably stuck in traffic. It's dreadful today. Call me if they're not home in twenty minutes.'

Joyce gave her a quizzical look.

'Jia Lin's not home from school yet.'

'Who takes her home?'

'We have a Filipina domestic helper who doubles as body-guard and cook.'

'I thought you weren't allowed to have Filipina domestic helpers here.'

'You aren't really. But lots of people do. She's listed as an employee of my ex-husband's company. Anyway, she and I take turns collecting Jia Lin from school. Well, to be honest, she does it nearly all the time, and I do it occasionally. That was my cousin. She's at home waiting for them.'

'The traffic's been dreadful all week.'

'That's right. I'm not worried. They must be on the bus on the way home. It can take more than an hour to go that tiny distance when the traffic's as bad as this. Now stop loitering and get the cleaning stuff.'

Linyao leaned back in her chair and a gramme of the worry that she had dealt with earlier bobbed up again like a drowned man who sinks out of sight and then dramatically resurfaces. At that moment, the lucky dip of her life was evolving into something a little more serious: not a fairground game at all, now, but a game of roulette; maybe even Russian roulette. The potential pain quotient in the situation quietly rose. The delivery of a child from school to home should have been straightforward: it always had been in the past.

Scenarios crowded into her mind. She chose the most comforting and focused on them: they may have stopped off to see someone, or go to a shop. After all, what could go wrong when a child is released by one responsible adult, her teacher, to the care of another responsible adult, her domestic servant? Yet, however long the odds, she found it difficult to set the worry aside. The fact that the ball was in play was enough to cause a tiny knot in her stomach, a weight in her bowels, the beginnings of an ache in the centre of her chest.

Linyao worked hard to control her mind, slamming her thoughts forcefully back to the situation at hand. 'Anchovies,' she spat. 'Vega would have killed us, and I may even mean that literally – how many other vegans can you name who carry guns?'

☯

Joyce stepped out into the residual sunshine of the darkening day. It had been an unusually chilly week, and the morning had started out cold, with a stiff breeze shaking the trees and shrinking people into their army-surplus greatcoats. But the sun had come out by midday, and warmth had begun to creep into the air as the afternoon wore on. Now it was just after five thirty, and becoming cold again.

The Shanghai evening rush hour was beginning in earnest. A cacophony of traffic sounds filled the air as Joyce tripped along the wide, uneven pavement: cars hooting, the air-brakes of trucks farting, bicycle bells jingling, motor scooters buzzing, the roar of heavy buses dragging their twelve-tonne loads. It was hard to believe what her guidebook said – that just twenty years earlier, Shanghai had been a city mainly of bicycles, with just a few black 'Red Flag' limousines for the officials and business people. Today, you could still see hundreds of bicycles on the main roads – but they were squeezed like toothpaste into thin lines by hundreds of cars jostling their way to dominant positions at the heart of the main routes.

There had been an outcry two years earlier, when officials had proposed banning bicycles from the city centre. After all, since people of importance had cars, why did they need to cater

38

for the rabble? The car lobby argued that in the 1930s, before the communist takeover, there had been more cars in Shanghai than in all the other cities in China put together, so it was right to return the city to being a motor capital. But the Shanghai press took the rare step of actually reporting the outcry of common citizens, and the plan was eventually withdrawn.

Yet now, day by day, an increasing number of cars of all shapes and sizes filled the city, and bicycles were again in danger of being completely squeezed out. During rush hour, the steaming vehicles inched along, radiator to bumper along every road, whether major highway or small side lane. They became trapped, grille-to-grille in the narrow roads alongside the courtyard houses in the older parts of town. They made life difficult for pedestrians as they perched half on the pavements, or sometimes simply drove along them.

In the single week during which Joyce had lived in Shanghai, the evening rush hour had stretched from being forty-five minutes during which the traffic moved more slowly than usual, to seventy-five minutes in which vehicles barely moved at all, topped and tailed by an hour each side during which cars rolled forward in bad-tempered jerks – which was also a pretty good description of the people driving them. And if an extra factor was ever thrown into the mix – an accident, bad weather, a VIP visit, a small conflagration in a shophouse on the main road – then traffic came to a complete halt for an unpredictable length of time.

Yet central Shanghai's road problems had never quite reached the world notoriety of Bangkok traffic jams – until four days ago. On that Saturday, two major sets of roadworks began on the eastern stretch of Nanjing Dong Lu, joining the three which were already there. Five major sets of roadworks in a relatively short space were too many. On the Monday, there had been a period of steaming, angry gridlock between five thirty and six forty-five, interspersed with spasmodic bursts of movement.

Worse was to come. This being China, with all the attendant fawning on officials, VIP visits were the worst thing. Joyce knew that later in the week, some sort of international summit was due to be held in Shanghai, with politicians flying in from around the world. Those were the worst interruptions of all. The previous Friday, a European prime minister was in town, and the main north–south road, Xizang Lu, was blocked for fifty minutes during the morning rush hour. Almost everyone had been late for work that day: one of the newspapers carried a photograph of a school morning assembly with just three pupils. Later this week – was it tomorrow night? – some sort of meeting was taking place in Shanghai involving the Presidents of China and the United States. There was also an anti-American demonstration planned, to coincide with the visit. There was much speculation as to whether the march was organised by independent activists or activists employed by the Chinese government – but whichever it was, it would bring the city to a halt for everyone except officials. It would be worth completely avoiding the centre of the city for the next couple of days, Joyce realised.

She had spent a lot of time thinking about cars and driving, since she signed up to take driving lessons as soon as she got here. Her father, who spent most of his time in New York, had been horrified to hear that she was learning to drive in China. 'They don't know how to drive in that country. They just *buy* driving licences – they don't have to do any tests or anything. You'll be flattened on your first day on the road.' But his warnings had not been heeded. It was probably true that in parts of China you could get a driving test just by paying money to the right person – the abysmal lack of motoring skills among many rural drivers seemed proof of that. She'd heard stories of one province where the only driving test was a written one. As long as one could memorise rules, one could get out onto the street as a licensed driver without ever having driven a car.

But in Shanghai the system proved to be similar to that in

other countries: there were driving schools, and there were lessons to be taken and a test to be undergone. Joyce had signed up for twenty lessons – the rule of thumb being that the average person needed roughly as many lessons as she was years old – and the first was scheduled for eleven o'clock the following Tuesday. Joyce had been very careful to specify the time, so that the morning rush hour would be over, and there would be a pause before the lunchtime rush hour kicked in and jammed the streets again.

But she was wondering whether she had made the right decision. Flip had had his test the previous week, and ended up with a time slot of five thirty to six. In the event, the car turned onto the main road, got stuck in a traffic jam, and barely moved. The examiner gave him a pass mark, despite his having skipped many of the official manoeuvres he was supposed to do. 'He should really have extended de test, but I de the las' one for de day, and he obviously wan' go home,' the young man said afterwards. She liked Flip and had initially wondered whether he might become her first Chinese boyfriend – until he confessed to her that he was trying to decide whether he was gay. And then she had met Marker Cai: gorgeous Mister *Sigh*, whom she was going to meet for coffee one of these days.

The thought put a grin on her face as she gingerly trod the busy pavements leading to the hardware shop. The early evening gridlock brought one bonus to pedestrians. During the earlier parts of the day, it was hard to cross a road of weaving, jerking, stop-start traffic. But during rush hour, the cars sat still most of the time, crawling forward only once or twice every few minutes. That made crossing the road easy. The main streets of the city became long thin car parks of stationary vehicles.

Strolling down the side road, she quickly found the hardware store and chose a bottle of super-strong stain remover. Although she knew that Flip had been joking about the presence of steak in cleaning fluid, she carefully checked the ingredients list to make sure there was nothing objectionable in it. After all, who would have thought there would be fish in Lea & Perrins? Of course, the bottle of cleaner she wanted was three times the price of the one next to it. It was always the way in China, and the thing that made life difficult and expensive for people from overseas. Products which were recognisable and had bonuses such as believable lists of ingredients on them were usually imported, and thus pricey. But there were always tempting local versions of everything, at a fraction of the price, but bearing no information in English, and often very little in Chinese. Does one take the risk? No; better to pay the premium.

Two minutes later, she was walking back across the main road and noticed that she was walking in between precisely the same cars; none of them had moved. And a minute after that, she slipped once more through the doors of the Shanghai Vegetarian Café Society.

Linyao and Flip were working at a table, chopping vegetables.

'He scares me,' she was telling him.

'I too, now you tole me dat,' the young man replied.

Joyce had intended to go straight to the wall and start the stain removal process, but decided instead to join the others. This conversation sounded too good to miss. She guessed they were talking about the mysterious visiting god of animal-lovers. 'Vega?'

Linyao nodded. She was tense: her right leg was vibrating on its heel.

'Relax. He's on our side,' Joyce said. 'It'll be fine.'

The older woman nodded again. 'True enough. Or so it seems. But he's extreme. You know how this sort of movement attracts extremists sometimes.'

'You mean he goes around rescuing animals from labs and all that?'

'That's just for starters. Let me tell you what I've heard about Vega.'

Her conspiratorial tone inspired Joyce to pull her chair in more tightly. Clearly, there was some good goss about to emerge, and good goss about a celebrity they were about to meet was irresistible. Was he young and good-looking? She was tempted to ask Linyao whether she had a picture of him, but was worried she might appear crass.

Linyao leaned forward into the conversation. 'There used to be two main animal rights groups in Shanghai. There was one north of Suzhou Creek called All Living Things – it was a very Buddhist group – and there was one that came out of Hongqiao called Friends of Creation, which was more a humanist sort of thing, a mixture of Chinese and Westerners. The Friends put out a lot of leaflets and stuff, and occasionally picketed the wet markets and things, but nothing too controversial.

'All Living Things was a bit more lively. It was run by this young woman called Zhong Xue Qin. She was brilliant at press and publicity. She was always on TV, campaigning outside restaurants, harassing the stallholders at the wet markets and writing articles in the newspapers about animal welfare. She was also incredibly tall and thin and beautiful, which helped – classic Shanghainese blood, you know. But one time her group actually got into a fight at a restaurant serving southern Chinese food – you know how in the south they like rare animals freshly cooked. The cooks had got some endangered stuff – flying squirrels and the like. But the restaurant was owned by some-one high up in the Party. Zhong and two of the group went to jail for a week. After that, we thought she would quieten down. But she became even more extreme.'

'What sorta ting dey do?'

'They found labs where animals were being experimented on, and stopped people going in. They got students at the universities to stop going to vivisection classes. And then she started campaigning against this supermarket chain, owned by a powerful family.'

'Which one?' Joyce asked.

'Mee Fan Trading in Chinese,' Linyao said. 'It's owned by a family named Mee. Actually, the real name is Memet, or something like that – they are from the far west, Urumqi – but the *Guoyu* version is Mee. The far west of China has lots of problems, and several members of the family moved to Canada, and some moved to London. Anyway, there were various meetings and eventually the second son of the Mee family, a UK-based guy, flew into China to join the family firm and was giving the task of sorting out the problem with Zhong Xue Qin. They met. And the predictable thing happened.'

'What?' Flip asked.

'You typical man,' Linyao scolded him. 'Can't you guess? She's dirt poor but beautiful and fiery. He's got no principles at all, but is stinking rich.'

'They fell in love?' Joyce ventured.

Linyao gave a single nod. 'They fell in love. They got married three months after they'd met. Which was kind of weird, because she was born in Shanghai and he was born in London from an Urumqi Muslim family in a sort of self-imposed exile. She managed to convert him to being a supporter of animal welfare, and now she had his endless buckets of money behind her. The Mee Fan supermarkets started carrying organic food – her influence. One day she broke into a lab at Shanghai Second Medical University to release some mice. But while looking for rodents, she went through all sorts of no entry doors, and touched all sorts of things she shouldn't have touched. She caught some horrible disease and died within three days.'

'*Aiee!*' said Flip. 'Like Ebola or someting?'

'Something like that. Maybe Ebola or Marburg or SARS.

I don't know exactly. None of this was ever printed, of course, but you hear things in the right circles.'

She seemed to have stopped speaking, but Joyce felt the story was unfinished. 'I thought you were going to talk about Vega – where does he fit into all this?'

'Her rich husband went crazy with grief and anger. He fled

to London. Dropped out of sight. This was maybe two years ago. Then, about seven or eight months ago, people in my circles started hearing about a new animal rights group coming out of London. It was called the Children of Vega and it was run by a young man codenamed Vega. It had a special focus: animal welfare in China.'

'You reckon that was him? The husband?'

Linyao nodded. 'I reckon he had decided to glorify his wife's memory by starting a group in her honour, to fight for animal welfare in China. They don't do leaflets. They don't do picketing. They don't do interviews. They are a real civil disobedience type group – and they have huge budgets: his pockets seem to be bottomless. Their first action was to stage a major raid on a live food market in Guangzhou. A great team of people in black masks descended on the place and held up the stallholders. They stole loads of amazing animals – there were red and white flying squirrels, masked palm civets, Chinese muntjacs, martens, leopard cats and so on. The really cool thing was that they left behind some money for the stallholders – so that, technically, they had *bought* the animals rather than stolen them.'

'Wow,' said Flip. 'Soun' like he got style.'

'Style and scale. He only does big jobs. Their second job was to close down a bear bile farm in Sichuan. They used their weapons in that one, and a security guard got killed, which upset a lot of people in vegetarian circles. But the police never traced it to anyone. Everyone wore masks. I mean, no one knows officially whether either of those jobs were Vega's gang – no one claimed responsibility for them. But to people in veggie circles, it seems obvious. Who else could it have been?'

'Why is he coming here tonight?' Joyce asked. 'Does he want to sign us up? Masked people and weapons and things – it all seems a bit heavy.'

Linyao shook her head, to the younger woman's relief. 'He doesn't want to sign us up. I told him that we had a small group and were not very into civil disobedience. We just cook tofu. But he's planning a few operations here, I think, in the next week or two. He's had the Shanghai Friends of Creation and All Living Things working for him for some time, setting up something. He's very strategic. He sends an advance team who work with local activists, suss out the scene, and prepare a project. Then he and his main team fly in, do the job, and disappear. He said he needed to be here for a few days and wanted some place where he could be sure the food was strictly vegan, to his personal standards. That's where we fit in.'

'Phew,' said Joyce. 'So we're not part of the action. We're just the caterers.'

'Exactly.'

'Armed break-ins, like, so aren't my thing. But cooking up a decent lentil loaf – that I can manage.'

A tinny burst of pop music erupted below the table. 'My mobile again,' Linyao said.

'You like Cheung Hok-yau?' Flip commented, his admiration for her ring-tone evident from his face. 'Classy mama.'

Joyce walked over to the wall and started spraying it with the stain remover. 'Better get this meat sauce off before they get here.'

'Lemme help.'

With Joyce spraying and Flip scrubbing, the stains started to fade. They worked in silence. Despite her outward appearance of calm, Joyce, who spent much of her time anxious about nothing at all, was becoming increasingly nervous about the short-fused, gun-toting god of vegans from London. To her way of thinking, there was something horribly illogical in the concept of animal welfare activists carrying guns. If you didn't want animals to be hurt, then you shouldn't want humans to be hurt – humans were, after all, just a particularly big, ugly, stupid, troublesome breed of animal.

Linyao spoke on the phone in rapid Shanghainese, interspersed with bits of Mandarin and English. Her eyes were wide with fear and excitement when she finished the call. 'Change of plan.'

The others turned to look at her.

'He's doing some sort of operation in town tonight.'

'Tonight? What sort of operation?' Joyce felt a wave of distaste at the prospect of being linked with any activity that might include violence. After all, she had practically been through an earthquake today – excitement enough to last her a month.

'I don't know. But it'll be big, knowing him. And stylish.'

Flip pointed to the semi-prepared food laid out on the kitchen table. 'Does dis mean he not comin' after all? Can we eat all dis ourself?' The prospect produced a theatrical expression of big eyes and lip-licking.

'No. They're going straight to the event. They've been working on it for days.'

'So what do we do?' Joyce asked.

'We need to meet them at the site, with hot, packed, Code 3 sandwiches.'

'Let's get this straight. They'll do some sort of stunt, rescuing animals or something, and we are just the outside caterers. We make the food available, deliver it and we leave?'

'You've got it.'

Joyce shrugged. 'It's okay, I guess. This reminds me of something I read about the movie business in *Teen People*. People in the business love to talk about being in it because it sounds so glamorous, but every movie is really six people doing glamorous things and four hundred holding lights or making sandwiches and coffee.'

'It won't be difficult,' Linyao said.

Flip moved over to the kitchen and started assembling the wraps.

'Gloves on,' Linyao barked at him. 'Germs are animals and I don't want any animals in Vega's sandwich.'

The younger woman's brow wrinkled. She'd thought of a

problem. 'Where's the operation and how are we going to get there? The traffic's chock-a-block outside.'

Linyao moved to the window and took a look. Traffic was stationary for as far as the eye could see. 'You're right,' she said. 'It's bad. It's been terrible all week.'

'Wait till tomorra night. Dat when de summit start. De two Presidents? It not wurt getting outta bed. 'cept I tinking I might go to de demo tomorra evenin'.'

'If we take the van, we won't get there until next month. We're just going to have to walk or go by bike. If we can be ready to go in twenty minutes, we'll make it on time.'

The three of them were soon energetically preparing food in the kitchen: peeled grilled peppers and roasted eggplant slotted into home-made whole-wheat wraps lined with cos lettuce and yellow tomatoes, with a fresh carrot stick inside.

Linyao's phone rang. 'Not *again*,' she said. 'Now what?'

She'd forgotten that her child had not reached home. But the spinning had stopped. The ball was landing.

She wiped her hands, picked up the phone and listened to the caller's voice. And the irritation in her face was quickly replaced by fear. 'Oh,' she said, quietly. 'Oh dear.'

Joyce and Flip stopped breathing, stopped crinkling paper, stopped moving.

'I'll come and see what's happening. Ring me immediately if they turn up. It'll be fine, I'm sure it will be.' Her tone failed to reflect the confidence of her words. Linyao slowly let the handset drift downwards, forgetting to hang up.

'Jia Lin?' Joyce asked.

Linyao's voice lost its hard edge and became vulnerable. 'Jia Lin and the maid are *still* not home. Now, I must admit, I'm a bit worried. I'm going to go and walk the route from the school to home, and then I'll ring friends, in case she and the maid decided to visit someone and forgot to tell us or something. You'll have to—'

'I'll deliver the stuff; don't you worry,' Joyce said. 'I'll use my bike. It'll be a piece of cake.'

'You've got to leave it at a place called the Herborium: you know it? It's a health food shop on Rujin Yi Lu. The operation is at the Jin Jiang Plaza Tower, which is nearby at the junction of Maoming Nan Lu. They're going to storm some animal restaurant or something near there. Some new dining club called This Is Living. What a stupid name.'

Joyce's fist flew to her mouth.

3

In 61 BC, Emperor Xuan of Han made an avenue of eighty-eight rare deciduous trees for the people. Each had different coloured leaves.

It was beautiful, but the ground was soon covered with leaves. They fell so fast the royal gardener could not keep the ground clear of them.

The Emperor asked the wise man: 'What shall I do? The path to the palace is buried.'

The wise man told him to announce a new currency in the land: leaves. He said: 'The exchange rate will be five hundred leaves for one gold coin.'

From that day on, the avenue was kept perfectly clean. No leaf even touched the ground before a loyal subject snatched it up.

Some people gathered leaves and swapped them for gold. Others collected leaves and hoarded them. The king was happy to pay a small sum for such a great service.

Blade of Grass, all things can be achieved by uniting the right human beings together in the right combination.

From 'Some Gleanings of
Oriental Wisdom' by CF Wong

Twin doors slid apart and welcomed him on a high-speed journey to the heavens.

Elevators, CF Wong had long believed, were little cuboids of good feng shui – and especially external glass lifts like the one into which he was about to step. For a start, they were more or less square, the simplest of the recommended room layouts in the ancient texts, although this one, like most glass elevators, extended outwards slightly in a bay-window shape to ensure that the riders got the widest possible view. Second, they were in full control of the person inhabiting them, thanks to the buttons. Third, and most importantly, there was an element of magic in them. Of course, most people didn't see this magic at all – people today were so blasé, they failed to register any wonder at the modern miracles surrounding them. How quickly people's minds closed and became tragically desensitised to the world!

The feng shui master had spent a great deal of time thinking about this. It was all to do with natural physics, he reckoned. When one was young, one learned basic physics. That's *all* one did. One was carried around by one's mother and one's entertainment was to watch adults interacting with the world. The laws of physics accumulated in one's head. Adults communicate with other adults by making sounds. Days are bright, but nights are dark. Water flows, but the ground does not. Pictures of people in picture books look like people but have no life. Birds live in the sky, but people do not. The rules pile up in the child's head and the world starts to make sense.

And then comes the day when electricity arrives in the village, and things start to change. Now the dark is not dark – there are bright suns shining in the blackness (sometimes so bright that you can't actually see anything). Then a box appears in the village headman's house where the pictures laugh and talk and move, like live, albeit grey-skinned, people. The first time Wong saw television he assumed that the reason Westerners were called *gwai lo*, or ghost people, was because they had greyish white skin, as they did on television in Guangdong in the 1960s.

And then comes the day when the child, now grown up, goes from the village to the big city and discovers that all the most fundamental laws of physics have been overturned. The gradual trickle of modern magic into China's rural areas becomes, in the urban parts, a *Changjiang* – a Long River – of marvels. In

Guangzhou, the ground moves, up, down, and sometimes crawls flat along the ground, or snakes around corners. Water flows, not just in rivers, but elegantly out of stone carvings in the middle of buildings. Buildings stand like glass mountains, higher than the trees and hills around them. And Guangzhou was on the flight path of two airports, so up there in heaven, just above the clouds, there was a constant line of tubes filled with people – he used to think of them as trains of the air – flying as high as any bird has ever flown.

And then there were the elevators. He recalled the first time he stepped into one. He was twenty-seven years old and had just entered his first skyscraper, an office building in eastern central Guangzhou, near the trade halls. He had heard of the things, but had never tried one himself. Initially the experience was very unpleasant. For a start, the space was small – claustrophobically small, especially since six people had entered it with him. Then there was the fact that the walls and doors were metal. He felt sealed in, almost as if he was in a standing-room-only tomb of some sort. But worst of all, he had no feeling of control. The doors appeared to close without clear human intervention – only later did he become aware that some of the individuals who had entered the small room had been applying their fingers to the side wall panel.

But it was when the door reopened thirty seconds later that his attitude changed. The elevator had not appeared to move. There was a slight jerk and a shake, but there had been no perceptible vertical movement. He did not feel as if he had flown up a tall building. Yet when the door opened, the scene outside had changed. Instead of a narrow pale green corridor and an aged security guard, there was a pale mauve corridor and no security guard. The doors whisked shut again, the room shook itself once more, and this time the doors opened to reveal a large red-carpeted office. It seemed to be some sort of magic – every time you spent half a minute in this tiny room, the world outside the door changed. He knew how it worked, but that did not lessen his amazement.

Wong spent half an hour going up and down in the elevator on that first occasion, and had arrived late for his appointment. At first, the lack of apparent movement mystified and intrigued him. Why did one have no real sensation of movement, except for a slight tremor in the stomach when the elevator stopped? Then he worked out the answer. Since each person was the centre of his own existence, what was really happening was that you and your elevator-room were staying still while the world outside moved up or down. This accorded perfectly with the saying of Mo Zhou in 479 BC: 'The wise man knows that he is the centre of the world. Throughout his life, he never moves an inch, but the world runs and jumps and leaps around him.'

That experience took place thirty years ago, but CF Wong had still not lost his love of elevators. And he particularly liked glass-walled elevators on ultra-high skyscrapers, where one could see the world changing shape before one. This elevator was an external one, clinging to the side of a glittering glass-walled tower. He watched with eyes wide as the Shanghai cityscape rearranged itself gracefully in front of him. One moment the office blocks towered above him. The next moment, they seemed to elegantly throw themselves down, and he was level with the tops of the highest ones. The buildings seemed to morph and shrink as he watched. And then, seconds later, he was up in the sky and the buildings and streets had all laid themselves out as toys below him, the biggest city in China becoming a doormat at his feet.

Standing next to Wong was Bi Yun, a vice-president of the company that owned the hotel at which he was about to dine. His eyes were on the feng shui master's face, and he had noted his guest's obvious pleasure in the elevator ride.

'Gorgeous view, isn't it?' Bi said in Beijing-accented Mandarin. 'You feel like you are blasting off into outer space. It's like being in a glass rocket or something, right?'

Wong nodded. 'View very beautiful, yes.'

'Well, we want people to feel they are blasting off to heaven, because that's exactly where they are going,' the businessman gushed. 'Wait till you see the final table settings. It's a gourmet's paradise, it really is.'

The elevator continued to fly smoothly on its way up to the 45th-storey penthouse restaurant. 'Do you know how fast we're moving?' the businessman asked.

'Yes. We are not moving at all. The world moves down.'

'No, you'll find that we're moving up at almost three floors a second – that's about thirty feet a second. Think about it. Three floors a—'

'No,' said the feng shui master. 'Each person is the centre of his own universe, as Mo Zhou said. When you go in an elevator like this, you do not move. What happens is the universe falls forty-five storeys down.'

Bi's eyebrows rose a centimetre. 'I'll have to think about that one.' He gave Wong the kind of smile one gives to a child who believes his own fantasies.

People who knew Wong as a taciturn old man would have been surprised to see him now. He stood tall, his chest thrust out. Had he been walking, they would have noticed the spring in his step. There were even the early glimmerings of a smile curling at the edges of his lips, although Wong was not generally a smiler. The fact was that the past months had been a remarkably profitable time for him. For years he had dismissed northern China as any sort of viable market for his skills. Following the war on Falun Dafa in the late 1990s, feng shui was placed on the frowned-upon-activities list, along with most other non-materialistic codes of belief – although they could do nothing about the feng shui-influenced architecture that was already going up. All unregulated spiritual activities were disliked by the government.

This had upset Wong, as he was in the feng shui business for largely materialistic reasons, and was happy to interpret it as materialistically as anyone wanted. You want an excuse to buy a load of gold trinkets? No problem, I'll give you one. But in the past two years, feng shui had become fashionable in China again – absurdly, as an import from Westernised, British-flavoured Hong Kong. How can you import something to a country from where it originates? There was an idiom in English about this – sending coals to castles, or something? And a matching one (much older, of course) in Chinese: herding ducks to Guangzhou. Yet now there were feng shui 'waving cats' at the entrances to all the shops, and Shanghai people were filling his bookings diary. He could afford to turn down all but the biggest payers.

He had had so many commissions from Shanghai over the past year that he had decided to base himself in the city for a few months, mop up whatever cash there was, set up a satellite office, and a branch of his association. East Trade Industries, the property company which paid his biggest retainer, had bought land, office blocks and several strata titles in Pudong, so it was happy to underwrite the costs of the move. It was cheaper than flying him up and down from Singapore every few days.

The money was great. Normally, that would have been more than enough to satisfy him. But on visits to Shanghai in recent weeks, he had gained more than cash: he had gained status. One of the people who had hired him was a tycoon, another was a senior Communist Party official, and a third was a senior security agent working for the President's office. In the last of these assignments, Wong had been asked to find the safest spot in the vicinity, in case 'important people have to hide or find shelter for any reason'. This had not been difficult. Wong could do it without a map. He simply pointed out that Tsz Lum Cove, a bay cut into a nameless barren rock in the Yangtze Estuary, was sheltered in every way: physically and spiritually. A steep cliff hung over a small plateau just above sea level. The sides of the cliff surrounding the bay were so steep and the material it was made of was so thick (limestone and granite) that nothing could penetrate it – bad vibrations or the blast of major weapons. 'Even if you dropped a bomb on Shanghai, a fisherman in Tsz Lum Cove would be just fine,' he'd said.

And he had been thrilled at how seriously the security chief had taken the pronouncements, laboriously writing down everything he said in simplified characters. In the end, the man had declined to pay his bill, calmly explaining that, 'The President's office does not pay for consultancy work; to work for us is an honour.'

Normally, the feng shui master would have been furious at such a cop-out. But not this time. He had been content to bite his tongue and say nothing. Although he had never thought of himself as status-conscious, he was pleased to think that his words were being added to the emergency files for evacuating top people in the event of war in China. It made him feel important and, more significantly, it made him feel he could do some name-dropping and raise his fees.

'We're here,' Bi said. The lift came to a halt, the internal elevator lights went out and the doors *wooshed* open.

'Lights not working?' Wong said, noting the darkness of the lift and the gloom of the corridor. 'Power cut?' The only light leaked out of the floor, like the emergency strips leading to exit doors on an aircraft.

Bi shook his head. 'No. We use an automatic dimmer to turn them right down so you get more of an effect when you enter the restaurant.'

They followed the spooky floor-lit corridor around a turning to the left and came upon the main door of the restaurant. As Bi had said, the darkness enhanced the drama of the entrance. The doorway was bathed in multicoloured light and surmounted by a temporary sign: a neon light with the name of the dining club which was meeting tonight: *This Is Living*. The letters were in luminous yellow-green which gradually changed to shocking pink as they entered. Wong stopped and stared at it for half a minute, wondering about the feng shui implications of a light which changed colour (yet another modern artefact that broke the recognised laws of physics). Bi, impatient, grabbed Wong by the elbow and pulled him through the doorway.

In shape, the restaurant was much as Wong remembered from the previous week – a large, elegant, oval-shaped room on two levels, with a balcony rail making sure no one tripped off the higher level, which had been turned into a sort of stage. But in another way, it looked very different – the lighting engineers had given it an otherworldly atmosphere with low-slung lights, focused beams, and mixed colours. The room was reddish on one side, blue on the other, and had a clear, balanced tone only in the middle.

Wong looked up with delight at the suspended ceiling. Modern ceilings, to him, were one of the marvels of room design. Suspended ceilings, by definition, lowered the height of a room. But clever layering and lighting effects meant that the net result was to make it appear higher than it would otherwise have seemed.

The room was dotted with tables – thirty-one of them – at intervals large enough for people to have discreet conversations: not like in most Chinese restaurants, where diners ate shoulder-to-shoulder with strangers. In the middle of the raised area was the display table – a high-standing platform where chefs would perform their culinary party tricks from time to time.

There were only four people in the restaurant when they entered, but a steady flow of couples joined them. Each person was welcomed effusively by celebrity chef Jean-Baptiste De Labauve, who gushed over them. He clearly had not been able to decide whether to wear a professional chef 's outfit or something stylish that a haute cuisine restaurant host might wear, since he liked to do both jobs – or at least to take the credit for both. As a result, he was wearing chef's whites, but in ivory silk, and without the stovepipe hat. Around his neck he had a natty Hermès scarf knotted to one side. He had no fear of getting the outfit ruined, as most of the actual cooking was to be done by his staff, overseen by his deputy, a Japanese chef named Benny Tomori.

Virtually all the diners were Asians, and about three out of four were male. It was a strongly testosterone-dominated group. The few women present were mostly young, attractive and rather quiet: mistresses, trophy wives or doting personal assistants, which in Shanghai was a widely recognised term for concubines. There were to be only eighteen guests tonight, all of whom – well, all the men anyway – were founding members of the This Is Living dining club. Wong was not an official member. He was well out of his league as all the others were wealthy businessmen or top officials (which often meant the same thing, not that anyone would be stupid enough to say so). Several were sons of tycoons. But during the preparations, De Labauve was delighted to learn that a number of the guests knew Wong and had employed him. And once he heard that the geomancer used to work in the seafood industry in Guangdong – centre of China's live and exotic food sector – he had invited him to join the founders' meal as a special guest.

Wong was looking forward to it, and his mood went from good to superlative when De Labauve handed him his payment for doing the feng shui reading of the restaurant – a fat envelope of cash. No records, no signatures. No need to declare anything for tax. He tucked it in his jacket pocket right over his heart and from time to time stroked the pleasant bulge it made.

Within twenty minutes all the guests had arrived, and gongs were pounded to invite everyone to move from the bar area to their tables.

De Labauve mounted the raised area and beamed at each table in turn. He spoke in Mandarin, made semi-unintelligible by his French accent. 'Welcome, ladies and gentlemen, to the founding meal of the most remarkable dining club in Shanghai. Most of you will know that we offer the freshest, most delicious food in China. This is true. But we offer more than that. We are, I believe, offering the only culinary experience in the world in which all the main ingredients will be alive as you start the meal.

'The fish you will eat are all swimming in the aquarium, which is in the room to my left, through the blue-lit door. The poultry is clucking away in cages in a room to the left of the kitchen. The crabs, lobsters, prawns and crayfish are swimming in tanks on the east side of the aquarium. The vegetables are growing in conservatory trays in the climate-controlled greenhouse on the floor below us. The giant sea turtle tried to escape twice but has been apprehended and is now in safe custody in the care of the sous chef.'

Pause. Cue laughter. The speaker bowed slightly to acknowledge the audience reaction. 'And now, let the magic begin. The food will inspire you to repeat to yourselves, ladies and gentlemen, I hope, the exclamatory phrase which has given this restaurant its name.' He switched to English: 'This Is Living.'

He banged a gong, and the lights dimmed. A Japanese chef appeared from a door on the left, with a massive knife in one hand and a sharpening tool in the other. He rubbed them together, making sparks fly in the darkness. From the other wing, another chef hurried into the room holding a large fish in a net. He dropped the shiny green creature onto the carving table and the two chefs started to dissect it. It wasn't easy. The beast wriggled and flapped – and was clearly quite strong. The diners looked on with a mixture of horror and morbid fascination as the heavy knives chopped through its twitching, frantic green skin. Dark blood spurted.

De Labauve was back on the microphone, this time providing a commentary. 'This dish has been nominated by Mr Tun Feiyu. Thank you Mr Tun. My sous chef Benny Tomori and his assistant aim to get the fish filleted and onto your plate while it is still flapping. This is not an easy job and needs great skill on the part of the chef. You may think that removing the fish's spine will render it unable to move, but the flesh of the fish can continue to contract and expand even after the backbone has been extracted.'

Right on cue, the two chefs pulled the spine out of the fish and held it up. It looked like something from a children's cartoon.

'It will be served with the beating hearts of frogs, which the chefs in the kitchen have prepared for you in the past few minutes,' De Labauve continued.

While Tomori and his assistant rapidly began slicing the filleted fish into small pieces, two other chefs appeared with a dish of animated objects – the frogs' hearts – which were swiftly placed on small plates and distributed to diners, who broke into a spontaneous round of applause.

Then diners stared at the twitching morsels of flesh on their plates with either horror, delight, or delighted horror, before the braver ones among them splattered them with soy sauce and wasabi, and popped them into their mouths. Wong was thrilled and ate his portion with his eyes closed in rapture.

'Astonishing,' said Park Hae-jin, a Korean businessman sitting nearby, who chewed slowly with pleasure in his eyes.

'Eat, eat,' Chen Shaiming, a Beijing factory owner, said to his nervous-looking wife Fangyin.

'Ew! Does it hurt it to be cut up like that?' she asked.

'No, it likes it. Fish and frogs don't have feelings. They don't feel pain.'

After a slow start, all the portions were consumed (although several of the women surreptitiously passed their portions to their male partners to consume).

The second dish was Shanghai hairy crabs, nominated by a Shanghai-Indian import-export businessman named Vishwa Mathew Roy. A rack of the creatures – unusually large, female specimens – was wheeled into the room. The crabs' pincers were tied shut with pink ribbons, and their legs similarly incapacitated. Yet one of them had somehow come loose. It was scuttling sideways across the top of its fellows, towards the edge of the tray and freedom. One of the chefs caught it and turned it upside down to retie its bonds.

Once the display was tidy again, a junior chef quickly went

along with his fingers, flicking the eyestalks of each crab to make sure they flinched, proving that they were all still alive and thus truly fresh.

This job done, thick, steaming-hot soup was poured into a massive tureen under the crabs. A glass dome was placed over the entire structure and then the flames were turned up high. The soup quickly started boiling, steaming the crabs to death. After just sixty seconds, the flames were turned off and the transparent lid removed. The crabs were picked up with tongs and placed on the diners' plates. Waiters laid gloves on the tables.

De Labauve strode to centre stage again to provide commentary: 'Most of you probably know how to eat hairy crab. But for those who don't, this is what to do. Stick your fingers under the edge of the shell like so – and rip the top half off the crab like this,' he said. 'Don't worry. It's almost definitely dead by now – and if it isn't, it soon will be.'

Inside, the crab was a steaming and delicious white. And since they were female crabs, there was succulent yellow roe to eat, too. Wonderful.

Food, Wong decided, should always be served or cooked alive if at all possible. Certainly if it was going to be presented to men. (The women appeared to be less enchanted with the process.) Males should eat just-slaughtered food several times a year if possible, he decided – preferably this should include some food that was alive when it went into the mouth. The consumption of meat, after all, was not just a way of getting nourishment into the body. It was symbolic of the struggle to live. Just as early man had to battle sabre-toothed tigers to keep his family alive, so modern men needed to be involved in some sort of physical activity to make his meals really satisfying. Buying slices of them dead in plastic wrappings, Western-style, from the supermarket – what kind of True Man would do a thing like that? No, food should be grappled with, and the winner should eat the loser.

In a situation like this, the food was alive and could, in theory, win the battle. The lobster could snap at the fingers of the human trying to eat it, jump off the table and run to the elevator. The turtles, De Labauve had said, had already tried to make a break for freedom. But of course, no one wanted the animals to escape, so the odds were weighted in the humans' favour. And the deep, primal satisfaction of killing an animal as or just before one eats it – what a shame that the vast majority of people would never know that feeling. It seemed fitting that business people in China, who were proving to be masters of innovative entrepreneurialism, had successfully arranged a way to let people experience death as part of living. Killing was part of eating, and it was wrong for them to be separated.

After the crab, a drink was distributed as a palate cleanser. It turned out to be a broth of tiny live fish that wriggled and squirmed as you swallowed them.

The third dish was baby octopi, nominated by the Korean businessman, Park Hae-jin. These tiny bright red beasts, barely a mouthful each in size, were provided with a spray container of red chilli sauce and herbs. You blasted one of the creatures with the red stuff, which drove them wild – and then popped it straight into your mouth.

Wong, joyfully crunching his live baby octopus, reflected on how fortunate he was that Joyce was not present. His pestilent assistant, he knew, was stupidly fond of animals and would find this whole show objectionable, hard though it might be to believe. (He would never have chosen her as a colleague: she had been foisted on him a year earlier because she was the daughter of one of East Trade Industries' clients.) How could anyone see any harm in this wholesome display of consumption of fresh, healthy food? Indeed, to object to something like this going ahead was cruelty – cruelty to human beings, who needed fresh food to live.

He had hardly finished his baby octopus before De Labauve was back on stage. 'Now we have a treat for you. A classic dish with a new interpretation. I'm proud to introduce to you Drunken Prawns Flambéed in XO Cognac, nominated by our very own feng shui master CF Wong – who, incidentally, assures me that this restaurant has the best feng shui of any eating place in the whole of Shanghai.'

Wong smiled and bowed his head to acknowledge the reference, although he wished De Labauve had not repeated the praise he had given to the room – praise which he had given to at least six different restaurants in Shanghai in the past year. Remarkable how that phrase alone could guarantee a generous tip on top of his agreed fee.

Chef Tomori reappeared, trailed by two junior staff. They wheeled in a large, low-walled glass-sided bowl perched over a gas burner and containing giant tiger prawns swimming in consommé, along with chives and spring onions and sliced ginger. The chef then emptied a bottle of XO brandy into the bowl – and at the same time, turned up the heat. The tiger prawns started thrashing around.

'See how the prawns are disco-dancing as they become inebriated,' De Labauve laughed. 'They're really enjoying themselves.'

It was clear to everyone that this was not the case, but it would have been churlish to spoil the manager-chef's fantasy. 'Look at that big one on the right – it's breakdancing like Michael Jackson. *Formidable*,' he said, his voice cracking with glee as he slipped back into French. 'What a happy scene.'

The creatures writhed for another half-minute before Chef Tomori gave his staff the signal that they were ready to take the next step – which had to happen before the prawns died of alcohol poisoning and were boiled alive at the same time.

'But now the dancing party must end,' De Labauve said. 'Just like humans get hot after a wild party, it's time for our drunken prawns to get really hot-hot-hot.'

The prawns were moving slowly now, as the heat drained their ability to move. Chef Tomori threw a flame into the pot and *fwoom* – the whole dish was suddenly ablaze. At the same time the lights were dimmed, so that the blue inferno in which the prawns were being immolated became the only light in the room. The creatures thrashed in their death throes while diners watched fascinated (several personal assistants staring through gaps in their fingers). After thirty seconds, movement had more or less come to a halt. A lid was placed on the dish to put the flames out.

The main lights came back on in the restaurant and the junior chefs used tongs to transfer the steaming prawns out of the soup and onto plates, which were quickly distributed to the tables.

The room was filled with another spontaneous round of applause before the diners began tucking into the steaming morsels on their plates. Some of the women looked a little queasy, but again, most managed to get the prawns down.

Wong was proud to have chosen this dish, and bowed his head to acknowledge the thanks of the people sitting near him – Tun, Chen and their partners. The feng shui master was delighted at how the evening was going. Now this was Chinese cooking at its best. It took him back to his younger days in the fishing villages of the Pearl River Delta. He had been much too poor to eat in fancy fish restaurants, but had spent a year working with an uncle who had a fishing boat: and ultra-fresh fish and seafood, in some cases eaten raw, had been his diet throughout.

However, even the feng shui master felt a little disquiet at the next two dishes. A live civet cat (nominated by Bi Yun) and a live pangolin (nominated by De Labauve himself) were wheeled through the room in cages. Wong did not feel any compunction about eating such beasts – indeed, he knew that both could be delicious and was anxious to try them out cooked and spiced in De Labauve's signature East–West fusion style – but he was discomforted by the fact that both now might well be illegal items, and he tried to minimise the number of occasions on which he broke the law, since he'd become the pet feng shui master of the law enforcement agencies in east Asia. But then he scolded himself for being so soft. Any police officer would take a bite if offered such rare delicacies, he told himself. And why shouldn't he? After all, this was just a bit of fun, nothing serious. Besides, much of the power base in Shanghai was probably in this room, so they had no need to fear the authorities.

In the event, the pangolin proved a little tough and chewy; and the civet cat, although tender, was rather dark-tasting. The first needed more marinating, he decided, and the latter should have been caramelised with honey in some way and served with garlic, ginger and oyster sauce.

The soup course – which came late in the meal, as it should – was Live Scorpions in Old Turtle Broth, nominated by Chef Tomori. Each dish had two whole scorpions boiled alive in it. It was warming, spicy and delectable.

Before the next course, there was an interruption. Chen Shaiming rose to his feet and held up his glass of 1996 Lynch Bages. 'I would like to propose a toast to our host tonight. When he first sent the word around about starting a dining club called This Is Living, featuring live food, most of us thought that this would be a good idea, but probably not possible today, what with all the rules and regulations and animal rights and SARS and avian flu and what not. But he has done it. And I say: who cares about animal rights? What about human rights? Humans have a right to enjoy what God has put on this planet for us to eat. And by God, we are going to exercise that right. Right, Jean-Baptiste?'

Wong clapped loudly.

De Labauve smiled and raised his glass in reply.

'This is living,' said Chen, raising his glass.

'This is living,' the other diners echoed, rising to their feet.

The noise of the scraping chairs hid another sound – although the diners were probably too drunk to have registered it, even had they heard it. It was the sound of bodies – at least two, maybe more – falling over heavily in the corridor outside.

☯

Lu Linyao was exactly halfway across the junction at the crossroads of Nanjing Dong Lu and Jiangxi Nan Lu on her way to Jia Lin's tutorial school when her phone's now-annoying melody burst out of its tiny speaker. She had been holding it in her hand, willing it to ring, and willing it to be the voice of her cousin Milly saying that Jia Lin and their domestic helper Angelita had returned safely.

'She's back?'

There was silence on the other end.

'Milly, is that you?'

'Mama! I—' Jia Lin said before her voice became muffled, as if a hand had been placed over her mouth.

'Jia Lin. Jia Lin!'

A woman's voice came on the phone: it was neither deep nor dark, but the words it spoke turned Linyao's world into a black and hateful space. 'We have your daughter.'

'Who are you? Where is she? I need to get her back. *Please.*'

Linyao froze in the centre of the junction. The lights turned green and cars started surging across. But she remained in place, her palm cupped over the speaker of the phone as she struggled to hear. A truck stopped less than a metre away and blasted its air horn centimetres from her face – but Linyao was not shifting. She moved her mouth from the phone just long enough to scream in Mandarin at the truck driver: 'Shut up. I'm talking to someone here.' And then she said into the phone: 'Where is she? Is she okay? I want to speak to her.'

The voice remained exceptionally calm. 'She's fine. And you can have her back in one piece. As long as you follow my instruct—'

The truck and two cars started honking at her, as did a van from the other direction. Linyao bent her head low and began

66

marching around in a mad square dance in the middle of the junction, trying to hear. As a result, she blocked two more lanes of traffic and more cars started blasting their horns. A traffic officer in a blue and grey uniform raced towards her.

'I can't hear you. Too much noise here.'

'I said, she'll be fine, as long as you follow my instructions.'

The officer arrived and screamed at her in Shanghainese: 'Idiot *tai-tai*, move out of the road.'

'What instructions? What do you want me to do?'

'Get out of the road NOW.'

'Tell me what I have to do to get her back.'

'I said move it, crazy woman.' The traffic officer grabbed the top of her arm and started pulling.

Linyao turned and spat at him: 'Get away. This is important.' She wrenched her arm out of his grip with such ferocity that he was taken aback. He stood and stared, unsure what to do next. The watching drivers were so astonished they started laughing, and two of them applauded.

She turned back to the phone and screeched down it: 'Come on, woman, spit it out. What do you want me to do? I'm in a situation here. Some idiot in a uniform is trying to arrest me.'

'Uniform? Do not speak to the police. You speak to the police and you will never see your daughter again.'

'I'm not speaking to the police. Some traffic cop is speaking to me.'

The kidnapper sounded distinctly worried. 'I'll call you later with the instructions.'

'Be quick. My battery's running out. It might be dead. Give me your number, I'll call you.'

'Are you kidding? I'm not giving you my number. We'll call you later.'

'I told you. My phone is nearly out of power. You won't be able to call me later.'

'Buy a charger.' She hung up.

Linyao marched off, with barely a glance at the astonished

traffic officer, who was too shocked (and judging from his expression, too scared) to try to detain this suicidal and clearly demented woman.

Eight minutes later, shaking with distress, Linyao was standing outside a huge pile of rubble that was supposed to be the address of the offices of CF Wong and Associates (Shanghai). Her mind was numb. Looking at the rubble, she wondered what it meant. Buildings don't just disappear. Not in real life. Children didn't get snatched. Maybe none of this was happening. Maybe this was all some sort of awful nightmare. She touched a fence post to see if it was solid. It was.

She tried to call Joyce, but the young woman's phone was switched off. She must be on her bicycle, delivering the food.

Standing nearby, also staring disconcertedly at the demolished building, was a tall gentleman of Indian origin. He had white hair and wore a dark grey, almost black, Nehru suit. He looked over at her. 'Excuse me,' he said. 'Do you speak English?'

Linyao nodded, although she was too emotional to be able to say anything in any language at the moment.

He leaned towards her and his eyes filled with concern as he noticed hers were full of tears. 'I'm so sorry. Was this your home? Your office, perhaps?'

She shook her head, and then managed to splutter a few words. 'No. I wanted to meet someone who had an office here.'

'Me too,' said the stranger. 'CF Wong is his name. Do you know where the people whose offices were here have been moved to?'

Linyao blinked her eyes dry. 'You're looking for Wong? Me too. Do you work with him? I need – I need someone to help me,' she said. 'My child . . .' She trailed off into sobs. 'Someone has taken my child.'

'Dear, dear.' The kindly man gently took her by the arm and led her down the road to a small, grubby noodle shop, where he helped her onto a stool. He said to the waiter in slow English:

'Please bring her a cup of *lai-cha*, hot, sweet – two spoonfuls of sugar.' The man recognised the words *lai-cha* and disappeared to fetch some milky English tea.

'My name is Dilip Sinha. I do a lot of work with Mr Wong. We are both members of the Union of Industrial Mystics. We do some work with the, er, law enforcement people, and have enjoyed some success helping them. Clearly you have a problem. I wonder if there is anything I can do? Would you like to tell me about it?'

Over disgustingly sweet, lukewarm tea, Linyao brokenly related her story.

Sinha spoke little, but gently encouraged her to share every detail. She explained that she had been warned not to go to the police – but she knew that CF Wong, with whom she was familiar because he was the employer of her new friend Joyce McQuinnie, did some investigations for the police and might be able to help.

'You are quite correct. Our group, I am pleased to say, has had a lot of experience in dealing with criminal elements. One of Mr Wong's specialties is the feng shui of crime scenes. My recommendation is that you should go to the police anyway. However, I think—'

Her phone rang. She snatched it up and scrabbled to find the green button.

'Yes? Yes?'

'I hope you chose not to go to the police, Ms Linyao.'

'Yes, yes. I mean, no, I did not go to the police. Where is my daughter? I want my daughter back.'

The voice on the phone was relaxed and nasal, almost sleepy. 'You can have your daughter back. All you have to do is follow my instructions really, really carefully.'

4

Joyce pedalled as fast as she could. The wind whipped her hair. Her hair whipped her face. Strange bits of particulate matter and wisps of chemicals from factories far and near entered her mouth and nostrils, and began their journey to her lungs. Here was a speck of sulphur dioxide from a coal-burning plant on the plains of Mongolia. And there was an infinitesimal particle of diesel exhaust from a Siberian truck. And here was a trace of nitrogen dioxide from a power plant in Wuhan. Not all the matter was man-made: a proportion of the matter slipping into her system was soil from the windswept plains of the lower Urals. Sixteen of the world's worst polluted cities are in China, but they do not hold on to their by-products: they generously share them with their neighbours for miles around. Shanghai is a city surrounded by one of the biggest urban conurbations on the planet – some seventeen million people, or two Londons side by side. The air is frightening.

There's a significant downside to cycling in Shanghai, which can be summed up thus: if the traffic doesn't get you, the pollution will. The roads are poisonous, yet it is a city in which uncovered food is often carried by bicycle – obscenely pink plucked chickens, their skinny strangled necks dangling out of baskets, collecting fumes in their dead beaks, feet and pores.

Conscious that she was serving a man who had a short fuse and a big gun, Joyce was being extra careful. She had managed to pack the hyper-vegan meals in an airtight box and covered it securely with a cloth to keep at bay the blackish particles in the air. Linyao referred to it as Siberian black pepper. In this city, Joyce was moved to ask herself, was there any actual air left in the air? In urban China, living itself was lethal. But then it probably was anyway, sort of.

Despite these morbid, confusing thoughts, Joyce was moving and she was happy. There was a lot to be said for the traditional way of travel in China. While the sheer number of bicycles filling the streets sometimes made it difficult to move any faster than the speed of the slowest of the other pedal-pushers, at least forward movement remained a little more constant on bikes than in cars – a clear case of the turtle and the hare principle in action, slow and steady winning the race.

On several main streets bicycles had their own lanes, and could keep crawling forward when motorised vehicles ground to a halt. Sometimes the bicycle lane was marked merely by a white line on the road. On other streets there were little metal picket fences holding the cars at bay. And every few minutes one came upon blocked junctions where the canny cyclist could either ignore the traffic lights or simply dismount, cross the road as a pedestrian, and then resume her journey while jealous car-drivers watched, frustrated and immobile, angrily picking their noses and glaring at the traffic cops.

One of the challenges of negotiating Shanghai – indeed, all China – was that the most important road rule appeared nowhere in any Chinese motoring manual or driving lesson. You had to work it out for yourself. It went like this: The Heavier Entity Has Right of Way. Thus, bikes could pull out in front of pedestrians, motorbikes could pull out in front of bicycles, cars could pull out in front of motorbikes, vans could pull out in front of cars, and dirty big ten-tonne trucks could do whatever they liked, whenever they liked, whether their actions caused death and disaster or not. A second crucial rule was this: the only exception to the first rule was when the driver of any vehicle was carrying people wearing uniforms: this raised the weight category of the vehicle by one notch, or two notches if the uniform-wearers were visibly armed. People who did not know these rules did not live long on Chinese roads, and thus neatly removed themselves from the gene pool.

At regular intervals the official road rules clashed with the unwritten rules. For example, the law said that pedestrians had right of way if the green man was shining, and cars turning right had to wait until walkers were off the road. In these instances, the unwritten rules took precedence – cars were heavier than people – and vehicles would simply honk their way through the pedestrians. Foreigners did not know this and could often be seen arguing with pushy drivers while the reflections of the green man flashed across windscreens.

Joyce had been riding on Shanghai streets for six days now, and no longer felt that death was both imminent and inevitable every time she got on the saddle. But being on the roads was still stressful, as one regularly passed crowds which had gathered to stare at the human and vehicular results of traffic accidents. When she cycled past such a scene, she was always tempted to speed up and continue along the road with her eyes tightly shut – another reason why she was poor proof of evolutionary theory.

Her present level of stress should have been increased by the fact that the delivery was running late – but then no one could blame the Shanghai Vegetarian Café Society for that. It was the short-tempered Vega who was really running late, and who had changed the plans at the last minute. Now Vega – he was a question mark, for sure. What would he be like? He had become a legend in the international vegetarian community so quickly. It was interesting that Linyao had unabashed admiration for his work in freeing bears and so on, but then added the comment that he was 'a bit extreme'. What did that really mean? She pictured a masked, caped crusader – a sort of superhero figure hovering between good and evil: there was something attractively Darcy-ish about the concept.

There was another simple but important reason why she was intrigued by him: he was male and English-speaking. Three-quarters of the vegetarian society in Shanghai were women, and the few men were of the spotty, wimpy sort – not really men at all, in her book. Only two spoke reasonable English, and of those, only Flip had any sense of cool about him. Vega, whatever his faults might be, sounded like a seriously bloke-ish bloke, to use the language of her British mother.

The lights changed to green and Joyce stood heavily on the pedals to get the clunky machine moving again. Murderous fellow road-users aside, she enjoyed cycling – it reminded her of being eleven and pedalling furiously up and down the prome-nade near the apartment where she and her sister used to live in New York with a nanny and their father, an Australian property developer who travelled on business all the time. But it was a shame the Chinese had such crappy bikes, she said to herself, not for the first time that week. How could a civilisation which took cycling so seriously not have discovered the delights of the titanium-framed, ultra-light mountain bikes which filled the bike parks of New York schools? Here in Shanghai, one did occasionally see colourful imported bikes, but the great ma-jority were still the old, Forever brand models. No longer were Chinese bicycles available only in black, but they were still ponderous old-fashioned models. Whenever one had to ride uphill, it became apparent that they had been carved out of solid blocks of wrought iron, or perhaps lead. Flip had told her that there was a shop somewhere selling foreign-style mountain bikes for 400 yuan, but she had not been able to find it.

When she first arrived in Shanghai from Singapore she had assumed, pityingly, that Chinese people would be unable to afford expensive imported bikes. But she soon learned that assuming Chinese citizens were poor was always a fallacy. Big cities like Shanghai and Beijing always seemed to be over-flowing with things that most people – even in London or New York – would not be able to afford. It was what she quickly learned to call 'the no small numbers' principle. Since China had so many people, the smallest proportion of them – ten per cent, two per cent, a quarter of a per cent, whatever – was a big number anyway. She'd read that by 2009 there would be more middle-class people in China than the entire population of the United States. *Plus* a billion others aspiring to join that class. Middle-class people would want decent bikes, so they'd have to import a few more nice shiny ones, hopefully with chrome fittings and whitewall tyres. Joyce could hardly wait.

By standing up and putting the full weight of her 53 kilos on the pedals, Joyce managed to get her wrought iron bike accelerating up to a reasonable speed, despite the fact that she felt like she was dragging a bicycle factory with her. Then she turned the corner from Ruijin Lu to Changle Lu and approached Maoming Nan Lu, where she came within sight of her destination: the Jin Jiang Plaza Tower. It was a skyscraper in the classic Western mould – gold and glittery, with thousands of watts of light bulbs focused on it from ground level, turning it into some sort of glowing monolithic monument. It was gorgeous and crass. Looking at the spate of new angular spikes rising from the Shanghai cityscape, it became obvious that human nature had really not changed an iota from the days of the Tower of Babel. Let us build a tower to heaven and then we shall be as gods.

She turned the bike down a side street just before the hotel and looked for a sign which identified her drop-off point. There it was: Herborium, written in English and Chinese over a small shop with packets of herbal medicines in the window. She took out her mobile phone and dialled the number Linyao had given her.

'*Wei?*' barked a young woman's voice.

'Er, I'm from the Shanghai Vegan Café Society? I bought the hyper-vegan meal packs? I'm outside the Herborium place?' Joyce spoke in slow, careful English, still not confident enough to use her halting Chinese on the phone.

'Leave them in the shop doorway,' a female voice replied.

'When's the operation actually going to—' Joyce began to

ask, but the signal clicked off. Vega's staff were obviously in no mood for idle conversation.

She placed the basket of food in the doorway, taking out one meal pack – she'd made a spare – for herself.

Instead of heading for home, she walked smartly to the Jin Jiang Plaza Tower. While Vega and his crew were eating their lovingly prepared meal, she planned to go to the hotel's new restaurant, find Wong, and tell him to leave immediately. If Vega and his gang were somehow going to stage some sort of stunt to spoil the opening party or humiliate the individuals there, her boss needn't be among the victims. In fact, she might earn some major brownie points with Wong if she persuaded him to leave before Vega turned up and embarrassed all the unfortunate people who stayed.

As she walked, she straightened her clothes as best as she could; dressing to be a cyclist in Shanghai did not really leave one chic enough to swan through the receptions of fancy hotels. But she had quickly learned that being a Westerner gave her a certain power of entry in China. Since young Western people tended to dress in such class-inappropriate ways (the poor ones often dressed stylishly, the rich in denim rags), hotel staff could never tell whether you were a backpacker or a child of the billionaire banker in the presidential penthouse suite. Thus she'd stick her nose in the air and wander through fancy hotels at will.

Donning a snooty expression, she waltzed calmly across the dazzling, over-lit, over-air-conditioned lobby and marched past the reception desks. When she reached the private elevator that took guests to the 45th-floor restaurant, she found a sign outside explaining that the restaurant was closed this evening for a private party, the name of which was given simply as TIL.

She sneaked around the sign and took the elevator up, enjoying the glittering view of the city through the external glass wall almost as much as Wong had. Reaching the gloomy corridor at the top, she followed its curves till she came to the blazing, neon-lit doorway that her employer had entered an hour earlier. 'This Is Living' said the sign. This was it – the dining club which Vega and his storm-troopers planned to attack this evening. The door was shut. She tried to push it open, but it was locked.

After tapping on the door for a couple of minutes, she heard someone unlock it from the inside. A man in a Mandarin-collared staff uniform eyed her suspiciously. 'Yes, missy? You want?' He looked from side to side, as if he expected other people to be present. He looked genuinely surprised that there was no one in the corridor other than herself. Had the other guests left servants or bodyguards outside? And if so, where were they?

'Yes, missy?' the doorman asked again.

Missy missy missy. What a funny title she had had to get used to. Or was it missee? The whole -ee ending thing had been a problem for her, as was the 'L' and 'R' switching thing. When people in China spoke that way, it made her think of the worst sort of mock Chinese from the old days of British television: 'You wantee drinkee tea, missee? Velly nice.' It was the Chinese of her father's old Peter Sellers' videos. It was *Goon Show* Chinese: 'Ying Tong Yiddle I Po'. It was not the sort of Chinese that decent, aware, politically correct young people would dream of acknowledging. But what to do when you went to China and some people actually did say: 'You are Blitish, missee?' You couldn't comment on it or quote it or correct it or laugh at it or even admit to noticing it.

The truly awkward thing with stereotypes was not that they were inaccurate; it was that they were sometimes on target. Over the past week, she had learned that the Blitish Missee thing was only a minor factor in what was known locally as Chinglish; there was a host of other linguistic switches she had to get used to. Instead of *yes* or *no*, people sometimes answered a question by repeating it as a statement. Almost everyone pronounced her name as two syllables: Joy-Si. And everyone pronounced Q as CH. And ZH was J. And R was the hardest of all – it kind of hovered between the sound of J and R and SH. One thing she had discovered that was a great comfort to her: absolutely no Chinese person ever said: *Ah so*. The Western comedy screenwriters had got that one dead wrong. To her surprise, she found that the only linguistic group which used that phrase regularly were expat Germans.

'Missy?'

'Yes. I'm with Mr Wong. I'm a bit late.'

His eyebrows rose. He was not happy. She was, indeed, very late. But was she meant to be there at all? His irritated look said that his instructions specified there were to be only eighteen guests, and according to his restaurant diary, all eighteen of them had arrived more or less on time – so who was this girl?

'Your booking is for tonight, missy? Is a private party tonight. This Is Living Club.'

'Yes, I'm with Mr Wong. CF Wong? He's the feng shui master working for Mr De Labauve, the manager?'

The expression in the door captain's eyes changed. She had said the magic words: the name of the boss. She must be legitimate after all. How could a mistake have been made? His brow wrinkled and he looked down at his bookings diary. 'Sorry. We expected eighteen guest tonight. Eighteen are here.'

Joyce laughed nervously. She was terrible at lying, but knew she had to try. 'Well, er, ha ha, I didn't know whether I was free so I was on the list and then I was off the list and then I was back on the list and then maybe they took me off again and well, ha ha, here I am, you know how it is?'

To her surprise, this little speech did the trick. The captain nodded with his hooded eyes betraying contempt – he was quite familiar with the moronic fickleness of the ultra-rich who made up most of the clientele.

'I think you are off the list, but does not matter. I think you can go in.'

'It's not full then?'

'The restaurant has space for seventy person, thirty-one tables. We have eighteen only at special party tonight. No one is sitting with Mr Wong.'

He opened the doors and led her in.

Inside, the room was almost as dark as the corridor outside, despite the brightness of the doorway and the spotlights trained at unusual angles. The doorman handed her into the care of another staff member, who blandly led her to the table where Wong sat.

The feng shui master looked up and glared when he saw her. His eyes narrowed and the space between his eyebrows tied itself into the sort of knot only a sailor could undo.

'What? What do you—?'

'I got an urgent—'

A gong sounded, cutting off their conversation. It was time for the next course.

Joyce sat next to him and whispered: 'I've come to tell you that you gotta split. You shouldn't stay here. It's because—'

Wong sighed and raised one palm to silence her. 'I know you like animals, but I like animals, too. I like to eat them. Man got to eat. Man got to eat to live.'

'No, I don't mean that. I mean you gotta go because something bad is going to happen.'

'What something bad?'

Joyce's eyes darted from side to side. There was no sign of Vega, or anything odd going on. She saw nothing but a group of fat rich men and thin rich women finishing tiny portions of something from huge plates. 'I don't know. I don't know exactly. Just something, like, really bad. You see there's this guy—'

De Labauve stepped out onto the little stage to do his spiel for the next item on the special *menu dégustation* for tonight.

Wong shook his head in a studied display of disbelief. 'Some guy will do something bad. But you don't know what.'

'It's just that, you see, there's this guy. His name is—'

Wong interrupted her. 'You say you don't know what something bad is going to happen. Well, I know what is going to happen. Something good is going to happen. And I know exactly what it is. Some good food is going to go into my stomach. That is what is going to happen.'

De Labauve spoke in his bad French-Mandarin about the delicate flavours of crustaceans and a pair of chefs appeared carrying the largest lobster Joyce had ever seen. It was a metre in length, and had a bluish, rainbow-tinted shell.

'I think this guy is going to break in here or something—'

'Shh,' Wong said. 'I want to listen. Afterwards you talk.'

'And the lobster is the king of seafood,' De Labauve continued. 'And this beast is the king of the lobsters. It is one hundred and two centimetres in length and weighs almost eighteen kilos. It was captured three days ago and transported here by aircraft just for you tonight. This dish has been nominated by Osato Miyake in the name of his lovely wife Kami.' This triggered a round of applause, plus bowing and arm flourishes from Mr Miyake.

Joyce turned to the stage and her face filled with horror. 'Oh dear God,' she said. 'I hope that doesn't mean they are going to *kill* the poor thing.'

Wong gave her a look of utter contempt before turning his chair slightly so that he wouldn't have to look at her. He put his hand against his head so that he wouldn't even see her out of the corner of his eye.

Chef Tomori raised the lobster high to show everyone. It swayed its long antennae, almost as if it was waving a regal goodbye to the audience. Then he raised it over a large glass dish of boiling water. He tensed his arms, preparing to drop the massive petrol-hued beast into the transparent cauldron.

Joyce gasped: 'No!' She clapped her hand over her mouth in horror and stood up.

Wong, embarrassed, spat at her: 'Sit down. Shut up, crazy *gwai mui.* You spoil the party.' He had visions of all the insulted guests pledging never to use his services again.

The lobster was dropped. A shriek of escaping air came from its shell as it plunged into the boiling water. Then there was a deafening crack from the side of the room – so loud it had everyone reaching to cover their ears. The tank of boiling water shattered loudly. Several people screamed. Gouts of boiling liquid splashed on the guests sitting nearest the stage. They leapt from their seats, squealing and brushing the steaming water from their arms.

Joyce and Wong ducked down, both of them knowing the sound of a gun being fired. Water and broken glass cascaded into the fire, extinguishing it with a loud hiss. Clouds of steam filled the stage. Shrieks, noise, chaos, confusion.

Then a loud, clear voice from the back of the room said: 'Good evenin'.'

Everyone turned and stared. A young man stood in the corner, near the kitchen door. He was dressed entirely in black and was holding an AK47 in one hand, Rambo-style. He had a mask over the top half of his face, rather like Batman. Curls of long, dark, greasy hair ran down to his shoulderblades. He was flanked on both sides by other individuals similarly attired.

'Everyone keep absolutely still,' he said in a London accent, pronouncing *still* as *stiw*. 'And you won't get 'urt. *Yet,*' he added menacingly. 'Now stand up and put yer 'ands on yer 'eads.'

The intruder's assistants raced quickly and efficiently to each table. When they got to the table behind which Wong and McQuinnie were crouching, they levelled guns at them, forcing them to stand with their hands in the air along with everyone else. The diners and staff were frisked for weapons. Two of the diners were found to have handguns on them, as did one of the waiters. The pistols were dropped into a tureen of consommé which was simmering quietly in a corner. 'Where's my cursed bodyguard?' Tun Feiyu snapped, but there was no answer to be had.

The giant rainbow lobster lay still on the ground, killed either by the boiling water or the bullet. His saviours had been too late to rescue him and there were only a few things left on the menu: a chicken and egg dish and something called 'curling oysters'. Vega, well-organised though he seemed, appeared to have some time management issues.

'This your friend?' Wong whispered to Joyce. 'You said there was some guy . . . ?'

'Yes. No. Yes, this is the guy I meant. But I don't really know him. He's not really a friend. I only made his dinner.'

'What?'

The young man in the mask approached the stage. He slung his gun over his shoulder and faced up to the cowering, terrified De Labauve. 'Please don't hurt me,' the chef begged. 'You want my *pochette*?'

'No fanks.' Vega, who was as thin and scrawny as a stale green bean, easily picked up the much larger man by his lapels and threw him across the stage where he landed on the griddle with a hiss. As he struggled to get off the burning metal surface, De Labauve's wig fell off, revealing him to be bald. This elicited a single scream, from the chef's girlfriend, who was sitting at a table to the far left – but whether she was upset that her boyfriend was being roughed up or because she had not known that he was hairless could not be ascertained. Scrambling off the griddle, the chef picked himself up and grabbed the nearest drink – Tonyboy Villaneuva's glass of Chateau Lafite '82 – and poured it onto parts of his body which had been burned: the back of his bald head, and the sides and fingers of his hands.

The sudden violence had silenced everyone.

'The slaughter of the innocent 'as TO STOP, awright?' Vega said. He spoke in an odd, slightly slurred way, as if he were drugged. His words varied illogically in terms of pitch and volume, with some words almost screamed.

'But for now, I 'ave only one word LEFT to say to YOU.' He made a hand gesture and he and his gang swiftly pulled something out of their shoulderbags: something dark, plasticky and glinting – gas masks.

Wong realised what was about to happen and grabbed a serviette to clamp in front of his face. He turned to look for the exit doors, but they were all guarded.

Joyce put her hand up in junior school fashion and squeaked in Vega's direction: 'Excuse me. I'm actually—'

But her words were drowned out by thuds and hisses. A number of gas bombs were set off and the room immediately filled with smoke, darkness and the sound of coughing individuals falling to their knees. The gas had a medicinal smell, rather like cough syrup.

'One word. And THE WORD is: Goodnight. Awright?' said Vega, with a laugh.

CF Wong and Joyce McQuinnie fell into a deep sleep.

5

'Where is my child? Just give me my baby.'

'Calm down. Jia Lin is fine. We need to do a little deal with you, that's all.'

'Just give me my child back. I'll do anything you say, but just give her back to me.' Her voice cracked and trembled.

'You'll get her back. But you need to give us something.'

The kidnapper spoke in English, but it was with neither of the accents Linyao knew best: Chinese or north American. Was it some variety of British English? 'Anything. You can have everything I've got. I don't have much money but you can have all of it. Please!' She burst into tears again.

'Calm down, Ms Lu. We want one thing only. We want your security pass for the Shanghai Municipal Stables. We just need to borrow it for a while.'

'My stable pass?'

'Yes. That's all. Just give us your – just lend us your stable pass, and you'll get your daughter back.'

'When do I get her back?'

'Bring the pass to the park south of Yan'an Dong Lu, opposite the Main Telecommunications Building, and sit on one of the benches near the centre. Take your mobile phone with you. We'll call you at seven o'clock exactly.' Then the soft voice hardened: 'You call the police, or anyone in the authorities, and the deal is off – you'll never see your daughter alive again, do you understand?'

Linyao's reply was just a sob.

'Do you understand?'

'Yes, yes, I won't tell anyone.'

The phone went dead.

She turned a bleary, red-eyed face to Dilip Sinha, and wept as she spoke. 'They want my stable pass card. I have to deliver it to the park. At seven.'

Sinha's face betrayed no emotion, remaining calm and reassuring, although his right eyebrow lifted itself two millimetres.

She rose to her feet.

'Sit down,' Sinha said. 'Getting there too early will do us no good. It's better that you keep as calm as possible. We need your brain working at full capacity. It will work better if it is calm. We can take comfort from the fact that the child is alive and well, and the persons with whom we are dealing have a plan to get her back into your arms. Also, we can take comfort from the fact that they want to swap her for something that you have, rather than something you don't have, such as a million dollars. Now tell me. Your stable pass – what does that do?'

She lowered herself back to the stool. The light was disappearing. A truck roared by. The evening was getting colder. She shivered, but would have done so had she been in a sauna. Linyao buried her face in her hands for a minute. She took deep, slow breaths. Then she looked up, sniffed once and spoke calmly: 'It gets me into the place where they keep the animals for government use – the horses for parades, the performing animals for shows, and so on. I'm a veterinarian. My job is to look after these animals if they get sick.'

'I see. Is there any money associated with the place?'

'No, nothing. There's the animal block, and there's the offices, and there's the storerooms where we keep the fodder, medicines, bales of hay, that sort of thing. There's no money there.'

'If it's not cash they are after, it's something else – are any of the animals valuable in any way?'

'Not really. Horses, birds, the occasional performing elephant or tiger. They all have some monetary value, but not a lot. Elephants are expensive, but they're not easy to sell on the street corner.'

'Could they use your card as a front to get in somewhere? For example, to escort a performing horse to a parade to entertain the Politburo members, or the visiting dignitaries from the United States or something?'

'No. My card only gets me into the stable block. It doesn't get me into any other building. Even if the horses were entertaining someone important, I wouldn't – or someone with my card wouldn't – be able to go with them.'

'But the horses, et cetera, can go to buildings where top dignitaries are waiting to be entertained? At the presidential summit which starts this week, for example?'

Linyao thought about this. 'Yes. There will be a few animals at the summit's first night cultural show at the Grand Theatre tomorrow. But I don't see how my pass could help anyone in? ltrate those events. No – they can't be planning to sneak into the parades with the horses or anything. There are separate passes for the animal handlers. Even the animals themselves have passes – photo passes with their pictures on them.'

Sinha sighed. 'Perhaps they don't understand that your stable pass only lets them have limited access. Perhaps this is all misconceived.'

'I'll tell them when I speak to them – when they give my baby back.' She looked down at the phone she was clutching tightly: now this tiny device was her precious lifeline to her child.

The *vaastu* master looked away, his eyes appearing to sweep the dingy street as he searched for answers somewhere in the middle distance. 'No – there's something wrong here. Their planning is too good. They wouldn't make a mistake like that. Our train of thinking must be wrong. I think we should assume that they know your pass will only get them into the stable block. Is there access to any important government building from the stables? Is it adjacent to anyone's office?'

'I don't know. It's just north of the creek in a building off Zhejiang Bei Lu. There are lots of nondescript buildings around there – I have no idea what's inside them.'

'Let's look at a map.' Sinha had purchased a street map of Shanghai at the airport bookshop to help him find Wong's office – now, his ex-office. They pored over the map and noticed that next to the stables were dozens of blocks, including some government offices. 'It will take forever to try to work out who is in them, and who they're after – but I think we're going to have to try.'

'You are going to have to try. I am going to the park.'

Sinha shook his head. 'I don't think you should, madam. They said seven o'clock. It will do you no good to go ridiculously early. Indeed, it may make them feel uncomfortable. I suggest we follow their instructions closely. Let's spend some time looking at the map and working out what they want your pass for. And then, in good time, we'll head to the park.'

After some thought Linyao decided that he was right – engaging in some activity would help her pass the time without going mad with worry. 'I'll take you there,' she said. 'To the stable block. Come on.'

Before Sinha could react, she had raced off down some gritty streets. Walking at a brisk pace, she led him over a small hump-backed bridge across an ugly brown river to the stable block in Zhejiang Bei Lu. It took less than twenty minutes to get there. Then they carefully walked the streets surrounding it. Sinha took notes in a small notebook as Linyao told him what each building contained. She knew some of them, but there were several she couldn't identify. In those instances, they simply strolled up to the main entrances and examined the nameplates. There was one large office building, to the east of the stable block, which had no nameplate at all – something that piqued Sinha's interest. The guards standing outside looked particularly hostile. All the windows were covered with reflective panels so passers-by could not see inside. Stone barriers prevented cars pulling up outside the main door, and a guard checked every approaching vehicle before allowing it to proceed into a tunnel to a basement car park to the right of the entrance. This black hole swallowed up a succession of cars, most of which were black and had tinted windows.

'Very suspicious,' said Sinha. 'No identifying marks whatsoever. It strikes me that this building is significant, given the vehicular activity and the fact that it gives no clues as to what it is.'

Linyao shook her head. 'That's where the spies hang out. It's one of those secrets that nobody tells anyone else because everyone already knows it.'

☯

Seven o'clock – or actually, six forty-nine – arrived with glacial slowness. Linyao waited at the Yan'an Road park. She sat on a bench, but she was shaking so much that she looked as if she had delirium tremens. She had the stable pass – a piece of laminated plastic bearing her photograph – in her sweaty right hand, which was in her pocket, and her mobile phone was on her lap.

The little digital clock on the screen of the phone moved slowly. It said 6:49. She waited for what seemed like hours before looking at it again. It *still* said 6:49. Had the damn thing stopped? What a time for the clock to give up! Did this not prove that she was cursed? Her life had become a waking nightmare. If she and Jia Lin came out of this alive, she would burn incense at the temple every day – twice a day, if that's what the gods wanted.

Then the time on the tiny Motorola screen switched to 6:50 and she realised that the phone was still working, but the rawness of her nerves was slowing time down for her. There were ten minutes to go. She closed her eyes and replayed, in her head, the conversations with the kidnapper. Did she recognise the voice? Were there any clues in what was said, or in the background noises? Were there any background noises? She couldn't bear to replay Jia Lin's little cry – it broke her heart even to think of it. What must the poor girl have been suffering. When she got her back, she would never let her out of her sight again. She would pull her out of school. She could come to work at the stables, in her office. She would learn more from her mother than from that useless school that allowed kidnappers to snatch children and their minders from its doorstep.

Her mind played on these things for a while, and when she next looked at her watch it said 6:54. The phone was due to ring in six minutes. Again and again, her eyes swept the thinning crowds of people ambling through the park, looking for a small girl with pigtails. Where could she be? When would she appear?

Several groups of people with small children were strolling home through the park and a number of times Linyao's heart jumped as she saw someone who she initially thought was Jia Lin – but on each occasion, just as she became sure enough to leap to her feet, the child would turn and she would see that it was not her.

Finally, *finally* – the pop song burst out of the phone and Linyao started so much that it almost slid to the ground. She snatched it as it fell. Her trembling fingers found it hard to find the talk button.

'Yes, yes, yes,' she said. 'I'm here.'

A female voice started talking rapidly in Mandarin: 'Good evening, honoured client. This is a short, recorded message from Unicorn Delight Trading to give you the exciting news that you can cut your telecoms bill by fifty per cent – yes, a full fifty per cent – by switching your accounts to us with no transfer charge. All you have to do—'

'Die, die, die, die, die, scum,' she screeched into the phone. She slammed the red button with her fist so hard that the phone flew out of her hand and fell to the ground. The back cover snapped off and the battery fell out.

Oh no, no, no. Not now, not now. Feverishly, she picked up the pieces and reassembled it, cursing continuously. Within seconds of her sliding the back cover into place, the music started playing again.

'Yes, yes, yes? I'm at the park.'

'I know. You're here early. Which is why I'm calling a few minutes early. Did you bring the pass?' The voice had lost some of its tranquillity and betrayed signs of excitement. It was the voice of an Englishwoman.

'I did.'

'We can see you. Can you hold it up?'

The news that she was being watched sent a fresh tremor through her system. She held up the small photo card as if she was examining it. Then her eyes scanned the park again. Who was it? Where were they? The park was still busy. There were some families playing in the distance, there was an elderly couple near a hedge, there were two young lovers on a bench, there was a park keeper and a gardener chatting by a tree, there were several idle old men walking and smoking, and some dirty-looking migrant workers were camped under a tree.

'Where's my daughter?'

'Look over to your left. Far left. See those trees?'

'Which trees?'

'See those thick trees near the bench?'

'Yes.'

'Look at the third tree, counting from your left.'

As she stared, a figure stepped out from behind the tree. It was impossible to tell whether it was male or female in the evening gloom, but Linyao's heart leapt when the figure pulled a child out from behind the tree. It was Jia Lin; it had to be: she recognised the distinctive floppy hat and the satchel.

Linyao leapt to her feet and started running towards the tree.

'Stop,' said the voice on the phone.

At the same time, the figure by the tree held up one hand in a keep-away gesture.

Linyao slowed down but did not stop.

'*Stop*. Go back to the bench where you were sitting, and put the card down on it. And then walk slowly towards the tree.'

The child and the adult disappeared from view. Linyao stopped and reluctantly turned around. She quickly marched back to the bench and carefully placed the card on the seat. Then she turned around and walked as fast as she could in the direction of the tree.

She was dimly aware of someone behind her, walking briskly to the place where she had been sitting, but she didn't turn round. Who cared about the blasted card? Anyone who wanted could have every card she owned. She wanted nothing but her baby back. She strode as quickly as she could towards the tree and broke into a run as she reached it. 'Jia Lin,' she called out. 'Jia Lin!'

The child stepped out from behind the tree and Linyao reached out to grab her. But then she saw her face and recoiled. It was not Jia Lin but a child she'd never seen before, wearing Jia Lin's hat and carrying her school bag. There was no one else behind the tree.

Linyao burst into tears.

❧

In the first century, a desert bandit and his gang came to the cave home of the wise man Luo near the Plain of Jars.

The bandit said: 'Give us your money or we will kill you.'

Luo said: 'I have nothing to give you except my wisdom.'

The bandit said: 'Then we will take your life.'

Luo said: 'But my wisdom is valuable. I can show you a mountain where diamonds grow on trees.'

He led the bandit chief on a journey of many li to Cold Mountain. They camped at night close to the summit.

At first light they emerged from their tents. The trees and hedges were glittering with jewels on every leaf. Even the cobwebs were hung with diamonds.

The desert bandit chief's jeweller looked at the gems through a magnifying glass. He said: 'These have amazing designs, the finest work I have ever seen. Each is cut into intricate six-sided patterns, and no two are alike.'

The bandits let Luo go. They filled chests with the jewels and took them home. But when they reached the desert, their treasure boxes contained nothing but water.

Blade of Grass, to the dweller in the desert, there is no gem more magical than the frost. To the dweller in the frost, there is no gem more magical than the sun. The foolish man labours hard to create wealth. The wise man merely recognises it.

From 'Some Gleanings of
Oriental Wisdom' by CF Wong

It was the ache in his bony hips that brought him back to consciousness. He had been dimly aware that every time he turned over in his sleep, there was a bruising pain at the points where his hip bones stuck out. It was almost as if someone had replaced his mattress with a slab of concrete. And it was cold. Where was his blanket?

Wong, his eyes still tightly shut, moved one hand along what should have been the surface of his bed, groping for his blanket – and what he found made him open his eyes with a start. This wasn't a bed. He was sleeping on the floor: a frozen, unyielding slab of concrete. His head ached. His bones were stiff. His muscles weren't responding. And he was groggy. He felt as if he had been hit on the back of the head with a plank.

It gradually came back to him: they had all been gassed at the restaurant. So where were they now? Not at the Jin Jiang Tower Plaza Hotel. That had been thickly carpeted with the finest double-thick *tai ping*. He was in a totally dark room. But although there was no light, there was sound. He could dimly hear other people breathing, occasional stirring noises, dormitory sounds. Quite a few people were here – perhaps everyone from the restaurant. And there was something about the quality of the sound that suggested they were in a big space: a hall, a factory, a godown of some sort.

He pulled himself into a sitting position with some difficulty. His joints hurt as much as his head – not just from having spent an unspecified amount of time sleeping on a hard floor, but from the gas, too. It must have been very powerful stuff to knock him out so quickly, he reckoned.

Now his eyes were functioning, he closed them again, to make them more sensitive to the light, and then opened them as wide as he could and stared about him. There was a slightly greyer quality to the light ahead of him: there must be a window or door or something in that direction, emitting light through a crack. But nothing else was visible. He put one hand out blindly in front of him and felt something: hard, metallic, upright, tubular. Prison bars. He was in a cage or cell of some sort. Behind him, he heard slow breathing. There was someone else unconscious close by. He guessed it would be Joyce. Reaching out his hand, he felt a hideous, shaggy scarf and realised he was right.

But where were they? Had they been kidnapped by that mad young man for whom Joyce had made dinner? And what were they going to do with them? What did they want? The man had talked about 'the slaughter of the innocent'. What did he mean?

A spotlight flashed on, burning his eyes. He covered them with his hand. It was a tightly focused beam, illuminating only him and leaving the rest of the room in darkness. He squinted below his fingers to look around, but could only dimly gain confirmation that he and Joyce appeared to be in a cage of some sort.

A voice seeped out of a set of speakers set into the ceiling of the room – a large, echoing space. 'Good mornin', Mr Wong,' Vega said. 'I trust you slept well. Better than most of the animals waiting to be eaten in the cages of yer bloody restaurant.' That London accent again: *well* was pronounced *waiwoo*, and *animals* was *animoles*.

92

'It's not my restaurant,' Wong replied. 'It belong—'

'Don't bovver speakin'. Can't hear you, mate. Can just see yer mouf flappin'. I've gotta closed circuit TV camera focused on where you are, but I didn't trouble with microphones. I decided I'd be better off not being able to hear you. I'm a famously soft-hearted man and may be driven to feeling a bit of sympathy by yer pathetic cries. But that won't 'appen if I can't hear you. So this conversation is going to be one-way only, awright?'

'Who are you? What do you want?' Wong shouted. Realising that he probably could not be heard, he spread his hands out, palms to the ceiling, in a questioning gesture.

'Yes, of course you 'ave questions. I guess you wanna know what's going on. Well, I shall make a presentation about that when the rest of yer mates 'ave woken up. Me drugs expert told me that it would be between nine and twelve hours for most of yer. You've woken up after only eight, so I imagine you'll be feeling pretty dizzy. Tell you what, Mr Wong, I don't want anyone to miss the fun, and I don't feel like explaining myself individually for each one of yer who wakes up early, so I suggest you 'ave a little nap and then I'll wake you all up in two or free 'ours' time. Does that sahnd like a good idea to you? Cheerio and goodnight.'

Wong decided he had no choice. Sleep would be good: his head was swimming. He stole Joyce's scarf, folded it into a pillow for himself, and then almost immediately felt himself dropping back into a state of deep unconsciousness, his last thought being that he hoped he would wake with this awful headache gone.

The next thing he knew, the room was glaringly bright, there were shouts and calls and someone was crying. He blinked his eyes and wiped some dribble from his chin. He guessed that he had been asleep for another hour or two. He recognised the voice of the man shouting. It was Tun.

'Let me out. How dare you put me in a cage like a common criminal. Let me out,' he shrieked in Mandarin.

There was no response. As Wong's eyes got used to the light, he realised that they were all in cages, each with one or two people in them, in a large, warehouse-type space. Each cell had its own spotlight beaming down on it. As people woke up, the lights were being switched on remotely to illuminate their cells.

Behind him, Joyce snored on. The gas must have hit her hard.

Tun turned around and saw Wong awake. 'What's going on, feng shui man? What idiot has dared to cage us? Is this some sort of hostage situation?'

'Sorry,' Wong said. 'I do not know. I think we have been kidnapped, all of us. By the people with the masks who came into the restaurant last night.'

Tun shook his head in disbelief. 'It can't be. Who would dare to do such a thing? I mean, do they know who I am?'

'Maybe they took you because they know who you are.'

This grimly uttered reply silenced Tun, who was clearly having visions of kidnappers demanding a portion of his large fortune.

'But maybe not,' Wong continued, to comfort him. 'Maybe they kidnap you because you are rich, but maybe not. They kidnap me too, and I am not famous and rich. I am a poor man only.' As he spoke, he scanned the room and realised that there were more than a dozen other prisoners. Were they all individuals from the restaurant? He thought he could see people whom he did not recognise from that meal. By this time, there were eight cages visible, and people were stirring, or sitting in a stupor, looking at Wong and Tun, the only two alert enough to have a conversation.

'But who has done this? Who are these people?'

Wong shook his head. 'I don't know. I know nothing about them. But my assistant Joyce – she knows them. She made dinner for him, she said.'

'Who made dinner for them?'

'Here,' said Wong, indicating the sleeping figure behind him. 'My assistant. But now she is a victim, too.'

Tun shook the bars of his cage. 'Let me out,' he shouted, 'or you will regret it. You will pay for this with your lives.'

There was a loud echoing click – the sound of a public address system being switched on.

'Good mornin',' said the preternaturally calm voice of Vega. 'I 'ope you slept well, Mr Tun. Or actually, to be honest, I don't. I 'ope you slept really, really badly. And I hope you have a bloody awful stinker of an 'eadache.'

Tun switched to English: 'Who are you? Get me out of here. Now. Right now.'

'I can see your lips moving, but I can't hear what you are saying so you might as well shut it. How about some music to wake everyone else up? It's time for all the 'appy campers to rise and shine. Wakey-wakey.'

Bach's *Brandenburg Concerto* began to pump through the speakers at loud volume. Over the next twenty minutes, most people woke up. As an increasing number of lights went on, the room began to reveal itself as an abandoned theatre. The ceiling was high, and the remnants of old stage lighting systems and pulleys were visible overhead.

As each cageful of individuals woke up, Wong and Tun did their best to brief them with what little information they had.

'So we've been kidnapped by some lunatic gang?' Park Hae-jin said, rubbing his eyes with his palms. 'Are they Iraqis or neo-Nazis or what?'

'I have no idea,' said Tun. 'Probably terrorists who want to hold us for ransom. My guess is that they are some sort of extreme fundamental Muslim insurgents. What do you think, Wong? From Iraq?'

The feng shui master shook his head. 'No. I think they are vegetarians.'

Park blinked. 'Vegetarians? What do you mean?'

95

'I don't know,' said Wong. 'But my assistant seems to know them. And she is a vegetarian. So maybe they are, too.'

'I thought vegetarians were Buddhists,' Tun said. 'Those people did not seem like Buddhists.'

Wong shrugged. 'Other people are vegetarians, too. Joyce says that rock stars are all vegetarians.'

'Maybe these people are rock stars. The guy with the gun – he had long hair. Greasy, dirty long hair. That Geldof guy, maybe.' Tun evidently felt they were on to something.

'But why would rock stars kidnap us?' This was Tun's partner, a thin Chinese starlet named Bingqing, who was checking her make-up in a compact mirror.

Tun said: 'In the past, vegetarianism in Shanghai was associated with gangsters. Triad gangs. But these people – they are foreigners, no? You must wake up your assistant. See if she can tell us the answer.'

'Yes, good idea.' Wong kicked Joyce's left leg repeatedly until she woke.

'Ow!' she squealed. 'My leg. Ow. My head.'

'You must wake up,' her boss said unsympathetically.

'*Cheese*. I've got a stinking headache. Where are we?' Joyce's eyes were puffy and her hair was a jungle. 'This is like ten hangovers rolled into one. And I didn't even have anything to drink last night.'

'Who are those people?' Wong barked at her, worried that this whole ghastly mistake might even be Joyce's fault – and thus, by association, his fault. What if he had to pay compensation to all these rich people or something? It would mean bankruptcy. He needed to disassociate himself from her. 'They are friends of yours, Ms McQuinnie?'

'Are they Iraqi insurgents?' Tun asked.

Joyce looked around. 'Dear God. Where are we?'

'Captured by those mad people who came to the restaurant last night,' Tun explained. 'They seem to have kidnapped the lot of us, can you believe it, young woman? Are they friends of yours? You had dinner with them or something, Wong said.

96

Are they insurgents from one of the Muslim countries? I bet this is all to do with George W Bush.'

Joyce shook her aching head. 'No. They're vegans. There's this guy called Vega—'

'I told you,' Park said. 'Vegans are Muslims.'

'No, they're not,' Bingqing said. 'I thought vegans were like aliens. From *Star Trek* or something. The first *Star Trek* movie, remember, "The Curse of Vega" or something?'

'Where do they come from, these vegans?' Wong asked.

'What? Oh, I don't know. But there's a group from London, and they've hooked up with some local groups here. He sounds like a Londoner. The guy with the gun?' said Joyce, rubbing her temples. 'Oooo, my poor head.'

'But what *sort* of group are they?' Tun asked, getting exasperated. 'Are they like Triads or mafia or something?'

'No, of course not,' said Joyce. 'They're vegetarians. Vegans are a type of vegetarian.'

Wong looked smugly in Tun's direction. 'I said, already.'

'Vegans are people who don't eat leather shoes, I think,' Bingqing said. 'I've heard of them. Is that right?'

'They don't *wear* leather shoes, usually,' Joyce replied. 'I'm not sure about eating them. I never heard of a specific ban on eating shoes. They don't eat meat, eggs or dairy products.'

'Clearly some sort of weird cult,' Park said. 'Eating shoes, not wearing leather, not eating meat – they sound like strange and dangerous people.'

Joyce opened her mouth to explain that vegans were not strange and dangerous people, but then shut it again. The Children of Vega definitely did seem to be strange and dangerous people. Look what they did to that poor French restaurant guy yesterday, throwing him onto the griddle thing. Where was he? He didn't seem to be here.

Someone stirred to Wong's left and a spotlight went on, illuminating a middle-aged Chinese woman he had not seen before. She sat up in her cage, rubbing her head and groaning.

'Look,' Wong said to Tun, 'it's not just people from the restaurant. There are other people here, too.'

Bach finished abruptly, in the middle of a movement, and the public address system burst into life again.

'Mornin', luvvies. You must be awake by now,' Vega said. 'Stand by for a moment. The Court of Poetic Justice will soon be in session. The first 'earin' will begin shortly.' The sound clicked off again and they were left in silence.

'We need water,' Tun shouted.

'Can I have coffee?' Joyce called out. 'I think I better have decaf, because I've got a really bad headache.'

'He can't hear us. Can only see us.' Wong pointed to small cameras in the ceiling, angled at the cages.

'I'm hungry,' whined Bingqing. 'I couldn't eat that awful food last night. I hate food that wriggles when you try to eat it.'

'You can share this,' said Joyce, patting a paper bag sticking out of the pocket of her coat.

'What is it?'

'It's a vegan wrap.'

'No, thank you. I don't like to eat shoe leather.'

Joyce shook her head. 'It's not shoes. I didn't say vegans ate shoe leather. I just said there was no ban against them eating shoe leather.'

'There *should* be a ban on them eating shoe leather,' Tun said. 'It's not natural.'

Wong nodded. 'This explains why they are a bit crazy. All the chemicals in the shoe leather. Makes them *ji-seen*, you know, crossed wire.'

Joyce gave up trying to explain.

There was a loud bang from the public address system as Vega switched it on again. 'Sorry,' he said. 'Bloody knockoff Chinese sound systems. Next time I'll bring me own B&O system. Much better than this crap. You want breakfast? Put up your hands if you want somefink to eat or drink.'

Most of the people in the room raised their hands, although

some of them were still feeling too queasy from the effects of the gas to even think about food.

'I just want to go home,' Bingqing shouted. 'And have a nice long bath.'

'So do I,' said Chen's wife Fangyin.

'So do all of us,' said Park.

Vega chuckled: 'I could easily bugger off an' slaughter some INNOCENT chickens and pigs an' give you eggs and bacon. But I'm gonna teach you a lesson. Yer gonna starve.'

'You can't do this,' Tun shouted. 'If this is a joke, I don't think it is very funny. Get me my lawyer. I demand that you get me my lawyer immediately.'

'But you won't starve to deaf,' Vega continued. 'That would be too kind. Yer all going to be punished, and some of you will DIE – perhaps all of you. But most of you will die in different ways. I fink you'll all find this to be a learnin' experience. Unfortunately, you'll be dead at the end of it, so yer noo knowledge won't be of any use to yer. 'owever, you will not die in vain. All yer deafs will be recorded on videotape and WIDELY distributed, so that people everywhere will learn from yer fates.'

'What is he talking about?' Tun said to the group as a whole. 'He's mad.'

'I don't like it,' Bingqing said, bursting into sobs. 'Talking about killing us and stuff. If this is a joke, this is a horrible joke. Tell him to stop, Feiyu. Tell him to stop all this and take us home. Where's the car, and the driver, and the bodyguard?'

Vega's outburst had sent a chill through the room. Several women started crying softly – and the men sat in grim silence. Most of them, by now, remembered the violent scene from the night before, and realised that Vega might be capable of anything – even murder. Where was De Labauve? Had he already been killed?

Joyce was stunned at Vega's words. This must be some sort of trick, she was sure. No vegan would kill any living being

99

intentionally, and definitely would not commit multiple murders. No, Vega was trying to terrify people. That was the only logical answer. He was trying to scare them into realising the value of life. That was what veganism was all about: appreciating the inherent value of sentience. Perhaps he would tell them that if they signed a promise to be vegans for the rest of their lives, he would let them go. Yes, that must be it. It was some sort of psychological game. Deliberate mental torture. He was putting them in the shoes of the animals they had killed, to teach them a lesson they would never forget.

Wong asked Joyce: 'Who is this man?'

'His name is Mee something. His dad owns a supermarket chain. His family comes from China, but they have family members in Canada and London.'

'Mee Fan Supermarket?'

'I can't remember. My head's like porridge. Linyao knows all about him. She was talking about him last night.'

Bingqing said: 'But why is he saying these awful things? Is he really going to kill people? I can't stand it.'

'I don't know,' said Joyce. 'I hope not. I hope it's just some sort of horrible joke. Vegetarians don't kill anyone. Not real ones. They are nice people. They are the nicest people. Like Paul McCartney?'

Wong looked blank.

'You know . . . "Eleanor Rigby" and all that?'

'Eleanor who?'

'Never mind.' Thoughts were running at high speed through her mind as she worked hard to convince herself that the threats of killing could not be genuine. It was clear that Vega was rich, powerful and crazy – a dangerous combination of traits – but no one, surely, would go from freeing caged animals to killing humans? On the other hand, Linyao said that they had killed a security guard on one of their previous missions. She decided to keep that piece of knowledge to herself to avoid panicking people.

The lights went on to illuminate the other side of the room. They could see now that the old theatre in which they were being held had been roughly refashioned, with the prisoners in cages where the seats had been, and the area on the stage made into a kind of court room, with a raised table for a judge and a dock for a prisoner.

There was the click of a key being turned in a lock, and all eyes swivelled to the stage. The door opened at the back of the raised area, and Vega walked in, this time wearing the curly-haired wig of a traditional British judge over his masked face. He was holding a machine-gun of some sort in his right hand.

''ullo, lads and laddesses,' he said. 'PLEASE be upstanding for the entry of the judge.'

No one moved.

He raised his gun and shouted: 'Stand UP or I'll bloody well kill the lot of you and good bloody riddance.'

The prisoners wearily rose to their feet.

'Awright. That's better.'

Two more masked individuals entered – they were small, slightly built and dressed in shapeless black clothes: probably women. They stepped off the stage and walked towards the cages. They stopped at the one containing the small, wizened middle-aged woman whom Wong could not remember having seen before. One pointed a gun at her while the other undid the cage door and let her out.

Vega sat at the judge's bench and hammered on it with a mallet. 'The Court of Poetic Justice is open for business – I mean, in session. Okay, wot 'ave we 'ere, the first case, methinks? Put the prisoner in the dock.'

The woman's hands were cuffed behind her back and she was manhandled into a space behind a wooden divider on the right side of the court.

Vega picked up a piece of A4 paper and read from it. 'Your name is – bloody 'ell, 'ow do I pronounce that? Xin Pei Yi, aged fifty-one. You are accused of locking up bears in coffin-sized cages and keeping them alive in a state of intense suffering for years on end. 'ow do you plead?'

The woman, who clearly did not understand a word of English, replied in a stream of furious Mandarin.

'Translation,' Vega barked.

One of the female guards turned the accused's words into English: 'She says you are a pig and a dog and should let her go before her sons come and – the rest is obscene, sir.'

'Given the bloody great PILE of evidence in front of me, namely the reports by operatives codenamed Rescuer, Lockbreaker and 'ero, I find the plaintiff guilty as charged.'

'Accused,' Joyce called out.

'Wot?' Vega looked around.

'That's the accused. The person who makes the complaint is the plaintiff. You got them muddled up.'

'SILENCE. I will not have this court brought into disrepute by outbursts from the public gallery. One more word and I'll charge you wiv contempt of court. The PUNISHMENT for contempt of court is deaf, awright?'

'Yes, sir,' Joyce said, and then realised that this would count as two more words. So she changed her reply to a servile nod.

Vega looked back at the papers in front of him. 'Where was I before I was so rudely interrupted? Oh yes, Mrs Xin, aged fifty-one, the bear-bile woman, the bear TORTURER. On the evidence I 'ave before me, I find Mrs Xin to be guilty as charged on all counts.' He slammed the hammer onto the table. 'The Court of Poetic Justice sentences her to a taste of 'er own medicine.'

The door opened and two more of the Children of Vega walked in, trundling a narrow, coffin-like metal cage on a trolley. It was about eighty centimetres high and one metre deep. The bars were rusted and on one side there were dark brown stains which looked like blood.

'We have a genuine bear-bile farm cage for you, transported

at great expense from Sichuan province,' Vega explained. 'I 'ope you'll find it very comfortable. 'ome from 'ome, so to speak.'

The woman screamed in a different Chinese dialect as the guards manhandled her into it. She struggled hard, and it was obvious to anyone watching that both victim and guards were acquiring a significant number of bruises during the operation. Eventually they padlocked it shut with three chains. She yelled and kicked and rattled the bars.

'Oh dear,' Vega said. 'Dear, oh dear, oh dear. She's 'appy enough to put uvvers in the cage, but she don't like the SAME treatment for 'erself. Well, that's not very fair, is it, luv? We have to be fair, don't we?'

The woman continued to shriek, her screech becoming increasingly loud as she began to panic.

'I sentence you to – 'ow long shall we give her? Lemme see, the reports say that you keep bears ALIVE in the cages for many years at a time. I'm gonna be really kind-'earted and sentence you to just two years in that cage. Of course, you probably won't be in there for that long. I imagine you'll die of loneliness, bad food and bedsores LONG before yer sentence is up, so that will be nice, won't it?'

The screaming redoubled in volume, and then stopped and turned into a wail of misery.

'I can't STAND this bloody noise,' Vega said, camply smoothing his hair off his shoulders before putting his fingers in his ears. 'Get 'er out of 'ere.'

Mrs Xin the bear-bile farmer was wheeled away through the double doors to suffer her punishment alone.

'Next,' the judge barked.

The guards went to a cage next to Tun and dragged a small, sleeping fat man out of it. It was Chef Tomori.

'Aha! It's time for the first execution,' Vega said with a look of glee. 'That is, if we don't count Monsieur De Labauve, 'oo was standin' TOO CLOSE to the gas last night and didn't make it.'

'This is not funny,' Park shouted out.

'And the first person to die today will be Chef Tomori! Let's give him a BIG round of applause.'

The chef was woken up and manhandled into the dock. Vega picked up a sheet of paper and scanned it. 'Wotcher, Tomori-san. Lemme see. You are accused of murdering an 'uge succession of sentient bein's in a variety of ways, in a killin' spree that 'as literally lasted decades. You are pretty much the Jack the Ripper of the animal kingdom, ain't you? But today's sample charge will be the DELIBERATE murder of thirty-six live scorpions yesterday. They were killed by being dropped alive into somefink you call Old Turtle Broth. I would 'ope that the *old* in that sentence refers to the age of the soup, but sad to say, I expect that it refers to the age of the turtles, since nothing touches your stony 'eart – sentient bein's 'oo are old, young or just babies – you eat 'em all, and organise the most PAINFUL deafs for 'em, don't yer?'

Tomori was in a state of terror. 'Please,' he said. It was one of the few English words he knew. 'Please. Please-please-please-please.'

The double doors on the other side of the court room – really the side wings of the old theatre – swung open. Four men in black clothes marched in, grabbed the trembling chef and tied him into a harness. It had a hook dangling tail-like from the rear, as if designed to dangle the wearer from the ceiling – or lower him into something.

'Ooh, goodie-goodie, I like a bit of theatricality,' chuckled Vega.

Once Chef Tomori's arms and legs were tightly strapped together, the men hoisted him aloft and disappeared back the way they had come. An ominous cloud of steam drifted through the swinging doors.

'Now 'ow does Chef Tomori like to treat animals?' Vega pondered. 'Oh yes, he likes to drop 'em ALIVE into a vat of boilin' water.'

From the backstage area, Chef Tomori's screams could be heard as he realised the fate that was planned for him. Also audible were the sounds of a pulley system being operated. 'Ready,' a voice shouted from backstage.

Vega smiled. ''Aving read all the evidence, I PRONOUNCE the prisoner guilty. And sentence him to poetic justice.' He clumped the table once with his hammer.

There was an ear-piercing shriek, cut off abruptly by a splash.

The caged audience screamed as loudly as Tomori did.

'Ew,' said Vega. 'Gross . . .'

6

At 8.42 a.m., the kidnappers dropped Angelita Consolacion Balangatan (known to her friends as Peachie), blindfolded and hooded, out of a car crawling along the edge of Hengfeng Lu in north Shanghai, near the railway station. The maid found help from a tourist, who loaned her a mobile phone.

'Ma'am,' she wept into the phone, 'I've been released. I'm so sorry. I'm so, so sorry.'

'How's Jia Lin? Where is Jia Lin?' croaked Linyao, who had been up all night, and had trouble using her voice.

The maid sobbed for a while before she could speak again. 'I don't know. I mean, she's still there. They only let me go. I don't know what they're – they separated us this morning and took me in a car and pushed me out. I tried to tell them that I needed to stay with her, I begged them not to separate us, but they wouldn't listen. I'm so sorry.'

By the time Sinha had arrived at Linyao's Hongqiao apartment – where she had waited the entire night by the phone, helped by her mother, cousin Milly and a pint of black coffee – Angelita had been back home for an hour and had been questioned in detail numerous times about the experience.

Linyao reported her findings to Sinha before he had even sat down: 'They kept her blindfolded the whole journey there. She has no idea where they took her. Then they kept the two of them in a room with no windows, and pushed food through a flap in the door. They gave them a pizza between them.'

'I told them she only likes plain with extra cheese,' the maid wailed. 'But they wouldn't listen. I had to take all the pepperoni bits off myself and eat them.'

'How is the girl?'

'She's okay,' the two women said together.

Linyao continued: 'I mean, considering. She wasn't as upset as Angelita was, she said. There was a colour television in the room and a big pile of DVDs. They watched *Friends* episodes until nine thirty and then Angelita put her to bed.'

'I'm sorry. I'm so sorry,' the domestic servant said.

Sinha smiled at her. 'Don't worry. There's absolutely nothing for you to be sorry about. None of this was your fault. You did very well in keeping Jia Lin fed and unworried and ensuring that she got enough sleep. You did absolutely the right things.'

Linyao continued: 'My daughter apparently slept through the night. Angelita stayed up all night trying various ways to break out of the room. She dismantled her watch to try to use the edges of it to unscrew the door hinges. But she got nowhere. The kidnappers fed them at about seven in the morning, and then took Angelita out of the room. There were three or four of them, all masked, some Chinese, some *lao wai*. Before she could get a look at anything, they put a blindfold and a hood on her head and took her out of the apartment.'

'I begged them not to separate us,' sobbed Angelita. 'But they wouldn't listen.'

'How did Jia Lin react?'

'She didn't say anything. Not while I was being taken away. But I could hear her asking the kidnappers something as they took me out of the door.'

'What did she ask?'

'She asked if there were any more *Friends* DVDs.' The maid looked up at him. 'Are you a policeman?'

Sinha shook his head. 'No. I am a master of *vaastu*.'

'I don't know what that is.'

'No matter. I shall explain it to you – on the journey.'

'Journey?'

107

He stood up. 'Come on. Both of you. We're going for a drive.'

Shortly afterwards, they were in Sinha's car, a Renault Megane he had hired from the Avis office at Shanghai Hongqiao Airport, on his arrival the previous afternoon. He drove slowly, speaking in his languid drawl. 'Interesting driving techniques they use here. Rather like India. But slightly less use of the horn. You know they say that in India people use the horn in place of the brake? Whereas here they sort of nestle up against each other and use their size to intimidate other users to give them space. Still, it's more like India than Singapore. I must switch my brain over to Indian Driving Mode, which will give us a better chance of survival.'

'What good will this do?' Angelita asked. 'I didn't see anything. I couldn't see anything. I had this hood thing on. I don't know where they are.'

'Let me tell both you ladies about *vaastu*. The *Shilpa Ratnam*, a Sanskrit book, says "*Vaastu* is the unmanifest. *Vaastu* is the matter of all matter. *Vaastu Purusha* is the spark of the soul within." *Vaastu*, like feng shui, is really not a thing you can see. It is about awareness – awareness of what you can see and what you can't see.'

'Meaning . . . ?' Linyao's head was spinning and she was in no mood to concentrate on anything – particularly not a lecture on arcane Indian beliefs.

The old man thought for a moment before continuing: 'For example, the pupils of your eyes focus on various objects and then move on to other objects. But the peripheries of your vision detect much more – information which you see, but don't *see* that you see, if you get my meaning.'

Angelita whined: 'But, sir, I could not see anything at all, from the edges of my eyes or anywhere else. I had a blindfold and a hood, which I had on almost the whole time.'

'But there's more to awareness than seeing. Perceiving is not just seeing. There's so much information that you detect without your eyes. What were you aware of? Where did you feel you were? What did you sense, with your five senses, and your sixth sense? What did you hear? What did you smell, what did you touch, what did you intuit?'

'Sir, I don't know what that means.'

'Never mind, never mind. One detects things in many ways. That's all I'm saying. That's the spirit of *vaastu*. One detects bits of things without realising. We need to put it all together. Some people believe that all these underappreciated ways of detecting things add up to something called intuition, which is something that enables us to know things without being told them. Other people think intuition is an entirely different thing; an additional source of information which women in particular have in generous quantities.'

'But I couldn't see anything and I didn't hear anything – any address or anything.'

It was hard to remain patient, but Sinha was aware that an infinite amount of tolerance was necessary. 'Ms Balangatan – or may I call you Angelita? – you are perhaps not hearing me properly. Which is understandable, since you are very tired, and very worried. What I am trying to say is that it doesn't matter if you couldn't see anything clearly, or see anything at all.' He stopped the car and turned in his seat to look her in the eye, trying to appear serious but kindly, like a family doctor from a television drama.

'Now, let's stop here for a minute and gather all the information that is available to us. First, location. In *vaastu*, we always start off with the sun and its relation to us. Because we and the sun change our positions relative to each other, directions and times of the day are where we always begin. Now, Angelita, when you were taken from the school to the place where they kept you overnight, how long was the journey?'

'Quite far, sir.'

'Quite far. Can you be more precise? Did you feel yourself

travelling a long distance? Or was it just a long time? How long did the journey take?'

'I don't know. I couldn't see my watch or anything. I had my head all covered up.'

'But how long did it take? There's a clock in your head, you know, which is good for estimating things. In everyone's head. Was it half an hour? An hour? Two hours?'

'It was about an hour. Maybe more.'

'A lot more, or a little more?'

'Just an hour, I think, or an hour and ten minutes.'

'Good. That is nice and precise. Were you moving the whole time, or were you in a traffic jam? Remember, you were close to the middle of town and rush hour was about to start.'

Angelita thought about this for a while. 'It was stop and start and stop at the beginning, but then we began to go faster, and then it was stop and start and stop again.'

'Were you aware of turning left or right at any point?'

'There were lots of turnings, some left, some right. I can't remember them.'

'Can you remember the first one? That's all I am asking for. Was the first turning to the right or left?'

'It was left.'

'Okay. Given the location of the school and the direction you were going, that probably puts you on Sichuan Nan Lu heading north. That narrows it down to a place on this part of the map. Possibly Hongkou or Yangpu or somewhere around there. It narrows it down to an area where – just a few million people live.'

Linyao said: 'If she was driving for an hour and ten minutes, they could be anywhere. You can go a long distance in a good car.'

Sinha shook his head. 'Yes, but not at rush hour. They snatched them off the street just after five. For at least half that journey, they were moving through rush hour traffic. It would be quite possible to drive for seventy minutes and only travel a few miles, perhaps five. I've spent a lot of time in this city on business, and I've suffered the rush hour often enough. It seemed to be much worse than usual last night, when I came from the airport.'

'It's going to be worse this evening,' Linyao said. 'There's the American President visiting, and the demo. Nothing's going to be moving.'

The *vaastu* master turned to Angelita again and took both her hands in his. She giggled with embarrassment. Sinha ignored this and spoke with gravitas: 'Listen to me carefully. Now I want you to think about this morning. Short journeys have more potential to be of help to us than long ones. There are two locations which are relevant to us. The train station where you were released – let's call that Location B. And the location where you and Jia Lin were held. Let's call that Location A.'

'How do we know she's still there?' Linyao asked.

'We don't. We don't know anything. We are working only on probabilities, enhanced by our deductive powers. We work on the basis of anything we can get, including guess-work. But the salient fact is this – the kidnappers went to some lengths to keep Angelita unaware of the address of Location A while releasing her. This strongly suggests that Location A remains important to them. They don't want anyone to know where it is. It may have been just a temporary transfer station or holding pen, but given its importance, it is likely to be more than that. It may be the place where the kidnappers are based, and/or the place where Jia Lin is still being held.'

Linyao nodded.

Sinha drove to the corner of Jiaotong Lu and Hengfeng Lu by the North Railway Station, where Angelita had been pushed out of the car.

'Which side of the car were you pushed out of?'

'This side, sir,' she said, indicating the right.

'And you landed on the kerb? The pavement, here?'

'Yes, sir.'

'Now that tells us that they were on this side of the road, so came along this way. Where exactly did you land? Where were you when you stood up and took off the blindfold and the hood?'

'Just there, sir.'

He screeched the Renault to a halt.

'Okay. So that's where you landed. Let's work out where you came from.' He slammed the car into reverse gear and started driving backwards.

The car squealed at a high pitch. There were shouts and honking of horns, which he ignored. They reached the previous junction. 'Now, Angelita. Did you turn left or right into this road?'

'I don't know, sir.'

'You turned a corner? Which way?'

'I don't remember.'

'But you did turn a corner.'

'Yes.'

'How do you know you turned a corner?'

'Because the way the car moved made me lean over until my head touched the window.'

'Ah. Can you show me?'

Angelita leaned to the left, pretending to knock her head against the car window.

'Thank you.' He revved the car backwards and turned it sharply to the right. Angelita, who was not wearing a seatbelt, leaned over and hit her head lightly against the window.

'Just like that,' said Sinha. 'Right?'

She nodded.

The *vaastu* master continued to drive in reverse gear, causing more shrieks and blasts of car horns from shocked motorists behind them.

'That indicates that you turned sharp right, just here. Then what? Were there any other turns before that?'

'I don't know.'

'Did you do any other leaning over?'

'Yes. I lean over one time before that time.'

'Did your head touch the window again?'

'No. It went the other way. There was nothing to lean on. I felt myself leaning against the shoulder of the girl. Leaning to the right, right over, a lot.'

'The girl?'

'One of the kidnappers was a young woman.'

'How do you know the person next to you was a girl?'

'She smelled like a girl. She was smaller than the others. Her voice came from lower. She was wearing Estée Lauder. White Linen.'

'And the other one: woman or man?'

'I think a woman, but I'm not sure. And the driver was a man.'

'Did the other person guarding you say anything?'

'No.'

'Did he or she cough?'

'Yes, one time.'

'And from that do you think it was a man or a woman?'

The domestic helper thought for a while. 'Yes, it was a girl's cough. A young woman, maybe.'

Sinha nodded. 'Good detection work, well done. Can you show me exactly how you leaned?'

Angelita listed heavily to the right. 'The girl's shoulder was here, and I was pressing on it. For a long time.'

'Good. That means the car turned sharply left. Any more leaning to the left or right before those two instances?'

'No. They stopped the car after those two corners.'

'Now let's get down to establishing some facts. How long did it take to go from Location A, the place where you ate pizza and watched *Friends*, to Location B, the station?'

'Not very long.'

'Now that's not a good answer. I don't need to tell you why. You are an intelligent adult woman. I will ask again: how long did it take to go from Location A to Location B?'

'Just a few minutes. Five or ten minutes.'

'There's a big difference between five and ten.'

'I think maybe seven minutes. Or less. Maybe six.'

'Good. That's a nice, clear answer. Was the vehicle moving continuously during the six minutes, or did it start and stop a lot?'

'Mostly it was moving. But it did start and stop a bit.'

'Did it stop because the traffic lights were red? Or did it get caught in a traffic jam?'

'How can I tell? I had the hood and the blindfold on.'

'Traffic jams and traffic lights – and train crossings, come to that – have a different effect on how cars move. Did you hear any beeping noises? Did the car stop moving completely for two minutes, and then move again? Or was it stop-start-stop driving?'

Angelita thought. 'Both. The first time it was stop-start-stop for a while. And the driver, or someone, was getting very impatient. He kept saying curse words, and things like: "Come on, come on." Then, after about three minutes of hardly moving at all, we went fast for a while, but then stopped. I think that stop may have been traffic lights.'

Linyao slumped into silence, fascinated to realise that this man was actually getting some significant information out of the maid.

'A little while? How long do you mean by that phrase?' he asked.

'After the traffic jam, we moved for a minute, maybe two, very fast. And then we stopped at some lights.'

'Did you hear crossing sounds?'

'Crossing sounds?'

'You know, b-b-b-b-b-b-beep. That sort of thing.'

'Yes. I think so. I don't know.'

Sinha took the map and studied it carefully. 'They dropped you at this point here. So if you turned this way and then that way, and before that through a traffic light junction, and before that in a straight line, but in a stop-start fashion, that means you probably came from around here – or around there – or up here somewhere. Or perhaps somewhere around here, if your time estimates are poor.'

Linyao leaned over to look at the map. She shook her head and sighed. 'But those are really big areas you are looking at. How are we going to find one room in one apartment in one building?'

'We've only just begun,' Sinha said. 'Awareness of the unseen. That's the key. Now let's talk about sounds and smells. Did you hear anything, smell anything, anything at all?'

'Yes. There was a coffee smell outside, before they took us into the building.'

'Excellent.' He pulled open his briefcase and extracted a packet of ground coffee beans. 'As it happens, I am partial to a good espresso and like to carry my own supply. Was it like this?' He ripped open the packet and held it under her nose.

'Yes, a bit like that. Bitter. Strong.'

'Okay,' said Sinha. 'Probably a real coffee shop, as opposed to a local noodle eatery with weak instant muck. We need to locate all the coffee shops in the designated area.'

They studied the map and drove around a network of roads, but there was not a single coffee shop on any of the streets Sinha had marked on his map.

'Close your eyes, Angelita. Does any of this seem familiar?'

'No, sir, sorry, sir.'

'Any smells, sounds, anything at all?'

'No, sir. Nothing, sir.'

They drove around for another ten minutes, but Angelita

115

continued to recognise nothing. She kept apologising: 'I don't know anything, sir. Can't recognise any place, sorry.'

'Don't apologise. It's helpful that we can eliminate these roads from our search. Besides, it's not you who has got it wrong. It's me. There are no coffee shops here. We must be in the wrong place. Let's try this street.'

They turned into a small road in the Yangpu area, but it contained nothing except nondescript apartment blocks.

'Damn, damn, damn, damn,' said Sinha. 'This is bad news. We have seriously slipped up somewhere, but I can't think where.'

Linyao said: 'Maybe there wasn't a coffee shop. Maybe someone was just making a cup of coffee in their home and she smelt it through a window.'

Sinha shook his head. 'Unlikely. Sales of coffee-bean grinders for home use are not exactly widespread in this country – not yet, anyway, and certainly not in Yangpu. It's more likely we've made a serious mistake somewhere. Let's try going a couple of streets to the west. Can we turn left at the end of this road?'

Linyao looked at the street guide. 'No. I think it's a one-way road. We have to go right to go left. Turn right, go down for two blocks, and then turn left.'

'This place is like Alice in Wonderland,' said Sinha. 'You have to turn right to turn left. You have to go away from your destination to get to it. You have to – hang on.' He slammed his foot on the brake and the car stopped, throwing its occupants forwards. 'I've got it. Give me that map.'

'What do you mean?'

Sinha showed her the page. 'Look here. We believe that the kidnappers turned left from their base to take Angelita to the station. Because she leaned to the right "for a long time". So we've been assuming that the kidnappers came from over here – from here it would take a left turn to get onto the main road heading this way, to the station.'

'Ye-es?' Linyao said. 'But—'

'But there are situations where you have to turn left to go right. You have to do that in three places in the land of Alice in Wonderland, on expressways, and on roundabouts. Remember Angelita said she leaned over to the right for a long time? We assumed that indicated the car was turning left. But what if she ended up leaning over to the right for a long time because the car was going right round, or almost right round a roundabout and turning right?'

'Could be.'

He stabbed a major junction on the map with his thick, blunt finger. 'And if my thinking is right, then this may be the junction. Let's go and see if there's a roundabout there – and a smelly coffee shop here, on this road.'

Minutes later, his face brightened. There was indeed a roundabout at the junction he had identified. And the road that led off it had two coffee shops on it. Another road, which splintered off the first at a slight angle, also had a café on it.

The brief period of despair had passed and they were once again energised. They got out and walked rapidly up and down the streets, identifying several places where they could detect a specifically coffee-ish smell.

Angelita was becoming excited. 'Yes, maybe it was here. The smell was like this. This coffee. There was another smell. A cooking smell.'

'Also from the coffee shop?'

'No. When I came out of the building, I smelled coffee. And then they walked me along for a little while – maybe two minutes. And then I could smell a strong cooking smell. Chinese food.'

Linyao asked: 'How can they walk her along the road with a hood over her head? It must have looked weird.'

Sinha shook his head. 'You're right. It would have looked too strange to risk. I suspect the walk she made would have been down a back alley, and then perhaps down into an underground car park or something. Somewhere hidden away from the main road.' He thought for a while. 'Tell me more about this cooking smell. And let's walk around as we talk about it.'

They marched along in a grid pattern across a collection of streets while Angelita used her ears and nose to see if she could detect anything familiar. On the third corner, she stopped them. 'That's it. That's the smell.' She widened her nostrils and took a deep breath. 'It came from there.' She pointed to a vendor of fried stinky tofu. Although he was about two hundred metres away, the smell was sharp and noxious.

They hurried over.

'Stinky tofu is bad news for our investigation,' said Sinha. 'You can smell it for miles. And it drifts in the wind.'

'No, it was near here. It was a strong smell. We were almost on top of it. I could hear the man calling out. Something like: "*Jia chang dow-foo, jia chang dow-foo*".'

'Home-style tofu,' Linyao translated.

They approached the tofu-seller and Sinha encouraged the maid to look around with her eyes shut. 'I know it sounds crazy, but I strongly believe that keeping your eyes shut will better help you recreate where you were.'

She did as she was told. She stood in the middle of the street with her face up to heaven and her eyes closed, looking beatific, like a nun high on ecstacy, spiritual or otherwise.

While she concentrated, Sinha's eyes darted around. One house to the left had an alley along its east wall. And there was a building on the other side, fifty metres up the road which also had a side alley, along which one could speedily push a woman in a blindfold from a back door to the road.

'It would help if we knew which side of the road you were on,' he said. 'Can you tell us that?'

'I don't know, sorry.'

'*Vaastu* teaches us that the most important thing in life is the sun. If you know where the sun is, everything else follows.'

'But I couldn't see anything. And the room we were in had no windows.'

'The sun does not produce only light. It gives us heat. Were you aware of any warmth?'

Angelita stopped to think. 'When I was taken out of the room in the morning, we had to wait half a minute until the driver got something – the keys or something. I think they were undoing the locks of the front door. I could feel warm on my arm. There was sunshine and breeze and noises – it made me think they had the window open.'

'Excellent,' said Sinha. 'Now you've got the idea. The sun is the origin of all things, but also it is the starting point of all places, the *vaastu* masters say.'

She closed her eyes as she tried to conjure herself back into the scene. 'There was heat on my arm, just here.' She stroked her left forearm. 'And there might have been a window open, but I'm not sure.'

'Which direction was the window?'

'This way. I was facing the door, and the window was this way.' She pointed to her left.

Linyao stepped in, impatient as ever. 'But which way? North, east, south, west, that's what we need to know.'

'I don't know, ma'am, I'm sorry.'

Sinha raised one hand. 'You think you don't know, but you do. You felt the sun's warmth on your arm. That's all we need to know.' He marched back to the centre of the road, looked at his watch and then up at the sky.

The *vaastu* master knew a trick which enabled him to use an analogue watch to tell the directions of the compass at any time. First, you locate the sun in the sky. Then you look at the hands on your watch and find the middle point between them and then line up the sun with the middle point of your watch. The numeral 12 on your watch will point due north. Then use any rhyme – Never Eat Shredded Wheat was the one he had been taught in a New Delhi grammar school – to place the other major points of the compass clockwise at the right spots: N, E, S, W. Do a bit of mental extrapolation to find the location of the sun at other times.

'At eight ten or eight fifteen this morning, the sun would have been about – there,' he said. He pointed low on the horizon, at a building which seemed to be a school or some sort of government institution.

'The sun's heat would come from the east, and – I would think – might hit the top few floors of that building over there, and perhaps that one, and maybe the one next to it. If you could feel the sun's heat on your arm, it was almost definitely shining directly at you, through the window, which may or may not have been open. That gives us only a few options. It was one of those buildings along there, probably.' He pointed to the three blocks which were catching the sun on their upper storey. 'Let's check each of them in turn.'

Sinha made Angelita enter each foyer, close her eyes and take a deep sniff, and then listen for a while. But she couldn't differentiate between them. 'They all smell the same, and sound the same,' she said. 'Sorry.'

All three buildings had aged security guards at the bottom. The third one they questioned gave them an interesting lead – after Linyao had slipped him a 100-yuan note. 'Black people,' he said in Shanghainese. 'Fifth floor, back flat.'

'You mean people in black clothes?' Linyao asked.

He nodded. 'Always black. Foreigners.'

Linyao translated for Sinha.

'Were they foreigners?' asked Sinha. 'The voices on the phone were not Chinese?'

Linyao said: 'I think it must be foreigners and Chinese working together. Anyway, to the older generation in Shanghai, people from outside the city are called foreigners, or outsiders: *waidiren*. Whether they come from London or Fujian or Beijing or the moon, they are all just outsiders.'

'*Waidiren*,' the old man repeated in a grumble.

Linyao, her face set, headed for the staircase.

'Stop,' Sinha called, reaching for her arm. 'We need to—'

'I am not stopping. I need to find my child.'

'I know, I know, you want to see your daughter as soon as possible. But they may be armed. It may be dangerous. At this stage, I strongly recommend that we get professional help from the law enforcement authorities. It is vital to—'

But Linyao wasn't listening. She raced up the stairs. The *vaastu* master and the domestic helper looked at each other – and were soon puffing up the stairs after her. 'I tried,' Sinha said to the domestic helper. 'You're my witness. Did you hear me? I did try to dissuade her, didn't I? This could get nasty. I advise you to keep your distance. No heroics, please. Heroics make me nervous. They are very unspiritual. Neither *vaastu* nor feng shui can protect one against heroics, which are a very bad thing.'

Outside the door of the flat at the back of the fifth floor, they noticed three discarded Pizza Shack boxes. Sinha whispered to Angelita: 'There they are. One for you and Jia Lin, two for the kidnappers. That suggests there are only three or four of them.'

Linyao picked up one of the boxes and rang the bell.

'Who?' said a female voice in Mandarin.

Linyao replied in the same language. 'Pizza Shack. You ordered three pizzas last night. You win a special prize. Free pizza.'

'Don't want it. Go away.'

'What? Can't hear you.'

'Go away.'

'Can't hear you. Open the door. Get your free pizza.' She rang the doorbell again.

The door opened a crack. It was chained so that it could not swing wider than seven or eight centimetres.

'Here is your free pizza,' Linyao said, holding up one of the boxes as if it was still full. 'Open the door, please.'

The door closed, a chain was removed, and the catch was released again.

Instantly Linyao slammed the door with her shoulder, knocking over the woman on the other side, who fell backwards, yelling curses.

The furious mother stormed into the room, with Sinha and Angelita behind her.

The young woman in black clothes rose to her feet and pulled out a gun. Linyao batted it out of her hands with the pizza box. 'Where's my child, you bitch,' she yelled, falling heavily on top of her. Never mind scorned women: there is no fury like a mother parted from her child. Angelita picked up the gun from the floor and held it lightly with her fingertips as if it were a dirty nappy. She decided that the safest thing to do was to get rid of it, so she threw it out of the window.

Sinha said disapprovingly: 'If you ever find yourself in a repeat of this situation in Singapore, I would strongly advise you not to throw guns out of windows. They don't like that sort of thing over there.'

Angelita, trying to be helpful, fell heavily onto the woman with whom her employer was struggling, landing on her stomach and causing her to groan. While the two women grappled with the kidnapper – who appeared to be alone in the flat – Sinha scanned the apartment for a windowless room. He knew that a room with no window would almost definitely be a maid's room, and would likely be reached through the kitchen. So he raced past a two-ring cooker and entered a utility area containing a washing machine and an ironing board.

Beyond that, he saw the door of a maid's bedroom, bolted from the outside. He slipped the catch and slowly swung it open. Inside, a small girl was watching television. She looked up at him briefly, registered no interest, and turned straight back to the screen.

'Come, Jia Lin. I'm a friend of your mother's. We've come to take you home.'

'After this,' she said.

'I'm sure your mother will buy you a DVD of this movie for your very own.'

Seconds later, Linyao and Angelita both appeared behind Sinha. 'Jia Lin,' they shouted, simultaneously.

'Hi,' the little girl said, her face lighting up with happiness. Jia Lin jumped off the bed, and ran past Sinha and her mother, burying her face in the domestic helper's legs.

7

The atmosphere in the underground theatre was tense and feverish. Silence, broken only by the sound of people weeping or trying to comfort each other, had followed Vega's exit. Murmuring noises then broke out as the religious among them started beseeching various deities to effect their release from this nightmare. Even to the only nominally religious, these seemed to be a good idea, and a steady drone of mumbled prayers to the Almighty or mantras to the collective will started to hum through the echoing chamber.

A few people wept openly, and one man curled himself into a foetal position and started calling for his mother, which, if the truth be told, made most of the others feel like doing the same. God or mum? Now there's a choice. The Catholic route of combining the two with a Holy Mother seemed to make excellent sense to several people for the first time. For the entirely non-religious, a great truism became clear to them: if religion is a delusion, it is a useful, even necessary one, and people too intelligent or self-possessed to delude themselves are greatly to be pitied.

As time passed, the misery level fell. The very texture of the air in a room containing people condemned to death is somehow changed: it is filled with life and light as the inhabitants start to feel grateful for the most mundane realities. Thank you for dirty floors. Thank you for stale air. Thank you for this minute of breath and thank you in anticipation of the next. The notion that you don't know what you've got till it's gone is wrong. People who have been given a glimpse of the end of the road don't have the luxury of waiting until life has gone to miss it. To lose the confidence that the sun will rise on another day is a type of death in itself.

This mental barrier of despair was broken through in silence, without pain or panic. The room felt like the cabin of an aircraft falling slowly out of the sky. People sat quietly and thought about their families, their parents, their children. If the purpose of the Children of Vega had been to make animal-abusing diners feel guilty for their crimes against four- or eight-legged friends, the exercise was proving a dismal failure. Not a soul was feeling remorseful about having eaten large numbers of innocent, fun-loving lobsters. The few who were not praying but having coherent thoughts about the situation were thinking only about how they had fallen into the hands of madmen, and whether there was the slightest chance of fighting or arguing their way out.

'We nominated curling oysters for the meal,' business-man Chen Shaiming suddenly said. 'There's nothing cruel about eating oysters. We shouldn't be here. They should let us go.' He raised his voice, in the hope that someone outside would hear him. 'Are you listening? You should let us go.'

His corpulent wife Fangyin chimed in, a whiny nasal echo of her husband: 'Yes, everyone eats oysters. Can you tell them, please?' She turned to look at Joyce, who was assumed to be the in-house expert on the ways of killer vegans.

Joyce pursed her lips. Traumatised by what she had seen, she was curled up motionless at the back of the cage. It seemed so unfair, especially since she had last year become a vegetarian herself. She decided that she might as well talk – it would take her mind off the horror that kept replaying itself on the screen in her mind. 'Well, maybe a vegan might think that eating oysters *is* cruel. I mean, you eat them alive, right?'

'Yes, but not in a *cruel* way,' Fangyin objected, feigning surprise at any such implication. 'I think they rather like it.

125

Much better than just rotting there on the ocean floor for years and years. Dying of old age is a slow, nasty death.'

'But how do you actually do it?'

'You pick up the oyster in the shell,' her husband explained. 'Then you squeeze lemon onto it. If it sort of squeezes itself up, that means it's fresh. That's why we call them curling oysters. Then you add a bit of chilli sauce – that usually makes it curl again – and then you pop it in your mouth. You chew it quickly and then you swallow it. That's all there is to it. No cruelty at all. A quick, painless death.'

Joyce spoke carefully, thinking about each word: 'But, if you – if the thing winces when you put lemon on it, maybe the lemon, like, *hurts* it?'

'But you have to put lemon on it,' Fangyin said. 'And you have to see it wince. Otherwise it is not fresh, and you can't eat it. If you eat an oyster that doesn't curl, you can suffer a fate worse than death – you can have an upset stomach.'

'That's not a fate worse than death.'

'It is to me.'

If anyone was upset by Fangyin's crassness in the face of what they had just seen, they didn't say anything. But several closed their eyes when she used the word *death*.

There was a noisy interruption from the cage next to the one Wong and McQuinnie shared. 'That's the same with me. I nominated Korean spiced baby octopus for my dish,' said Park Hae-jin. 'You put chilli and garlic sauce on it, and then you eat it. It's not cruel to animals or anything. They *like* the chilli sauce. They do a little dance.'

Joyce's brow furrowed. 'But if you put lemon or chilli on a creature and it writhes about, it probably means that it doesn't like it. It probably hurts.'

There was a loud snort from another cage. 'Of course it hurts,' said Tun. 'Haven't you ever accidentally wiped your eye or something when you've touched a chilli? It hurts like crazy. Lemon, too. Ever squirted a bit of lemon into your eye by mistake? You're idiots, pretending that it doesn't hurt.'

Joyce nodded, her face suddenly very disapproving. 'Yeah, he's right, I'm sure. When you stick stuff on those creatures, you're really hurting them. It's ever so cruel. That's why you're here.'

There was silence as the Chens took in this unwanted information.

'But what will our punishment be?' Fangyin asked. 'Will they sprinkle a little lemon into our hair? I think that would be a fair punishment. I don't mind even if they squeeze a whole lemon into my hair. It would spoil my hairdo but I am prepared to accept that as a punishment, if I have to accept something as a punishment. Can you tell the man?'

Joyce was exasperated. 'He can't hear me or any of us, so no one can tell him anything, okay?'

Park, the octopus eater, looked depressed. 'But I'm sure it's a happy dance. I know the difference between a happy dance and an unhappy dance. They *like* the chilli sauce.'

'Shut up, you idiot.' This comment came from Tun, who clearly had a volcanic temper. 'Chilli sauce contains capsaicin, an extremely harmful and painful chemical compound. Those baby octopuses are writhing in their death agonies, not dancing. And besides, you crunch them up in your mouth while they are still alive. Are you going to tell us that they enjoy that as well? Would you enjoy that – being doused with burning chemicals and then being eaten alive?'

Joyce said nothing, but a vile thought ran through her head: *Perhaps he will find out.* She blocked the thought immediately and stared around to distract herself.

Park opened his mouth to defend himself, but shut it again without saying anything. He took his jacket off and shaped it into a pillow before lying down on it. 'My head still aches,' he said.

A rather handsome if chubby youngish man sat in the back corner of the room, in a cage with a short dark-skinned woman dressed in bright colours. 'The thing we nominated was not cruel, I'm sure of that.' His accent, similar to but not exactly like that of a Hispanic American, gave him away as Filipino.

'What was it?' Joyce asked.

'*Balut*,' he said.

'What's that?'

'Eggs. Just eggs, that's all. Even vegetarians eat eggs, don't they?'

'Well, some do. Vegans don't.'

'There's no cruelty in eating eggs.'

His wife nodded furiously. 'We only nominated eggs, which even vegetarians eat,' she repeated, to make sure everyone had got the point.

Park was not standing for this. 'Tonyboy, don't you pretend your dish is cruelty-free while the rest of us are guilty.'

'What? Eggs are eggs.'

'Not if they are *balut*.' Park turned to direct his comments at Joyce. 'May I introduce Tonyboy Villanueva and his wife Girlie. What they have neglected to tell you is that *balut* refers to fertilised duck eggs.'

'Oh,' said Joyce, as if she knew what he was getting at.

'They are fertilised,' Park repeated. 'Think about it. They have little bird foetuses growing inside. The creatures are alive. They have tiny wings and tiny bones and tiny feathers.'

Tonyboy shot back: 'But it's not cruel. We cook them, sometimes.'

'And sometimes you eat them raw,' Park said. 'Even if you cook them, what are you doing? You are throwing some poor live baby bird into a pot of boiling water. I suppose you are going to tell us that they like it – that it's like going to a swimming pool for them?'

'Shut up, Park,' Tonyboy said, defeated. 'You made your point. But I still think—'

'I thought you said we nominated chicken?' interrupted Girlie Villanueva.

Her husband lapsed into guilty silence.

'Tonyboy, did you nominate – ?'

'Yes, but I think better we keep quiet about it. Eating eggs will probably seem less upsetting to these people than, than – the other thing.'

'What was the other thing?'

There was a long silence during which Tonyboy looked the other way. 'I nominated *balut* with *pinikpikan*,' he said quietly.

'Mother of God, bless us.' Girlie covered her head with a pashmina scarf.

'What is *pinikpikan*?' Park asked.

'It's a Filipino chicken thing, what we call an Igorot dish.'

'And?'

'It's roast chicken.'

Park refused to let him get away with this. 'Come on. This is a live food restaurant. Roast chicken is not just roast chicken. Talk, Tonyboy, talk.'

The Filipino businessman sighed. 'Okay. You might as well know. With *pinikpikan*, you hold the chicken down by its head and then you beat it all over. When its whole body is bruised, it starts to swell up – the blood creates haematomas under the skin. Then you pluck it and roast it. It gets big like a melon, swollen because of the beating. The meat is more juicy and tender that way.'

'That's bad news for you guys,' Park said.

'What about us?' said a new voice. In a cage at the back was an Indian couple in their fifties. 'We nominated the Shanghai hairy crabs. If they are going to steam us to death, then I cannot think of a more painful way to go,' said Vishwa Mathew Roy. His wife burst into tears.

Park let out a long slow breath. 'Death by steaming. That's—'

129

He was interrupted by the click of the door at the back of the stage opening.

Vega re-entered the room and walked over to the judge's bench. ''aving a nice little conference, are we, chums? Well, sorry to interrupt the sweet little nuffins you animal-murderers are swapping, but it's time for the next 'earing, okay, folks?'

Everyone tensed.

The double doors on the other side of the stage opened and six masked men entered, several of them carrying guns. Three walked to the cage containing the Chens, while others went to the cage Park occupied with his dazed, silent wife Yon.

'It's all a mistake,' Fangyin pleaded. 'I don't even like oysters. I just pretend to eat them. Really I don't eat anything at all. I'm a Venusian, just like you people. I'm always on a diet. Ask my husband. I don't eat *anything*.'

Ignoring her pleas, the guards lifted the two cages onto a wheeled pallet and trundled them to the area to the left of Vega's court. All four of them were talking at once.

'Please, this is all a mistake—'

'Mr Vega, if you would just let me—'

'I could make you rich. Just say—'

'Please don't—'

Vega held up his hand. 'SILENCE,' he yelled. 'What a bloody awfoo racket.' He took a pair of airline-style earplugs out of his pocket and twiddled them into his ears. 'Much better.' He looked at the papers in front of him. 'You four 'ave been accused of – blah, blah, blah, blah. I really can't be bovvered with all this stuff.' He tossed the papers aside and looked over at his victims, terrified in their cages. 'Let's just cut to the chase, shall we? You guys have been found GUILTY of being extremely unpleasant little shits, why not leave it at that?'

The four people in the cages started pleading for their lives again. Chen Shaiming dropped to his knees, and Fangyin followed suit. 'Please, please, Mr Vega,' he said. 'I am a multimillionaire. We can pay you—'

'THIS is the Court of Poetic Justice. We've gone to a whole HEAP of trouble to make sure the punishments suit the crimes. I'm very proud of these next devices we've prepared specially for you. Bring 'em on, mates, bring 'em on. Let 'em rip.'

Two staff appeared with large plastic canisters which appeared to be topped with some sort of spraying device. They looked like equipment a farmer might use to blast pesticides at crops.

By this time, three of the victims were pleading on their knees and the fourth, Park's wife Yon, was curled up in a ball on the floor.

The guards aimed the chemical blasters at the cages and pulled the triggers. Gobbets of vivid red gunk flew at the victims, who screamed and writhed and started frantically clawing at their skin to get it off.

'Lovely jubbly,' Vega said.

He let them scream and scratch at themselves for a full minute before making a dismissive gesture with his hand. The guards wheeled the cages out of the room. 'Put them in the basement wiv the bears,' Vega said. 'I don't normally approve of any sentient bein' eatin' meat, but we might make an exception this time. That Korean bird looks a bit tasty, knowwotimean? Ha ha.' He glanced at his watch and then rose to his feet.

The guards moved over to the cages where the remaining prisoners sat, almost all of them with their eyes shut, and many of them with fingers crammed in their ears. The Children of Vega used their gun barrels to make the prisoners who remained conscious stand up.

'I do apologise that these 'earings may be a little GORY for family viewin'. Especially since I notice that some of you businessmen have rahver young trophy wives, naughty, naughty. But just REMEMBER one fing: all this is yer own bloody faults.'

Joyce turned a tear-stained face to Wong. 'I guess he thinks I'm your wife. What was the dish you nominated?'

'Prawns,' said the feng shui master, his face filled with dread.

'Just prawns? What sort of prawns?'

'Drunken prawns,' he said. 'Drunken prawns flambé.'

Joyce closed her eyes. This was going to be bad.

'Oh bother,' she said, and fainted.

☯

'Those brave enough to kill will be killed. Those brave enough to not kill will live.'

Lao-zi, sixth century BC, quoted in 'Some Gleanings of Oriental Wisdom' by CF Wong

Thirteen minutes later, the doors burst open again. Most of the prisoners looked up. Others preferred to remain curled up in denial. But this time, it wasn't Vega who stepped into the room. Wong peered at the newcomer. It was a smaller figure, with red hair tied severely in a tight ponytail, sticking out from Vega's theatrical judge's wig.

'Please be upstanding for the deputy chief judge,' said an armed young woman accompanying her. The guard had something Japanese about the lower half of her face, which was all that was visible.

A few people rose wearily to their feet, exhausted by the horror they had seen, while most remained incapacitated by anticipation of what might come next.

The new judge, overlooking the fact that many of her audience ignored her, took her position in Vega's seat. She read from the papers in front of her in a much more formal manner than her predecessor in the hot seat: 'I hereby declare by the powers vested in me as a voluntary representative of sentient beings that the Court of Poetic Justice is in session. In the ongoing trial of the Children of

Vega versus the This Is Living Dining Club, the next defendants—'

'Where is he?' Wong called out in English.

'Silence,' she replied angrily, in a strict, schoolmarmish tone. 'Vega is working on another major assignment. I will be presiding over this hearing, as he has to attend to important business elsewhere. And in future, you will not speak unless I ask you to, is that understood?'

Wong was intrigued to note that although the redheaded woman had a stern, unyielding edge to her voice, she lacked the note of vicious gleefulness that Vega had displayed. He hoped she would find it harder to torment people.

'As I was saying, the next defendants are—' She checked the pages in front of her. 'Mr and Mrs Wong.'

The guards went to the feng shui master's cage and stuck their guns through the bars.

'Excuse me,' said Wong, pointing to the comatose figure on the floor of the cage. 'She has fainted. Also, she is not Mrs Wong.'

But the guards were not listening. Red Hair leaned forward to look at the papers in front of her. 'If you can't move, you can listen to the evidence from there. Mr and Mrs Wong, you are accused of ordering the painful torture and death by chemical poisoning and burning of more than two dozen live creatures in a dish called Drunken Prawns Flambé. How do you plead? Be warned: if you plead not guilty and are found guilty, the court will add the charge of perjury to your sentence, and your punishment will be correspondingly heavier.'

How could a death penalty be made heavier? 'Not guilty,' he said, anxious to stall for time while looking for ways to escape.

'You plead not guilty. Very well.' She started to leaf through the paperwork in front of her. 'Okay. Here's the stuff. We have the menu, which clearly lists a particular dish for the meal last night, and specifies that it was – I quote – "nominated by Mr CF Wong". It then names the dish as Drunken Prawns Flambé and describes the dish thus: "Live prawns marinated alive in ginger and onion soup to which a generous portion of Martell XO cognac is added before the whole dish is flambéed".' She looked up. 'I think that's admirably clear. So this court finds you guilty of the charges as laid, plus the additional charge of perjury for pleading not guilty.' She gave an elegant tap on the tabletop with the hammer.

Wong scrunched up his nose. That had not gone well. Now what? 'I am not CF Wong,' he said.

'I'm not listening. Okay, here's the sentence. You two will be securely tied up and then dropped into a bath of hot soup. We'll turn the heat up, add something flammable to the mixture and then set it on fire. That should be fitting. Is that big bowl thing with the burner ready?' This last comment was directed at a stocky Chinese woman who seemed to be taking the role of stage manager.

Wong, unable to think of anything to do, desperately scanned the tiny cage to see if there was any tool he could use to defend himself. There appeared to be absolutely nothing. He put his hands in his pockets, but they were empty except for some sheets of paper and the packet of money he had been paid – surely not enough to buy his freedom, not after the tycoons' offers of cash had been ignored. And then there was his *lo pan*. But it seemed unwise to pull that out. All that would achieve would be to confirm that he was, indeed, CF Wong the feng shui man.

He slipped his hands into Joyce's jacket pockets to see if she had a penknife or anything similar. Certainly, she used to carry one as a key-ring. He found nothing but crumpled tissues in most of her pockets. In one, he discovered her sandwich.

He pulled it out and stared at it. Was there any way he could break out of a metal cage using a vegetable sandwich? Could he overpower the guards with it? Threaten to smear it on their nice clean black clothes? No obvious answer sprang to mind. Had it been some sort of hard snack – a watermelon or something – he could have thumped someone with it. But a soggy, day-old sandwich? There was no hope. Unable to think of anything else to do, he absently started to unwrap it.

An alarm went off – a ringing sound triggered by someone watching from the stage. 'Meat alert, meat alert,' said the Japanese girl, who appeared to be the security chief of the outfit. She raced up to Wong's cage, the click of her steel-reinforced heels echoing from the hard walls. 'No dead flesh is allowed in these premises.'

'Except dead people,' Wong said. He continued to unravel the greaseproof paper to reveal a tortilla wrap. He pried it open and noted that there were red, yellow and purplish-green things inside.

'No meat is allowed in these premises,' the young woman barked. 'Prisoner Wong, you are ordered to throw the sandwich outside the cage immediately.'

He ignored the commands and continued to poke around inside the roll, pleased to be unnerving the guards.

She marched right up to the edge of the cage and pointed the barrel of her gun directly at his temple. 'Put that thing down, *now.*' And then her eyes suddenly widened. 'What – ?'

The fury in her face changed to shock, and then puzzlement. 'Is – is that a hyper-vegan?'

Wong had no idea what she was talking about, but quickly replied: 'Yes. Yes it is.'

The woman was confused. She dropped to her knees and peered closely at the tortilla. Wong picked up a slice of something slimy and held it up to her: It was unmistakably a limp piece of grilled, peeled yellow capsicum. Next he held up a slice of seared eggplant. 'Fried *qiezi*, very nice,' he said. 'My favourite.'

'You are CF Wong, the feng shui master?'

'No. My name is Eric Wong, and I am a chef. A vegetables-only chef. I kept trying to tell you. I make these things.'

'And are you – are you a hyper-vegan?'

'Yes.' He spoke firmly. 'A big one.'

The guard stood in silence for ten seconds, and then jogged back to the judge. She spoke quietly but Wong could just about make out what she was saying. 'Chief? I think there might be some sort of mix-up here. We may have got the wrong guy or something.'

'Not a chance of that,' Red Hair replied. 'That guy's the restaurant feng shui guy. And one of the diners. Vega identified him before he left. He was there, in the TIL group, eating live animals.'

'Can't be. This guy's a vegan. A hyper-vegan. Look at the food he's carrying with him. He says his name is Eric Wong. He's carrying the same sort of hyper-vegan wrap that we had last night from the veggie café. There must be some mix-up. Maybe this was one of the kitchen staff or something.'

'Shit.'

Red Hair reached for her hammer. 'The court is adjourned.'

Five minutes later, Wong and McQuinnie were in a white room off a dark corridor outside the theatre being interviewed by Red Hair and Japan Girl. The Children of Vega kept asking questions that Wong could not answer, so he stalled by pretending he was concerned for Joyce's health. 'My assistant needs help. Is there anything we can do?'

Joyce had been poked and prodded until she had woken up and been made to stagger out of the cage at gunpoint, but had slumped back into unconsciousness as soon as she'd sat down in the interview room. Her body was in a chair, but her head was against the wall and she was snoring.

'Drugs?' Red Hair asked Wong, pointing to Joyce with her eyes.

'Drink,' Wong said. 'Tsing Tao and your gas stuff don't mix

too good. Also, she is young, can't take it, all this trauma. Is hard for vegetable-eaters like us.'

Red Hair's lips became a thin line, almost invisible. It was evident that she was quietly furious. No doubt she had been thrilled that Vega had left her in charge, and was upset that a problem appeared to be emerging on her watch. Had a mistake been made – a serious error? No: this had to be CF Wong, and he had to be the prawn-murderer. But the hard evidence of the grilled vegetable sandwich sat on the table glowing like a 100-kilowatt football stadium floodlight. It had been dissected and found to be distinctively vegan. Perhaps it wasn't his. 'I don't believe you, Mr Wong. I think you stole that sandwich, and this whole thing is a trick to help you escape your fate as a murderer.'

'They probably found the sandwich somewhere,' Japan Girl added.

Red Hair slammed her pen down on the desk. 'Okay. We don't have time for this. We have to bring this session to a close. Answer this question exactly right and we may just take you seriously. Get it wrong and you are in the soup – literally.'

She glanced up at the light bulb to think. Then she lowered her piercing pale blue eyes to stare at Wong. 'Got it. Who were the founders of veganism and what year did they do it? Answer correctly or die.'

The feng shui master swallowed hard. His mind raced, but no possible answer presented itself.

'Elsie Shrigley and Donald Watson founded the first vegan society in the UK in 1944. They were disgusted with the number of vegetarians eating eggs,' Joyce said in a sleepy mumble, having just woken up. 'Where are we?'

'Hello, Joyce,' said Wong, with a degree of bonhomie that she had never heard him use before. 'How are you? I was worrying so much. You fainted, you know, after you see what happen to those poor meat-eaters.'

'Oh *cheese*, yes,' Joyce said, rubbing her temples. 'Dear God. Dear, dear God.'

'But I have explained to these people that they should not do the same to us, because we are, er, hop, er, hippo, hypo, the same things as they are. After all, why should they hurt someone like me, a vegetable-only eater called Eric Wong?'

Before the women could analyse Wong's unconvincing statement, Joyce ripped into them. 'Yeah, I can't believe you are doing what you are doing. You're crazy. How can you kill people? What are you doing? I mean, *what are you doing*? Vegans are supposed to love and respect sentient life. That's what it's all about. You can't just boil people alive. That poor – You can't—' She burst into tears.

'Name six famous vegetarians,' said Red Hair, who was still suspicious, her lips shutting so tightly that they disappeared once more.

'What?'

'Name six famous vegetarians. If you are really a vegetarian, you should be able to do that.'

Joyce took a moment to compose herself, and then said, sniffing: 'Er, Einstein, Elvis Costello, Mahatma Gandhi, Reese Witherspoon, Bob Dylan, Michael J Fox, Natalie Portman, Alicia Silverstone is a vegan, so is Moby, and Shania Twain. In fact, most geniuses were veggies, like, er, Isaac Newton – and did I say Einstein? – and Steve Martin, Damon Albarn from Blur, and—'

'Paula McCarthy,' put in Wong. 'And Eleanor Rugby.'

The two women in black looked at each other. Japan Girl sighed. They *were* veggies. This was a bloody awful mess.

Joyce was still angry and glared critically at their captors. 'There's too much death around. More birds and mammals are raised and slaughtered in a single year in the United States alone than the entire human population of Earth. We need to cut the number of deaths in the—'

Red Hair turned on her: 'Listen here, bitch. I am in charge around here, and no one tells me what to do. If you are very, very lucky, I may allow you to escape with your lives. But I haven't decided yet, so I would advise you to SHUT UP. Got it?'

Cowed, Joyce shrank back into her shoulders and nodded. The door opened and another Child of Vega marched in, a European woman not much older than Joyce. She didn't have her mask on, and her face was as white as a sheet. 'Jesus, Minnie, I need to talk to you,' she said. 'I just got a call from Harriet. There's – there's some really weird stuff happening. He's – you need to know what he's really – what's happening out there. I—'

Red Hair lifted up her hand to stop her. 'We'll talk outside.' She and Japan Girl followed her out of the room. They slammed the door and locked it carefully behind them.

☯

Wong and McQuinnie waited in silence. Just outside the windowless basement cell, the women talked in low voices. The minutes ticked on and five painfully slow ones grew to eight and then ten. There seemed to be some sort of dispute going on. The voices, although whispering, were emotionally charged. It appeared that there had been some development that had the Children of Vega passionately divided.

After two or three more minutes, the whispered conversation came to a halt. Wong tensed himself for the reentry of their captors, but they heard footsteps decreasing in volume. The women were walking away, perhaps to gather opinions from other members of Vega's team, or members of the local groups who had been co-opted onto it.

This is our chance, he decided. He examined the room to see if there was anything they could use to break out with. There was nothing – except a copy of the *Shanghai Daily* that Red Hair had used to cover the table while she carefully dissected Joyce's tortilla. It would have to do. He unfolded it and dropped to his knees in front of the door. Then he opened the pages and slid them out through the crack between the door and the floor.

'You got anything I can use to push key out?' he said.

Joyce searched her pockets. 'Nothing,' she said. 'I had a penknife but it's gone. They must have taken it out of my pocket after they knocked us out.'

'I need something, anything. Something thin, long, like a pencil. Did she take her pen when she went outside?'

She looked at the table, and even lifted the tortilla to see if it was underneath. 'She did. Bugger.' There appeared to be nothing they could use. Then her eyes fell upon the half-demolished wrap on the table. 'Hang on a minute,' she said. 'How about this?' She picked up a chilli pepper.

He shook his head. 'Too soft. Any hard vegetable?'

Joyce bit her bottom lip as she searched through the detritus. 'We always put a piece of nice raw stuff in the bottom of a vegan pack – hang on, what about this?' She pulled out a small, peeled carrot stick. 'This is hard.'

Wong peered at it. 'Too fat. Eat some, please.'

Joyce nibbled at it with her front teeth, Bugs Bunny style. 'Hmm,' she said. 'It's quite good. We sprinkle balsamic vinegar and black pepper on it to bring out the sweetness.'

After a frantic minute of sculpting the carrot with her teeth, it had become a thinnish twig. 'Will that do?'

'Let me try,' he said, taking it from her. The carrot was still too thick to fit into the keyhole, but he forced it in and the middle part of it entered. He wriggled it a bit from side to side and then came the sound he was waiting for – the clink of a key falling. They heard it bounce.

'Cheese, I hope it landed on the newspaper,' Joyce said, crossing her fingers. 'That sounded like a big bounce.'

'Old key very heavy. Not bounce too much.' He carefully pulled the sheet of newspaper back into the room. Almost at the end of the sheet, they both saw it at the same time: the key.

'Yay.'

'Shh. Keep quiet. We are not out yet.'

He picked it up, listened carefully at the door, and then gingerly unlocked it from the inside. It swung open with a B-movie creak. There was no one outside.

They tiptoed out of the room and found themselves in a dark corridor with several doors leading off it. Voices came from a room about four metres ahead of them on the left. Four or five people were talking simultaneously, and one was sobbing. 'This isn't what we thought it was,' the crying voice was saying. 'This is evil. He's going to blow up the whole bloody place, isn't he?'

'We don't know that,' came another voice, a stern one which Wong recognised as belonging to Red Hair. 'We don't know that for sure.'

'Get real, Minnie. We do,' a third voice said. 'He is. You just don't want to admit it to yourself.'

'How many people will be killed? All this killing is wrong. There may be vegetarians in the crowd. That's different. They don't deserve to die. And children! Babies. *Babies*. We can't be part of this,' the distressed voice continued. 'This is mass murder.'

No one replied to this. Then a young man's voice spoke: 'Can't we just call the Grand Theatre anonymously, and tell them that there's a bomb? Tell them to cancel everything, evacuate the place?'

'Who's going to believe us?' Japan Girl replied. 'They get hundreds of crank calls like that every day when something like this is going down. Look at the size of the anti-American demo. No, there's nothing we can do. I think we should split.'

The crying voice sniffed and added: 'Perhaps if we give them precise details, tell them that the bomb will go off at six eighteen, tell them how we know, who we are, maybe they will believe us.'

Another voice spoke, a voice they recognised as the white-faced woman who had entered the interview room. 'I say we split right now, cover our tracks. If Vega succeeds in killing the leaders of the two most important nations on earth and we get blamed for it, there's going to be nowhere to hide. We are going to be hunted down and killed by every member of every military organisation on earth. Killed slowly. If the Americans Guantanamo us, everyone in the whole bloody world is going to applaud. Are you ready for that?'

'Let's just go,' said the male voice.

Wong and McQuinnie heard the sound of chair legs scraping against the floor. Holding their breath, they raced through a fire escape door and ran up the stairs. At the top, they moved into another corridor and then found an un-locked door leading to something that looked like an adult education classroom.

They raced into a walk-in cupboard at the back of the room and then stopped and looked at each other, each wanting confirmation from the other about what they had overheard. '*Aiyeeaa*,' the feng shui master whispered. 'Vega is going to bomb the two Presidents. Did you hear? Big bomb, kill lots of people. *Aiyeeaa. Ho marfan.*'

Joyce was enraged. 'That is SO not a vegan thing to do. That is like so *totally* non-veg.' She stamped her foot. 'And to think, I made him dinner.'

'What is the name of this guy again?'

'Vega. Like Vegan without the "n" on the end.'

'Weega?'

'No, Vega. With a "V".'

Wong's mind began racing. 'No, I think *Weega*.'

'Look, I know how to spell Vega.'

'This man, he have any connection with western China? Far west? Northwest?'

Joyce nodded. 'Yeah. He's from this family in one of the provinces in the west. They were unhappy there so they moved to London and—'

'Xinjiang? Urumqi? Is he from Urumqi?' 'I don't remember.

142

Maybe. I know it was something I couldn't pronounce, anyway. Room something.'

'You mean Urumqi, Xinjiang province,' Wong whispered to himself. His eyes were wide and full of fear. 'Now I understand. Now it make sense. The bombs. The targets. *Wah.*'

'What, what, what?'

He breathed out slowly before replying. 'I tell you why he calls his name Weega. It's for a reason. Is not really short for vegan. He just want you to think that, so that you support him. Really, his name is not Vega, but Uyghur. U-Y-G-H-U-R. He is the Uyghur bomber, I think.'

'Who?'

'The Chinese government have big problems in a place called Xinjiang, where the Uyghur people live. They don't treat the people so good. They are not Chinese.'

'If they're not Chinese, how can the Chinese government do stuff to them?'

'The place they live in is part of China, but they are not the same as Chinese people. Wrong race. They are Muslim. They have strange names. Some of their buildings have – how do you say it in English? Onion-shapes.'

'Like domes? Okay, but what has this got to do with bombs?'

'The Chinese government treat the Uyghur people badly. Always bullying, fighting with them. Some get lost, get shot, get killed, disappear. Thousands locked up. Some of the Uyghurs campaign against Chinese government. Some get explosives, start bombing campaign.'

'So you think our Vega is one of those?'

'He is using your group and other Shanghai vegetarian groups to help him get secret network in this city. But his real mission is not this. He want to explode bombs in the name of the Uyghur people. Probably he want to get notice worldwide.'

'How come I never heard of any of this stuff?'

143

There was an obvious answer to this – idiot Westerners were only interested in pop music, Hollywood movies and hamburgers. 'If he sets off bomb near the Chinese leader and the US leader, then the whole world will be talking about what is happening in Xinjiang. For the Uyghur people, this is a very clever plan.'

'I guess.'

'But we got to stop it.'

Less enthusiastically: 'I guess.'

A minute later, Wong and McQuinnie peered out of the classroom at the corridor. They had still not been traced. The building was a maze of corridors, all of which looked exactly the same.

'How do we find our way out?' Joyce asked.

Wong was staring at his compass. 'Big question is: how old is this building?'

'What?'

'If it is before 1949, maybe it is built with feng shui principles. But after that, no good, unless very recent.'

'We better just go out of a window or something. We can hardly call the guards and ask them whether they have a book detailing the history of the building, can we?'

'No need for book,' said Wong. 'I can tell. This building very bad, very boring architecture. Communist style, 1960 something. No feng shui.'

'So how do we find our way out?'

'We find something from before 1949 – that will help.'

'Like what?'

'Like that,' said Wong as they turned a corner and saw a guard shuffling along a corridor away from them. He looked to be in his late fifties or early sixties.

Wong raced to the shabby workstation the guard had just left and found what he was looking for: an old picture of a green dragon taped on the wall for good luck.

'Okay,' he said. 'So this mean front wall is that way and back door should be over this side.' He pulled out his compass to check the directions. 'Back way faces northeast. Back door will not be so heavily guarded. Probably there is also delivery bay or staff entrance on back side.'

They raced through another corridor until they found the back entrance – but it was heavily guarded, probably by a security company hired by Vega. So they turned and ran back along the corridor, trying door handles until they reached one which was unlocked. They raced into the room – another empty classroom – and then carefully climbed out of the window into a Shanghai back alley. They were free.

'I can't believe we broke out of that place so easily.'

'That was the easy job,' Wong said. 'Now come the hard one. Now we have to break into the place where the Presidents of China and USA will have their meeting and tell them to cancel it.' He paused. 'Or . . .' He lapsed into silence.

'Or what?'

'Or we go far, far away. So when bomb blows up, we are not near.'

'Let's do both. We'll race over to the Grand Theatre, tell them that there's a bomb in the place, and then we'll get as far away as possible, leave the bomb squad to switch it off or whatever you do with bombs.'

Wong ran to a fruit shop and offered to slip the vendor a small sum of cash for permission to use her phone. She quickly agreed. He expected her to point to an old Bakelite handset, but the woman reached into her apron and brought out a tiny, shiny chrome mobile phone. 'Twenty yuan a call,' she said in Mandarin.

'That's outrageous,' said Wong, shaking his head and returning his envelope of money to his pocket.

Joyce saw what was happening. 'Give her the money. We need to call the police. Save all those people locked in the basement.'

Her boss's face darkened. He passionately hated extortion

unless he was doing it. But Joyce was right – there was no choice. Handing over the money, he took the phone and called a contact from the Public Security Bureau to come and raid the premises they had just left. He didn't give any details except to say that 'people led by Western foreigners' had kidnapped 'high-ranking Chinese citizens'. He knew that would get them excited. Then he dropped the names Tun Feiyu and Chen Shaiming, and could hear the law enforcement official sitting up straight and paying attention. 'Who are you? Who is this calling?'

Wong rang off, unhappy that if there was any reward going, some petty policeman would get it.

'Give the old lady some more money,' Joyce said. 'I want to call Linyao.'

The feng shui man slowly pulled the envelope out again – and Joyce snatched it from his hands. She opened it wide, and the fruit vendor noticed the huge wad of money inside. '*Wah!*' the old lady exclaimed, and switched to English. 'Missy, gimme two thousan' *kuai*, you keep phone.'

'Okay, that sounds reasonable.' She counted out the money and walked away with the phone.

Wong snatched the envelope back. 'You don't spend my money, please,' he said.

'This is an emergency,' she said. 'Besides, this is a Samsung D900. It costs way more than two thousand.'

'Truly?'

'Truly. Marker's got one. It's five hundred US. It's got a built-in MP3 player and a three megapixel camera.'

Wong wondered why the woman had sold it cheaply, and then realised that it might have been stolen.

His assistant pounded Linyao's number into the keypad.

'Lin? It's Joyce. Where are you? We have just had the most incredible night. It was totally bizarre. Wait till you—'

'I had an amazing night, too, but let's compare them later. I got an emergency.'

'So have we. We think there's a—'

'There's something weird going on at the summit. Someone went to an amazing amount of trouble to get my pass to do something to the animals that are appearing in the show at the Grand Theatre tonight.'

'Uh-oh. My news is also about the summit. We reckon someone has put a bomb in the theatre. Where are you?'

'On the way to Renmin Park – the People's Park, right in the middle of town. That's where the sum—'

'So are we. See you in – however long it takes us to get there. I'll call you when I arrive.'

☯

'The key thing to remember is that the earth is square,' Dilip Kenneth Sinha said. 'Obviously.'

Buoyed by his triumph in locating Jia Lin, he was treating Linyao to a free lecture on the key principles of *vaastu shastra* as he drove her to the centre of Shanghai. His plan was to drop her there so she could hook up with Joyce and Wong, and then he would track down the union's local contact. Shang Dan had lived in the city for years, had a good feel for local politics, and was the person most likely to be able to deliver useful information about the bizarre events of the past twenty-four hours.

Linyao, who was sitting in the front passenger seat as he manoeuvred the Renault, not without difficulty, through the Shanghai traffic, was only half listening. Her sleep-deprived, adrenaline-filled head was reeling. It had been hard to tear herself away from her daughter, but she had found the idea of Jia Lin heading out of the city for a few days irresistible. Occasionally, something in his droning voice would catch her attention and she would react.

'Square? The earth is square?'

He nodded. 'Yes. Not physically, but in cosmological terms. We think of it having four directions: sunrise, sunset, north magnetic pole and south magnetic pole.'

'But that is just a different way of talking about north, south, east and west, yes?'

'The Western way just treats them as points. The Eastern way gives each direction its own individual character. For example, sunrise – what Westerners boringly call east – delivers warm, healthy, life-giving, beneficial rays. The other directions do not. The energy of the north is heavy and grand, for example, and is associated with the head. So that's why we never sleep with our heads to the north.'

It took a few seconds for the apparent contradiction in Sinha's words to filter into her brain. 'Run that by me again. The head is north, so why don't we sleep with our heads to the north?'

'The body is a type of cosmological magnet. The head is the north of the body. We never sleep with our heads north because two magnets oriented in the same direction repulse each other. This is the opposite of feng shui, which considers north the area of sexuality, and thus recommends that beds be sited with the sleepers' heads pointing north. But most regions of the planet have their own geomantic systems.'

'Not Canada,' said Linyao, who was using the conversation as a means of keeping awake while trying to avoid touching on subjects that might engender emotional strain – such as thinking about exactly what lethal plots the kidnappers' gang had concocted, and where she fitted in.

Sinha expertly spun the wheel to swerve around a truck which had pulled out without warning in front of him. 'Even the Western world has its own geomantic traditions,' he said. 'Consider *De Architectura*, written by Marcus Vitruvius in the first century BC. It purports to be the first book of architecture, but in fact deals with all sorts of human issues, ranging from art to morality to the gods. In chapter three he talks about the perfect human body.' The car bumped up onto the pavement to avoid a man wheeling a barrow and squeezed between two flatulent buses. 'Vitruvius says the face should be exactly one-tenth of the height of the body. The distance from the chin to the nostrils is exactly one-third of the length of the face, and the same applies to the distance from the nostrils to the space in between the eyebrows.'

Sinha rambled on, meandering from topic to topic as they slowly approached the centre of the city and Linyao felt herself finally surrendering to sleep.

8

Agent Thomas 'Cobb' Dooley did not walk to the front office of the Shanghai Grand Theatre. He surged, tsunami-like, his personality filling the full volume of the corridor the way a subway train fills a tunnel. Even in the widest corridors, people would flatten themselves against the side walls as if he were four or five people rather than one. This quality was so pronounced that he almost needed to be thought of as a plural entity. Here come Dooley, Dooley are arriving, Dooley are here and are surrounding us. Get a bus: Dooley need transporting. It was not because of his physical size. Indeed, he was below average for an American male, topping out at a fraction under five feet nine inches, which qualifies you for the nickname Hobbit in the US military or similarly macho, hierarchical bodies.

Not that he was puny. Hours spent in the gym meant that he had a stocky body which made his shaven head seem two sizes too small. But the muscle was a bonus, and not the key part of his character. He always tried to use his personal presence alone to fill any enclosed space he entered. He attempted never to smile, he worked at keeping his posture aggressive (head down, upper body poised for action, fists clenched), and he kept permanently attached to his face an expression which warned people that they were talking to someone with the shortest fuse in human history. During high-stress, climactic days (such as the next forty-eight hours, which were the culmination of three months' planning) there would be something about his eyes and forehead which said that he had just lived through the worst hour of his life and if one more thing annoyed him, it would be the very last straw of all the final straws that had ever existed since the dawn of straws.

The first time a person encountered Tom Dooley, they would wonder what terrible thing had happened that day. Some people would actually ask a member of his staff what had put Agent Dooley into such a bad mood, and would be shocked to hear that this state of rabid, bitter ferociousness was normal. If he had the ability to be in moods other than bad ones, no one was aware of it. There was a rumour that he had been caught smiling last week, when a secretary entered his office without knocking on the day he had laid off three staff.

'Git Carloni. An' Felznik,' he growled to the officer following behind him (given the size of his ego, there was no room to walk alongside him).

'Yes, sir,' barked GS-9 Special Agent Simon Lasse, his nervous voice nasal and high. He started squeaking rapidly into his walkie-talkie.

Dooley smiled inwardly at the man's terrified obsequiousness, working hard to keep the downturned set of his lips firmly in place. For the truth of the matter was that the entire tough guy personality was a bit of an act. Well, to be honest, more than a bit. It was entirely contrived. Dooley had been as soft as margarine left in the sun for most of his life, but had spent the past four years perfecting a persona in which he appeared to have the warmth of a glacier. He had been an undersized, bullied wimp during an unhappy childhood in south St Louis and had overcompensated for it every day since he joined the most prestigious department of the United States Secret Service.

He had made his major move four years earlier, transmuting from a smiling wimp to a grim-faced tyrant. His epiphany followed an assignment in which he had been so impressed with the power of the personality of a previous SecTreas (no one in the USSS used full titles for anyone) that he had copied the man's characteristics with the care of a professional impersonator. Every detail of the way the man expressed himself, from the threatening manner in which he walked, to the shortness and gravelly nature of his utterances, to the hostility of his smile, to the way he seemed to be in a permanent foul temper, had been minutely studied and recreated. Dooley had painstakingly conjured up the SecTreas, complete and unabridged, late at night in front of his bedroom mirror, and eventually rolled his stolen persona out for public consumption when he got a major promotion to number two of the USSS's highest-profile department.

Only when he had comfortably slipped into the SecTreas's personality did he make a shocking discovery. He had been suffering from a serious psycho-physiological ailment all his life without realising it: he had been born without a personality. He was a void, just like all the other voids in his department, in his office, in his college, in his school, in his street. He had no passions. He had no interests. His opinions were held lightly and could be swayed from one extreme to the other merely by the reading of a newspaper opinion column. He realised that that was why he had slipped into the older man's personality so easily – he was like a naked man who had been given a coat for the first time. He made himself comfortable inside it, and he had never looked back. And now, after four years, the coat had bonded to his skin.

The new, revised edition of Tom Dooley suited his present position perfectly. He had achieved high rank, and he was determined to be superlatively good at it. Since his job was to inspire his team to achieve the impossible, he had to scare them into devoting more hours and more energy to the job than was good for their health. That was what good bosses did, wasn't it? It was the secret of capitalism, that you quietly destroyed other people's family lives in order to get a good result for your company, aka your paymaster, and ultimately yourself. And once you got to management level, you delegated every part of your job to others, reserving for yourself only the problems that no one else could deal with. And then you made sure things were so tightly organised that there wasn't anything in that category. Which was the situation he had achieved.

Or had he? One of his staff had dared to call him with a problem they couldn't handle, that they thought warranted his attention. One of the most important aspects of Dooley's carefully cultivated image was to demonstrate regularly that he did not suffer fools gladly; that he did not suffer fools at all; that he did not suffer anyone in any way; that the only thing to do was to do one's job so well that he never had to notice one. This might be another opportunity to demonstrate that, he thought.

Yet somehow, as he reached the end of the corridor and saw his staff with two women, a Western teenager and a Chinese woman, there was a sinking feeling in his gut. These didn't fit the usual profile of fools to be suffered, of cranks, trouble-makers, time-wasters. He could be looking at the birth of a headache, less than seventy minutes before POTUS, the President of the United States, was due to arrive. This could not be allowed to happen. Chaos had been exiled from every cubic millimetre of the Shanghai Grand Theatre and not the slightest fragment could be allowed to re-enter.

Ten minutes later, he was struggling to keep his composure. 'Ladies, ma men've checked ever' inch of this building. Ever' inch,' he growled. 'If there was a bomb the size of a goddam pea in this building, we would have found it – not once, but six times over.'

Dooley narrowed his eyes and beamed an unspoken message to McQuinnie and Lu: *If you are implying that I don't know my job you better realise that people have died for less.* He was wondering how the hell the two women's vague allegation got all the way to his level. The kid was clearly high on something. There was an unfocused look in her eyes that unmistakably said *drugs*.

'Yes, yes, look, sorry about this and all that,' Joyce blurted, blinking and rubbing her eyes. 'But I just, well, really think there's a bomb in here, and I don't want anyone to get hurt. I had to tell *somebody*.'

'You think there's a bomb in here? Well, we think there ain't. Want some hard facts, kid? Some numbers?'

'What do you mean?'

'You know how long we bin here? You know how many times we bin through this building? You know how many staff we got here, checking things out?'

'No, I don't—'

'Well, I'll tell you.' Dooley liked interrupting people. With him, it wasn't just an obnoxious habit. It was *policy*. Riding roughshod over people trying to converse with you or each other when they should be silently, respectfully listening to you – that had always been a key technique of the SecTreas that he had admired. 'Ma team have been studying these venues for three months. We bin here, physically, on the ground, for six weeks. You know how many people are here with the President of the United States? Do you know, li'l lady?'

'I don't know, but—'

'I'll tell you. Seven hundred and twelve. Normally we have a couple a hundred. Sometimes we go up to four or five hundred. But on this trip we are being really careful. And when I say really careful, I mean it – that's why there are seven hundred and twelve American souls here, advising, running around, checking and rechecking ever' inch of ever' building that the President of the United States will place his dainty little toes into.'

'Yeah, look, you don't have to listen, but we just thought we should tell you because—'

'So where is it? Where is this bomb that you have a feeling jes' may be in here?'

A pause. And then: 'I don't know.'

His much-practised look of being irritated beyond endurance became even more pronounced. His next statement was little more than a low, rumbling whisper. 'Okay. What *sort* a bomb is it?' His staff, hearing his voice drop to dangerously bass level, sidled a step backwards in formation, worried that he might go off at any moment. They already knew that there *was* a dangerous bomb in the building, and its name was Thomas Dooley. They prayed that Joyce had an at least half-reasonable answer to the question.

'Um. I'm not sure,' she said, and bit her lip.

Dooley wondered whether to continue the conversation or just explode now. And what sort of explosion should it be? A quiet one in front of the civilians and, after they had left, a loud one to the staff who had disturbed him to talk to these crazy women? Or a massive one to shut everyone up at once? And should he use foul language? He normally didn't in front of civilians – you never knew what could get into the media, and they were all wary of the media these days. He decided that he would try one more question, which he also delivered with menacing quietness. 'What 'zackly makes you think there's a bomb in here? You have a dream about it or somethin'? A vision, mebbe?'

Joyce had no immediate answer to this. The only thing to do would be to explain in detail about the strange group who had kidnapped them yesterday, and what they had overheard. It was a long story, but there was no other option. She opened her mouth to speak, but Linyao got in ahead of her.

'Because I put it here,' the mother-of-one declared.

Dooley took a step back and raised his right arm. Four officers standing behind him pulled out guns and levelled them at the Chinese woman.

The Secret Service agent's eyebrows rose. What in hell was all this about? A drug-crazed backpacker kid talking vaguely about a bomb threat carried zero weight – but an actual confession from a calm, obviously intelligent, bilingual Chinese woman in her thirties: this sounded like something they might just need to take seriously.

'Now this is gettin' serious,' he said. 'I want you ladies to know somethin'. Of course putting a bomb somewhere is a major crime. But jest *telling* me that you put a bomb somewhere is also a serious offence in my book, whether you did or not. *Capisce?* You gone beyond the pale. Now, ma'am, you gonna tell us about this bomb that you say you put in here?'

Linyao nodded.

Her self-assurance made Dooley begin to feel uncomfortable. He could feel his cheeks fall, so that his face no longer registered Powerful and Irascible but merely Unhappy and Ill-At-Ease. This was not good. There was only an hour or so to go before POTUS walked in and he did not want to be pulled out of his comfort zone. Normally, he knew what to do about situations that threatened to drift out of control. You bully people around you into working so hard that they rebuild the walls of your comfort zone. He had done it before, and would do it again. That was the nature of the job. But if an Actual Crisis arose at such a late stage – anything that could be classified as a Potentially Serious Incident just before POTUS arrived – this would be a major development. It could not be allowed to happen. After all, he was the ASAIC. His official title was Assistant Special Agent in Charge. But for the past twenty-four hours he was actually Acting Special Agent in Charge, his supervisor having been in? ltrated by a dangerous enemy agent – a stomach bug. By taking prime responsibility for security during this meeting, Dooley had taken on a degree of responsibility that could make or break his career. Nothing could be allowed to spoil it.

Dooley turned away and looked out of the window. He could feel the tension rise in his neck and shoulder muscles, his deltoids and trapezius tendons becoming stiff.

People in normal jobs could never understand just how intolerant of failure the Secret Service had become in recent years – especially at this level. When he had first been assigned to the Secret Service Presidential Protection Detail, he felt like a princely suitor in a fairytale who is given a list of Three Impossible Things To Accomplish By Noon – only in his case, he had a couple of months to do them (which was good) but the list had stretched to several thousand impossible things (which was bad). Yet the punishment for failure was similar to that suffered by princes in fairytales – off with his head. In most cases the word 'head' in this context referred to the boss, who would have to resign to take responsibility for the shortcomings of his staff. And now he, Thomas 'Cobb' Dooley, was the boss. The buck stopped with him. And this buck could stop his meteoric rise dead.

His voice lost a little bit of its subterranean resonance: 'So where did you put it? And how did you get in? We don't remember seeing you in here before and, believe me, lady, we see ever'one who comes in here.'

Linyao moved towards the chair.

Four guns were cocked to fire.

'No sudden movements,' barked Dooley.

'I was just going to sit down,' she said. 'I've been up all night.'

The Acting Special Agent in Charge gestured at her to take the seat. 'Talk. Fast. If this is some sort of joke, your ass is grass, which is an American phrase you probably won't find in your English language textbook in this goddam country.'

Linyao took a deep breath before speaking, wondering whether to add that she was Canadian. Probably best not to. Didn't Americans have an even lower opinion of Canadians than Axis of Evil residents? 'I didn't personally put a bomb in here. But I am indirectly responsible, I believe, for a bomb of some sort being here. I'll give you the facts, and you make up your own minds whether this is a serious issue or not. Does that sound reasonable?'

'Yes, but make it quick. We got no time for time-wasters. You got two minutes, and then you're out of here – both of you.'

Linyao painfully told the story of how her daughter Jia Lin had disappeared on her way home from school the previous night. She explained that she was a government veterinarian working for the Shanghai municipal authorities, and how an access card to the stable block north of Suzhou Creek was the only thing the kidnappers wanted in advance. And she told them that several animals from that block had been transferred a few hours ago to the back stage of this very building. She believed the kidnappers were somehow involved with a bomb plot because of some information that Joyce had. She explained that her young friend – who had also been temporarily kidnapped, they believed by a separate branch of the same group – had overheard that a large explosive device had been sneaked into the premises and was due to go off at six eighteen precisely. It might have been smuggled in with the animals.

During her recitation, Dooley's heart speeded up. There was something just a little bit plausible about the woman's wild story. And six eighteen was exactly halfway through the performance that both presidents would be watching – which did involve animals from somewhere, God knows where, perhaps from this woman's stable block. Like all law enforcement agents, teachers, reporters and mothers, Dooley had a lie-detector built into his eardrums. It had not beeped once during Linyao's tale. She was telling the truth, or thought she was. Of course there was no bomb in here – that was impossible, with all the security measures in place. But something weird had occurred, and it involved space for which he was responsible. He had to check it out. He had a mission to keep the World's Most Important Man safer than safe and that meant that in a very real sense he, Dooley, was the World's Most Important Man at this moment. And he could not fail. *He could not fail.*

'Come,' he ordered, his basso profundo voice scooting up to a nervous mid-baritone. 'We needta go for a walk.'

They marched at almost running pace to the main auditorium, and then through a staff-only door that led them to the wings at the back of the stage where human and animal performers would wait for their entrance. Thomas Dooley's brain raced as they strode. Even though his legs were relatively short, he had learned to stride in such a way that normal people had to scurry or half run to keep up. The anxiety made him move even faster than usual. A little nodule at the back of his mind was saying that it was just possible that the make-or-break moment of his career had arrived. The possibility that real trouble was afoot was still low, but it was there. And if something bad was happening, he was going to be on top of it.

Dooley had come from an embarrassingly working-class background (his father was a low-ranking operative in a factory which made American Standard toilets), and so had always been hungrily ambitious. As a youngster, he had always thought that secret agents were hired through a furtive approach made in a bar late at night. But he had actually joined the Secret Service by the most mundane route imaginable: he had wandered past their stand at a career fair in St Louis. He signed up on the spot, soon started doing cop-like duties in his local office, and then moved to the Uniformed Division at the White House before shifting to credit-card fraud and counterfeiting. He did a short stint on a team looking after Bill Clinton, and then rapidly rose to almost the very top of the Presidential Protection Detail – and today was number one, with the help of the enterovirus bug which had temporarily promoted him.

He liked people to know that the protection service, known as the SSPPD, was not like other branches of the Secret Service. Everyone had heard of the SS, but few people really understood it. The Secret Service had been set up by Abraham Lincoln, who signed the bill, can you believe it, on the day he was assassinated at the theatre: 14 April 1865. There had been one local patrolman assigned to guard him, and the man had wandered away to get a better view of the stage, not realising that the real action was going to take place in the audience. Yet protecting the President had not been part of the original brief of the newly founded USSS. It was set up for the specific purpose of stopping the printing of fake money, which was considered a far greater threat to the health of the country than the mere killing of the President.

Lincoln's death did not inspire Congress to take serious action to protect their leaders. And so gunmen were allowed to kill President Garfield (not related to the cat) at a railway station in Washington in 1881 and President McKinley at an expo in Buffalo in 1901. Only then did Congress decide to assign somebody to take the blame if more Presidents got killed: the Secret Service, thanks to the catch-all nature of its name, got the job. Those who understood the SS had argued that it was really just a type of commercial crimes bureau which accidentally had a moniker that belonged in pulp fiction. But no one listened.

So the USSS continued to grow with two non-matching core functions. Over the years it had developed a good relationship with the Mint, and the two organisations prided themselves on doing their job well. The fact that the US dollar had more or less become the world's currency appeared to be proof of this. Fighting fraud and counterfeiting – especially in these days of high technology – was relatively straightforward.

The other core function, protecting the President, was not. The SSPPD, the Presidential Protection Detail, had evolved into the organisation which probably ran the most complex logistics operations in history. Its work had nothing to do with sitting at computers and devising systems to catch tech-savvy criminals. PPD officers were out there, on the street. They were visiting venues. They were prowling along alleyways. They were sneaking up stairwells. They had to be the eyes and ears of large patches of ground, because they had responsibility for unimaginably wide areas. If fifty thousand people came to see the President, they had to ensure that not a single one of them could harm him. If he went on a tour which involved him being visible from eighty buildings, then all eighty of them had to be checked out and 'secured'. If he drove one hundred miles, then every one of those miles had to be made safe.

If all those things had to be done away from Washington – say, in Chicago – the job was ten times harder. If the President's trip was outside the United States – say, in London – the job became one hundred times harder. And if the task was on one of the Hard Targets list – problem countries, like China – the task became one thousand times more difficult. He thought of Europeans as semi-foreigners and Asians as 'full' foreigners. And so on this occasion, at the recommendation of his department, the President was travelling with a team of seven hundred and twelve individuals, of which some three hundred were minders, plus a huge amount of equipment, including a fleet of armour-plated vehicles. The one that everyone knew about was the bulletproof limo, but other vehicles were always present, including the communications van and the military ambulances.

Since 9/11, assignments had become harder. Not only did the Secret Service PPD have to secure every inch of the ground, they were also responsible for the air. The 'equipment' list on this occasion included a small air force. In this case, permission had been obtained (after weeks of negotiations) for U-2 reconnaissance missions to be flown over Shanghai. There were also two helicopters available – one was a Bell attack chopper, known as the Topchop, prepared for quick escapes if the Prez had to be zipped to a safe location. The second was a Sikorsky Blackhawk AH-60, on permanent standby at a nearby helipad for 'contingencies'.

The incongruous crocodile of rushing, unhappy people arrived at the wings of the main auditorium of the Shanghai Grand Theatre, which was carefully guarded by four individuals. After a word with the men at the door, they were allowed onto the stage. There were very few performers there as most had been asked to do their rehearsals on a similar stage at the other end of the building.

'Lasse,' Dooley growled. 'Explain the system to them.'

'Everyone who comes in here has a Theatre Zone 1 pass or is accompanied at all times by someone with a Theatre Zone 1 pass,' the jumpy junior agent said. 'Everything that is carried in here is checked. Every box, every bag, every piece of paper. Even the animals are all individually checked, their cages, their food trays, everything. You couldn't smuggle anything in here. You couldn't smuggle a beer can in here. If there is a bomb in here, it would have to be microscopic – the size of a thimble. Too small to cause any trouble.'

Lasse called a man in blue overalls over and asked him: 'Leong, what animals do we have in here today?'

The man, who appeared to be Chinese-American, spoke in Shanghainese with a local man, similarly dressed, and then turned back to translate into perfect English: 'Very few, he says. There will be six white doves, but they haven't arrived yet. They should be here in a few minutes. The Spinning Acrobat Sisters are bringing them. There is a parrot that appears with Mystic Megiddo. There's the elephant that he makes vanish. The ceremonial horse. And there's a kennel on standby, since one of the guests is bringing a seeing-eye dog. That's it.'

'Megiddo makes a real elephant vanish?' Joyce asked, looking through a box of props on the stage. 'Look at this – amazing,' she said, pulling out a pack of Mystic Purple Smoke Bombs.

Lasse nodded. 'Yeah, apparently. I don't know how he does it but there's all sorts of trapdoors and fake walls and things on the stage. You know how it is with these magic guys.'

A stagehand pulled a heavy rope and a pink curtain fell noisily onto the middle of the stage.

'Careful with that,' Lasse squeaked, unnerved by the sudden movement and loud sound.

'Show me the elephant,' Linyao said.

Leong made a call on a walkie-talkie and two other men laboriously brought the white elephant to the stage from a passage that opened onto the stage-left wing.

162

'It's not moving very well,' the man in overalls said in Shanghainese to Linyao, vaguely recognising her as a Shanghai government vet he had seen before. 'I think it's sick. It's sweaty, too, and smells funny.'

'Can we keep as much of this conversation as possible in English, please?' rumbled Dooley, annoyed at losing full control of everything going on.

'He's saying that the elephant is sick,' she said.

The pale-skinned beast approached slowly, its weight clearly detectable through the sprung floor as it lowered each of its oak-like feet to the ground.

'Aha. There's the problem. There's the crack in your security.' Dooley stared. 'Are you telling me that this is not an elephant but some sort of terrorist bomber? Dressed up, is he?'

Linyao shook her head. 'No, I'm not saying that this is not an elephant. I'm saying that it's not Jin-Jin. That's not the elephant which I had to health-check and clear for the job. It's not even the same sex. This is a male.'

'It's an elephant, but the wrong elephant. Fine.' Dooley turned to Leong, who pulled out his clipboard and started scanning the pages. 'Got any others in a cupboard somewhere? Bring me a spare.'

'Look,' Leong said, holding up an image. On one page of the thick pile of papers clamped to his clipboard was a photograph of a white elephant. He gestured at the beast. 'It looks the same to me.'

'Rubbish,' said Linyao. 'There's no similarity at all. Look at the forehead. Look at the eyes. Look at the wrinkles at the top of the trunk. This one's much older, for a start. And, as I said, it's male.'

Leong pointed under the beast. 'Male? Well, where's its things?'

'The testicles are inside. That line is where its penis is.'

He shook his head unhappily. 'They all look the same to me.'

'Okay,' said Dooley, now feeling confused. He straightened his back. When you are a five-foot-nine boss, you cannot afford to relax your spine, not for a second. He filled his chest and deliberately lowered the pitch of his voice half an octave. 'So we have established that our security ain't quite as flawlessly airtight as we would have liked to think. One impostor has managed to penetrate the inner sanctum. But it is an animal, for chrissake.'

'Yeah,' sneered Lasse, anxious to back up his boss. 'An elephant. What's it going to do? Spray water through its trunk at the Prez? Throw a banana at him?'

'Shut up, Lasse,' said Dooley, who liked to abuse those who worshipped him. He turned to Linyao. 'Look, ma'am.

We don't like being fooled in any regard whatsoever when it comes to security matters. So ah'm grateful to you for pointing this out to me. But ah'm finding it damn difficult to see where the logic of all this lies. Why would someone go to all this trouble to switch one elephant fur another?'

Linyao knelt down in front of the animal. 'Look at this,' she said. She pointed to a scar which ran along the elephant's stomach. She felt its leathery skin. 'It's badly distended.'

'The Trojan Horse,' Joyce put in. 'Maybe they've done something to the elephant. It's like the Trojan Horse, you know, where all the baddies were hiding inside?'

'There are bad guys waiting to leap out of this elephant?' Dooley scoffed.

'I didn't mean it literally.'

By this time Linyao had pulled out her extra-large veterinary stethoscope and was listening carefully to the underside of the beast, moving the instrument along the scar. After half a minute she stood up and faced the Acting Special Agent in Charge. 'This elephant has two heartbeats. One of them is its heart. The other is something else.'

'Gimme that,' said Dooley, snatching the stethoscope viciously out of Linyao's hands. He placed the end of it on the elephant's skin. 'I don't hear nothin'.'

Linyao took hold of the pad end of the instrument and moved it further down the beast, towards its stomach.

'Hear something there?'

'*Shit.*'

Dooley's exclamation, although quietly spoken, had a tone which silenced everyone. If the Acting Special Agent in Charge was worried about something, then it was time for everyone to be worried.

Linyao had an I-told-you-so look on her face but resisted letting the same comment form itself on her tongue.

The Secret Service boss rose slowly to his feet. '*Shit*. It's ticking. This elephant is ticking.' POTUS was due to arrive in this room in one hour and *something was ticking. Geez.*

Dooley snatched up his walkie-talkie from a nearby table: 'Code red, code red, twenty-one, twenty-one, we have a situation in Auditorium One. Possible presence of an explosive device. Explosives Unit One and Two immediately to Auditorium One. Repeat, BD Unit One to Auditorium One. Ah want Donaldson.' He thought for a moment, and then added: 'Code red, forty-two, seven. Armed Units One and Two should proceeded to Auditorium One immediately. Bring arms, code forty-two, seven.'

Running feet could be heard immediately. Within thirty seconds the doors of the theatre burst open and a bomb disposal squad appeared, followed within seconds by dozens of men with guns.

A man in orange overalls with the letters BD over his breast pocket was at the head of the pack. 'Where's the blaster?'

'Donaldson, you ain't never going to believe me.'

Three more bomb disposal officers approached.

'Where is it?' one of them asked, looking at Dooley.

'In the elephant.'

'Get out of here.'

'In the goddam elephant.'

'Shut up.' Donaldson, his eyes on stalks, approached the beast. Dooley held out the stethoscope to him.

'How do I get to it?'

'Tell the elephant a funny joke and while he's laughing, slip in through his mouth.'

'Thanks, Dooley.'

'It's all yours.'

'You kidding us or what?'

'Have you ever known me to kid anyone? Ah don't kid people. The bomb is in the goddam elephant.'

'Shit.'

'Shit is right.'

'What are we supposed to do? This is not exactly a standard situation in the bomb disposal manual.'

'It's not in mah manual either. But it's a bomb, so it's your baby.' The Acting Special Agent in Charge was trying to sound cocky but was sweating like a pig – no, never mind pigs, like Niagara Falls. His whole body was suddenly wet.

The two men dropped their voices and walked to the back of the stalls, talking intently. Several other armed men had entered by this time. Lasse barked at them to stand by in the front stalls while Dooley and Donaldson decided what to do.

On the stage, Joyce whispered to Linyao: 'What do you think they'll do?'

'Shoot it. Then cut it open.'

'We can't let them do that.'

'I know.'

Slightly more than one hundred metres away, the two senior officers were having a similar conversation.

'Shoot it,' said Donaldson.

'What if it sets the bomb off?'

'Geez, Tom, you don't shoot the bomb. You shoot the thing in the head. Your guys can hit a friggin' elephant, I hope? You shoot the thing in the head, and it goes down, and then you cut it open and then you get the bomb out, and then you clean it up, and then you put it on a silver platter with a little pink ribbon on it, and then you give it to me, and then you say please and then you say pretty please, and then, maybe, if I am in a good mood, I will disarm the bomb for you.'

'We'll take the elephant out. But you take the bomb out.'

'I may be a vet, but I ain't that kind of vet.'

'Neither am I. But my guys aren't qualified to move a bomb. We aren't qualified to touch the damn thing. That's your job.'

'Yeah, but we aren't qualified to hack the thing out of an elephant's gut. That's not our job. You need a – I don't know what you need.'

They heard footsteps. Linyao had raced down the aisles. They turned to face her as she reached them. She had caught the tail end of their conversation. 'You need me. I'm a veterinarian. I'm a surgeon. I know the right person to do this job. There are not many specialists in large animal surgery, but I know who they are. If you can't reach the specialists, I'll try to do it myself. I've never done anything with an elephant before, but I have operated on horses and other animals. Ideally, we should move the animal to a proper surgical theatre.'

Dooley shook his head. 'No, lady, we don't have time to play around. We don't know when the thing is due to go off. We're talking about the President. We can't take risks. POTUS will be here in sixty minutes – less. We need to deal with this right now. Finish it. This place has gotta be clean for the Prez.'

'You have to get the bomb out. What other choices do you have?' Linyao said. 'This way, the elephant survives, the bomb gets disarmed, everyone is happy.'

Dooley spoke to Donaldson: 'Can we whisk the thing out? Put distance between it and the Prez?'

'No way. Unless you got a giant-sized *Star Trek* transporter. Every road is jammed out there. You'd have to land a major aircraft carrier on the roof of the theatre. Impossible. Whatever we do, we have to do it here. We need to finish it as quickly and neatly as we can.'

'But let's not kill the elephant unless we have to,' Linyao pleaded.

Dooley puffed out his chest and glared at her. 'Listen, lady, ah perteck the President, and ah make all decisions involved with pertecting the President. We don't have time for fancy-nancy operations on your four-legged friends. Ah'm really sorry but we have to take the thing out. A few bullets in the temple – it won't hurt a bit. And then you can help us saw the thing open. And then Donaldson here will get the bomb out. How does that sound?'

Without waiting for an answer, he barked orders at his troops.

'Okay, Group One. Arm your rifles. We are going to take out one elephant. Serbis, Nozinsky and Walters, you are going to do the job for us. Assemble. When you are ready give me the signal, and on my count of three you will shoot the beast behind the right eye. We want a quick and painless death. Not too messy, please. Do it backstage somewhere.'

The three men prepared their weapons.

'Now where is the damn thing?'

'Behind the pink curtain,' Donaldson said. 'That's where the other girl took it.'

'Move that curtain,' Dooley shouted.

A stagehand yanked the rope and the curtain flew up.

But Joyce and the elephant had vanished.

9

The King of Ji was raised from a baby on the finest wine. From birth to adulthood, he drank nothing but the greatest wines from the most celebrated vintages.

Then one day he went exploring among the common people and saw a peasant drinking a liquid that was perfectly clear. It was not red, not white, not yellow.

He said: 'What sort of wine is that?'

The man said: 'It is the wine of heaven. It falls from the sky and I catch it in my rain barrel.'

The King was amazed and asked to taste it. It was the greatest wine he had ever tasted. He swapped all his wine for the peasant's rain barrel.

One day he went exploring further and discovered a freshwater lake. Later, the peasant who found his body said he had drowned with a smile on his face.

Blade of Grass, drink water before wine, even if the finest wine is open and ready waiting for you. The foundations of a joyful life are laid by Heaven and our enhancements are not enhancements.

Blade of Grass, discovering the world in which you live is the chief part of your education. As the Emperor of Xuan said, 'He who has to ask questions looks like a fool for a minute; he who does not ask questions remains a fool forever.'

From 'Some Gleanings of
Oriental Wisdom' by CF Wong

'Come on, boy. Come on. This way. Good boy.' Joyce kept wanting to pat him and say 'Good dog', because that was the sort of thing one said to large, lumbering pets. 'Good elephant' didn't trip nearly as naturally off the tongue. But she kept up the flow of encouraging murmurs, stroked the top of his trunk and gently pulled his lead – and he kept moving forward, so that seemed to be the right thing to do. 'Come on. Good boy. Come on. Joyce will buy you a little treat if you keep moving forward. Come on.' She wondered if elephants liked the same sort of treats as cats and dogs – biscuits and stuff. In cartoons, they always ate bananas. Why was one never carrying a banana when one needed one? As a proselytising vegetarian, she decided she ought to always have one about her person.

What astonished her most was his eyes. Huge, intelligent, pinky-brown orbs in a nest of pale grey wrinkles, they shone with kindness – and a great deal else, too. Joyce believed she could see a stunning range of things in there – wisdom and suffering and knowledge of things that will be forever unknown to human beings. Overall, the most striking thing about the creature's eyes – or actually, eye, because one could only see one eye at a time – was its obvious humanity, or what we arrogantly define as humanity, anyway. She mused that it was when one glimpsed this that one instantly reached enlightenment about the fundamental brotherhood of sentient beings. Children were often aware of this, as were vegetarians of all ages, but the majority of other adults had little notion of it – except on occasional visits to the zoo, when they were startled to catch the eye of an orang-utan or a gorilla and see just how 'human' they were.

From childhood, Joyce had had the ability to do a 'soul stare' with monkeys. You could see the subtlest emotions in a chimpanzee's face. Then, in her early teens, she had worked really hard at developing the ability to connect with other species. These days, especially since she had become a vegetarian, she could tell – or imagined she could tell – exactly what was going on in the minds of many small creatures. Her friend's hamster looked mildly bilious most of the time but could occasionally pull a deadpan glare that cracked her up. A white-eye in a cage she'd seen at the Hong Kong bird market looked surprisingly philosophical and had a ribald sense of humour. The neighbour's dog looked manic-depressive most of the day but had a devil-may-care smirk at night. She had even spent time staring at animal faces to learn how they smiled – her sister's cat, for example, did it the opposite way to human beings: she turned the edges of her lips down.

But you didn't need to have a spiritual connection with animals to realise that this elephant was not smiling. It felt seriously ill. There was a dizziness in its brow. Its movements – slow and halting – suggested that it was in pain, and its trunk was not swinging and probing as she expected it to be; it hung loosely, like a dead limb. Joyce's eyes filled with tears as she became aware of the deep unhappiness of this beautiful, innocent creature, which had probably been mistreated all its life and now had been turned into an instrument of death.

The elephant stopped moving and turned to stare at her.

'What do you want, boy? Can I get you something? You want water?'

They had escaped to a sort of underground car park. She noticed a drinks machine nearby and found enough change in a secret pocket inside her jacket to buy a plastic bottle of mineral water.

The beast turned its hurt eyes to the bottle and then reached out with its trunk to touch it. Although she felt him try to grip it with a sort of webbed finger thingy at the end of his trunk, she didn't let go, realising that it would do the creature no good to swallow a plastic container.

'I'll feed you. Let me do it.'

She unscrewed the cap and showed him how she could splash it out of the bottle. Then she moved close to him and put the bottle to its cracked, pinky-grey lips.

'There you go, boy, there you go.' It opened its lips and she emptied the entire bottle into his mouth. The creature's mouth was bizarre: the bottom half was like two giant lips pressed together, making a groove that pointed straight ahead. There was something very labia-like about the elephant's mouth. It was like pouring water into a fleshy, pink conduit. It seemed to enjoy the drink, and then closed its mouth and made a smacking noise.

There was a steep ramp leading out of the car park, and they were drawn to it by the flood of natural light coming from it. The ceiling was low – 2.1 metres, a sign said, but the beast lowered its head, apparently used to walking through human-sized spaces.

As they emerged into the light, the elephant turned its head to Joyce and swung its trunk at her. It seemed to indicate its back. Again, it pointed to her and then pointed up at the valley where its back joined its head.

'You want me to go up there? Is that where your minder used to sit? Okay, I guess I could try.'

She steered the beast towards a concrete parapet and used it as a stand to get herself halfway up. And then she gripped the elephant's rough skin and pulled herself to the top. It was surprisingly comfortable up there – albeit rather smelly. The skin at the neck was softer than the skin on the sides, and she found that her legs fitted snugly around its upper back. Here, the Special Relationship kicked in. Just as daughters have a special relationship with fathers, and sons with mothers, so young women have a special relationship with large, muscular animals such as ponies and horses. Okay, so this particular beast was not part of the *familae equinus*, but Joyce felt a similar instant bonding with the powerful beast between her legs. Freud, had he been alive and watching, would have applauded.

Joyce knew how to ride a horse and was curious as to whether the same techniques would work on an elephant. She shifted her hips around, squeezed with her knees and patted its head. 'Come on, boy. Let's move. Let's go. Come on, let's go. Good boy.' She jerked her hips back and forth. The creature started to lumber forward. It worked. Now where was CF?

Unhappy about approaching a building crawling with armed men, he had said he would wait outside for them.

☯

Wong's narrow eyes had never been bigger. He looked. Then he shook his head. Then he looked again. It couldn't be true – but apparently it was. Yet it couldn't possibly be. There were things that could be and there were things that could not. And this definitely fell into the category of something which could not. There was only one possible explanation. He had actually gone insane. Temporarily, he hoped. The gas that the mad Venusians had pumped into the room must have had some sort of hallucinogenic drug in it. He was having what Westerners called 'a trip'. Or maybe it was the trauma of watching all that violence. Whatever, his brain was seriously malfunctioning. That was the only satisfying explanation for the vision that his deranged mind was projecting in front of his goggle-eyes: Joyce McQuinnie, lumbering up from the car park ramp of the Shanghai Grand Theatre on the back of a white elephant, like a junior maharani from 1880s India.

But what really shook him was the realisation that this was not just a random hallucinogenic vision. It was a vision *with a message*. He recalled the uncomfortable episode yesterday morning when he had seen a picture of a white elephant and felt that it was a significant omen. Up to now he had stupidly thought that the extraordinary near-death events of the past twenty or so hours were the incidents that had been foretold. But now it was evident that this interpretation was wrong. An actual meeting with an actual white elephant – that was the really important thing that Heaven had decreed would happen this week.

The vision moved closer. It looked incredibly real. He felt he could reach out and touch the animal's wrinkled, leathery side. He could hear Joyce saying: 'Come on, boy. Good boy. That's it. Keep going. Good boy. Good boy.'

173

He reached out a finger and – gingerly, tentatively – poked it. Solid. Unyielding. Rough to the touch. Fibrous, almost wooden-feeling.

'*Come on*, CF. We have to get this elephant away. Good boy. Good boy.'

He looked up at her, in a daze. The white elephant was solid. So was she. Somehow, this was actually happening. 'What do you mean? You are *stealing* this elephant? Who belong to it?'

'There's a bomb in it. That's where the bomb was hidden. Every inch of the place was searched. Every human goes through a plastic explosives detector. The only place that Vega knew they wouldn't look is inside the animals. We've got to get it away. Are you listening to me? CF?' She started to repeat her story. 'Vega? The mad guy? He put a bomb inside . . .'

Wong's mind reeled. He dimly heard Joyce going through an exhaustive explanation of why he should help her get the giant beast away from the theatre where the opening event of the summit would be held, but none of it made sense to him. How could an elephant be a bomb?

'I don't understand.'

She spoke slowly, John Cleese talking to a foreigner: 'There's. A. Bomb. In. This. Elephant.'

Wong blinked.

Joyce continued: 'Vega did some surgery on it. Cut it open and stuck a bomb in it. That's why it's looking so sick. That's why it's walking so slowly. It's going to blow up soon. We need to do something with it.'

Wong started to come out of his daze. *This* was the bomb? Vega had put a bomb in the Shanghai Grand Theatre – and Joyce and her friend had somehow discovered that it was inside the elephant? This was ludicrously far-fetched. This was definitely a hallucination.

A spark ignited in another part of his slowed-down brain. *Bomb?*

Bomb = danger.

Danger = possible damage to his person.

Only possible reaction to possible damage to his person = rapidly remove person from scene.

Can bombs exploding in hallucinations do actual harm in the real world? Who knows? He had never had a vision as vivid as this one before. But it would be crazy to risk it. 'If there is a bomb inside this elephant, we should put him down. We should leave him here. We should go far, far away. Right now. Come. Get off. Let's go.' Animation returned to his body as fear set in. He grabbed her arm and tried to pull her down.

She shook her arm free and then used her hips to urge the beast to walk. 'No way. I'm not leaving it. They'll shoot it. It's not fair. What has he done to deserve to be shot? Nothing. It's not right. I'm a veggie. A true veggie. I will not be associated with any animal deaths. Besides, even if they do shoot it, what about the bomb inside? That woman said it was a big one, and it'll go off at six eighteen. Loads of people will die if we leave him here. We have to move him to somewhere safe. Come on. *Come on.*'

This was madness. Wong, losing his temper, wanted to shout abuse at her, but his mind had started working at high speed on various other tracks. He was not a generous man, and news that a bomb would soon go off left him thinking only about his own safety. Yet one grim fact stuck out of the lake of fog in his mind like the mast of a sunken ship: he could not allow the white elephant to die. What a terrible stroke of bad fortune that would be. It would be equivalent to him losing his own life. No – it would be worse than dying, because what would happen would be that he would remain alive but have the worst luck in the world every day for the rest of his days. This would be an unimaginable horror for a feng shui master. Death would be a far better option.

As for the crowds in central Shanghai – he wasn't particularly bothered about failing to halt the death of dozens or hundreds of Shanghainese citizens, pestilent and smelly over-tall people with stupid clothes, *ma da sao* men and frilly princess women. No, it was the death of the elephant which would cause the eruption of a mountain of bad karma of incalculable proportions. In karma, size mattered. Killing a bacterium was nothing. Killing a bird or medium-sized animal, unless it was for food, was not so good. Killing a horse was seriously bad luck. Killing an elephant – this would be catastrophic. And a white elephant! Symbol of longevity. Symbol of perfection. Symbol of royalty. Killing a white elephant after having the forewarning he had had the previous morning – it was not to be contemplated.

As Joyce lumbered away, he begrudgingly admitted to himself that the killing of innocent passers-by might actually be a factor to be considered in an indirect way, too – it would be messy and make the situation horribly complicated. The authorities would have to be involved. And in China, as he had learned to his cost many times, one did not want the powers involved in any way if it could be at all avoided. Somehow, Joyce was right: they had to solve the problem, not run away from it. The bomb had to be moved away from the city centre. It had to be placed somewhere where it could go off and do no harm.

The elephant was moving slowly and Wong caught up with Joyce in a few strides. 'We must move the elephant somewhere with no people before it booms. Where shall we put it?'

'Somewhere deserted. Let's get onto the main road and see what we can see.'

They turned out of the western approach to the theatre, looked out at Huangpi Bei Lu and stared. There were tens of thousands of people filling the road – the anti-American demonstration had reached as near as it would be allowed to get to the Shanghai Government Building, which was adjacent to the east side of the Grand Theatre. Bodies and banners filled the street for as far as they could see. Although the police had attempted to limit the demonstrators to Huangpi Bei Lu, many had spilled onto Nanjing Xi Lu, getting in the way of the cars, which stood nose to tail in a jam. It looked as if the entire pedestrian and vehicular population of the world had decided to descend upon the gates of the Shanghai Grand Theatre at this precise moment.

Both of them had the same thought at the same time.

'What time is it?' the feng shui master asked.

Joyce looked down at her watch: five eighteen. 'Gridlock time,' she said.

Right on cue, half a dozen trapped cars started honking.

☯

Panic creeps. As the mental precursor of frenzied action, panic should hit like a thunderbolt. It is usually connected to danger, and should therefore engender a rapid reaction. But more often than not, it meets an almost impenetrable wall, which is the human dislike of losing control. So instead, panic creeps silently around our synapses, head down, tiptoeing along. But as it travels, it grows, and we need to change our metaphor. It becomes a huge, expanding amoeba with many pseudopodia, and then grows into a full-scale stream of the stuff. It floods into an increasing number of sections of our subconscious, like an underground river breaking into new chambers. There are no visible ripples on the ground above, but nevertheless the firmament has become dangerously unstable.

This refusal to countenance panic is important, for panic may sweep through our cranial passages as liquid, but it is not water. It is a type of plasma which works like liquid nitrogen on the brain: it freezes the system, turns it cold and hard and unmoving: messages can no longer travel from synapse to synapse. The thought processes which should organise our escape stop working. So perhaps the correct thing to do in the face of extreme danger turns out to be to ignore it, and focus solely on solving the problem. Joyce, who tended to freeze when scared, was halfway there.

Wong sat down, his body facing away from the elephant, and started to think about what to do. This was a job for the intellect. Hard, cold logic, the computation of many facts at high speed, was what was needed. Some things one could do by instinct, but moving loaded elephants out of crowded city centres was not among them. This needed every one of the eight hundred thousand million brain cells in his cranial cavity working independently and in correct sequence.

Space. Peace. Absence of people. That's what was needed. If he could not save the elephant, it would at least have to die in a peaceful situation, willingly sacrificing itself so that others might live. He imagined the elephant exploding in a quiet, deserted field, with himself and other onlookers watching through binoculars from a safe distance – and preferably with a local mystic such as Shang Dan doing something to mitigate the negative forces unleashed by the beast's demise. This is what must happen. He must enable this to happen. Find an open green area. He looked at his watch. 'The bomb will boom in fifty-eight minutes. We need to find a quiet place quickly. Park, something like that.'

By this time people from the demonstration had spotted them and many had surged onto the pavement to have a close look at the beast – elephants were not a common sight on the streets of Shanghai. The first to reach it were children, and their families soon caught up with them. At the start, there were a dozen people, then fifty, then a hundred, and then they were surrounded by a sea of bodies growing larger and denser by the second.

'Sorry,' shouted Joyce. 'We need to move this beast. Excuse us. Can you keep away, please?'

No one paid any attention. From her vantage point on top of the grey mountain she shouted: 'Please keep away! This elephant is explosive!' Still no response. She realised she needed to switch to Mandarin, but this was not a subject covered anywhere in the first eight chapters of *Conversational Mandarin*

Book One. 'Bomb. Bomb inside elephant. Big bomb,' she shrieked.

Several people looked up, baffled, at the young woman on top of the elephant. 'Big bomb,' she told them.

'Bum?' a young man stroking the elephant asked. He pointed to his bottom. 'Big bum?'

'No, *bomb*. Big bomb.'

She leaned over to Wong. 'How do you say bomb in Mandarin?'

'*Baang.*'

'What? Bomb in Chinese is *bang*?'

'Not *bang*. *Baang*. High falling tone.'

'Weird. How do I say "This elephant may explode"?'

'*Zhe tou da xiang hui bao zha.*'

'Thanks.' Joyce shouted from the top of her voice: '*Zhe tou da xiang hui bao zha.*'

The crowd laughed. Several people applauded, apparently thinking that she was making some sort of witticism. The young man stuck out his bottom again and made a farting noise with his pursed lips. This elephant's rump might explode with gas, is that what she meant?

Cheese. What to do? Joyce closed her eyes in despair. Darkness often helped. Visualisation – that was the answer. She remembered the advice she had received from one of her favourite teachers at school: when you are in a bad situation, calm yourself, visualise the situation you would rather be in, and then try to conjure up the routes that would lead you from your present position to the one you want to be in. She took a deep breath. Where was she now? Trapped. Surrounded. Hemmed in. Where did she want to be? Alone with the elephant, far away from the city, preferably near a veterinary surgeon's clinic. What must she do to get from here to there? Move. Run. Gallop. Find a quiet spot. Escape.

She opened her eyes and jerked her hips forward. 'Okay, we have to get going now. Out of the way, please. Out of the way.'

She gently spurred the beast on with her legs, the way she had watched Jungle Boy do on television, and it jerked forward, swinging its trunk to get people out of the way. 'Which way?' she called out to Wong.

'Over there. I think is a park there. Not so crowded. We let it explode there.'

It took several minutes to travel a few dozen metres through the crowd towards the park gate, which Wong said was just past the two buildings on their immediate right – the Grand Theatre Gallery and the Shanghai Art Museum.

It was tough going. We talk of a sea of faces but actually human mobs are nothing like oceans – they have more of the quality of hot mozzarella. They stretch and become long strings. They pull against each other and they coagulate back into globules. They sometimes harden into tough little pools which won't break up, and at other times they turn into groups of threads, sort of together and sort of separate. Chinese crowds have particular qualities of solidness, nay, of impassable stolidity. In every mob there are always individuals or lumps of people that are totally immoveable – even in the face of large objects (trains, trucks, cars, elephants and, on one memorable occasion in Tiananmen Square in 1989, a tank). As a result, movement was painfully slow.

The elephant actually trod on one man's foot, causing Joyce to squeal in alarm. 'Ooh, *sorrysorrysorrysorry* – CF, the elephant stood on that guy. I think he hurt him. We better do something. He's probably got broken bones. Can you see if he's hurt?' But Wong took a resolutely Asian view of injuries to passers-by: if someone got hurt on the way, that was too bad. Since it was acceptable for cars to bash passers-by out of the way, why should an elephant not have the same right? The good of the masses was the important thing, and people in positions of importance (such as in an official limousine or on top of an elephant) could not be expected to pay attention to particular individuals in crowds they might encounter. It was the individual's duty to look after himself.

Wong, McQuinnie and the elephant moved gradually through the thick mob – Joyce continuously looking back in horror at the people they injured – until finally they succeeded in making significant progress along the road. Towering above them on the other side of the road was the JW Marriott Tomorrow Square, a huge shiny skyscraper the top half of which appeared thicker than the bottom – like a huge steel knife stuck into the ground. It made Wong shiver. Police, evidently assuming this was some sort of sideshow scheduled to perform at the park, held up the demonstration to let them through. And so they lumbered at crawling pace to Entrance Gate Number Seven of the People's Park, better known as Renmin Park. Joyce's heart was in her mouth. 'Dear God, I hope there are no people in the park today.'

It didn't look very likely, considering the crowd at the gates – there was a stream of people coming in and out, some holding balloons, children with candyfloss, mothers with strollers.

Entering through the iron gates, they walked a few steps through a narrow passage and past a signboard on the left in Chinese and English: 'Ethic or moral codes should be duly honoured, visitors are expected not to urinate or shit.'

In front of them the path diverged into three lanes: the middle one led to a lake, the ones on either side forming part of a ring road circling the park. All three were heaving. There were fence-to-fence people everywhere they looked.

The park, Wong noticed, had been beautifully designed – he couldn't have done it better himself. The path in front of them gently meandered, gracefully revealing a perfect scene: a pond-side viewing area, shaded by a large tree and focused around a body of water surrounding a wooden house on stilts. There were water-lilies standing tall out of the pond on one side of the bridge leading to the structure, and dragonflies standing on nothing over the surface of the water on the other: a perfect blend of the natural and the urban.

This was something that the Chinese and Japanese did so well, and no one else seemed to understand. Other peoples seemed to assume that environments had to be either human (flat and urbanised, with featureless green lawns and football pitches), or natural (protected wilderness areas where matted vegetation grew into impenetrable forests). But in ancient oriental garden design there was an attempt to do something really, really important: to find and recreate the perfect human–natural environment, the paradisical spot that is imprinted in every human being's race memory. This was why feng shui (and *vaastu*) were so vital.

'Oh no.' Joyce scanned as much of the park as she could see from her high seat: there were people in every corner. Indeed, in many places the crowds were so thick that it was difficult to see any grass. She looked down at Wong and noted the look of despair on his face.

The feng shui master was deeply torn about what to do. Try to save the elephant? Try to save the community? Try to save themselves? Only the first and third options made sense to him, but he had no idea how to effect them. Perhaps someone else could solve it. 'I think we go back to the hotel. Tell people. Leave the elephant and get out of here peedyqueue. Go back to hotel and phone. Is not our problem. Is problem for the authorities. They can fix it, maybe.'

'No way,' said Joyce. 'The authorities will shoot the elephant first. They like killing things. Then they'll run away and let it blow up. There's no time left to dig the bomb out of the elephant and switch it off. How long do we have left?'

Wong looked at his watch. 'Forty-eight minutes. Bringing elephant to park wasted a few minutes, did no good.'

'Well, it was your bloody idea.'

The feng shui master felt as if he could hear the tick-tick-tick of the bomb inside the elephant. It appeared to be getting louder and stronger and faster as the countdown headed to zero.

But then he realised that what he could hear was the thud of his own panicking heart.

10

'Okay, where is it?'

'Where is what?'

'This is not funny. Ah warn you, Miss Ling, ah do not have a sense of humour. People like me don't. We have them surgically removed when we join the US government.'

'My name's Linyao. Ms Lu to you.'

'Where is the elephant, bitch?'

'Search me.'

He cursed under his breath and reached for the radio. 'Dooley to SL-One. Dooley to SL-One. Come in.'

'Cap'n?'

'This is an emergency, I want you to locate an—' he paused, momentarily – 'an elephant. Repeat: an elephant. It's at loose somewhere in this building. It's been—' another embarrassed pause – 'er, stolen, taken, kidnapped, whatever, from the back stage area.'

'An elephant? Did you say—'

'You heard me.'

Dooley spun around just in time to see the shoulders of a thin young man named Ari Tadwacker moving up and down.

'Something funny, Tadwacker?'

'No, sir. Nothing, sir.'

Dooley turned his attention back to Linyao. 'You're coming with me.' He grabbed her violently by the arm and pulled her down the corridor into one of the dressing rooms. When they were alone with the door shut, he yanked her arm again to spin her around to face him.

She squealed and tried to shake herself free. 'Let go of me. Who do you think you are?'

'Who do you think ah am?'

'You're a security guard.'

Dooley's teeth ground themselves together. This was a situation he hated. He wanted to say who he really was – one of the top, top men in the Secret Service, a *legendary* United States institution – but he couldn't. For the truth of it was that the name of his organisation was oddly, ridiculously, painfully unquotable. As a child, the words 'Secret Service' were inestimably glamorous, conjuring up images of clandestine operations involving James Bond-like special agents on missions with cool gadgets and women in bikinis. But from the moment he joined the service at the age of twenty-eight, he had found the name of the organisation just plain embarrassing.

When a girl at a party asked you what you did, you couldn't reply: 'I work for the Secret Service and my rank is Special Agent.' It made people laugh. It made you sound like you were an eleven-year-old boy playing a game. It made you think of Maxwell Smart talking into his shoe. There was no way for an adult man to say it without sounding like he was joking. In off-duty social situations, he preferred to mumble that he worked for the government. Then people would ask for more detail, and he would brush them off in such a way that they would end up impressed. 'Nothin', ah'm jest a civil servant. Ah just do my bit. Cog in the wheel. Don't really want to say too much about it, know what ah mean? Heh-heh. What do you do?'

That little *heh-heh* said it all. But the truth was that the existence of the Secret Service was not in itself secret. They had 'Secret Service' emblazoned on their vehicles and on their badges. Their office address was in the phone book. Hell, they even had a website. When he had transferred from the service's financial side to the presidential side, his work title became less embarrassing, at least when talking to other government agencies. He and his colleagues referred to their group as the PPD, a nice boring set of initials, or sometimes as 'the Detail'. This was distinctive and also wonderfully suitable, as checking details – over and over and over again – was a key aspect of what they did. For it was the details that sometimes blew up into major problems, as he was finding out to his cost today.

'Okay, ah'm gonna ask politely one more time. Where's the elephant? How did your friend get it out of here? Ah don't like bombs wandering around in the same building and the same city as my President is wandering around in, got it?'

'I don't know. I wasn't looking. I was with you. She was behind the curtain. I think she used magic. Megiddo's magic.'

Dooley gritted his teeth. 'Okay, we are alone, so ah can use unofficial methods of interrogation. Ah warn you, lady, I can make Guatanamo look like *Sesame Street*.'

He grabbed the lapels of Linyao's jacket and heaved her off her feet. 'You talking?' he asked.

She said nothing.

He pushed her heavily across the room. She hit a chair, which toppled over, and then fell to the ground, knocking against a table. A flurry of coloured acrobat uniforms flopped on top of her. Landing heavily, she slammed her head against the floor and couldn't resist a yelp of pain.

Dooley strode across the room. 'Usually ah follow Miss Manners' rules, lady, but ah have one rule which overrides all other rules. And that rule is this: ah perteck the President. And if ah have to break all the other rules to keep that one, ah'm right happy to do it.' He placed the heel of his boot against her chin. 'Where's your friend?'

'I don't know. I didn't see.'

There was a knock on the door.

'What?' Dooley shouted.

It creaked open and a face appeared. 'I found the stagehand who operates the moving bits of the stage.' It was Agent Tadwacker, holding the arm of a man in blue overalls. 'He says there's a revolving wall on the left part of the stage which is how they make the elephant disappear.' The two men who entered the room tried desperately not to look at Linyao crumpled on the ground in the corner, but she kept drawing their eyes.

The stagehand spoke in broken English. 'Missa Megiddo and his people – they take out elephant with trick. The curtain come down. Go to the left. Elephant go with it. They press button and stage back part turn round. Elephant go backstage. Go in cargo elevator.'

Dooley turned back to Linyao. 'What's your girlfriend's name? And where is she going with the blasted thing?'

She glared at him.

He pulled out his gun and pointed it at her.

'Her name's Joyce,' Linyao said. 'Joyce McQuinnie. And I have no idea where she's going. Where do people with exploding elephants go to in Shanghai? This sort of thing doesn't happen a lot in this country, officer. It may happen in yours.'

Dooley turned to face the stagehand. 'Where's the cargo elevator go to?'

'To loading bay, underground car park.'

'Let's go.' To Linyao: 'You stay here. I want to talk to you later.'

On the way Dooley made a series of calls on his radio. He put Carloni in charge of rechecking security at the theatre – every damn inch – and Felznik in charge of informing all the other units who needed to know that a breach of security had taken place, and Tadwacker in charge of getting a group of men to fan out to find Joyce and the elephant. He himself took the most unpleasant job of all – telling the President's men that there had been a possible compromise of the venue and the meeting would have to be cancelled or moved. There was no other choice. There was an explosive device inside or near the building: precise location unknown. POTUS must not approach. The Secret Service was ordering the show to be cancelled.

To do such a thing at the last possible moment meant the highest possible level of pain – a level of corporate, official agony that was almost unbearable. The amount of planning that went into a visit by the US President to anywhere – even the local doughnut shop – was huge. To change any aspect of the trip (such as an ingredient in the hors d'oeuvres) was a significant deal. To have allowed something to happen that caused the whole thing to be cancelled was a rare occurrence that destroyed careers and made grown men weep – or throw themselves off buildings. The only light at the end of the tunnel would be to (a) make out that any security breach was entirely due to the shortfall of the Chinese partner security agency; and (b) to claim that any creditable action in the matter, such as the discovery of the problem, was entirely due to the American partner.

He called Agent Lasse over. 'Get me Captain Zhang. We'd better let the Chinese know that we have a problem.'

☯

Commander Zhang Xiumei of the People's Armed Police already knew that trouble was afoot. She and her team were technically sharing security duties at the Grand Theatre with the American Secret Service. But the Chinese team worked in a more subtle, low-profile way. There appeared to be fewer of them on the ground, but in fact there were more of them: you just didn't see them. Her men had already told her that the Americans were in a panic over something, and she was waiting for the call when it came.

Her reaction to the news she was given was predictable enough – the same utter disbelief that had been Dooley's reaction. But her way of expressing it was very different. She lowered the phone and showed no emotion whatsoever, other than a slight tightening of the forehead. She stood in perfect stillness, statue-like, while considering the information she had been given. Could this be some sort of elaborate American joke?

She had often pondered the mysteries of American humour, and had several times seen Hollywood comedies which left her cold. Western humour appeared to be largely verbal, and mostly focused on people saying things which meant the precise opposite of what was clearly stated.

'There's a bomb in the elephant.' She replayed the line in her head. She knew all the words in the sentence, but had no idea what it meant. The whole was not greater than the sum of the parts. In fact, while the parts each meant something, the whole meant nothing. She knew what a bomb was, and she knew what an elephant was. But why say there was a bomb inside an elephant, when such a thing could not be?

Her fundamental attitude towards Westerners was wariness and distrust. This had been triggered by an experience she had had twelve years ago, when she had first had a conversation in English with a group of British soldiers who were in China on some sort of information exchange visit. The words of the discussion had been entirely straightforward – indeed, they could have been lifted out of her English language school textbook. Yet the reaction to the conversation was bizarre, and revealed to her the enormous wealth of hidden associations behind the simplest Western phrases.

'Like yer uniform, Miss.'

'Thank you for the compliment.'

'It's real then?'

'Yes. It is a People's Armed Police issue uniform.'

'Not a pirate copy from Shenzhen?'

'No. It is authentic, from the quartermaster stores. Miniature replicas on dolls are available, if you would like to purchase one.'

'I heard Chinese military uniforms came in two sizes: too big and too small.'

'No, they come in four sizes: small, medium, large and extra large.'

Why this straightforward conversation should have left the British troops doubled up with helpless laughter left her baffled, even after she had looked up several of the words in the Chinese–English dictionary. She had tried the largest dictionaries she could find, in case there were alternative meanings or associations which were not initially clear to her. Later, she had phoned her English language tutor and recited the entire conversation for him. The teacher – a fifty-year-old Shanghainese named Wu Jian Min – had been as baffled as she was.

'There's a bomb in the elephant,' she repeated to herself. 'We should cancel the opening show because there is a bomb in the elephant.' The English language appeared to have an infinite number of metaphorical phrases, most of which had no obvious connection with the thought they expressed. Heavy raindrops were cats and dogs. A superlative item was the knees of the bumble bee. Clouds had silver linings. Babies were born with silver spoons in their mouths. What was the metaphorical meaning of 'a bomb in an elephant'? It surely couldn't refer to a real bomb in a real elephant. Nor could it refer to really cancelling the actual pre-summit show. Both would be ridiculous. She phoned Teacher Wu.

'What does it mean, there's a bomb in the elephant?'

'What?'

'The English idiom: there's a bomb in my elephant. What does it mean?'

'Where did you see it? What are you reading?'

'I am not reading anything. One of the Americans called me and said it. I want to know what it means. It sounded important.'

'I'm not sure. Wait.'

She could hear the sound of pages being flicked in a specialist dictionary of English idioms.

'Bomb can mean to perform badly on stage. "The comedian's act was poor so he bombed." That's negative. Or it can be positive: "It goes like a bomb", meaning performs really well – typical English. Two meanings, each of which is the opposite of the other. No logic in the language.'

'But what about *There is a bomb in my elephant?*'

More flicking noises. 'Nothing. Not listed under bomb or elephant.'

'Old dictionary?'

'Not so old. About twelve years.'

'So what's the answer? Must be recent coinage. Can you guess?'

'Let me ask Tu Feng Rong. He was in Europe last month. I'll call you back.'

Zhang lowered the phone. Typical of the Americans to be so wily and unpredictable – and at the last possible moment, with the two Presidents due to arrive in a few minutes. Americans could never be trusted. The elephant, she vaguely recalled, was the symbol of one of the main US political parties, the Democrats or the Republicans. That must be something to do with it. And the single biggest US–China issue over the past few months, in the run-up to this summit, was the One China Policy which covered relations between China and the renegade province of Taiwan. The Democrats – or was it the Republicans? – were opposed to it, or were they in favour of it?

If that was it, it would only be a temporary problem, as it was just a matter of time before the Taiwan issue resolved itself. China's military leaders were acquiring foreign arms as fast as they could, aiming to hit 'the crossover point' as soon as possible – the point at which the People's Liberation Army was more powerful than the Taiwanese defence force, even with equipment from Western allies. Some said that China had already achieved it; others said it would be a year or two before the balance was clearly in the Motherland's favour. At that point, the leaders' noble dream of one China could be realised: the Taiwanese would have no choice. This was important to many people in power, particularly the elderly, but she had to admit that it meant little to younger people.

Commander Zhang was a Communist Party member, but

her card was in her breast pocket wallet, not her heart. There was a crucial two centimetres of difference. The ideological content of membership had somehow become detached and drifted away from its practical considerations. There had been quiet but important changes over the past decade. The Party card had begun to identify not your political affiliation but your age, sex and job. The vast majority of members – some said 80 per cent – were more than thirty-five years old. More than 80 per cent were men: membership had little attraction for women. Also, you had to be a member if you wanted to achieve anything in the Chinese civil service. It was almost a union card for government officials and army officers. So a Party card almost inevitably meant old, male and employed by the authorities. In her case – she was twenty-nine, the youngest commander they had ever had – in her case only the third of the three typical member characteristics was accurate.

The Party was changing. Every year or two campaigns would be launched to attract younger members, more females, and people in private industry. These programs usually worked. People quickly signed up once they heard what was on offer. There was a host of privileges, some official, some unwritten, that accumulated to Party members. Your children got into better schools, you heard what was happening before ordinary people did, and you had a much better choice of jobs. And most importantly of all, you were part of the network. You were linked in to the circles of people who had power – and that meant the military and paramilitary forces, and their allies.

The Americans did not understand this, nor did they understand how China's armed forces worked. Yes, they ostensibly guarded the borders of the country. But they also guarded the ideological borders of the Party. If there was dissent in the country, that was equivalent to the borders of the Party being attacked, so of course the dissent was snuffed out with great force. Taiwan and Hong Kong were on the fringes of the mainland in terms of both physical borders and ideological borders – so it was no wonder that both were kept on short leashes.

When Commander Zhang, who was from Nanning City, had originally moved to Shanghai, she had thought about joining the People's Liberation Army and becoming part of the 2.5 million-strong green-uniformed body that makes the biggest contribution to keeping the Party in power. But she found its business interests too anti-ideological: what was an army body doing running nightclubs and factories? It had been trying to cut back on its business interests for years, but the clean-up was going slowly. As a result, the PLA's prime motivations were blurred. She felt there was a lack of professionalism in the way it was managed. You run an army differently from the way you run a business empire. So instead, she had joined the People's Armed Police, a smaller body spun off from the PLA in 1983, but with key tasks such as guarding important government institutions. She had quickly risen to being a senior office in the Special Police, a unit of the Internal Guards Corps, although for this mission they were sharing duties with the State Guests Protection Unit.

Both the PLA and the People's Armed Police were managed by the Central Military Affairs Commission, an eleven-man group made up of senior generals plus the most important Party leaders. The small print in the articles said that the Commission's chairman was elected by the National People's Congress, a body which represented the masses. But that was a joke. The hot seat always went to the Party's top man. Mao Zedong, a charismatic but fatally flawed military leader, held the chairmanship of the Commission for years, and passed it on to Deng Xiaoping, another former soldier. Deng held on to power even after resigning as head of the Communist Party of China. How did he do it? He kept the seat of chairman of the Commission. When Jiang Zemin took the job in 1989, and Hu Jintao in 2004, there was concern that they lacked the military background necessary for the role. But both increased military budgets, ensuring that they kept the support of the real power base in China.

Americans always overestimated the importance of politics and politicians and political systems like democracy. In China, power was what counted, and the Central Military Affairs Commission was where the power lay.

Commander Zhang's phone rang. 'Yes?'

'There's a bomb in my elephant: Rong has never heard it either. He thinks it is something sexual. He says it is almost definitely offensive. Do not say yes. Do not repeat it to anyone else. I suggest you don't reply or react in any way.'

'Thank you, Wu *lao-shi*.' Zhang put the phone down and tried to dismiss Dooley's barked words. But the memory of the call would not leave her. There was an urgency in the American agent's voice that she found impossible to put aside. And the fact that he was talking about cancelling the event – how could he joke about such a thing just minutes before the two Presidents arrived? Perhaps the man was on drugs. Amercians did that sort of thing all the time, she knew. Even former president Bill Clinton liked to talk about inhaling drugs, didn't he? And wasn't it common knowledge that George W Bush was an alcoholic? Maybe Dooley was high on something. After all, had this been a serious emergency, the alarm would have been set off and sirens would be shaking the entire Shanghai Grand Theatre.

The alarm went off and sirens shook the entire Shanghai Grand Theatre.

☯

In a lake city in the fifth century, a rebel warlord named Xie killed the king and took his palace.

He searched for the ring bearing the royal seal but could not find it. He tore the building to dust but it was not there. His men even searched the stools of the young princes in case one of them had eaten it. But they had not.

194

The judges ruled that since no one had the royal seal, the land could have no king. Darkness settled on the kingdom.

The princes lived in the dust with only the birds to talk to.

One year later, the eldest prince turned up at the court with the ring and the judges proclaimed him king. The judges asked him where he had hidden it.

He said: 'I did not hide it. I put the ring on the foot of the bar-headed lake goose. Every year the geese fly five thousand li away for the winter. But they always return to their original homes.'

Blade of Grass, even people who live in the dust can get friends in high places, and sometimes unexpected ones.

Remember the saying of wise man Mo Zhou: 'You can go no further than halfway into a dark forest: from then on you are coming out of the other side.'

From 'Some Gleanings of
Oriental Wisdom' by CF Wong

The problem they had had outside the theatre was repeating itself at Renmin Park Gate Number Five, through which they were trying to leave the area: individuals and families were surging around them, wanting to touch the elephant.

'Don't touch,' Joyce said. 'Bomb inside. Big bomb. Bang. I mean *baang*.' But the crowds smiled up at her and ignored everything she said. What was the Mandarin phrase? Already she had forgotten it. She shouted down to Wong: 'A farm. Fields. That's what we need. Crops. They go for miles, and there's no one around. Paddy fields, maybe. Where's the nearest farm?'

Wong grimaced and gave her his how-stupid-can-you-get look. 'This is city centre. This is middle of biggest city in China. There is no farms here.'

'Oh. Any other parks?'

'No empty ones.'

'So what's plan B?'

'What?'

Joyce closed her eyes again. 'What are we going to do?' she said quietly to herself. She decided she needed to try again to visualise the answer. She placed her palms over her eyes to create true darkness. In her mind's eye she saw a picture of crowds of people milling around – and then she saw a truck speeding along with the elephant inside, rushing past all the crowds, heading for the wide open spaces. It was a low-sided vehicle, and the elephant was happily waving its trunk at the people they passed. They were approaching a massive, clean, flower-lined animal hospital away from the city. That's what they needed: a large vehicle to take them to an animal sanctuary filled with veterinary surgeons pulling on their gloves ready for an operation. 'We need a van or a truck or a pickup or a horse box. See if you can hire one. How much time do we have left?'

'Forty-five minutes, thirty seconds.'

Wong liked the idea – it seemed the only option, and a similar notion had occurred to him as soon as he realised how crowded the park was: they definitely needed vehicular help. So he stepped into the road near the north exit to the park and started examining vehicles rolling slowly past. By standing in the middle of the road and waving a handful of banknotes, he managed to persuade the seventh large vehicle which passed him to halt. It was a heavy van, fortunately with a low floor and a high ceiling. The driver, naked from the waist up despite the cool temperature, leaned out, a cheap cigarette attached to his lower lip. There followed a rapid conversation in Mandarin and Shanghainese which involved a lot of numbers and pointing to the elephant.

The phone Joyce had acquired from the fruit-seller rang. It was Linyao, who had managed to slip away during the panic at the theatre. 'Joyce, it's me. Where are you?'

'We went into Renmin Park, just behind the theatre. Now we've headed out of the park again, out of Gate Number Five. Come and meet us here. We don't know what to do. We need your help. Wong's trying to get someone to take the elephant away from the city centre in a truck.' By the time she had given directions to Linyao, agreement had been reached between Wong and the truck driver. The feng shui man looked grim – clearly the price had been high. 'They'll take us,' he told Joyce.

'Thank God you found an empty one.'

'It's not empty. That's why I have to pay so much.' He shook his head and groaned out loud, suffering physical pain as he pressed a pile of banknotes into the driver's hands.

The men in the cabin quickly unloaded wardrobes and other furniture from the van and left it on the side of the road. One of the younger men was assigned to stand guard over it. The others urged Joyce to get the elephant inside.

It was not easy. The sickly beast did not want to enter a hot, dark, noisome, small room on such a cool and pleasant April day. But one of the men had a couple of green bananas in his lunch box, which eventually lured the creature inside. The men slammed the door shut behind the beast and Wong and McQuinnie hopped into the cabin with the driver and his brother.

'Where to?' the driver asked.

'Out of town,' Wong said.

'Which way?'

'Any way. Quickest way.' The feng shui master decided that it would not be wise to tell the men that they had just accepted the job of transporting a soon-to-explode bomb, so merely impressed upon them the importance of getting the elephant to some open air as quickly as possible.

'We need to get there in forty-two minutes,' he said, 'so drive.'

The men turned the truck left into Huanghe Lu, heading north, and stopped dead, caught in a traffic jam. Everything came to a standstill for two minutes.

Just as Wong was going out of his mind with impatience, there was a slight movement: each vehicle advanced twenty metres or so, and then the traffic stopped again.

One more minute passed.

'*Cheese*,' whined Joyce.

'Yes, cheese,' Wong agreed. Why this extremely common English expression was not included in his book *Advanced English Idioms Book Two*, he had no idea.

He kept looking at his watch. It was awful how quickly time passed – and how slowly they moved. A metre. Then two metres. Then a whole minute with no movement at all. They had thirty-nine minutes left. And then thirty-eight. And they had moved less than fifty metres from the park gates.

Cars, Wong decided, were the root of all societal evil. It was not money. It was not the love of money. It was cars. You could see this very clearly in China, which had developed a taste for the motor car later than most other countries. Cars introduced two great evils. The first was the removal of all relationships outside the family. In foot-powered communities, people fulfilled their needs from their neighbours: people within walking or cycling distance. They bought their rice or pancakes or *choi sum* from the farmer next door, their child was taught by the local teacher down the street, and the shoemaker around the corner made their footwear. And they in turn bought things from you. The interrelationships were vital, strong and were renewed every day. But once cars entered the picture, people drove to fashionable stores five or ten or a hundred minutes away, and bought things from people they did not know. They soon forgot the names of the vendors in their own villages. Soon, no one knew anyone outside their immediate families. Strangers dealt only with strangers. People no longer knew their neighbours. Natural human communities broke down. This was a huge, negative change which could be seen happening in rural villages, and blame for it could be laid squarely at the feet of Western capitalist car-makers such as Henry Ford.

The other bad thing that cars had introduced was the destruction of relationships between travellers. When Westerners designed cars, they built them with a one-word vocabulary:

Honk, which was autospeak for 'Get out of my way'. What a tragedy that this decision had been made by some Westerner one hundred years ago. What a shame that cars were not given a bigger vocabulary, or, if it had to be just one word, at least a more expressive word. Had cars been invented in the East, they would surely have been given a more subtle, versatile, pleasingly ambiguous word.

In Chinese, positive notions were often expressed negatively, because this added a delicate layer of civility to them. For example, the Mandarin phrase for 'You're welcome' was *bukeqi*, which literally meant 'No need to be so polite'. In Cantonese 'thank you' was *mm-goi*, two characters which literally meant 'not required'. The thought it contained was 'I gratefully acknowledge that you have done a service for me despite the fact that we both know that you were not required to do so'. What a better world it would have been if the motor car's one-word vocabulary was *Honk* meaning: *Mm-goi*.

In front of them, the cars sat immobile as mountains. There were Santana 2000s and Santana 3000s – it looked as if all the cars in Shanghai were a single brand: the locally produced models that the German Volkswagen company manufactured on the outskirts of the city. The vehicles may have had fancy German high-performance engineering inside them, but if there was nowhere to drive, there was nowhere to drive. There were said to be forty thousand taxis in Shanghai, and it looked as if every single one was stationary in front of them.

'*Aiyeeaa*,' Wong said, as another minute passed.

Next to him Joyce stared at the names of the buildings they were failing to pass. Prominent on Huanghe Lu was a boutique called Foreign Trade Finery. She couldn't imagine a funky clothes shop in Sydney or London or New York with a name like that. People just seemed to think differently here. The stuff was all frilly and silly and brightly coloured. There was not one garment in the window that she would have worn, dead or alive. Shanghai had created its own fashion sense, taking bits from all over the world. Women in their twenties liked to wear denim hot-pants, as if they were in Arizona cop shows. Older women sometimes had a remarkable (to Joyce) ignorance of the horror of VPLs – visible panty lines. Just the previous day she had seen a woman in layers of transparent chiffon through which her underpants – large, ugly briefs that would have looked awful even on a man – were showing. And the men: when the sun came out, the men would roll up their shirts or T-shirts to get some cool air on their pot-bellies. Nothing could have been less attractive.

A moment passed, and she was still staring at the unenticing window display of Foreign Trade Finery.

'It's quicker on the elephant than in this truck,' Joyce said.

The feng shui master nodded.

The elephant, in seeming agreement, knocked at the walls behind them and trumpeted a moan.

'Plan C,' Joyce said. 'Abandon truck and return to riding the elephant.' She threw open the cabin door and, ignoring the shouts of the driver, jumped out. There was no danger, since all the vehicles around them were stationary.

The men were initially reluctant to let them go, especially since Wong wanted his money back. The dispute on this point threatened to drag on. But Joyce barked at her boss: 'Tell them to keep the money. There's no time for fighting. We've got thirty-seven minutes left.' She raced around to the back to open the door. The elephant was happy to see her – the dark, cramped room had not improved his day. He slowly but gratefully backed out of the van.

Joyce again closed her eyes and for the third time tried to visualise an answer – and another picture eventually came. She saw herself cantering along on the elephant, riding it as if it was a horse. She saw the two of them galloping down a freeway at high speed, and then reaching a country village where a veterinary surgeon would appear, operate on the elephant, remove the bomb and throw it into an empty field, whereupon the elephant would trumpet its thanks to her and rise to its feet, fully recovered and grateful to her for the rest of its life (elephants never forget, after all).

But when she opened her eyes, she saw that the beast had closed its eyes, and she began to despair again. The elephant had stopped moving altogether. It was generating a lot of heat. It was covered in sweat – large drops of it. It stank. It looked as if it was on its last legs. There was no way it was going to gallop, canter, or even walk.

'Joyce.' Linyao leapt off a bicycle she had stolen and it clattered to the ground behind her. She ran towards them. 'The American agents are really upset that you ran off with the elephant. They want to "locate and destroy" it. They're looking for you. You better hide.'

'Not without Nelly,' Joyce said. 'Hang on – is this a boy or a girl elephant?'

'Boy.'

'Not Nelly, then. How about Nelson? Let's call him Nelson.'

'When is the bomb going to go off?'

'Thirty-six minutes,' Wong said. '*Aiyeeaa*. You are animal doctor: can you take the bomb out?' He realised that separating the explosive device and the beast would be the only way that this day would end without the death of the white elephant – and the end of all positive fortune in his life.

Linyao shook her head. 'The truth is, I don't think so. I've never done anything like this. Even if I did it in a proper operating theatre. To do it in the street, without the proper tools – it's impossible.'

'He looks like he's really suffering,' Joyce said, her eyes again becoming wet. She patted Nelson's head and rubbed its trunk affectionately.

Linyao agreed. 'The thing in its stomach must be making it feel terrible. Or it might be the pain from the operation. They must have anaesthetised it heavily to cut it open, and given it gallons of painkillers. I'm guessing the stuff is probably wearing off now, so it's starting to feel the pain again.'

'What can we do?'

'You'll have to let it rest.'

'But we can't. We have to keep it moving, get it out of town.'

'It's not going to move if it's sick. You'll need to let it rest.'

'We don't have any time. Can you give it some painkillers?'

'Yes.'

Linyao took out a huge syringe from her bag, filled it from a plastic bottle, and stuck it in the elephant's butt. 'This will make him feel better.'

The elephant did not complain as at least a litre of medicine was emptied into its flank.

Wong was intrigued. Could modern medicine really solve the problem for them? 'Now will it move fast?'

Linyao shook her head. 'No. In about two minutes' time, it will fall fast asleep.'

'Thank you,' said Wong, on possibly the only occasion Joyce had heard him make an ironic comment. 'Thank you very much.'

11

Dooley raced up the stairs.

'Where we going?' puffed Lasse, following three steps behind.

'Roof,' the Acting Secret Agent in Charge shot out, not willing to expend his breath on more detail – going up the stairs to the top of a tall building needed every cubic centimetre of air in his lungs. In cases of emergency he hated taking elevators. It seemed to him the height of madness to enclose yourself in a small metal box when maximum freedom of movement was your bottom line. Especially with mad bombers lurking who knew where. Those damned terrorists. Now that the security forces were looking out at every juncture for swarthy adult males with beards and Islamic names, the bastards were using animals, white female teenagers and Chinese doctors to smuggle bombs into places. At the top of the stairs he pushed open the door to the roof, only to find himself staring down the barrel of a gun. He raised his arms and barked: 'Acting Special Agent in Charge Dooley.'

The officer on guard realised who it was and lowered the weapon. 'Sorry, sir, I didn't know you were coming up here. Once the alarm went off we all went on defcon red. I didn't have any inf—'

Dooley brushed him aside and marched onto the roof proper. There was a squad of snipers, in pairs, fanned out to cover the building from all directions. They turned to stare, feeling the waves of stress emanating from him. 'Listen, men,' he shouted. 'Anyone seen an elephant coming out of the building?'

Two of the men laughed – not because it was funny, but

because everyone was simultaneously bored and tense, an uncomfortable combination which makes you over-react to everything. Further, laughing seemed to be the most obedient reaction, and obedience was what one had to demonstrate in front of Thomas Dooley if one did not want one's butt kicked. One sniper tried helpfully to make a follow-up crack: 'I thought Janet Remo had retired.'

But the sternness of the lines on Dooley's face – there was not a hint of a smile there – mowed down the first vestiges of polite laughter at their roots.

Dooley felt he was moving in slow motion as it sank in that this situation was so far out of the box, he would have to cooperate closely with the Chinese – perhaps even do the unthinkable and let them take the lead. A bomb was walking around the same part of town that POTUS was occupying. Commander Zhang Xiumei: it had to be her. She was the only one capable of handling this – more's the pity. He was already worried that she was far too capable and knowledgeable and smart and well-informed for his liking. And even worse, he almost sorta kinda actually *liked* her, or would have liked her had he been capable of liking anyone.

In his position, he had a cast-iron policy not to find pleasure in any relationship, or even to feel indifferent to anyone. Indeed, it was policy to actively hate everyone, if at all possible. But Commander Zhang sparked other emotions in him. Anger, jealousy, and something else; some other emotion he did not want to look at too closely. She was not pretty in the normal sense – and he was immune to that sort of thing, anyway – but she shone with intelligence, drive, animation, courage and loyalty. Her staff jumped to her every order with a level of instant, adoring obedience that he had never achieved with anyone, not even skinny, servile Lasse. She was the perfect government agent. He enjoyed watching her in action, marshalling her troops with staccato commands. But he was angry with himself for having nonnegative emotions about her. To have an involuntary reaction to a person was bad enough. To have such an unpredictable response to someone On the Other Side – hell's bells, a kind of madness was overtaking him.

Two days ago, the last time he had had a meeting with her, they had continued to talk for almost eleven minutes after the formal business was over. He realised that had she been an American officer, he would have been tempted to suggest meeting for a drink 'after all the craziness is over'. But she was a member of the People's Armed Police: it was not an option. A slightly elongated and semi-personal chat after a formal exchange of notes was about as far as it could go.

The scary thing was that they had talked almost entirely about non-official things, as if they were two normal human beings, capable of normal social activity, which they decidedly were not. They had swapped details about their families – what their parents and relatives did. Yet even that basic Dale Carnegie conversation had been full of minefields. He had told her that his parents lived in Kentucky where Kentucky Fried Chicken came from. This had meant nothing to her, but the term 'KFC' elicited a nod of recognition. They had those in Shanghai. He asked her where her folks lived. She replied Nanning City, which meant nothing to him. 'That's nice,' he said. 'Uh. Where is that? Near Beijing?'

'Guangxi,' she had replied – another name that meant nothing to him.

'Sorry, ah don't know where that is, either. Is it north or south?'

'South, near the border with Vietnam.'

He then asked what seemed like the most obvious, banal question of all: 'And do you have any brothers and sisters?'

'No,' she replied, quietly.

And then he felt mortified when he recalled that in China, most people weren't allowed to have siblings, not in the urban areas, anyway. Goddam.

He racked his brain for a quick change of topic. The standard subject of social conversation between agents cooperating on behalf of different countries (as he had experienced in presidential protective assignments in London and Rome) was a comparison of pay and conditions. It seemed a safe enough topic.

'Enjoy your job? Good pay – ah mean, compared to other jobs?'

She nodded. 'To be paid is good,' she said, which was not quite the response he had expected. Then: 'How much do you get paid?'

This had thrown him momentarily. He blurted out: 'Well, an agent's pay is pretty good, about the same as a middle manager in business or a bit higher, that sort of thing. But we work hard for it – as ah'm sure you do.'

'Yes, but how much do you get paid? In United States dollars?'

Dooley had stopped. The information was not classified. But it might be embarrassing. What the heck – he could open up a little bit. It might even inspire her to defect from China and become an American. That thought gave him a smile, which he kept deep inside. What a shame a woman like this was stuck in such a godawful job in a godawful country.

'Weel, you start off pretty low, on the pay scale, ah mean. But then it climbs up at a reasonable speed. After an average of five years in the field, a special agent can get assigned to a protective detail, which lasts four to five years. We start at what we call the GS-5, GS-7 or GS-9 pay levels, depending on qualifications, and so on. And then, after a few years, we climb up through GS-11, GS-12 until we get to GS-13, which is what is called the Journeyman Grade. But we get good extras, too. We get twenty-five per cent of base salary in addition as LEAP money – that stands for Law Enforcement Availability Pay. 'cause we're never off duty sort of thing, always on standby. Then there's SOT, which is scheduled overtime.'

'Yes, but how much do you get in dollars?'

There was no escaping it. 'Weel, the average new agent can expect to pull down maybe fifty-five to sixty-five thousand, and then it climbs up to GS-13, Journeyman Grade, at something over a hundred thousand per year. Oh, and there's one really good perk. Agents in the field also get G-Rides. These are government vehicles. Uh, cars.'

She thought about this. 'One hundred thousand US dollars a year. That's a lot of money. That's almost a million yuan. That's more than our President gets. And a free car.'

'Yeah, well, it's not really a free car. We can only use it on government business and to go to work and to come home and other stuff.' Hell, what was he saying, it *was* a free car. 'And it's different for you. The cost of living here is like nothing. Ah mean, nothing compared to what we have to pay. Ah mean, a cup of coffee at Starbucks at home is like four dollars.'

'A cup of coffee at a fashionable restaurant here is five dollars. officers of the People's Armed Police get two thousand yuan a month. That's two hundred and forty US dollars. A day's pay works out as one and a half cappuccinos. Rank and file military men get meals plus an allowance of three hundred yuan a month. That's about one dollar a day.'

He hadn't known what to say to that. 'Gee, ah'm so sorry, that stinks,' he said – and then decided that that was the wrong response. 'Come and join my lot – ah'll see to it that you get a pay rise.' He had meant it mainly as a joke, but he saw alarm in her eyes. That was also the wrong thing to say.

'I can't join your service. I am from mainland China.'

She was dead right, of course. That was the end of that conversation.

A movement to his right brought him back to the present. A tall individual using a long-range weapon to cover the west side of the building gestured with his hand. 'Sir? An elephant, you said? Yeah, there was a girl and an elephant came out a few minutes ago. I thought it was pretty strange, but then I remembered there was a show tonight – magicians and circus-type things. Was the elephant part of the show?'

Dooley ignored the question. 'Where is it now?'

The man pointed along Nanjing Xi Lu. 'Down there some-where. Ah – it went in that direction. A big crowd gathered around it, made it hard to move. I saw it cross the road, head up there, past the Marriott Hotel. I think it's over there some-where, maybe near the park.'

The three of them peered over the edge of the parapet but could not see the beast.

Lasse said: 'Do you think we should go down there and have a look, boss?'

But Dooley was already heading to the staircase.

☯

Commander Zhang had dispatched an English-speaking lieu-tenant to get more information on the emergency: a young man named Wan. He reported back within minutes with the same information that she had been given: someone had put a bomb in an elephant. They were, apparently, talking about a real elephant. And then someone – a foreign woman working with a local woman, apparently – had escaped with the beast. At this moment, no one knew where the girl or the elephant had gone, but they could not have gone far, and the Americans requested the People's Armed Police and any other public security body to provide immediate help in tracking them down as soon as possible.

Zhang phoned Dooley. 'You told Wan about this elephant business. With the bomb inside, yes?'

'Yeah, Zhang, we may need your help in sorting this one out. We've found the elephant. They're about a half-mile or so up the road, due north of the Grand Theatre. They're heading north or east. We haven't exactly got a plan about what to do when we catch up with them. We've told the President's people – uh, both Presidents – that the show is off. They are being diverted to a secret location outside the

208

city.'

'You are talking about a real elephant, a real bomb.'

'Yes, of course.'

'This is not a sexual thing?'

'What?'

'This elephant and bomb, it's not an advanced English colloquialism for a, ah, sexual thing?'

'What are you talking about?'

'Never mind. What do you want me to do?'

'I'll tell you what you can do that might be real useful. Find me some sort of location – perhaps a warehouse or something – where we can explode the bomb safely.'

'Can you disarm the bomb?'

'Negative. We don't have the expertise to get to it. Nor do we have time now. We're going to have to blow the thing.'

'I'll start looking for a suitable location. Where is the elephant?'

'On the main road behind the park – waddyacallit, Nanjing Xi Lu, is it? Or just off it somewhere.' There was the sound of a map being crinkled. 'They may be on this road called, er, Huanghe Lu. We're chasing them.'

'Understand.'

'And, uh, Commander?'

'Yes, Special Agent Dooley?'

'We might need a bit of local advice. We're not that great at getting around here – especially not with this traffic and this demo and stuff.'

'Understand. I will send officer Wan to help you.'

'Thanks. I appreciate that.' Dooley rang off.

Zhang slowly lowered her handset and turned to Wan. 'The Americans are up to some sort of trick. And the President of China may be the target. What else can it be? This is exactly what we expected from them. Remember I warned you? We need to pretend to play along with them. Call the rest of the team.'

As Wan got on to the radio phones, Zhang wondered what

exactly she should say to her chiefs: they would be in a state of panic. This was a highly significant development. And which chiefs? Her superior at the People's Armed Police needed to know, but so did the Politburo, the Communist Party leaders and the Central Military Affairs Commission. She thought it would be wise to get an urgent message to her senior-most contact at the main leadership compound of Zhongnanhai in Beijing.

Zhang had a brief conference with her squad of twelve key officers, then outlined the plan. 'Wan, you will cooperate with the Americans and pretend to help them. But don't help them too much, you know what I mean? You will really be gathering information for us.

'Xin, you and your team will cover all activities at the Grand Theatre.

'Chen, you will seek out a location – a factory or warehouse or construction site, perhaps north of Suzhou Creek or out in Pudong somewhere, or Caohejing – which can be evacuated in case the bomb needs to be detonated.

'Tan, we've got a squad stationed at The Bund. Call them and inform them about the situation. Tell them to head straight down Nanjing Dong Lu. The elephant and the terrorists will escape from the Americans and run due east – straight into our waiting arms.'

She rose to her feet and headed out of the back door. She had not told anyone what she herself was planning to do. But she had her own transport and believed she could beat any traffic jam.

☯

'*Wei?*'

'Marc? I mean, Marker? Is that Marker?'

'Yes. That is . . . ?'

'It's Joyce. From CF Wong and Associates? You moved all our stuff? Last week? And then moved it all again yesterday?

Remember me?'

'Remember.'

'I said I'd call.'

'Yes.'

'How are you?'

'I am fine. How are you?'

'Yeah, fine, ha ha. Er, actually, not so fine. I've got a little problem. I mean a big problem. Er, hey, are you free right now?'

'Yes. You want to meet?'

'Yes, definitely, yes, yes.'

'You want to drink some coffee or something sometime or something?' He sounded excited.

'Yeah. Great. That would be fab. But there's just one thing.'

'One thing.'

'Yeah. Er. I need to move something. Can you help me move something, and then we'll go for a coffee somewhere?'

'Yes. Okay. What do you want me to move?' She believed she could hear the delight in his voice starting to evaporate as soon as the social invitation showed signs of transmuting into unpaid work. Joyce felt suffused with guilt. He must think he was being used – he must think she only wanted to see him because he was a removal man and would help her move something. 'Listen,' she said. 'I'm not just using you, ha ha, I wouldn't want you to think that.'

'Think that.'

'Yeah. You're a really good friend and I nearly called you after the first time we met, last week, on a Monday, or was it Tuesday? Actually, I nearly called you a few times. But you know how it is. I meant to, but I didn't actually call you. I just thought about it, you know, ha ha.'

'You just thought about it, ha ha.'

'Yeah. Ha ha. Anyway, what I am trying to say *is*.' She thought about what she was trying to say.

He waited patiently for a few seconds. 'Hello? Joy-Si? You

are there?'

'Er, yes-yes-yes. What I mean is, let's meet lots of times, for lots of coffees. I mean, ha ha, it would be good to get to know each other. I mean, even if I didn't want you to help me move this thing. Do you know what I mean?'

'Yes. I think so. You want lots of coffee. Many cups of coffee. You are very thirsty.'

'Um, yes. Well, I suppose that's true. What I am saying is that I'm not just using you. I'm not calling you just because you are a removal man and I need something moved. That's just a small part of it. *Apart* from that, I really want to meet you, you know, for social reasons. Meeting you for social reasons is more important than the little job I want you to help me with. Understand?'

'Yes. Understand,' Cai said. 'So we have lots of cups of coffee first, very important, then do little moving job afterwards, because not important.'

'Ah. No. I think. Ummm. No, let's get the little job out of the way. Then I can feel more relaxed. It's kind of an emergency sort of thing, know what I mean?'

'Yes,' he said, but she could tell from his voice that he didn't have the slightest idea what she was talking about.

'Look, can you get to the corner of Huanghe Lu and, er, Fengyang Lu in the middle of town as soon as possible? Just up above Renmin Park? Do you know where I mean? Then you'll understand what I'm on about. Thanks so much. I'm really, really grateful. Ha ha. Bye.'

She clicked the phone off. *Cheese.* Where had her brain gone?

☯

Jappar Memet sat in his suite in the Howard Johnson Plaza Hotel holding the document he was about to send out to the world. It had been prepared by Dilshat Tohti, the wisest scholar in the membership of the exiles, but would be issued jointly under their names and those of the other Children of

Uyghur.

'Final draft?'

'Yeah. 'ave a read. I can't fink of anyfing else to add to it,' said Tohti.

'Awright. Lemme 'ave a gander.'

Jappar tossed his lank, greasy hair out of his eyes and peered at the sheets in front of him:

We the undersigned claim responsibility for the Shanghai bomb which has this evening changed the course of world history. By killing/seriously wounding the two most powerful men in the world, we draw, for the first time, the attention of every human being on earth to a hitherto unnoticed calamity that has killed thousands of innocent people and sentenced millions of others to a life of servitude. A calamity that has destroyed not just two lives, but has wiped an entire nation off the map. A calamity which is close to genocide, the destruction of an entire people. But to set right mistakes that will no doubt be made by the world media, deliberately or otherwise, we wish to make certain points clear at the outset.

This bomb was set off in the name of East Turkistan, a country that no longer appears on any map. But this bomb was NOT set off by the people of East Turkistan, or any of the Turkic resistance groups. They are gentle and non-violent people who have been greatly wronged over many years but have borne their suffering with silent fortitude. This bomb was set off by outraged supporters from outside the community.

East Turkistan is the true and only name before Allah of the area which now appears on maps as the Xinjiang Uyghur Autonomous Region of China. It is 1,626,000 square kilometres (635,000 square miles) in size. It is a significant size: it is the size of all of Britain plus France plus Germany plus Spain. It is one-sixth of the land mass of China. However, its true size is larger still, measuring 1.82 million square kilometres. Significant parts were annexed into Qinghai and Gansu provinces as part of an illegal invasion in 1949.

Our fathers knew East Turkistan as a place where one truly experienced the Grandeur of God. It is a huge country with every type of scenery, from mountains to lakes, from dry deserts to lush forests. It has wonderful natural resources, including petroleum. But most wonderful of all are its people. It is the home of the 8.7 million Uyghur people and fellow peoples who live in peace with them. The community includes Kazaks, Kyrgyz, Tajiks, Tatars and Uzbeks. They are also Central Asians, they are also Muslims, and they count for an additional 2.5 million people. It is also the birthplace of a great Islamic civilisation, and has produced fine works, such as *The Knowledge for Happiness* by Yusuf Has Hajip. Below are some FAQs about East Turkistan.

Q: Is East Turkistan part of China?

A: No. It is part of Central Asia.

Q: Are the people Chinese?

A: No. The majority are Central Asian. Since 1949, the proportion of Chinese living in the area has risen from six per cent to about forty per cent today. This is a result of forced immigration, where the Chinese government has planted Han Chinese people on land owned by the people of East Turkistan.

Q: Is their language Chinese?

A: No. Their language is Turkic.

Q: Do they speak Chinese?

A: No, most don't.

Q: Do they consider themselves Chinese?

A: No. They consider themselves part of the Turkic peoples.

Q: Do the Chinese consider them to be Chinese?

A: No. They think of them as Central Asian Muslims.

Q: Historically, who does East Turkistan belong to?

A: The Uyghurs have lived there for more than four thousand years. They played a key role in the growth of the Silk Road as a channel between East and West.

Q: How did the Chinese invade?

A: The Manchu Empire invaded East Turkistan in 1876. The people bravely resisted for eight years, but eventually were overtaken by superior numbers. The Manchus renamed it 'Xinjiang' (New Territory) in 1884. The Manchus were overthrown by the Chinese Nationalists in 1911, and the innocent people of East Turkistan found themselves being brutalised under a new regime. The Uyghurs bravely fought back in 1933 but were crushed. In 1944 they rose again, and this time succeeded in re-establishing the free, glorious land of East Turkistan, an independent Muslim republic. However, from 1949 onwards, the communist rulers of China arrived and took command over the area by force.

Q: What is the situation since then?

A: Since then, the situation has been dire. The new rulers moved large numbers of army and police into the area. They use the Uyghurs' land for a range of military activities, including the testing of nuclear weapons. They have built prison labour factories in their valleys. Their blue skies and shining lakes are now filled with pollution. But worst of all, they have destroyed the culture. Any expression of their traditions results in harsh crackdowns, arrests and imprisonment. Their young men are taken. Some are tortured. Others disappear. They shut the mosques at will. The Uyghur language is banned from university so that all progress and resources are reserved for Chinese. They make the Uyghur work unpaid as slaves to construct pipelines to transport their petroleum to other parts of China. If they complain or protest, they are subject to summary execution. Execution is often carried out in public venues, to instil a sense of fear in the populace.

Q: How has the international community reacted?

A: It has done nothing.

Q: Is the situation getting better or worse?

A: The people thought that things could not get worse, but they did, in September 2001. After the attacks on the Twin Towers in New York, US President George W Bush proclaimed a 'war on terror'. The world's mainstream media, without exception, picked up this phrase and ran with it. Yet it was not a war on terror. It was a war against Muslims unconnected with the bombing in New York, as was aptly demonstrated by the illegal invasion of Iraq, a country un-related to the terrorists who brought down the World Trade Center. The Chinese government jumped on the bandwagon. They used this opportunity to label the Uyghur people (a tiny minority of whom had been driven to produce a few small-scale explosions) as terrorist Muslims who should also be stamped out as part of the 'war on terror'. Now, every time they make any nostalgic utterance about their lost culture, they are labelled Islamic terrorists.

Only a few organisations have paid any attention: Human Rights Watch and Amnesty International and the BBC.

Until the world is forced to wake up to the tragedy taking place in East Turkistan, the people there will continue to live in misery.

We are supporters living in exile. Our actions tonight will ensure that people around the world know the cause of the lost people of East Turkistan. We apologise to the families of those killed or hurt.

Signed,

Jappar Memet, Dilshat Tohti, Erkin Wayit, Etam Ablimit, Abdulghani Abchjreyim, Gulnar Yusuf and Aygul Alptekin
The Organising Committee of the Uyghur Children in Exile

12

In ancient western China, there was a god-emperor of fertility who had green eyes.

But his fifteen-year-old wife gave him no children. He was furious. The prophecies said his offspring would number one hundred or more.

So he spent his time with harlots. One of them quickly became pregnant.

'Even a harlot is more fertile than you,' he said to his wife, and threw her out. He also threw out the harlot's baby, although he kept the harlot for entertainment.

Heaven looked down on the heartlessness of this god-emperor and decreed that he should have no more children, from other wives, concubines or harlots.

But his barren ex-wife raised his abandoned baby. That child grew up and, at the age of fifteen, had her own child, the first of six boys. That boy grew up and had the first of his six girls when he was fifteen. And that girl, in turn, had the first of her six boys when she was fifteen.

Fifty years later, the barren wife, now sixty-five, returned to the palace with more than one hundred children. Many had green eyes.

The prophets declared the prophecy fulfilled and replaced the barren king with his ex-wife and her family.

Blade of Grass, the ultimate victory of love and goodness of spirit are built into Heaven's plan, although we may not be able to see it for a very long time.

From 'Some Gleanings of
Oriental Wisdom' by CF Wong

Marker Cai arrived on Fengyang Lu, skidding his racing bicycle to a halt in front of Joyce with an elegant twist of his handlebars. 'Hello, Joy-Si.' Then he noticed the elephant. 'Oh. An elephant.' What else can one say?

'Er, yeah. Hi, Marker.' Her heart was beating like a techno-trance drum machine. *Cheese* – she must look terrible. She hadn't washed or brushed her hair or anything. And what must her scrappy make-up look like? It probably looked like a toddler had applied crayons to her eyes. How long had it been since she looked in a mirror? She laughed nervously. 'Ha ha. Sorry about the hair and all that. I was up all night, and, uh, anyway, I got this elephant. Long story. We need to move this beast out of town. There's a bomb inside it which is going to go off very soon. We need to get it somewhere where there are no people. We've got—' She looked at Wong.

'Thirty-one minutes.'

'Thirty-one minutes. But the traffic's gridlocked. We can't drive him out. He's just about to fall asleep, so we can't ride him out. We need to move him another way.'

'Okay,' Marker said slowly. 'You have to move this elephant. Move it very quickly. Because there is inside it a – ?' His face was open, his brow raised and questioning.

'A bomb.'

'A bomb. There is a bomb inside the elephant. Bomb?'

'Yeah, bomb. As in *booooom*.'

'*Baang*,' explained Wong in Mandarin. '*Zhe shi yi ge bao zha wu.*'

Linyao spoke to Cai in Shanghainese to make it absolutely clear: 'Yes, we know this all sounds crazy, but it's true. Someone wanted to bomb the theatre show where the US President and the Chinese President were due to meet, so they put a bomb inside this animal.'

Marker Cai slowly nodded, as if he encountered this sort of assignment several times a week, particularly during elephant shifting season.

Joyce knelt down and pointed to the line of stitches along the creature's stomach. 'Plastic explosives and a timer. Some evil, evil person put them here. Cut open the elephant and inserted them and sewed it up. That's just so utterly totally horrible, don't you agree?'

Marker nodded. 'Agree. Okay. I help you move this elephant. And the coffee?'

'Yes, afterwards we have coffee.'

Sirens erupted in the distance – yelps, wails and wow-wow-wows.

Wong gave his own yelp. '*Aiyeeaaa!* Move fast, fast. Those American bad guys are coming this way.'

'We gotta go,' Joyce said. 'These guys are after us. Can you move the elephant for us, please?'

Marker was deep in thought. 'Can. One time I had to move a big piano quick-quick for concert and the truck broke down. We use platform on wheels. Ms Lu, you stay with elephant. Joy-Si *xiao-jie*, Wong-*sheng*, come with me.'

They followed Marker as he trotted down a side street called Beiha Lu. Although only a few hundred metres from the centre of town, it looked like another world. The buildings were two-storey houses with sloping roofs, divided by small alleyways decorated with what looked like lines of bunting but which were actually washing lines. Many older people were engaged in the standard Shanghainese evening activity for their generation: sitting on the pavement in ragged deckchairs, enjoying the evening breeze and watching the world go by.

Ducking down a narrow side lane, Cai led them to an old factory. At the door, he had a heated discussion with an elderly man who appeared to be acting as guard and general factotum.

'Okay. He needs money. One thousand *kuai*.' Marker looked at Joyce and Joyce looked at Wong.

'Money? What for?'

'For something which will help us move the elephant.'

Cursing, the feng shui master pulled his fast-dwindling stack of notes out of his pocket and carefully counted out a thousand yuan for the old man.

The elderly guard pulled a chain. With a fearsome rattling noise, the old metal shutter rose and disappeared into the roof. Inside was a live chicken warehouse – and it stank of guano. The smell hit them like a wave, and the fumes made their eyes sting.

'Ouch,' said Joyce. 'And *ew*. What are we here for?'

'That,' said Marker. He pointed to a wooden pallet piled high with cardboard boxes of eggs. 'They've got some big, strong ones here. We need the biggest.'

A minute later, Cai and the doorman trundled out of the entrance a large wooden pallet. It was about three metres square, twenty-five centimetres high and had some forty-eight wheels underneath, most of which worked. It rumbled like a distant thunderstorm as it moved. On top were several blankets that Cai had asked the old man to throw in for the price.

'Will it be strong enough?' Joyce asked.

'Yes. My job is to estimate the weight of things and then move them. That's what I do. You trust me, please. I move your elephant.'

Joyce sighed with pleasure. She felt like giving him a round of applause. Now a real man was taking charge of the situation. This was exactly what was needed. She felt, for the first time during this nightmare day, that they might actually succeed in getting Nelson away from the city centre to some place where the bomb could go off without harming anyone else.

'How are we going to get the elephant up on top of this?'

'Steps. That is the secret of moving heavy objects. Always use as many steps as you need.'

He borrowed bricks and wooden boxes from a hardware store on Fengyang Lu and took them to where Linyao remained gently rubbing the white elephant's boulder-like forehead. He was standing still, swaying slightly, with his eyes half closed.

'He's almost asleep,' the veterinarian said.

'We've just got to persuade him to climb up onto this platform. Then he can sleep for as long as he likes,' Joyce said. 'He likes you best, Joyce. You go on one side, and I'll go on the other.'

Between them the two women persuaded Nelson to mount Marker Cai's wheeled pallet, and then the beast lowered himself down to his knees and toppled over into a sleeping posture, slumped on his left side. Joyce threw a blanket over him. 'Okay, sleep tight,' she said. 'Time to go.'

Linyao was given the job of running interference. She moved to stand in front of the platform, ready to direct them and clear people out of their way.

Wong, McQuinnie and Cai leaned down and tried to push it along, but it wouldn't budge – not a centimetre. They strained. They heaved. They lowered their heads and placed their feet against raised bits of paving stone for leverage. It simply would not move.

'Shoot. There's no way we can move this thing,' Joyce said, her face red. 'Not even an inch. I mean, Nelson must weigh tons. How are we going to push this thing for miles?'

Marker, sweat dripping down his face, said: 'No need to push this for miles. We need to push it one metre only.'

'Meaning . . . ?'

'One metre only. This is the secret of moving heavy weight with wheels. Just start it moving, and then the weight will carry itself. Linyao, you please help also. We count to three, all push. *Yi. Er. San.* Push!'

The four of them strained against the platform with all their strength – and it started to budge.

The wheels rumbled and squeaked on the pavement and the load was suddenly in motion. As it started to move, Joyce realised what Marker meant. It seemed impossibly heavy at first, but once it had momentum, it rolled along by itself. It went from a crawling pace to a steady canter very quickly. And once it was going, you no longer had to push particularly hard.

You only had to fine-tune its journey, adding a push when the ground sloped up, slowing it when the ground sloped down, or nudging it to one side or the other if it needed to change direction.

Wong was fascinated – and delighted to have learned such an important life lesson from such a young man. If you were faced with a truly impossible task, a mountain to move, the only really important thing was to take the first step towards accomplishing it with sufficient determination. That in itself would set in motion the processes that would help you achieve the task. He must find a lesson in the Classics that taught this, and include it in his book. What he particularly liked about the principle was that it showed the power of the man who was in tune with the world. The man who relied on machines needed hundreds of units of horsepower to move a huge weight. The man in tune with natural physics used Heaven-given gravity to do the same job much more simply and cheaply.

They were rolling. Linyao raced ahead of them, clearing the pavements with shouts in Mandarin and Shanghainese.

They could hear the revving of the imported high-performance American cars being driven by the Secret Service agents a hundred or so metres away on Nanjing Xi Lu. But the drivers were disadvantaged by being on a log-jammed main road. They had to constantly force other vehicles off to the side to get through – and there were several points where the traffic was so tightly jammed that movement in any direction was impossible.

In contrast, Nelson and his team were moving at good speed along the pavements and gutters of Fengyang Lu. The pavements were relatively wide and mostly flat. There were slight inclines from time to time, but the momentum they built up enabled them to get over them with no trouble – so far.

'Out of the way, out of the way,' Linyao shrieked as the bizarre procession moved along. 'Coming through, big load coming through.'

They skidded off Fengyang Lu onto a much wider thoroughfare.

'Come,' shouted Cai. 'Down Central Tibet Lu.'

'No. That will take us back to Renmin Park area,' Wong replied.

'No. We turn left after Number One Department Store. To Nanjing Dong Lu.'

'Yes, yes, good-good, go-go,' said the feng shui master.

They zoomed past another large signpost in Chinese and English. This one said: 'Huangpu District will burst out with energy for the future development'.

Passing the Number One Department Store, they turned sharply to the left. Cai's plan was brilliant, Wong decided: Nanjing Dong Lu was a pedestrian precinct. It was long, wide and smooth. It would be easy to push a wheeled platform along there. But there was no way that men in cars could follow. There were regular bollards and other obstacles specifically designed to make it difficult or impossible for vehicles to get into the precinct.

Better still, the precinct started with a downward slope. It was only a gentle gradient, but it was enough to speed up their progress to a fast sprint.

Wong, unable to keep up with the younger people, trailed behind in a state of shock. From the evidence of his ears, he was amazed to discover that they were actually increasing the distance between themselves and the US officials' vehicles, which stood buzzing and angry in the gridlocked traffic just in front of the park, now almost half a kilometre behind them.

☯

Dooley thumped the dashboard with both fists. 'Is there no way we can git this traffic cleared?'

'It's difficult,' said Ari Tadwacker, who was driving in short bursts as agents ran ahead of them trying to clear the space. 'We asked the Chinese to clear the roads, but they said that there wasn't much they could do. They've kept the road to the west clear all day for Presidential access to the Grand Theatre, but that means all the other roads are much more chock-a-block than usual. Then there's the demo. I mean, this jam – it's incredible. I've never seen anything like it. It's worse than Bangkok.'

Dooley clenched his fists and ground his teeth. He was mentally writing the report he knew he would have to produce about this unbelievably ghastly afternoon. Bombs, terrorists, kidnappings – these things might work as excuses for their failure to remain in control of the situation. But being stuck in a traffic jam? There was no way a self-respecting ASAIC could even dare to mention that in a report. *In the end, I failed to completely fulfil my duties because the traffic was really bad.*

He turned to look out of the left-hand window – and was horrified to see Commander Zhang speeding past them on a Forever brand bicycle! Zhang Xiumei turned and waved, giving him a dazzling smile before she disappeared through tiny gaps in the traffic ahead.

'Goddam it, did you see that?' Dooley shouted.

'That police woman, sir?'

'It's Commander Zhang. She's travelling ten times as fast as we are and she's on a goddam Victorian penny farthing.'

It seemed criminally unfair. Dooley was sitting in his brand new Cadillac XLR, specially imported into Shanghai to provide motorised muscle for the mission. This car cost $77,000 plus $20,000 of Secret Service extras! And they had just been overtaken by his goddam Chinese counterpart on a goddam vehicle that he wouldn't have paid ten goddam bucks for in a goddam garage sale.

'Why don't we have some of them?'

'Penny farthings, sir?'

'Anything. *Anything* that can bloody well move.'

Dooley, losing his cool, stuck his head out of the window

and screamed: 'Move, move, move, damn you, move your butts out of mah way.'

But his performance merely made the other drivers on Nanjing Xi Lu turn around and stare at him, bringing forward movement to a complete halt.

The Acting Special Agent in Charge made a snap decision.

He called the senior bomb disposal officer. 'Donaldson. Dooley. Get me a bike. Big one. Your Harley. I'm on the main road behind the theatre, behind the park, stuck in a jam. The only way to move forward is on two wheels. If it's not here in two minutes' time, your butt is toast. I'm starting to count right now. Over.'

☯

Commander Zhang sped along on her bicycle, the wind in her face, reflecting, as Joyce had done the previous evening, on how in practice old technology was sometimes superior to the new stuff. Fifteen years ago, Shanghai road traffic had moved along at a steady twenty kilometres an hour on foot-powered vehicles. Now many people had cars – and vehicles crept along at five kilometres an hour in turbo-charged, computerised traffic jams. Thank heaven for pedal power. Passing that strange American spy leader in his fancy, chunky racing car had been fun.

The radio she had clipped to her bicycle handlebars, next to the old-fashioned thumb-rung bell, started to crackle.

'Commander Zhang?'

'Yes, Xin. I can hear you.'

'Things are looking good. We have them surrounded. They are heading east along the Nanjing Dong Lu. You're right behind them. We've got another unit coming west towards them from The Bund. And we've found a car not far from them – in fact, not far from where you are now. If you can get to the junction of Jiujiang Lu and the south bit of Guizhou Lu, near the Ramada Plaza Hotel, you'll find Sergeant Xie waiting with a squad car. He's looking out for you.'

'Excellent work, Xin. I'm only about a hundred metres away from Jiujiang Lu now,' she replied, bumping her bike onto the pavement.

Seconds later, Commander Zhang had tucked the bicycle into the trunk of the car and was being driven along the roads parallel to the pedestrian precinct, confident that she would reach the women and the elephant well before the Americans. It would take a little thought: most of the side roads leading into the pedestrian precinct had steel bollards built into them to stop vehicular access. But not all of them.

'Zhejiang Dong Lu crosses Nanjing Dong Lu,' Zhang told the driver. 'If we head for that junction, we can actually get the car into the pedestrian precinct. Then we've got them for sure.'

☯

'Vega? It's Minnie.'

'Yeah, wot, wot? I'm really busy now, honeychops. How's it goin' down your end?'

'It's all up, Vega, it's all up.' She gave a watery sniff.

'Wot you talking about?'

'Someone escaped. They called the cops. It was that feng shui guy Wong and the girl with him.'

'*Wot?* I don't believe this. I don't believe—'

Minnie burst into tears. 'They got out. And now the Public Security Bureau people have surrounded this place. We've locked ourselves in. But I don't know how long we—'

'Don't worry, Minnie. Let me tell you somefink. That's just a subsidiary job. That's a small job compared to what's goin' down over here. Our names will be glorified in 'istory for ever more, fanks to what's 'appening 'ere. I'm sorry your fing has gone down, but believe me, baby, it's only a sideshow.'

'Vega, I don't want to go down in history. They're going to do us for murder, Vega, do you understand? Murder and kidnapping. I don't want to be part of anything else violent or which will kill people. None of us do. We're Vegans, Vega, we—'

'Gotta go, babe, see yer.' He rang off.

Memet turned to his deputy, Dilshat. 'Shite. The vegan thing's gone pear-shaped. Bloody typical. It was goin' fine while I was runnin' it, and the moment I leave someone else in charge, it bloody well collapses into a bloody heap of shite.'

'Sorry, boss.'

'Don't matter. Those bloody bitches will get what's coming to them. I hope the cops beat them black and blue and lock them up for years and *years*. It's what they deserve for lettin' me down.'

He slumped back into the expensive armchair and put his boots up on a delicate wine table. It was a shame the veggie project had collapsed, but it was not a big deal. He had only been using the veggie groups to get himself a good network in this town so they could pull off the operation they had been planning for the past year – ever since a date for a China–US summit had been announced. That project was not going to fail. He owed it to his family, to his cousins, to his people.

Memet, though raised in London, had been brought up in an atmosphere of bitterness and resentment against the Chinese government. The house in bland, chilly Crouch End had been such a step down for his parents, who had previously lived as royalty under the shadow of the sweeping plains and glorious mountains of Xinjiang. His father had continually stoked his children's anger by telling them that they would have been kings or princes of a place bigger than Western Europe had not the Chinese invaders made their lives intolerable.

When he had first visited China himself, three years earlier, he had been taken to a Uyghur restaurant in Shanghai. His countrymen were there, dressed in ridiculous clothes, dancing and prancing like buffoons for the entertainment of a party of Chinese officials. He quickly learned that in the main cities of China, Uyghur restaurants were thought of as places to go for a laugh. You ate disgusting food from a shocking menu and watched primitive ethnic people cavort in colourful clothes.

And the menus really were revolting, particularly to a vegetarian like himself. A standard Uyghur restaurant menu in Shanghai would offer kebabs and lamb pancakes, but people inevitably ordered the more bizarre items on the menu so that they could sneer at the weird stuff ethnic people ate. Adventurous diners would roar with laughter at the menu and then fashion themselves nightmare meals from it. They would typically start with Raw Cold Jellyfish (20 yuan), and then move on to Drunk Horse Intestines (25 yuan), before focusing on Raw, Cold Sheep's Head (39 yuan).

Chinese and Westerners would laugh and gloat over the horrors of the menu, and then sneer at the dancers. The men would wear white or red Russian-style outfits with belts that were thicker and more bejewelled than anything Elvis ever wore in Vegas. The women would be subservient, covered up in trouser suits and hats, flitting around the restaurant laying down dishes for people to guffaw at.

On that first visit, Jappar had watched with morbid fascination. His father, sitting next to him, had tears rolling down his cheeks at the circus acts to which his noble people had been reduced.

Previously Jappar had felt distanced from his past, thinking of himself more as a Londoner than a Uyghur, but that evening something angry and cold was born inside him: a patriotic fury against the people who had turned a rich, proud people living in majestic mountains into an oppressed and poverty-stricken tribe of desperate souls selling their millennia-old traditions for a few paltry yuan.

And then he had met Zhong Xue Qin. Initially, he had nothing but contempt for the willowy Shanghainese activist who was causing trouble in the family-owned supermarkets run by his uncles, but underneath her slogans he quickly found much to admire: she hated the Chinese government just as he did. She was a passionate vegetarian just as he was. She knew how to channel her anger into fighting for what she believed in – something that he wanted desperately to learn to do.

They had become lovers, then a married couple, and then partners in crime. He had encouraged and financed her operations – including the raid on Shanghai Second Medical University that had killed her. Her death had driven him to suicidal despair for months. But he had emerged stronger, harder, meaner, and more determined to fight for his beliefs and the causes for which she had died. It was the Chinese government that had cruelly destroyed the ancient Uyghur culture. And it was in China that the cruellest meat-eaters dreamed up the most evil ways to torture and kill live animals. And so he had founded the Children of Vega, to revenge Xue Qin's death and get China's oppression of the Uyghur people right to the top of the international agenda.

And how better to achieve that than to kill the world's two most powerful individuals: the pair of Presidents identified in his complex plan as Px2?

☯

Bomb disposal officer Sam Donaldson arrived on the biggest bike they had. Dooley abandoned the Caddy XLR to Ari Tadwacker and climbed onto the back. 'You drive. We'll go together. We kin talk. Git on the sidewalk if you have to.'

Donaldson twisted the handlebars and the 1450cc Harley Davidson Electra-Glide Classic roared into life, skidding its 800 pounds of shiny heft smoothly up onto the pavement. It seemed effortless. Dooley felt like he was sitting on an intercontinental ballistic missile. Now this was American power at its best.

The bomb disposal expert was clearly still struggling to get a grasp on what was going on. He flipped up his visor and talked through the side of his mouth at the man behind him. 'I know you heard something ticking inside the elephant, but how likely is it that there really is a bomb in the elephant?' he shouted. 'I mean, this could just be a trick that the Chinese are pulling, couldn't it? Something to distract us so that they can get POTUS?'

'Ah realise that. The whole thing cud be a set-up. A plot to kill POTUS. The trouble is, that makes it worse. Terrorists are bad enough, but to have the Chinese against us, here in their heartland – it don't bear thinking about. We jest better pray—'

'Yeah, but what I mean is, do we know it's a bomb for sure? The creature may just have, I don't know, eaten a bloody alarm clock or something, you know what I mean? It sounds unlikely that anyone could put a bomb into a live animal.'

'You'd need too much explosive material, you mean?'

Donaldson thought about this. 'Well – I don't know. You'd need a hell of a lot of material. I mean, to have a reasonably big effect.'

'Plastic explosive?'

'Got to be. Probably Semtex. If you had Semtex, I guess it could be done.'

'How do you figure that?'

Donaldson saw a gap suddenly open up in the traffic and he skipped through it, powering a good hundred yards before having to ease off and sneak into a space between two buses, creeping forward.

'Semtex is malleable,' the bomb expert continued. 'You could take the stuff and flatten it to fit in the fat layer, under the skin, under one of the layers of epidermis, I suppose. I mean, arguably they could even shape it to fit around the creature's organs in some way. That's why plastic explosive is used so much in demolition – you can flatten it or shape it in any way you want and get the bang exactly where you want it.'

'So you're telling me that it really is possible.'

'It might be. If you want God's honest truth, I reckon it just might be. A thin slab of plastic explosive might work,' Donaldson said, adding: 'It's probably Semtex A.'

'Relevance?'

'Hard to detect and, until recently, quite easy to get hold of. Comes from Semtin, a place in Bohemia.'

'There's a real place called Bohemia?'

'You live and learn, Doolster. The stuff is made by Explosia, a company in Bohemia. Semtex A is strong stuff: it's ninety-five per cent PETN, which stands for Pentaerythritol Tetranitrate, and five per cent RDX, which stands for Research and Development substance X.'

'Sounds like something from a James Bond movie.'

'In the explosives business, true life is way weirder than any James Bond movie. The story goes that a military research and development department created the stuff, and then temporarily labelled it RDX while they thought up a proper name. They blew themselves to pieces before they came up with a name, so RDX is what we're stuck with.'

'How much Semtex do you need to cause a big bang?'

'Hardly any. That's the problem. That's why it's such a headache. With two fifty grams, you can take down a 747.'

'Geez.'

'A single suicide bomber can carry sixty pounds of explosive. But we're talking about an elephant. If they had a hundred or two hundred pounds of the stuff in there . . .'

'You could cause a pretty big bang.'

'Yeah, I guess you could.'

The bus on their left moved slightly, making a gap big enough for the Harley to squeeze through. Donaldson spun the accelerator and the Harley sped back onto the pavement and roared forward.

They nipped nimbly between the bollards blocking vehicles from proceeding into the Nanjing Dong Lu pedestrian precinct and revved up, sending crowds of shoppers and sightseers scrambling out of the way.

'Thank God. Now we got 'em,' Dooley said, the ghost of a smile finally illuminating his cracked lips.

☯

'Does the name Vega mean anything to you?' Sinha was sitting in Shang Dan's luxurious apartment, a minimalist loft-style residence hidden behind a red-brick façade in Old Town.

Shang Dan stroked his long thin beard and considered the question. Dressed in silk robes, the local *ming shu* expert had clearly modelled his image on the statue of Confucius in the temple on nearby Wenmiao Lu.

'Of course,' he said. 'Of course.'

This was followed by a lengthy pause. Sinha said: 'Would you like to share it with me?'

'Hmm? Oh yes. Of course, of course.'

But nothing more was forthcoming for at least a minute. Shang Dan, like a nervous witness undergoing cross-examination in a court, liked to think about his answers before delivering them. 'Vega is a star,' he said eventually. 'It is in the constellation called Lyra. It is a key element of our astrological system, along with the Pole Star. We use Vega in many of our calculations in the *ming shu*.'

'Would there be any political relevance to an activist of some sort naming themselves after the star Vega?'

Shang Dan thought quietly for a minute. 'No.'

Sinha sat back in his chair. This was proving frustrating. He seemed unable to elicit any information from the astrologer that could prove useful. What other line of inquiry could he take? Perhaps he should lay the entire situation before the man and see what conclusions he drew from it.

'There have been a number of odd things happening over the past day,' he said. 'We need to find out whether they are connected and where they are leading. First, Mr Wong's office was unexpectedly demolished. Then, an associate of Joyce McQuinnie, Mr Wong's assistant, had her child kidnapped. This was followed by Mr Wong and his assistant being kidnapped by another branch of the same gang – a gang which appears to be run by someone named Vega. The gang is very interested in the meeting of the two Presidents.'

Shang Dan pondered for a while, and then shook his head. 'This is Shanghai. Offices get demolished every day. Kidnappings are not so common, but they happen. The newspapers usually do not report them. Everyone is interested in the meeting of the two Presidents. Everyone in the world. And Vega. That name means nothing to me.'

Sinha was disheartened. But then something that Joyce had said when he had dropped Linyao in the city centre stuck in his mind. She had told him to find out anything he could about Vega. And she had added: 'Oh yeah, Wong says it might not be Vega. It might be pronounced *weega*.'

'What about *weega*? Does the word *weega* mean anything to you?'

This time the man's response was immediate. His eyebrows rose. 'Uyghur?' he said.

'Yes.'

'Minority tribe. Good food. That reminds me. I am feeling hungry. But the Uyghur people are associated with social unrest. Bombs and things.'

'Ah. Now I think we are getting somewhere.'

☯

Wong looked around and noticed that a People's Armed Police car had moved onto the pavement and was rapidly gaining on them. '*Aiyeeaaa!* Police is coming! Move faster, move faster.'

Cai and McQuinnie were straining: they had reached a slight uphill gradient and the platform had become extremely heavy. Wong threw his hands onto the elephant's blanket-covered butt and started to help them push.

Out of the corner of her reddening, sweat-and-salt-filled eyes, Joyce noticed that they were passing what had become one of her favourite haunts in her first week in the city: Mo Jo's, a café on their right. 'Special: cappuccino with warm sweet potato and chocolate cake with ice cream, RMB50', the blackboard said. She would have loved to stop for a drink – although she might have given the potato and chocolate cake a miss. Joyce loved shopping and it felt weird to her to be passing through one of the most famous shopping streets in the world and not be loitering in front of the shop windows. On the other side of the road there was a string of Shanghai boutiques. Several had plaques in the window saying: 'Shanghai Tourism Consumption Recommendable Spot'. She also noted, out of the corner of her eye, the Shanghai Elephant Dressmaking Shop. Not a very enticing name to women shoppers, surely – and almost as bad as Hong Kong's Hung Fat Brassiere Company.

'Let's go in here,' Marker shouted, indicating a shopping mall entrance on their right. 'Must not stop it moving. Must not lose momentum.'

'Okay, but hang on a minute,' said Joyce, pulling something out of her pocket. She had several of Megiddo's smoke capsules with her. 'I nicked these from the magic guy's box.' She pulled out the ignition strings and threw them onto the ground. They exploded silently and purple smoke started to pump out.

With a loud grunt, Marker pushed the platform at an angle and the structure moved to the right, sliding with a bump into a somewhat grubby air-conditioned shopping mall filled with displays of cheap clothes.

☯

A dense cloud of purple-pink smoke drifted over the pavement. Commander Zhang's police car roared past the shopping mall entrance, lost in the tinted smokescreen. The car emerged from zero visibility to see a street stall selling toys and camera film directly in front of them. The driver, Sergeant Xie Zhen Ting, slammed on the brakes but there was not enough time to stop. The car hit the stall before screeching to a halt and spinning around. A roar of anger erupted from the stallholder, who had stepped out of the kiosk to smoke a cigarette and narrowly missed death. She and several other vendors gathered around the police vehicle and started screaming through the window. Shanghai citizens might normally be respectful of the authorities, but using a car to mow down people's licensed businesses on a pedestrian precinct – that was well beyond the pale, even for uniformed officers.

Zhang wound down the window to bark at the crowd to move away. But an old man rushed over to the car. He grabbed her lapels and pulled them so that her face was centimetres away from his. 'Idiot girl – you should be locked up. You drove through my wife's shop. You will pay, cop or no cop.'

'Please get your hands off me.'

'You will pay, idiot police woman.'

'Look, I'm sorry about your shop. You will be compensated. You must file a claim.'

'You will pay now.'

'Just file a claim with—'

'You will pay now.'

The crowd took up his chant: 'Pay now. Pay now. Pay now.'

Commander Zhang bashed Xie on the chest with her gloved hand. 'Money,' she barked. Senior members of the paramilitary forces in China often carried wads of cash for paying stool pigeons, distributing bribes and so on. Xie peeled off a few notes and Zhang offered them through the window.

The old man spat on them.

The crowd expressed the same thought verbally: 'Give more. Give more. Give more.'

Zhang grabbed the entire wad of money out of Xie's hands and placed it in the man's hands. 'Here. Now move.'

No one moved, but Sergeant Xie yanked the car into reverse gear and started to move it, unceremoniously bashing people out of the way. 'Sorry,' Zhang shouted. 'Sorry. Please move.'

The crowd cursed them with their hands and mouths as the sergeant disentangled the car from the debris of the stall.

'I think they went into the building behind us,' said Xie. 'We can't follow.'

'That's what you think,' said Zhang. 'Switch places.' She elbowed him hard and slid into his seat, while he got out of the car and ran around the front to get into the passenger seat. Before he had even closed his door, she floored the accelerator and skidded the car back the way they had come, and then spun the wheel, driving straight into the shopping mall. Screams filled the narrow space as the car entered the main corridor and people threw themselves against the walls to let it pass.

'They can't be more than a few metres ahead of us,' Zhang crowed.

13

In ancient China, the fire people of Panyi Lake used to have contests. Whoever could extinguish the temple's ceremonial floating candles quickest without water would be the headman for the following year.

The Rong family used wooden caps on long sticks to snuff out the flames. They always won the contest.

The wise man went to the Xin family and said: 'I have a new invention. It is called the bellows. You can use it to puff air at each candle and blow it out.'

The Xin family found that it worked. They bought the bellows from the wise man.

When the Rong family heard about this, they said to the wise man: 'Make a very big set of bellows for us.'

The wise man did so.

On the day of the fire contest, the temple abbots made the biggest ceremonial fire the temple had ever had. They grouped dozens of large candles together to make powerful flames and set them afloat in the temple pond. The Xin family used their small bellows to blow them out one by one.

Then it was the turn of the Rong family with their giant bellows. But the more they blew air, the brighter and more fiercely the fire burned.

Blade of Grass, if the scale of your response does not match the scale of the problem, your problems grow instead of shrink. Killing a gnat with a rock hammer breaks your table.

Remember that a glass of water is a drink; enough glasses of water is a river; too many rivers is a flood.

From 'Some Gleanings of
Oriental Wisdom' by CF Wong

Wong was not just skinny, he was skeletal. Yet here he was, using his weight to move a mountain – almost *literally* move a mountain, for what was a sleeping elephant but a huge, climbable mound of organic matter? Part of him had still not finished pondering the miracle of how four smallish human beings could transport this tremendous weight. It was one of those principles that provided an interesting mental game for him to play with. It was like rolling a boulder down a hill. It was tough to budge it initially, but once it had begun to roll, it would move of its own accord – and you eventually have the opposite problem: how to stop it moving.

Inside the shopping mall the floor was flat, and the rolling structure had not lost its momentum. The polished granite surface allowed the platform, with its forty-eight rattling, screeching wheels, to move along swiftly. An obese, gaping security guard gave chase, blinking his eyes in disbelief.

Linyao, hoarse and exhausted, had joined the team pushing the platform, while Joyce took over the role of running ahead, shouting at people to get out of the way. She had no idea what the Chinese was for 'Please move aside, there's an elephant coming,' but it didn't seem to matter. Waving her hands and shouting: 'Out of the way, please, out of the way,' seemed to do the trick. Indeed, had she known the right Chinese words, they would probably have done more harm than good, as people would have stopped to point at the *lao wai* running along and trying to speak Mandarin. As it was, a trundling platform alone was unfortunately diversion enough to cause a significant number of people to stop and stare – even when it was heading directly towards them. 'Move, please, *move*,' Joyce shrieked at people who stood open-mouthed as they were about to be run over.

When fresh screams erupted behind them, Wong turned to see what was happening. A strange, low, tearing sound could be heard from the location at which they had entered – and shouts and cries from the same direction. He listened intently – and realised it was the stop-start revving sound of a car engine echoing off the hard-surfaced walls of the mall. '*Aiyeeaa, ji-seen*,' he said out loud. Those crazy Chinese police officers had driven their car into the building. They were driving along the corridor, nudging people out of the way. In a speeding vehicle, they would catch up in a matter of seconds.

He was about to share these thoughts with the others when an ear-splitting howl filled the shopping mall. The police chief had turned her siren on, causing a diatonic wail to echo around the building like the cry of a giant, wounded wolf. Looking back, Wong realised that it was a smart move, as people turned to see where the sound was coming from – and then leapt to safety in shop doorways as they saw the police car flying down the corridor at them.

'They're inside. Inside the building. They're coming,' Marker Cai gasped.

'I know, I know.'

The cart reached the end of the corridor and rolled into an open space – a high-ceilinged area used for temporary shows and displays, the current one being a school concert. Seconds after entering it, they heard Joyce's voice from in front: 'Whoa, guys, whoa. We have to do a left. We have to do a left.'

Wong swung his head around the corner of the mound of sleeping elephant to see that they did indeed have to slow down. There was a large escalator directly in front of them. They would have to move left or right, and the corridor to the left looked notably wider, since the right side had seats spilling out of a café, narrowing the space. But slowing down meant that the police would catch up with them for sure.

'Whoa, guys, you gotta stop and take a left,' Joyce repeated.

Cai raced round to the front of the platform and managed to slow its forward movement.

At that moment, the police car skidded into the main atrium of the mall. It was now just one hundred metres away from them. The vehicle halted and stalled as a woman with a mobile phone and a stroller crossed its path. The shopping mall's own security guard, who had been chasing Nelson and his group, was now in a state of confusion and was rushing towards the police car.

Wong found himself staring directly into the angry eyes of Commander Zhang, who was revving the accelerator, using the car engine's roar to scare shoppers out of the way.

'What do we do?' Marker said.

'This,' Wong replied, whipping the blanket off the elephant. 'Elephant,' he called out in Shanghainese at the top of his voice. 'Come and see the elephant. Real elephant, come and see.'

Two families walking nearby ran over to get a look, and were soon followed by a school party taking a short cut through the building on their way back from a museum. An elephant was much more interesting than anything else they had seen that day. People poured out of a nearby shoe shop and filled the corridor.

'Come see an elephant, elephant, real live elephant,' Wong continued to holler at the top of his voice.

The word spread. Two hundred children who had been forced to watch the school concert in the atrium leapt out of their plastic seats and poured into the internal avenue where the elephant lay asleep on its platform.

The police car, which had been creeping forward, came to a halt as a river of infants poured into the increasingly crowded space between it and the elephant.

Commander Zhang restarted the siren and honked the horn at the same time. She leaned out of the driver's window and shrieked: 'Out of the way! Move away, move away.'

But the rush to see the elephant had turned into a stampede.

Zhang and Xie stopped the car and scrambled to get out, aiming to pursue their quarry on foot.

'Time to go,' said Wong, and all four of them started to push again. Fired by the knowledge that they actually did have the strength to get this seemingly impossible weight moving, they quickly managed to start the platform rolling, this time angled to the left. The rolling show quickly recaptured its momentum, chased by dozens of small children, and was soon speeding down a mercifully straight corridor towards a source of bright light which they hoped was an exit.

Wong looked behind them. He saw that Commander Zhang had leapt back behind the wheel, leaving Sergeant Xie to manhandle the crowds of school children out of the way. 'Move, brats, move,' the officer shouted, waving his pistol and kicking at them.

Ahead of them, the light *did* prove to be an exit – albeit one with three stone steps. Nelson and his handlers raced out of the other side of the mall and bumped down the steps, losing a few wheels on the way. They emerged onto a dark, narrow street and, thanks to a slight slope on the pavement, rumbled straight into the road, knocking over a scooter rider and sending a number of cyclists spinning away. The platform swiftly moved past a startled traffic cop just as the lights changed and cars surged through the centre of the junction. With a mammoth effort from Cai, Nelson's trolley moved slightly to the right and neatly slid up a cambered kerb onto the opposite pavement.

They were in a shabby inner city residential area, rumbling slowly along a mottled, crumbling sidewalk. Staring at the ground as she pushed with both hands, Joyce's mind idly revisited a problem that had been in the back of it for several days: who chose the colours of the small bricks that made up Shanghai's sidewalks, and why on earth did he or she think that dull orange and Robin Hood green were a good combination?

☯

Jappar Memet snatched up the phone. 'Yeah?'

'Number fourteen calling for number one—'

'Yeah, yeah, wot is it? What's goin' on? Spit it out. Yer already on scramble.' He had been standing by with growing concern as his spies travelling with the Chinese and American

Presidents had reported that the two targets had failed to leave the Shanghai Government Building and head to the Grand Theatre on schedule. And a team member who had a vantage point in Renmin Square reported that American and Chinese guards at the theatre were using their walkie-talkies a lot and running back and forth. Something was afoot.

'We been rumbled,' number fourteen whispered. 'The alarms have gone off. Everyone's going crazy. I'm trying to find out exactly—'

'It couldn't be our bloody operation. It must be somefing else. There's no bloody way they could have found out—'

'They have. I think they have. I heard someone say something about an elephant. They must have—'

Memet winced. 'Shite. No, no, nooo.' He gave a low, guttural moan. Everyone else in the room shivered and moved away. It was the sound he made when he was about to commit an act of violence: it might be against a sofa, a human being, a cat – you could never tell. If something serious had gone wrong with Operation Px2, he would be furious beyond imagining. They had spent a year meticulously planning this caper and thought they had covered every base.

Memet pulled himself together and put the handset back to his ear. 'Wot's 'appenin'?'

'I don't know. I don't know anything. The alarms all went off and then everyone started running around like crazy. My unit has been ordered to recheck lists A to C of the venue security checklist. But one of the guys said it was useless, because the thing has already been called off and Px2 has been diverted. But I heard someone in the corridor of Unit J-7 talk about an elephant. That's what he said – something about finding the elephant. The girl has run off with the elephant and they can't find them. They've got to have – that can only mean—'

'Who? What girl?'

'I don't know how it happened. Some girl came in here and

242

told them about it. She was young, maybe twenty or so, wearing a yin-yang necklace. She looked like a hippie.'

'Wong's assistant,' Memet growled. 'The feng shui people from the restaurant.' But how on earth could they have thought of looking inside a performing animal? 'They must've found it. Shit. Call C-6 when you have any more information.'

He turned to Dilshat. 'They've rumbled us. How, how, how?' The wineglass in his hand shattered. He flung the pieces down onto the floor. The wine stain on the carpet was joined by drops of blood from his palm. 'Somebody leaked. Somebody talked. Somebody *stole my bloody elephant.*'

Dilshat asked: 'Where are the targets?'

'Diverted. Don't matter. I'm gonna find 'em and kill 'em. But I'm addin' someone else to the list.'

'Yeah?'

'Yeah. We're gonna find those feng shui people and kill them, too, as slowly and painfully as we bloody can, awright?'

14

In 56 BC, Emperor Xuan of Han and Warlord Gao were due to send their champions to battle with each other. The two fighters were evenly matched.

During the training sessions, Emperor Xuan constantly criticised his champion, saying: 'You cannot win. You are soft as water, yielding as mud. I have no hope.' The fighter knew this was not true, but could not answer back. He learned the skills of patience and forbearance.

Warlord Gao praised his champion day and night and expressed confidence he would win. The man became proud and haughty.

On the day of the fight, the two champions prepared for the battle.

This time Emperor Xuan sneered at his opponent's man. 'He cannot win. His mother was a goat and his father a stick.'

The opponent, who was used only to praise, became red in the face and shook with fury.

In turn, Warlord Gao was rude to the Emperor's champion. 'Your mother was a monkey and your father a stone.'

But the Emperor's man, patient as an ox, shrugged it off.

When the battle started, the enraged opponent attacked in a fury, leaping into action with sword and fists flying. But Emperor Xuan's champion used strength, strategy, wisdom and calm, and won an easy victory.

Blade of Grass, anger is a sword with a blade for a handle. It damages the user before the victim. Do nothing in anger. If you need to show righteous indignation, wait until the anger is gone, and replace it with dissembled anger, which you can control.

The roads south of Nanjing Dong Lu were narrow but
considerably less traffic-choked than the main thoroughfares.
Yet there were plenty of obstacles to surmount. Desperately
looking over their shoulders, they trundled their rattling,
juddering load past endless roadworks in which teams of
men shovelled hot, steaming tar into wide holes as if they
were feeding hungry dragons.

Wong shouted to the team to turn left. He had pulled out his
lo pan and was looking at the compass needle. 'East, we need to
go due east.'

They turned into another road – and then found themselves
on a gentle downward slope. It was a relief to have gravity on
their side to start with, but they soon found Nelson and the
trolley threatening to run away from them.

'Whoa!' said Joyce, who was jogging ahead. The trolley
started to speed forward and was nipping at her heels; she had
to jump out of the way. She turned and warned her team mates:
'We're going seriously downhill. This could be bad news.'

'Hold tight,' Marker Cai warned. 'Try to slow it down.'

They tried from both sides to arrest the platform's acceleration but it was no use. Its wheels roaring, the trolley raced down
the slope increasingly quickly. Joyce couldn't keep up. She fell
onto the path and scraped her legs. Cai leapt up onto the
platform and rode it down the hill as if it were a giant
skateboard.

It reached the bottom of the slope, narrowly missing a family
having a picnic supper on a bench, and started up the slope on
the other side. When it was halfway up it ran out of momentum
and slowed down. Cai jumped off and caught hold of it as it

245

came to a halt. Joyce, breathless, reached him and started to help. Between the two of them, they managed to stop it sliding back down the hill, but they did not have the strength to push it up – not one millimetre. It was a gentle slope, perhaps only a few degrees off the level, but it was a slope none the less. Their chances of holding it steady seemed low – and the probability that they could shift it forward was zero.

'Now what?' said Cai.

'Uh. I don't know. Let's just hold it here for a while,' Joyce suggested. Since there was nothing else they could do, that became The Plan.

After barely ten seconds, her muscles ached so much it seemed as if her arms were on fire. She felt each separate muscle group burning in her upper body – the trapezius, the deltoids, the triceps and biceps ached, throbbed and started to tremble. But she didn't want to show weakness in front of Marker so she gritted her teeth and rearranged her feet to improve her position. It had little effect. She felt her side of Nelson's platform start to slip backwards – first just a centimetre, then two, then three.

'Hold on, Joy-Si,' her companion said, smiling at her. 'Try to hold on.'

The warm gaze from his boy-band face with its straight, floppy hair gave her added strength, but it was a hopeless task. 'I don't know . . . I don't know how long I can hold it.' The platform began to creep back downwards, pushing the two young people with it. They heard footsteps behind them as their older companions caught up with them.

Linyao arrived first. She wedged herself between them and helped take the strain. And then Wong arrived. He was skinny but wiry. Between the four of them, they managed to stop it moving back down the slope – but they still didn't have the strength to inch it forward.

An unspoken state of stalemate was declared. Four human beings pushed one way. The force of gravity pulled the other way. Force met resistance and each balanced the other.

'We're stuck,' said Joyce, who had a talent for stating the obvious. 'For a bit, anyway.'

Wong, his arms stretched on either side of his head, palms against the elephant's blanketed flank, thought about the situation. They were neatly balanced at the moment, a classic yin and yang of forces moving in opposite directions. But one side was human and imperfect and transient, so would get tired. On the other was the force of gravity, which was none of those things and would inevitably win the battle. He imagined the thought must have struck all of them, as no one was speaking.

'*Wei?*'

He heard a woman's voice behind him. Half turning his head, he saw the family they had almost run over at the bottom of the hill. Following out of curiosity, they had come to see what was going on.

The six of them – a typical urban Shanghainese family of five adults and one child – stood as mute observers for a minute. And then more passers-by stopped to have a look.

And then another family came along, walking from the other direction.

Eventually, a small child snuggled in between Wong and Cai and tried to help them push. It was an encouraging note, although she was too tiny to make any difference. Yet her decision to help changed the attitude of the crowd. It was one of those fairytale moments. Another small boy joined the team pushing the platform, and then so did a woman, and then a man. Then the crowd surged around the platform, somehow deciding without discussion that this should be a community effort. The elephant-on-a-trolley needed to get moving again, over this slope, and if it took the strength of twenty-five or thirty people, then that was what would be provided.

'Thank you, thank you, thank you,' Joyce said in English, and then she tried it in clumsy Mandarin: 'She'air, she'air, knee.'

'*Sha-ya-nong,*' Wong added in Shanghainese.

With the crowd pushing and pulling, Nelson's trolley started moving steadily up the hill.

'Thank God,' said Linyao.

Joyce, pushing until the veins stood out red against her temples, was totally breathless. She turned her head to Wong. ' Why – did – you – tell – us – to – come – this – way? Where – does – it – lead – to?'

Cai said: 'This road leads to The Bund – a very busy place. I think no open space here.'

'Yes,' said Wong, 'but look what is after it.'

They reached the top and felt the helping hands evaporating away, leaving the original team of four progressing at a steady pace. The trolley was now moving along the east end of Jining Lu, a narrow road which fed directly into the wide stream of traffic that ran in front of the line of tall, ancient mansions known as The Bund.

Joyce looked over the elephant into the middle distance and her expression changed as she realised what Wong meant. 'Now – there's an idea,' she gasped, her face brightening.

Ahead of them, on the other side of Zhongshan Dong Lu, the main road that skirted The Bund, was the Huangpu River.

☯

Dilshat was trying to sound confident but he put so much effort into wringing his damp hands that an observer might have thought there was one of those tiny airline face flannels in them. 'The US Secret Service people are after 'em. And the People's Armed Police. I fink we can leave it to them. They ain't going to get very far.' He was sitting, hunch-shouldered, on the edge of the sofa, sheltering from the storm in the room. A massively destructive force, in the shape of Jappar Memet's temper, was careering hurricane-like around the suite, knocking over furniture, and Dilshat now knew that it was only a matter of time before humans – perhaps even him – would be added to the list of items that were seriously damaged or even totalled. Dictionaries tell us that the word *mad* has two meanings – angry and insane. In reference to Memet, it was a single concept.

'Not bloody good enough,' the activist leader growled, sweeping a vase off the shelf and watching it shatter on the floor. 'They'll just lock 'em up. I want Wong found and killed. No, actually, I wanna do it meself. With me own bare 'ands. No one screws up my plans and comes out alive – not that my plans have been entirely screwed. They'll just 'ave to be revised, that's all.'

Dilshat knew his boss had a pathological hatred of admitting failure in any way. Projects never collapsed. They merely evolved and needed revision.

The scholar nodded subserviently. 'You always said you expected that we would 'ave to revise plans as we went along. So in a way, the fact that we 'ave to completely change the plan means that it is goin' exactly accordin' to plan, right?'

'No plan survives first contact with the enemy. Who said that?'

Dilshat caught the eyes of the other two men in the room. Both looked blank. Scared, but blank. 'No one said anyfing, boss.'

'No, it's a quote, morons. Napoleon, I fink. Or what's that geezer's name? Churchill.' He moved swiftly across the room, snatched Dilshat's binoculars and raised them to his eyes, despite the fact that they were on a leather strap around the scholar's neck. Yanked upwards by his chin, he rose awkwardly and stood at an angle to accommodate his boss.

There was nothing relevant to see outside the hotel window, but Memet had a hyperactive need to keep doing something, even while he was just thinking. 'Right, this is the plan. We'll let those goons take Wong and 'is partner into custody. Then, after a suitable pause, we find them and wipe 'em out. I'll fink of a suitably poetic way to dispatch them later. In the meantime, while everyone's distracted and running around like 'eadless chickens, we're going to find and kill Px2. We're gonna have to be a bit creative.'

'Sounds good to me.'

'Yes, yes, yes, yes, yes. We'll give chase. That's it.' He grinned. A classic manic-depressive, Memet was suddenly overjoyed again. All he needed was reassurance that he would eventually get his way. How easy life was when you had enough people, money, imagination and self-delusion to continually revise your goals. Large numbers of well-trained staff, flourishing pacts with like-minded groups, and a generous spattering of yes-men to keep the general feeling of the team positive: those were the assets that megalomaniac-run organisations needed to maintain.

And, of course, a few spies, so one could track one's victims down. It wasn't that difficult when you had contacts high up on the inside of organisations. There were passionate vegetarians everywhere. 'Present location of Px2?' he snapped.

An operative sitting by a computer on the other side of the hotel room rapidly pounded a command which sent a ping to Contact YW-32b – no voice, just an undetectable signal sent from one machine to another.

The computer showed a GPS-type map with a moving red dot on it. Memet looked at it and nodded. 'And now I know just where they are. Let's move it, guys.'

☯

Wong and Cai were deep in consultation. They needed to pool all their knowledge to get from where they were to the river – precisely one hundred metres ahead of them. The problem was that Shanghai was a sinking city, which gave rise to a particularly bizarre topology. The Bund was built entirely on an unstable foundation of mud. Its first major architects soon realised that they had to construct buildings with their front doors two metres in the air. By the time the buildings were finished, the front doors would have sunk to ground level.

Much of the city on both sides of the water stood on what were originally mudflats. As a result, the Huangpu River ran at a considerably higher level than the ground level of the city around it. Tall walls had to be built and rebuilt to line the water channel – otherwise it would simply flood the space on either side of it.

From the street level of The Bund, you don't really see the water itself. You perceive the river by the raised embankment, the lines of tourists taking photographs, the huge gap where there are no skyscrapers, and the occasional masts or funnels of tall ships passing through. People who wanted to see the actual water had to climb staircases that led to raised promenades filled with tourists and tiny green and white stalls with Fujifilm written all over them.

But how could a group of individuals wheeling a sleeping pachyderm get to the water? There was no way they could use the staircases everyone else used.

'Only one way,' Cai said. 'We cross the road – there's a break in the divider fence down there – and then move south. Then we slide into the parking section in front of the shops.'

'There are openings at ground level there, I think,' Wong said.

'Yes. They lead to the floating restaurants. That way we can get all the way to the river without any steps. I think that's the only way.'

'Come.'

Their route agreed, they set off. Although the traffic was congested, there was just enough slack in it for Cai to lead their progress. Fortunately, he was experienced in negotiating with drivers to leave space for heavy loads intruding from side lanes. With some difficulty, they managed to guide Nelson's trolley across Zhongshan Dong Lu to the waterside. Then they had to find an opening in the fence that marked off the car park and trundle the trolley through the vehicles to the turnstile area. Fortunately, there was a strip which had no barriers and had been left open to accommodate large cargo items. Reaching the water's edge, it was time for Marker Cai to make complex, harried negotiations to see if any of the boats would take them.

During this pause, Joyce took the opportunity to get her breath back. She cupped her hands behind her head – and was horrified at the huge wet patches under her armpits. How she must stink. What she would have given for a shower, or a dip in a clean, blue hotel swimming pool! There seemed to be not much chance of such a thing in the immediate future. She tilted her head back, arching her spine forward to get the kinks out. There was a slight breeze coming from the north which refreshed her. She straightened her aching back and gazed at the fast-flowing waters in front of her.

The Huangpu was a big river. It was wide – easily half a kilometre across, and seemed equally broad for as far as they could see to the south and north. It flowed serenely, majestically in front of them. Across from them was the futuristic half-city of Pudong, an architectural jumble of science-fiction structures, a space city designed by Walt Disney cartoonists. This contrasted dramatically with the architecture on their side, which had the stately splendour of streets lining the Thames or the Seine. When all this was over, she really must come back to this spot with a camera, she decided.

Next to her, Wong stood on the edge of the dock and inhaled deeply. It wasn't just the polluted air that he sucked up into his wide, flat nostrils. It was the whole scene. He expanded his bony chest and breathed in the entire river, the cargo boats, the floating restaurants, the distant east Shanghai cityscape, the massive cumulonimbus clouds hanging in the sky, the rotting mooring posts, the rusted chains, the acrid smell of burning oil, the muffled chug of shipboard engines, the squawk of birds, the yelp of an invisible dog, the whine of a pop song coming from a radio on a bench next to a kissing couple half a kilometre away.

He looked to his right, south down the river. The Huangpu goes through a number of styles (a 1980s interior designer might have said 'colourways') on its eighty-five-kilometre journey to the East China Sea, and this particular stretch was slightly south of the portion beloved of postcard-makers and guidebook publishers. As one proceeded south, the river started to become more practical and functional and far more characteristic of the Huangpu's true personality. In the distance, he could see a busy dockyard loading bay. Wong knew that whether they went south or north, they would float past clusters of old-fashioned sampan-dwellings and boatyards where people crawled antlike up and over small beached ships, plastering over cracks in wood and fibreglass. On their left, to the north, was the opening of Suzhou Creek, a not-very-attractive tributary where brown water surged in a solid channel through a gritty area of crumbling buildings. Ahead of him, the main waters of the Huangpu itself were medium crowded, with a steady stream of cargo and pleasure vessels moving in both directions, but it was not log-jammed in the way that the roads were.

Wong stood with his hands on his hips and took in everything that could be seen and everything that could not be seen. As a feng shui master, he was powerfully aware of the enormous unseen power that moving water has on the human psyche. Rivers exactly like the Huangpu gave birth to every major city in human history. All the great cities of the world are river cities. River cities evolved separately and almost identically in all primitive cultures, on all inhabited continents on earth. Groups of dwellings – first huts, then hamlets, then towns, then cities, then massive urban conurbations – grew outward from the river banks, the source of life, the source of cities, the source of society, the source of the whole phenomenon of the six billion pieces of humanity.

This was the crime of modern man – the offence that he, Wong, personally had to fix. For man had forgotten that everything he did was in relation to the great river that gave birth to him, that watered him until he grew, that was the life force that ran through society's veins. It was the job of the few people who remembered – the feng shui masters, the *vaastu* readers, the few enlightened people among city planners and architects – to remind man to construct his life with due respect for the river at the heart of his city, be it via a tap in his kitchen, a well in his garden or the Huangpu at end of the road. This was a place where the literal Chinese meaning of the term *feng shui* – living in context with the winds and the waters – became crystal clear.

'This is perfect,' squealed Joyce. 'The river. We can take him out of town on the river – look, there's not much traffic. Well, not compared to the road, anyway. Well done, CF. You're brilliant.'

Wong snorted gruffly. Now to work. They had to get their cargo onto some sort of vessel. Fortunately, the ramps to the boats themselves were not too steep.

Joyce had suddenly recalled that time was running out and had started hopping up and down with anxiety and nervous energy. 'We need to move *really* fast. Which way do we go?'

Wong, looking at his compass, pointed to his left. 'North. That way is quickest to the open sea.'

Marker Cai finished his negotiations with the boat drivers. He had found a boatman who had a small freighter and was willing and able to take a heavy piece of cargo. The boat turned out to be a type of container-shifting lighter, and was moored next to a crane for lifting heavy weights. The dockyard workers were experienced at loading well-laden pallets onto ships, and speedily managed to slip various lines under Nelson's platform and attach it to the crane. Fortunately, Cai had managed to get a trolley with standard connections, and the technical side of the operation was achieved quickly and efficiently.

Some of the burly dockside workers (several of whom were women) peered curiously at the shape of the blanket-draped lump they were lifting, but everything was happening so fast that there was no time to ask questions. Where big chunks of easy money were concerned, dockyard workers did the job first and left awkward questions until after they had the money in their hands.

The platform bearing Nelson was hoisted into the air. The crane made strange and eerie howling noises as the metal strained to take the weight: it appeared that Nelson was heavier than anything it had ever lifted before. Most of the watchers, who were standing on the main deck of the boat, held their breath. But the crane managed to carefully swing Nelson over the central deck space and lowered him down next to two large crates which were already there.

As the pallet landed, the boat lurched violently away from the dockside and started to drop fast in the water.

'It's too heavy,' the boatman shouted in Mandarin. 'Get it off.'

'It's too heavy,' Cai translated for Joyce. 'We're sinking.'

The crane operator, more concerned about his crane than the boat or the people on it, declined to hoist the elephant back up into the air.

'Chuck some stuff out,' Joyce said, grabbing some boxes and flinging them over the side. Cai also started heaving boxes overboard, until they were all gone. The boat continued to rock frighteningly and still appeared to be sinking. The boatman screamed and shook his fists. 'Get this thing off.'

Then Cai picked up CF Wong and threw him overboard.

Joyce put her fist to her mouth. 'I don't think that was a – '

'Us, too,' Cai said, grabbing Joyce's hand and leaping over the side, pulling her with him. Lu Linyao squeezed her nose between finger and thumb and leapt in.

The four of them were soon splashing in the dirty water – with Wong creating the biggest waves, since he was scrabbling around in a panic, despite the fact that Cai was holding him firmly with one arm and grasping a truck tyre nailed to the side of the river bank with the other.

'Calm down, old man,' he said. 'I got you.'

Several dock staff had also thrown themselves off the side of the boat, and now they all bobbed in the water, looking anxiously at the lurching vessel. Gradually it settled. The sacrifice had been worth it. The boat had not sunk, although it sat extremely heavily in the water, with waves splashing worryingly right across the deck.

The boatman was throwing an apoplectic fit over the boxes that McQuinnie and Cai had thrown overboard. Apparently the items inside – illegal satellite television decoders – would not have their performance enhanced by being dipped in dirty water.

The young man managed to calm him down with a few shouted sentences.

'What did you tell him to make him quiet?'

'I told him that your boss was carrying a lot of cash and would pay him handsomely for all his troubles.'

Wong paused during drowning to screw up his nose to show his disapproval. Joyce sprang nimbly out of the water, and she and Cai dragged the feng shui master out. Wong was steaming and streaming. He shook himself, and then began to count the wads of wet money from his soaked envelope, anxious to retain some of it for himself.

Linyao climbed out by herself. 'What do we do now? Look for another boat?'

Cai shook his head. 'No. Take too much time. I think we have to stay with this one. Let's ask the boatman to take off all the other cargo.' He grabbed the entire wad of money out of Wong's hands and started counting it into the boatman's calloused palms. When the pile was high enough, leaving Wong just one or two notes, the old man nodded and waved to his crew to use the crane to unload the other two crates – which Cai said contained stolen BMWs – back onto the dock. The boat lifted itself slightly, and the float line painted on the side bobbed a few centimetres above the water.

'We must go NOW,' Joyce shouted. 'There can't be much time left.'

Sixty seconds later, they were travelling north along the river. Wong, McQuinnie, Cai and Lu sat near the tiny bridge cabin of the freighter, which was piloted by the boatman's wife (her husband had raced off to 'put the money somewhere safe', which probably meant his mahjongg bookie's cashbox, judging by the twinkle in his eye).

Joyce, peeling her wet hair out of her eyes, said: 'CF, can you ask the woman how long it will be before we get to the sea?'

Wong rose wearily to his feet and shouted the question to the skipper. After a short conversation, he passed the bad news to his assistant. 'She says it will take at least twenty minutes to get to the part of the estuary where it opens wide into the sea.'

He sat down, saying no more.

'How long have we got before – you know?'

'Ten . . . ish'

15

Dooley sat twitching in gross discomfort on the motorbike. His buttocks shifted from side to side and he wriggled and squirmed like a restless child. There was nothing wrong with the Electra-Glide's padded leather seat. He was uncomfortable because he was really sitting on a massive pile of shards of broken dreams. There is nothing sharper: not glass, not knives, not razor blades. Jagged remains of what had been a pretty impressive career stuck out in all directions under him, some of them painfully piercing his tight-muscled butt.

Somehow, impossibly, he had lost his prey. Yes, every agent loses somebody sometime. A bin Laden or a Saddam slip through your fingers. But to lose some young woman and an elephant? How could one lose an elephant? In his mind's ear, he could hear the committee of inquiry asking him: 'Agent Dooley, tell us once again: how did you come to lose the elephant?' More importantly, how could a man who had demanded a virtually unlimited operations budget, *and received it*, lose an elephant? He would be the laughing stock of the White House. Of America. Of the world. Imagine the head-lines. *Men in Black Lose Jumbo*. This was the end of everything: his prospects, his job, his life. Along with the girl and the elephant, the meteoric career of Acting Special Agent in Charge Thomas 'Cobb' Dooley had vanished.

It seemed impossible, but somehow, in the two hundred metres between Nanjing Dong Lu and Hankou Lu – an area of nothing but crumbling old blocks, grubby commercial build-ings and small alleys hung with washing – his quarry had disappeared into thin air. He had radioed every other bike and car on the road. All had lost the scent. There was no alternative now but to ask the Chinese for help. Perhaps Commander Zhang had managed to catch the sons of bitches on her Jurassic era bicyclette.

He climbed off Donaldson's Harley, stretched his spine and punched in her number so hard he nearly broke the phone.

'Zhang? It's Dooley. We lost them. Kin you see them?'

'Hello, Agent Dooley. I know where they are, although I can't see them from where I am at the moment. But I can see you.'

'You can?' Dooley strained to hear as a thrumming noise in the background started to get louder. 'Where are you?'

'Right on top of you.'

There was something in the tone of her voice that seemed to add 'as usual'. He wondered what she meant. But it quickly became obvious. As the juddering sound in the background rose to a deafening level, the Acting Special Agent in Charge looked up and saw a Chinese helicopter moving diagonally across the sky.

Bastards. They had a chopper. 'Uh, ah kin see you too, now. Where are they? Where's the bomb?' Better to refer to them as a bomb; it sounded less ludicrous, less Hollywood than 'where's the kid with the elephant?'

'In the river. East of where you are now, about half a kilometre, just boarded a small cargo-boat.'

'Thanks, Zhang. Ah owe you one. Detain them 'til ah get there.'

Silence.

Dooley reluctantly allowed himself to remember that she was not one of his staff, and should not be given orders. 'Ah mean, ah would be grateful if you cud locate them and stop them moving, Commander Zhang. If that accords with your plans, of course. Then we cud decide what to do with them.'

'I've already thought about that. Move fast, Special Agent Dooley. I wish you good fortune. Over.'

Damn. She knew where they were and it sounded like she

already had a plan. She rang off and he stabbed the buttons to talk to the Mobile Command Centre. A red light flashed on to show that he was in contact. He heard the receptionist's voice: 'This is—'

'This is Dooley. Ah need a chopper and ah need it now,' he barked, not wanting to waste time with niceties such as procedure. 'The biggest, fastest, fanciest one we got.' He knew that the Presidential party arrived with at least two choppers, and it was an established fact that the US led the world in aerospace technology, building the biggest, baddest, speediest, meanest, wickedest jet-fresh choppers in the universe. Now he would show two-wheeled Zhang what he could do.

☯

Commander Zhang's helicopter paused thoughtfully in the sky over downtown Shanghai for a few seconds before dipping to the north and then east as it followed a bend in the river.

She was proud of the fact that the Zhi-9 multi-role army support chopper, better known as the Z-9, was built by a Chinese firm, the Harbin Aircraft Manufacturing Company. Of course the original design had not been Chinese. It was a licensed copy of the French Eurocopter known as the AS 365N or, better still, by its nickname *Dauphin II*. But the percentage of Chinese parts had risen steadily and was now over 70 per cent. So the aircraft were Chinese, in a very real way. The PLA had more than one hundred and fifty of them in three models, and frequently loaned them to the People's Armed Police for special operations. Zhang had flown in them all. The naval variant Z-9C was the sleekest, the attack variant WZ-9 was the fastest, but she preferred the army multi-role variant Z-9, which was by far the most versatile. The craft she was in now, the Z-9B, was a good mid-size chopper, its thirteen-metre body small enough to be fast and flexible, but with enough room to carry a heavy payload of communications equipment, or up to eight troops. It had a maximum speed of three hundred and five kilometres an hour, and she told the pilot to step on it and use full throttle to get to the river as fast as possible.

'See that boat over there?' she said to him. 'Get us right over it, as quickly as you can.'

☯

A wise man's son was going on his first journey away from home.

His father said: 'Don't worry. We shall be in contact, even though we are far apart.'

The boy said: 'How can that be? I may be more than one thousand li *away from you.'*

The wise man pointed to the sky. 'At noon every day, look up at the sun. I shall do so at the same time. It will be our go-between.'

The boy said: 'Can the sun really carry messages between us?'

The wise man said: 'Yes. When I think it is time for you to come home, I will wink at the sun and ask the sun to wink at you.'

The boy set off, and every day at noon he looked up at the sun and felt his father looking at the same sun, many li *away.*

Two weeks later, there was an eclipse. The boy said to himself: 'The sun is winking at me, passing on a message from my father. Now it is time to go home.'

But halfway home, the boy fell sick and could not move.

The sun saw this and winked at the boy's father.

The wise man, realising that no second eclipse was scheduled, raced to the boy's rescue.

Blade of Grass, pretend you can commune with nature and soon you will be able to.

As Luo, the sage of the Plain of Jars wrote, 'Be not afraid of things that make you grow. Fear only when you are not growing.'

From 'Some Gleanings of
Oriental Wisdom' by CF Wong

The boat was *slow*. It was a divine snail, walking in sleepy slo-mo over the surface of the water. It ambled. It strolled. It stopped and scratched its butt, spun around a bit in the current, and then chugged along a bit more. It was in no hurry at all. Because, hey, it couldn't go any faster, so why sweat? It would get there when it got there, and no one could do anything about it.

Wong and McQuinnie were sweating, despite the stiff wind blasting sideways across the river. The operation was running out of time. The feng shui master kept stealing glances at his watch. There was not the slightest chance that they would be able to get to the open sea by the time the bomb blew up. They needed yet another plan. They would have to choose a spot somewhere in the river itself for the explosion – and they would need to get themselves well clear of it.

His eyes darted from side to side, looking for a space that was relatively unoccupied. But the river just did not seem to get any wider – and every inch of both banks were covered with buildings, whether dwellings or godowns of some sort. Even worse, there were always people in the water around them. On some reaches, the banks were lined with wooden boats parked for the evening – what Wong called 'family boats', in which water-people spent their lives in tiny, damp, creaking rooms. Then there were the boats that nudged past them one way or the other – an unending stream of junks, sampans, water-taxis and cargo-carriers moving around on business or for pleasure. There was no stretch of even a few metres where he could imagine a major explosion taking place without sinking at least one boat and killing or injuring people.

'*Cheese*. You know that book, *Slow Boat to China?* It must have been written about this boat. How far now till we get to the sea?' Joyce asked, her voice little more than an unhappy sigh.

'Twenty minutes at least, I think.'

'And how long have we got before – you know?'

'Eight minutes. No, seven and a half.'

'What are we going to do?'

Wong turned to face her. 'I think now only one thing we can

do. Stop the boat. Tell everyone to go away from us. And then pull the plug.'

'What do you mean?'

'You mean sink the boat?' Cai asked.

'We can't do that,' Joyce objected. 'Nelson will drown. He'll drown in his sleep. That would be awful.'

Wong cursed in Chiu Chow – a dialect that he hoped none of the people listening understood. Stupid *gwai mui* cares more about the elephant than about humans. 'If we sink boat, elephant will drown. He will be dead before he explodes. That is more kind to him than letting him live until he explodes.'

Joyce looked doubtful.

Cai didn't like the plan. 'If we sink the boat, someone will have to pay for a new one.'

All three turned to Wong, who adopted a don't-look-at-me expression and found something to stare at on the eastern shore.

Linyao held up her palm. 'Hang on. Another problem with this scheme. If we tip him into the water, he'll probably wake up – the shock of cold water, the falling sensation.'

'So?'

'Elephants can swim. They can even use their trunks like snorkels.'

'He'll probably swim after us. He likes me,' Joyce said.

Linyao agreed. 'He'll swim after our boat until the bomb goes off. Bang – right up our butts.'

'Ouch,' Joyce said.

The feng shui master pretended he was not listening, but Ms Lu's words worried him. He did not like the sound of this. A massive swimming bomb following him around at heaven knows what speed while he was stuck in a slow-moving boat in the middle of the Huangpu River – not a pleasant notion at all. 'Okay. I think we need a different plan.' Trouble was, he couldn't think of one.

He turned to the boatwoman and spoke in Shanghainese. 'Where does the river get wider? Is it soon?' Please let it be soon.

'Yes, very soon,' she said.

'Six, seven minutes more?'

'No. Maybe thirty-five minutes more.'

Wong grimaced. It was madness to rely on this woman's estimates, as she appeared to be making up numbers as she went along. The only thing he was sure of was that it would take much longer to get to the sea than was available to them.

Suddenly the chugging noise of the boat started to change tone. The engine coughed once, and then twice more. The rhythmic thudding started to slow down. The boatwoman did nothing, nor did she looked concerned. But everyone else did.

'What's happening?' Wong asked.

'Run out of petrol,' the boatwoman replied. 'Never keep much in the tank. Petrol so expensive these days, you know. Carrying so much heavy weight uses up petrol faster. You give me more money, I send for someone to bring us more petrol.'

Wong winced. This was a standard technique that some of the more crooked boat-owners used with tourists: they kept a minimum amount of petrol in the tank so that customers became adrift in the middle of the water for an hour or two, until they agreed to pay anything to get moving again.

The engine coughed one last time before becoming completely silent. The boat bobbed helplessly in the water, drifting forward almost imperceptibly on the current, and then came to a complete halt. The boatwoman dropped an anchor into the river.

'Don't do that,' Joyce shouted.

'She might as well,' Wong said. 'We're not going anywhere.'

☯

Command Centre broke the news to Agent Dooley that the most powerful helicopter was already taken. While Lockheed Martin put the finishing touches to their current big-budget operation, the rotorcraft equivalent of AirForce One, to be known as the US101, the Bell supercopter they had brought was playing the role of official Topchop. His contact at Mobile Communications filled him in: 'The SecDef ordered the Topchop to be used to take POTUS and the Chinese Prez to an unidentified location, as they say.'

'POTUS and the Chinese Prez together?' Dooley was amazed.

'Yeah. Kinda cute, isn't it? Our side had the better vehicle, their side had better information on where to take shelter against a major bomb attack, so they decided to join forces. Apparently they had already prepared this joint escape as one of the options in the security manual for the meeting.'

'It's still weird.'

'It was the SecDef's idea. Think about it. If the American forces and the Chinese forces separate and both go on maximum defcon alert to protect their Presidents, then we've practically got a situation where everyone's on a war footing. Doesn't bear thinking about. One tiny slip or misunderstanding on either side and everything goes *ka-boom*. End of the world, more or less literally. But if both sides team up against a common enemy – these people scattering hidden bombs – then the whole thing has a different flavour. It's us against them. Brothers in arms. All in all, this incident could end up being positive for US–Sino relationships.'

'I guess it figures,' the agent growled. 'What other choppers you got?'

'You can have the number two. It's a UH-60. It's already in the air, somewhere over the park. I can probably divert it to you within a couple of minutes. I guess we'll have to land it on the pedestrian precinct.'

The Command Centre operative was as good as his word. Just over two minutes later, Thomas Dooley was climbing into a Sikorsky UH-60A, better known as a Black Hawk. He was happy. Now he felt powerful. The chopper might have been an old-fashioned model – it was first developed in 1974 – but the Hawk had never been bettered, although there was much talk in military mess-rooms of a new Bell attack chopper taking over the prime spot.

Dooley had been in a Black Hawk only once before, but he had never forgotten the feeling of speed and power it gave him. Normally the US Army's frontline utility helicopter used for air assault, air cavalry and aero-medical evacuation units, it was infinitely modifiable. Considerably beefier than the Chinese helicopter Zhang was in (oh yeah!), the Hawk was designed to carry eleven combat-loaded assault troops, and was capable of yanking seriously heavy equipment into the air: a 105mm Howitzer and thirty rounds of ammunition. It was three tons of pure machismo.

'To the river an' don't spare the horses,' Dooley told the pilot. This was his chance to grab his life back out of the bonfire. He knitted his fingers together in a gesture of supplication and would have prayed, had he been able to think of anyone to pray to.

16

'I hate to add to the bad news,' Lu Linyao said, 'but I'm going to anyway. I think someone's caught up with us. Look.'

They turned around to see something buzzing in the air a long distance away, approaching from the southwest, following the curves of the river. It was moving at high speed and evolved quickly from a dot into a military helicopter. Marooned in their floating prison, there was nothing they could do but watch as it caught up with them. Within seconds it was hovering right over their heads. A force eight gale blasted over the boat and whipped the blanket off the elephant. It danced in the air like a ghost freed from a coffin before spinning into the water, where it lay pullulating with the waves.

A female voice boomed down in English from the helicopter. 'This is Commander Zhang of the People's Armed Police. Stop moving and pull over, or we will fire.'

Wong clambered with some difficulty onto the roof of the boat's cabin. 'Already we have stopped,' he shouted. 'Can you not see? Don't shoot, please.'

Joyce scrambled up next to him. 'Let me talk to them. We need to get them to help us,' she said. 'There's a bomb in this elephant. A big one. There are loads of people around here. Families and tourists and boats and dockworkers and stuff. You gotta help us move him. Loads of people are going to get hurt. You have to do something.'

The same phenomenon that they had seen on land was happening on the water. News that there was a drifting lighter containing a strange, monster-shaped piece of cargo and a *lao wai* had quickly gone round the river community. Clearly something extraordinary was happening. Maybe a Hollywood movie was being filmed. Now that the blanket had blown away to reveal a genuine monster, the excitement was palpable. Large numbers of people were approaching the boat. They came in sampans, in junks, in rowing boats, in speedboats and some in a variety of coracles. Fisherfolk and dockworkers from two or three kilometres up the river were swapping the news and jumping into vessels to have a quick look. Have you heard? There's a circus in the middle of the water. It was the most excitement the north Shanghai river community had had for years.

Within minutes, flotillas of boats were heading towards Nelson and his crew from every direction.

Wong looked at his watch. Barely five minutes to go.

☯

'Shall I shoot them?' the pilot, a young man named Jin Peng, asked.

'Of course not, you idiot,' Commander Zhang snapped. 'There is apparently a large explosive device there. Blast them and you will probably kill half the boat people in the river, plus blow us out of the sky.'

'What shall we do?'

'Just hover. The boat seems to have stopped moving. They aren't going anywhere. I want to hear what they are saying.'

She opened the door of the chopper and strained to hear Joyce, who was still on the roof of the boat's cabin.

'This bomb will go off in a few minutes,' the young woman said. 'We need your help. Our engine has run out of petrol. Can you send down a line and pull the boat along or something? Please. Otherwise a lot of people might die. Please. We need—'

But the rest of her words were drowned out by a low-pitched rumble. A large American Black Hawk helicopter appeared above the tops of the buildings from the south and also moved to a hovering position over the water.

Down below, the young woman on the boat redoubled her pleas, gesturing first at one chopper and then at the other. 'Can someone please do something? Does anyone up there speak English?'

☯

'What do you want me to do? Is this an attack situation?' The Black Hawk pilot, whose name was Milo Peters, looked over to Thomas Dooley.

'Ah don't know. Ah really have no idea what our next move is. Gimme a second.'

'Are we talking enemy situation or hostage situation?'

'Neither. There's a bomb down there. Inside the elephant.'

'Geez. *In* the elephant?'

'Yes. Don't ask.'

A pause while Peters took in this information. 'Is bomb disposal on its way?'

'No. No time. It's due to go off in a few minutes.' Dooley looked at his watch. 'Mebbe four–five minutes, tops. We need to sort this one out ourselves. Don't ask me how.'

Peters pulled at the joystick, changing the angle of the chopper in a bid to get a better look. 'We could order the people to move and then blast the boat with an air-to-ground – a small one would be all it would take to sink that boat. Sinking the bomb may stop it going off.'

'Too dangerous,' Dooley said. 'Look at them gawking crowds. It would take half an hour to get everyone to move their boats away. Second, we shoot that boat, we'll likely set the bomb off. We have no idea how big it is. It may be a toy. It may be a biggie.'

He swung the door of the chopper open and stared down at the scene below.

Joyce's voice drifted up to him. 'Come on, you guys. You gotta help us. This bomb is gonna blow in a few minutes. It could kill loads of people. We've done all the work so far. Now it's your bloody turn, if you'll pardon my French.'

Dooley, dropping his visor against the sunlight, looked across the sky at the Chinese Z-9 hovering nearby. 'Whatever we're gonna do, we better do it quick.' He realised that Commander Zhang must already have been here for a couple of minutes, and probably already had a plan: she'd hinted as such, earlier. His keen sense of competition gripped him. He was not going to let some blasted Chinese female get the better of him, even if she was a hell of an impressive woman. *Especially* since she was a hell of an impressive woman. 'We gotta take the initiative before the Chinese do,' he said to Peters.

'And do what? Airlift people off the boat?'

'No.' Dooley spoke into his helmet mike: 'Command. Someone find out how much an elephant weighs, can you? It's urgent.'

'What? How—'

'I don't know how you find out. Phone the zoo. Use Google. Hey, no, Yahoo!'

'Ya who?'

'Look it up on Yahoo! I need the info quick. You got five seconds max.'

Dooley turned to the pilot. 'How much do you reckon that thing weighs?'

'I don't know, sir.'

'Can you guess? I mean, you're a helicopter pilot, you must be used to heaving big heavy things about, right? Can you estimate?'

'Yes, but . . . I've never had to move an elephant before.'

'What's the gross external payload on this baby?'

'Maybe eight thousand pounds.'

'I don't like the word maybe. It's not in my dictionary.'

'Okay. Eight thousand pounds.'

'So what would a lump like that weigh?'

'Maybe – I mean, I reckon it might weigh the same as a couple of trucks, at least, maybe three or four trucks.'

'So what's that, in pounds and ounces?'

270

'Ten to fifteen thousand pounds, maybe.'

'You're saying we can't lift it and whisk it out to some remote spot.'

'Yes, sir. That's exactly what I'm saying. No way could we lift that.'

The radio buzzed. 'Uh, Dooley? Yahoo! says seven thousand to twelve thousand pounds, but Google says the biggest one weighed twenty-six thousand pounds. Wikipedia says it depends whether it's African or Asian, but it could be up to six and a half tons.'

'Wassat in pounds?'

'Uh, I don't know.'

'Geez.' Thanks for nothing. Then a thought struck him. That Chinese vet woman, Ms Lu Ling-thing. She was probably down there on that boat with her young friend. She would know.

He switched his helmet mike to external loudspeaker. 'Ms Lu. How are you? This is Special Agent Dooley speaking from the US Black Hawk helicopter over your head. How much does it weigh? Repeat: how much does that elephant weigh?'

After a few seconds, a hard-to-hear reply came from a tiny voice. He couldn't understand what she was saying.

'Could you repeat your answer, please?'

'Four thousand, five hundred kilos,' came the reply from Ms Lu. 'Four thousand, five hundred kilos.'

Dooley cursed. 'How come every goddam nation on this planet counts in kilos and we count in pounds? What's wrong with them all?'

The pilot interrupted. 'Four thousand five hundred kilos is a lot. It's like ten thousand pounds. We'll never be able to lift it. Even if we were empty. We haven't got a hope.'

'Shit.' Dooley thought for a second and then turned back to Peters. He'd had an idea. 'What if we had two choppers?'

'If we had two choppers, we might have the payload capability, but it would be damn near impossible to coordinate the lift. Even in ideal conditions, it would be a stretch – but lifting something from a boat drifting in a harbour – it's a pipedream, sir, if you want my opinion, sir.'

Dooley radioed Zhang. 'Zhang? You there?'

Her voice came through the speaker: 'I can hear you, Agent Dooley.'

'There's a kazillion people in those boats there, and living on the river banks. We got to lift that whole goddam bomb and take it out to sea. It's going to blow in a few minutes. A lot of people are going to get hurt. Neither of us is going to be able to lift it on our own. What's the payload on your craft?'

'What are you proposing?'

'What's the payload on your craft?' Dooley repeated. 'That thing down there weighs four thousand five hundred kilos. It may well be more than I can carry. How much can you take?'

'That's classified.'

'We can do more than half of that. We can do eight thousand pounds. I think we may—'

'We can lift the other half.'

'We're going to have to work together. It's the only way. We're going over to the boat to drop our cables. Can you do the same? But we'll have to coordinate our movements very carefully, you copy?'

He knew that both choppers were going to have to get extremely close to the boat at the same time – a dangerous manoeuvre. The only way to accomplish it would be if they took different flight levels, with one flying much higher than the other. He decided that if he offered to take the lower and more dangerous level, Commander Zhang would feel comforted.

'We're going low – fifty to seventy-five feet. You take the higher plane, one twenty-five feet plus.'

Peters moved the helicopter. Dooley told him to drop steel cables down to the boat – and waited for his Chinese counterparts to do the same.

While Dooley was outlining his plan, Commander Zhang had already called her headquarters and asked them to send a second Z-9.

'You can have one, but it may take a few minutes, maybe ten,' military traffic control had replied.

'We don't have ten minutes. Is there anything in the air we can have faster?'

'I'll check. We'll send one as quickly as we can, but I can't promise anything. Over.'

'Over.' Zhang said nothing further, but her glances out of the window at the Black Hawk made Pilot Jin uncomfortable.

'If you are thinking—' he began. 'Commander Zhang. We are not allowed any joint manoeuvres with the Americans without direct permission from the Commission. You know that. If we need two helicopters to lift this item, we'd better wait until we have two Chinese helicopters.'

'There's not enough time. I'll take responsibility. The waters are crowded. We cannot allow so many people to die. My grandmother was born and died on a boat. Besides, the Commission has decreed that the Chinese President and the American President go into hiding together. So the two countries have already teamed up. We are just following their example. How much can we carry?'

'Externally? The official sling payload maximum is sixteen hundred kilograms. This souped-up model may be able to do a bit more, perhaps two thousand or two ten.'

Zhang did a quick calculation in her head. They could carry roughly half the beast each, but neither of them could do it on their own.

'We have no choice. Release the cable.'

☯

Joyce grabbed Wong's arm. 'Look. There's something hanging under that one. What is it?'

They all stared at the American helicopter, which appeared

to be dropping something. The noise level started to rise as the two choppers came close.

'I know what that is,' shouted Marker Cai. 'It's a steel cable.'

The two helicopters had between them dropped four cables, which Cai grabbed and expertly attached to retaining holes on the underside of the platform on which Nelson continued to sleep. Who would have thought that the most useful person to have around would be an experienced office removal man?

Dooley continued to shout down to them through the Black Hawk's external speaker system. 'Move it, guys, we got jest a few minutes before the bomb blows. We need to get her way out of range of all these people. Move-move-move!' He added: 'And by the way, kin someone tell us where the hell we should take it.'

Wong's face lit up. 'I know. I know where to take it. There's a bomb-proof cove near here. Northeast, fifteen or twenty kilometre only. Tsz Lum Cove. Very safe.'

Out of the back door of the Black Hawk, a rope ladder fell. 'Come on up.'

Wong stared at it in horror.

He turned to Cai, who nodded and said: 'It's for you. You have to go up there and tell them where to take it.'

He grabbed the bottom rung and tried to hold it steady. With enormous difficulty, and whimpering with fear, Wong clambered up the swinging ladder towards the chopper.

Rope ladders are like naughty children. The more you reach for them, the further they dart away from you. Wong's dangling left foot stretched out under him, probing for the rung which had swung away. *Aiyeeaa!* Eventually he froze in horror, finding it difficult to move in any direction. He had never felt so terrified. He was stuck on a string in the middle of the sky, there was a deafening noise above him and an about-to-explode bomb below. He must have done something terrible to deserve this. Lack of respect for the white elephant. Or for animals in general. That must be it. He must remember to be kinder to animals. Maybe this was punishment for ignoring Joyce's dictums about man's stewardship of all sentient beings.

Then he heard the American's voice shouting at him from somewhere above. 'Hold on tight. You don't need to move. Just hold on.'

There was no need to tell him twice. He was frozen with fear, unable to move, clinging to the rungs for dear life. Then he felt a sharp jerk on the ladder, and it started to vibrate before moving steadily, mechanically, hydraulically upwards – there was some sort of pulley system which retracted the entire ladder up into the helicopter. Thank Heaven. He looked up as the lower surface of the helicopter approached. Wong repeated the words of Mo Zhou in 479 BC: he was not really being snatched up into the sky. The world was leaping and jumping and dancing around him. He was really just standing still and the American helicopter was lowering itself onto his head.

As the feng shui master came within reach, Dooley grabbed the back of his jacket and yanked him into the cabin.

Wong, trembling with fear, fell sideways into the seat.

Below, Marker Cai checked the fasteners on the platform one more time before looking up to Dooley in the chopper. 'You take it now,' Marker screamed and raised his thumbs up.

In the Black Hawk, pilot Peters kept a radio channel permanently open to the Chinese Z9-B. 'Ready, Pilot Jin?' Dooley said.

The smooth reply came from Commander Zhang: 'We were ready a minute ago, Agent Dooley.'

With the two pilots carefully coordinating their movements, the helicopters gathered strength and gently rose, lifting the beast into the air.

The boat, suddenly bereft of the weight that had been holding it half underwater, heaved itself up with such violence that the lighter ones on board – Joyce and Linyao – were jolted off their feet.

From the floor of the now wildly rocking boat, Joyce

watched with her heart in her mouth as the two helicopters heaved Nelson into the sky. Then they moved rapidly towards the estuary opening where the Huangpu met the East China Sea.

'Maybe two minutes,' Marker Cai said. 'They better move as fast as the summer lightning.'

As the two young people heard the stuttering sound of the two helicopters disappearing ahead of them, they were surprised to hear a similar sound behind them – getting louder.

Joyce was the first to turn around and look up. 'Marker,' she said. 'There's another Chinese chopper coming this way. And it looks like it's dropping something.'

17

Wong pulled his wet *lo pan* out of his jacket pocket. 'That way, that way,' he said. 'There's a cove there. Tsz Lum Cove.'

'How far?' Dooley shouted.

'Not far. Very close. On the east side of a small rock in the Yangtze River estuary. Is the most sheltered place in the whole area.'

They flew away from the river due east overland towards the cove, and quickly came in sight of the sea, and several islands, some of which had steep rocks. There were other aircraft in the distance, apparently circling the area.

'Looks a bit busy to me – in the air, at least,' said Peters.

'No people live down there,' Wong said. 'Not on that island. No access. You can't get there without boat or helicopter. Thick stone cliffs behind. Bomb proof. Drop bomb there and then fly away quick-quick-quick. It can explode. No one will be hurt.'

Peters was maintaining open channels with Jin, telegraphing every coordinate change, however slight, before he made it. The two craft managed to move in tandem surprisingly well. 'We're doing it,' Peters said. 'I can't believe we're actually doing it.'

Within thirty seconds they were almost directly over the rocky cliffs. There were two bays visible. 'That one or that one?' Peters asked.

'That one, the far one,' the feng shui master said. 'There are cliffs on three sides so will hold explosion in.'

'I'll need to change angle.' Peters radioed details of the proposed adjustment in the flight path to pilot Jin. 'Yawing left, nor'northeast, twelve degrees.'

'Are you sure there's nobody there?' Dooley said, concerned that at least one boat seemed to be visible in the water nearby.

Wong said: 'A few fisherfolk in the sea only. Almost nobody knows about this cove except me – and the President of China. I told his security chief about it when they consulted me. Even I didn't charge them.' The feng shui man folded his arms proudly.

'Okay, we're nearly there.' Dooley turned to Peters. 'Get ready to release the load. We're going to have to do a coordinated drop and then escape at high speed.'

The two helicopters flew over the edge of the bay.

'Dooley here. Can you hear me, Zhang?'

'Yes, I can hear you.'

'Let's drop the cargo on three, as soon as we get over the beach. One. Two. Oh geez, what's that?'

A pair of fighter aircraft bore down on them, and two attack helicopters approached from another direction. 'Move away, move away,' came gruff instructions through the speakers. One of the craft fired a warning shot at them – there was a bright flash and a missile streaked past them.

'Abort! We need to abort – I'm moving forty – Jin, swing left, forty degrees, repeat, swing left forty degrees – hold on everyone,' Peters shouted as the Black Hawk banked steeply away and the Chinese Z9-B followed suit.

Dooley heard rapid speech in Chinese as Zhang and her pilot swung steeply to follow the Black Hawk.

Peters shouted into an open channel for the benefit of the fighter planes intercepting them. 'Don't shoot, don't shoot. We are aborting. We are aborting.'

'Move well away,' said the voice from the attack choppers. 'We are ordering a no-entry air zone covering two miles around this spot. Get out of range.'

Wong gripped the handles of his seat so hard his hands turned white. He was scared, but he was also outraged. What on earth was destiny up to? How on earth could quiet, isolated Tsz Lum Cove suddenly be full of army jets firing guns at anyone who approached? And why now, when they had urgent need of it? It was so unfair!

278

Dooley was worried that the abrupt movements had set the platform below them swinging, shifting the weight and making it difficult for the two pilots to keep their choppers steady.

'Sorry, you guys, okay?' he said to his Chinese counterpart.

'What is going on?' Zhang shouted. 'The sky here is full of Americans.'

'I don't know. I really don't know. There's half a squadron of aircraft keeping everyone away from that bay.'

Neither spoke for a few seconds. And then Zhang's crackly voice said: 'And I know why. Look what's down there. One of your American craft.'

Wong looked out of the window to his left. Sheltering on the sand was Topchop, the presidential helicopter, containing the Presidents of China and the United States.

The horrific truth hit the Acting Special Agent in Charge with the shock, and the stink, of a massive fish slapped in his face. They'd managed to bring the bomb to the precise spot where its targets were hiding. It was incredible that they had not simply been blown out of the sky without a word.

'Oh no,' said Dooley. 'Oh, no, no, no. Are we in deep shit.' His voice was a whisper as he took in the enormity of what they had nearly accomplished. 'We just tried to kill the President. The two Presidents. We tried to drop a bomb on the President of the United States of America and the President of China. The two most important human beings on earth. Oh shit.'

'We are in, as you say, deep shit,' Zhang agreed.

Peters said: 'We need to get right out to sea.'

Wong added: 'Quick, please, time's running out.'

The two pilots swapped details of the coordinates to which they were switching, yawed their craft to the east and headed straight out towards the open ocean.

☯

Joyce McQuinnie and Marker Cai were flying. Well, they were moving at high speed anyway and *sort of* in the air.

The second Z-9 chopper had dropped a rubber dinghy on the end of a steel cable just in front of their cargo boat. Guessing what was required of them, the two young people had dived off their boat, swum to it and climbed in. Commander Zhang had obviously told her colleagues to keep close behind them, and also to take custody of the other members of the group. By dropping a small vessel to them, the helicopter crew could do both things at once. Lu Linyao had hidden inside the boat cabin, deciding that she, as a government employee, was best keeping a low profile in this whole affair. Besides, now that they had succeeded in getting the bomb away from the city centre, she felt the main part of her job was done and she was desperate to get home and spend quality time with Jia Lin. Several years' worth of quality time, preferably in quiet, boring Vancouver, would not be too much.

The chopper had then picked up speed, dragging the rubber dinghy along the surface of the water. The pilots initially moved quite slowly, but had quickly picked up speed. After a couple of minutes had passed and the pilots saw that their two passengers were firmly strapped into the high performance marine police dinghy, they let the throttle out.

The dinghy was now flying along at high speed, bumping across the crests of the waves, spending more time in the air than on the water.

'This is kinda fun,' Joyce said, lying back in the dinghy, fine sprays of salt water reviving her spirits. 'Bit like a theme park ride. Wet rides – we call them log flumes or log fumes or something like that.'

'Yes,' Cai agreed. 'This is fun. Better even than go for coffee.' He leaned back too. They were travelling at speed, and the wind roaring into the boat meant that it was almost impossible to stay upright.

Joyce tingled all over. Two days ago she had been trying to think of a way to get to know Mister *Sigh* a bit better. Now here she was, zooming along the Huangpu River in a really cool

Mission Impossible mode of transport, and *lying down next to him*. This was so outrageous! This was amazing. This was incredible. Life was just like so totally, totally weird. As she felt his hard bicep against her, an expression of utter glee spread over her face. So what if she wasn't wearing makeup, her hair was a bowl of oiled linguine and she stank to high heaven? He was just as tired and dirty and sweaty as she was, and none of it mattered a jot to either of them.

He turned to her and smiled. 'This is . . . so strange,' he said.

She nodded. 'Like totally.'

She looked at his lips.

He looked at her lips.

She half closed her eyes.

He half closed his eyes.

They leaned towards each other.

Then he opened his eyes wide in fear. '*Aie*,' he gasped, sitting up and looking as if he had been stabbed.

'What is it? What's wrong?'

'I remember. Just around this corner is a bridge. A bridge. What will we do?'

They both sat up, the wet air tearing into their faces with the force of solid water. Through thin cracks in their almost-shut eyes they saw what Cai had just seen in his mind's eye: there was, indeed, a bridge ahead of them.

Cai turned to Joyce, fear in his voice. 'The pilot's not slowing down.'

'We'll smash into the bridge. Can you undo the cable?'

'I try.'

But as he leaned forward into the wind, the pilot's plan to get the unorthodox vehicle they were towing past the bridge became clear. The Z-9 chopper increased both its forward velocity and its height, and lifted the police dinghy high into the air.

'Whoa! They're gonna try and take us over it,' Joyce squealed.

The two of them screamed as their tiny dinghy suddenly rose high into the sky and literally flew over the bridge.

Joyce slammed herself back down onto the floor of the dinghy. 'I can't look. I can't look. How high are we? No, don't tell me, I don't want to know. How high are we?'

Cai looked over the edge. 'We're in the sky,' he said. 'Right up, up in the sky. *Wah!* This is better than theme park ride.'

'This is better than Disneyland.'

He turned to face her, lying stretched out in the bottom of the boat, strapped in with a seatbelt, high as a kite in every sense of the phrase.

Joyce looked at him and licked her lips. 'Marker.'

'Yes, Joy-Si.'

'Come here.'

❷

Anger, as Warlord Gao's champion discovered to his cost two thousand and fifty-five years ago, clouds judgement. And that is perhaps one of the key reasons why spiritual people will always defeat armed people in the long run. The brain is the deadliest device in any arsenal of lethal weapons.

Racing across the waters of the Yangtze River Estuary was a high-speed cruiser owned by the Mee Fan Supermarket Company. On board was the retail chain's estranged son.

Having located the two Presidents, Jappar Memet could have won himself a place in history, either small or large, by firing missiles at the helicopter in which they were hiding from his heavily armed ship. If he had hit the Topchop, he would have won himself the great prize he had craved for years – world fame for himself and his worthy cause. There would be no other major talking point in the world's media for weeks, months, years. He would appear in every history book to be written about this century. If he merely wounded the two Presidents or even just made them uncomfortable, he would still have put himself and his cause on the map indelibly.

But that is not what he chose to do. It was what he had been planning to do. And it was the reason why he had raced (in the family chopper he had kept on standby) to his armed cruiser and taken it out to sea to the place where his contact had told him the two Presidents were hiding.

But when he spotted his elephant being whisked away in a helicopter, he saw red. His beast. His bomb. His plan. That man Wong and his silly slacker girl. Those evil, murderous people who had spoiled both his noble schemes on a single day: ruined them both as each approached the point of success. He was filled with uncontrollable, raging fury. His heart thumped. He became blind, almost physically. He had trouble breathing. Clouds of anger obscured the fact that he had finally come within sight of the goal he had been moving towards for the past year with every fibre of his being.

'Bloody Mr Wong has now got 'imself an 'elicopter to take my elephant away from me,' he snarled to Dilshat.

'Forget him. Let's get the—'

'It's like he killed my baby.'

'What?'

'My plan. My plan was the child I've been nurturin' for years.'

'Jappar, we need to—'

'I'm going to shoot that bastard out of the sky. That's what I need to do. I need to do this. Gimme a minute. It probably won't take more than one shot. Then we'll get Px2, awright?'

Dilshat agreed. With Memet as a boss, there was nothing else one could do. He resolved to give up political activism after this and go back to studying religion – the more esoteric, obscure and lonely, the better.

☯

Special Agent Dooley was in a state of shock. No, it was worse than that. He had had so many stultifying shocks in a row this terrible day that his brain was seizing up. Part of his mind was saying that he had just been responsible for transporting and almost dropping a major explosive device onto POTUS and the President of China. The rest of his mind could not cope with this thought, and enclosed it in a little box which it set to one side, refusing to talk to it, look at it, or even admit it was there.

Next to him, below his visor, Peters' face was as white as a sheet.

Dooley spoke quietly: 'I thought things couldn't get worse, but I was wrong. They just did.'

And then they got worse still.

A loud crack shook the chopper, followed by another one. Someone was firing at them from sea level. Alarms jangled in the cockpit as bullets or small missiles roared upwards past them.

'Now they're shooting at us from boats,' the pilot said. 'Shit. I can't believe this.'

Dooley looked down. There was one vessel below them and it was not American. It couldn't be. It was some sort of large white speedboat. They had nothing like that on this trip.

'Must be Chinese forces.' He roared into the microphone: 'Stop them, Zhang, tell them we're retreating.'

'It's not ours,' replied Zhang. 'I think it's American.'

'It ain't ours.'

Another missile shot upwards, narrowly missing the Z-9, which tilted dangerously to one side.

Both choppers were now operating separately, causing the platform they were holding between them to swing wildly from side to side.

Peters tried to get the two craft back into line: 'Yaw left, fifty degrees, got it, after three?'

'Copy: yaw left, fifty degrees, after three.'

'One. Two – Jesus, now!' Peters shrieked as another missile fired from the boat clipped the end of the Black Hawk's 48-foot rotor, shaking the craft.

'Excuse me,' said Wong, looking at his watch. 'We have one minute before the elephant goes boom. Maybe less.'

Peters struggled to remain in control of the craft.

That was the moment when Nelson decided to wake up. Who knows what went through his mind as he found himself on a platform in the sky, being borne aloft by two noisy human vehicles? Whatever it was, he must have decided that he wanted to get a better view. With great effort, he rose to one knee – his front right knee. Then he added his front left knee, his back left knee and his back right knee, in that order. As the platform swung, he raised himself to a standing position. He glanced around. Everything was blue. There was a nice, cool breeze blowing. The fresh air was invigorating. His tail wagged, puppy-like. The medicine that had been pumped into his butt must have contained some sort of painkiller as well as a sleeping solution. He felt better than he had done for days. But where was he? Had he died and gone to heaven? He felt like he was in the sky. There was so much blue around – and clouds, white, fluffy, cumulus clouds.

The bad thing was that he felt a bit unsteady. It wasn't sleepiness or the medicine. It was the ground. He didn't like the way the floor was moving. It made him dizzy. He took one step backwards to steady himself. But, sad to say, there was no floor behind him for him to step onto.

☯

Joyce screamed as she saw the elephant fall out of the sky.

Their helicopter had lowered their dinghy onto the surface of the water with a rough but survivable bump and then jettisoned the cable. Whoever had decided that they should come along for the ride had obviously decided they had travelled far enough.

She and Marker sat in the boat, bobbing close to the coast of the Yangtze Estuary, and watched Nelson tumbling from heaven.

He descended slowly. Because it is rare to watch large, heavy objects fall – especially iconically large, heavy objects such as an elephant – it became an impromptu physics lesson. Which falls faster, a four-tonne bag of feathers, or a four-tonne elephant? The answer is that they fall at the same speed. Indeed, everything falls at the same rate, with a standard acceleration factor due to gravity of 9.8 metres per second squared, whatever its size or weight. This is what physics teaches us. And this is what physics taught Joyce McQuinnie and Marker Cai as they watched poor Nelson fall slowly from his platform in the sky down down down towards the water.

Towards the water? No. Wait. What was that below him? A boat. A boat between Nelson and the water.

He dropped from the heavens and landed, splintering the expensive-looking white cruiser to matchwood as he went down. But this didn't stop him. He was a heavy lump – 4,181 kilos, in fact – and the rate of acceleration he had gathered from falling 102 metres was considerable. Down he went, deep into the water, and down, down, pieces of boat all over him, down towards the seabed.

The two helicopters, suddenly freed of their heavy load, shot out of control – fortunately, both went upwards and away from each other, and both immediately jettisoned their slings, which gave the pilots a chance of regaining control.

Wong's watch had decreed that the bomb should explode in a minute or so. But his watch was wrong. He had purchased it cheaply in Shenzhen and it lost at least a minute an hour.

There was an explosion.

It was impossible to tell, without careful calculation, whether the bomb exploded on the elephant's way down, at the moment it stopped descending, a few metres from the seabed, or on its slow bounce back up towards the surface – but explode it did. That was evident from the tremor that ran through the sea and the land. That was evident from the huge underwater rumble that thundered from below the surface.

That was evident from the mini-tsunami – a wave two metres tall – that roared in all directions from the site of the blast. It was a big explosion. Jappar Memet's staff had done their jobs well.

The concentric rings of water moving outward from the matchstick remains of the Mee Fan Supermarket cruiser panicked people watching from the shore half a kilometre away.

The wave washed into the estuary, shaking the boats in the river and tipping Joyce and Marker out of their dinghy into the water.

They bobbed together in the cool blue sea.

'Poor Nelson,' she said, weeping as she trod water.

'Want a tissue?' said Marker, pulling a sodden pack of Tempo tissues out of his pocket.

'Thanks,' she sniffed, giving him a tearful smile.

'They're a bit wet.'

'I don't mind,' she said sweetly, her nose red. 'So am I.'

18

Getting everyone satisfactorily seated was often a problem at meetings of the Union of Industrial Mystics. Just doing boy-girl-boy-girl didn't cut it.

Shang Dan, who had a white beard and wore red and gold robes and looked like the god of wealth, circled the round table carefully. 'Now let me see,' he thought out loud. 'Which way is southwest? I think I had better sit facing southwest.' He glanced over at Wong, who was sitting, taciturn, in the darkest corner. 'You're in the east, Wong? I normally go for due west or northeast but I have been suffering from excess earth energy this week.'

'Does that give you bad luck?' Joyce asked Shang.

'No. Indigestion.'

'I've got antacid tablets. They're good for indigestion. I keep them for when there's nothing to eat but really spicy stuff.'

'I don't think you can use antacid tablets to counteract the effects of bad feng shui, but thanks for the offer.'

'We don't mind moving if you want to sit here.' Joyce got a little buzz from using the plural pronoun 'we' to refer to Marker Cai and herself.

'Thank you, missy, but you are sitting to the southeast. I suggest you stay there.' Shang eventually found the right seat and dropped heavily into it.

They had decided to abandon the popular Shanghai eateries. After the horrific experience of two days earlier, Wong couldn't bear the thought of eating at any sort of restaurant for a while. He quoted Mo Zhou: 'The man who is bitten by a snake dislikes ropes.'

So Joyce had arranged for a restaurant to cater a meal for them on Shang Dan's boat, which was making leisurely circuits of the prettier parts of the Huangpu River, looking at The Bund and the futuristic Lujiazui district opposite. It was a pleasant evening, with a purple-pink sunset and a cool breeze. As the sun set, the water was becoming inky black.

Sinha was next to be seated, and was delighted to find that the place left for him had a view of the twinkling lights on the east side of the river.

'You do realise, of course, that the people behind all this—' Sinha vaguely waved his hand to encompass The Bund and the line of mansions and the river and then the whole of Shanghai – 'were the Indians?'

No one rose to take the bait, most of them being too busy inhaling the fumes which had started pouring from the galley: the unmistakably and uniquely Shanghainese smell of authentic *jingcong rousi jia bing:* soy pork and scallion pancakes.

Eventually, Marker Cai looked over and said: 'The Indians? Not the British?'

Joyce said: 'Not the Chinese?'

Sinha was pleased to have successfully engineered an opportunity to share his wide knowledge of Asian history.

'Emperor Doaguang, in 1823, took a census and discovered that vast amounts of the silver of Chinese people were going to pay for Indian opium, imported by Western business people. The Chinese arrested British merchants and threw three million pounds of opium into the sea. Various battles followed, and the British took Hong Kong in 1841 and Shanghai in 1842. Now before the days of tugboat steamers, coolies – a Hindi word – got into the habit of pulling boats and barges of rice along the river just here.'

'Coolies? You mean people pulled boats?'

'Yes. It's amazing what a human being—'

'Can move,' interrupts Joyce. 'It's all to do with momentum.

Yes, we discovered that yesterday.' She glanced over at Cai, who smiled and moved a micron closer, so that their elbows were touching.

'Anyway, coolies pulled barges along the swampy banks of the Huangpu River. The steps they took in the mud had to be reinforced and eventually became what's known as a towpath. This path was called the *band,* which is another Hindi word, meaning 'embankment'. The British, struggling with the precise pronunciation of Indian vowels, recorded it on maps as The Bund. The Hong Kong and Shanghai Bank was built on it in 1865 and the former Indian towpath became one of the most famous streets in the world.'

Tonight there were seven diners. Madame Xu Chong-Li was not present. She had sent her apologies. She was busy with a series of unexpected events, including a visit from some long-lost relations and a minor surgical operation she'd booked and forgotten – a bit embarrassing for a fortune teller. But Shang Dan had brought some friends with him: a woman who was an expert in *ming shu,* or Chinese astrology, and a specialist in the *chien tung,* which was the use of yarrow sticks for divination. Cai was present, not as a removal man, nor as Joyce's official boyfriend, which he wasn't yet, but as a weigher of bones.

On the way to the harbour, the two young people had purchased a pile of newspapers in English and Chinese, and were whiling away the time before the food was ready going through them to see how the incredible events of the past two days had been covered.

There was not a word about any of them. The newspapers were all filled with bland pronouncements about government departments releasing positive statistics. Eventually, Marker found a line in one of the Chinese language newspapers which said: 'Due to time constraints, a scheduled visit by the President and the visiting American leader to the Shanghai Grand Theatre last night was cancelled.'

'Is that all?' Joyce asked. 'Nothing about mad bombers or helicopters or kidnapped businessmen or anything?'

Cai shook his head. 'Joy-Si, one day you will learn. All the interesting things that happen in China never get into the newspapers.'

At that moment, the waiting staff emerged from the junk's galley and started to place pungent, steaming dishes on the table.

Although this was the official founding dinner of the Shanghai Union of Industrial Mystics, the evening was proceeding rather gloomily. The main reason for this seemed to be that Wong, who usually came to life during events that included large amounts of exotic Chinese food, was in a state of sullen, silent misery.

Shang decided to probe the sore spot. 'It's the elephant business, isn't it, Wong? You feel destiny placed a white elephant into your hands and you failed to save its life, therefore your life is cursed?'

The feng shui master nodded. 'I am a living dead man,' he said. 'My life is over.'

Joyce looked up. She hoped that a man of authority such as Shang could persuade her boss that it might not be as bad as it seemed. 'He's wrong, isn't he, Mr Shang? His life isn't really over, is it?'

Shang nodded. 'Oh yes, he's quite right. It is very bad fortune indeed. A genuine white elephant is one of the most ancient signs of divine power and longevity in Chinese tradition – and Vietnamese and Indian and Thai and so on. Allow harm to come to a white elephant and – well, you never get over it. Wong is right: he is a living dead man.'

'Oh.' Joyce didn't know how to react to this, so lapsed into silence.

The Shanghainese god of wealth continued: 'There are five elements, as you know: earth, metal, water, wood and fire.

291

Modern weapons are usually categorised as belonging to metal, although they can include other physical elements in them. In the cycle of destruction, fire leads to metal, and metal leads to wood – Mr Wong is represented by wood in this instance. So with fire and metal and wood in such a harmful conjunction, it was inevitable that a destructive thing happened.'

Joyce tried to remember the feng shui precepts she had learned. 'But you can mitigate things, can't you? Metal energy can be mitigated by water, right?'

'Yes, my child.'

'So would water mitigate it in this case? It happened on the coast.'

Shang Dan sadly shook his head. 'Not really. Dead white elephants, huge bombs: these are massive negative forces. You can't mitigate them unless you had an unbelievably large amount of water directly between you and them.'

Joyce thought for a moment. 'How much?'

'What do you mean?'

'How much? How much water? A litre, a hundred litres, a swimming pool?'

'A very large amount indeed. A lake,' Shang said.

At this point, Sinha interrupted. 'I see what Joyce is getting at. How about an ocean? If I understand the events of yesterday correctly, the bomb inside the white elephant blew up after the unfortunate pachyderm had fallen more or less to the bottom of the East China Sea, correct?'

'Yes,' Joyce said. 'The bottom of the East China Sea. I was there. Splash. Down he went.'

'So there really was a very vast amount of water indeed between the elephant and Wong. More than a lakeful.'

Shang picked at his beard, intrigued.

'In fact, I would say millions of cubic metres of water,' Sinha continued. 'Millions and millions.'

'An ocean of water,' Joyce said.

'The meeting place of the *Changjiang* and the Pacific Ocean,' Cai said.

Shang Dan thought. He stroked his long white beard and screwed up his lips.

Wong looked up at him.

Shang Dan made his pronouncement. 'That's very interesting. I would say this. If the bomb went off and the white elephant died right at the bottom of the sea, and there were a million gallons of water between it and Mr Wong, then we are looking at a very different cycle indeed. Instead of a fire-to-metal-to-wood cycle, which is very destructive, we have a metal-to-water-to-wood cycle, which is very positive. It is one of the most positive cycles you can have,'

This comment was followed by a moment's stunned silence. It was broken by Joyce, who said simply: 'Yay.'

Marker Cai's heart leapt to see her smile. The two young people leaned further into each other.

'So that's that, then,' said Sinha.

'It may well be that if you look at the circumstances closely enough, the forces are actually in your favour,' Shang Dan said, indicating Joyce and her boss with his glass.

Everyone turned to look at Wong.

'Let's eat,' the feng shui master said, stabbing his chopsticks into a dish of crispy squirrel fish in garlic sauce. 'I'm hungry.'

☯

The Acting Special Agent in Charge was on the phone.

'Commander Zhang? This is Dooley here. I guess you kin call me Tom. I mean, that's ma first name, I mean ma personal name. Ah'm gonna be leaving Shanghai in a few days, and ah just wondered if you might, I mean, if it would be okay if we had one last sorta debriefing, if you know what ah mean? Just talk things through.'

'At your office or mine, Agent Dooley?'

'Weel, I thought we cud go to a restaurant or something, git a coffee, you know – I'm buying, heh-heh. Mebbe git something to eat afterwards? There's this place called M on The Bund which is supposed to be nice. Say, five thirty?'

'Okay. Whoever gets there first can find a nice table. I know my way around and I'll be on my bicycle so it will almost definitely be me.'

'Yeah. You're probably right.'

☯

POTUS was on the phone to the President of China.

'You know that time we skipped the official cultural performance doodah because the SS was going nuts – as they do – and we played rummy and blackjack in my Topchop – that's the official presidential helicopteral vehicle – that's what they call it –   I mean like the official terminologogical term – anyway, we played cards down on the beach in where was it? The Yankee River?'

'In a bay on a small island in the Yangtze River Estuary. I remember.'

'Let's do that every time. No offence to you or to the small minority of people for whom the culture thing is important, which includes me, but I would much rather do that again than watch the cultural stuff, which has no interest in me, if you see what I mean. It's just not at the tip of my propaganda.'

'I agree.'

'But that's not what I was calling about. You gonna be at the G8 in July?'

'Yes.'

'Good. Me too. You gotta give me a chance to win all that stuff back. You play a slow hand, you son of a Satan, you. Okay?'

'You're on.'

☯

People who understand others are wise.
People who understand themselves are enlightened.
People who overcome others need force.
People who overcome themselves need strength.
People who are content are wealthy.
People who persevere have will-power.
People who do not lose their centre endure.
People who die but maintain their power live eternally.

Lao Tzu, from Tao Te Ching,
sixth century BC, quoted in 'Some
Gleanings of Oriental Wisdom' by CF Wong

150